L U D A

Grant Morrison

LUDA

Europa
editions

Europa Editions
8 Blackstock Mews
London N4 2BT
www.europaeditions.co.uk

A catalogue record for this title is available from the British Library
ISBN 978-1-78770-485-5

Morrison, Grant
Luda

Art direction by Emanuele Ragnisco
instagram.com/emanueleragnisco

Cover design and illustration by Ginevra Rapisardi

Prepress by Grafica Punto Print – Rome

Printed and bound in Great Britain by Clays Ltd, Elcograf S.p.A

CONTENTS

For Max

Φ

Then crying "I have made his glory mine!"
And shrieking out "O fool," the harlot leapt
Adown the forest, and the thicket closed
Behind her and the forest echoed "fool."
—TENNYSON, *Idylls of the King*

LUDA

1
The Phantom

Where to begin?

That's the big question, I hope you'll agree.

You. Me. Where do any of us "begin?"

Face it. An ill-judged wink across a crowded dance floor invites a lifetime of school bills. An inebriated fumble in the dark, on the playing field, in the cloakroom, gets the same job done just as well.

Even you, hearing this, you might be the product of a case of mistaken identity that wound up in the maternity ward.

I'm not judging.

Judging is *your* job. You'll have to reach a verdict after all the evidence in the case has been presented. That's how it works.

Off we go; the pistol cracks, jump-starting a spirited, high-heeled lunge from the starting blocks as we jostle for position in the "Human Race;" digging in for the long haul; and what starts as a marathon sprint, winds down over decades until it's a hundred-metre medicated crawl to the finish line.

That's what you'd say if you were trying to be clever, I suppose.

Lucky me, I don't have to try. I've got the front stalls and balcony eating out of my handbag most nights. I can bat an eye, purse my lips, and bring the house down like a drone strike any night of the week.

"Tonight" happens to be a Wednesday. Like yours truly, it can go one way or the other on a Wednesday but the weather's rotten outside, as my dripping, demoralized umbrella will confirm, and that's generally enough to guarantee a packed hall from the orchestra pit to the gods and nosebleeds.

So, if you ask me, and on the clear understanding there's nobody else here in the dressing room, you may as well take the plunge: It doesn't matter where we begin, does it, babes?

When all's said and done, we start off with nothing. You and me both, and all the rest. Hardly matters what happens in between; we arrive with nothing and we finish with nothing, am I right?

Zip. Zilch. Nada. Nought. Nil.

What better place to "commence my narrative" than here, with nothing at all?

At Ground Zero.

What makes me so certain I've got nothing? you may ask.

I can tell you it's because I know for sure I've got nothing to lose.

If you're already asking yourself, How long can she go on and on about nothing, settle in, I've only just gotten started.

Nothing is a blank canvas, you see. Nothing is a mirror waiting patiently for an anticipated reflection to show up. A lonely-looking glass in an Oscar Wilde fairy tale, aching for that special face to drift into view, bringing purpose to its blank existence.

Which returns me to me, unsurprisingly, looking in a glass like that one in the story Oscar forgot to write. Me and the wicked queen from *Snow White*.

Honestly, if I could sum up my whole life in one image, there's a mirror on the wall and there's me, looking in, or looking out, it's hard to tell with mirrors.

If anyone ever asks, I describe myself as an artist, and an artist needs a *carte blanche* to get started.

This *tabula rasa* I call my face has, for quite a long time, been every bit as vacant as it gets: symmetrical, bland, uninhabited, you could say. A halfhearted sketch for a grand, abandoned project. Even these reluctantly-accumulated lines and folds and cracks appear to me as if they'd much rather be somewhere else; livening up an Etruscan vase in a museum or adding texture to some moth-eaten rolled mediaeval tapestry.

Faced with that crumpled imprecision, the only reasonable response is to sanction a scorched-earth policy. Vietnam. The Gulf. Afghanistan. Agent Orange. Edit out the errors, blitz the flaws, illuminate the trenches with colour and contour.

Let scarlet poppies bloom on the graveyard pillows of my lips, soldier dear!

Come to think of it, you could say I've been touching myself up my whole life if you wanted to lead with a blue note.

As if to prove my point, having prepped the canvas with Derma Shield, the foundation goes on first—and these days, I might as well layer it on with a trowel, or a bulldozer. My sponge has to work harder than a navvy spreading tarmac on a highway surface pitted with artillery potholes.

I dip two fingers in the pot to scoop up a generous cool blob of W5 Kryolan pancake base before rubbing my palms together nice and slow, so the emulsion squishes through my fingers in creamy prayer. Then, placing the tips either side of the bridge of my nose, I draw my digits down in a tribal chevron.

It'll take as long as it always takes, time enough to say everything that needs to be said. If Luci LaBang is ready when it's curtains up, everything else is secondary.

She's on her way, floating up from the depths to the mirror's surface to replace my vacant features, Narcissus in middle age, in all her airbrushed Hollywood splendour.

Soon, she'll shatter the surface tension of the glass. She'll float up through the bulrushes, like Lizzie Siddall doing Ophelia, and screen-print herself onto my skull.

No matter how smooth your skin is, how good your diet's been, how "young you still look" for your age; no matter how much Botox you reluctantly forked out for two months ago, at Luda's request; there's no escaping fifty years of age. It's that five-knuckle rap on the door you can't put off answering. That sinister, long-anticipated stranger, sidling up to whisper a bedtime horror story you'd rather not hear, let alone live through. Until you're left with no choice.

Mine is the character arc, mine the "journey," no one would choose to take: hot young Drag Princess with a weekly show on TV to ageing Pantomime Dame in the blink of a mascara-clotted false eyelash.

As for Luda, we'll get back to that soon enough.

Some of you may require a sympathetic context for my howls of outrage, so allow me to digress briefly on the pantomime, an arcane form of art so coarse and lowbrow it wasn't deemed fit to share a pigsty on Noah's Ark, let alone passage to the Americas in the company of Charlie Chaplin and the first rollicking wave of music hall immigrants.

While the Little Fellow invented the idea of global stardom, pantomime elected to stay behind in the old country, determined to continue its backward Bedlam scuttle down the theatrical tree of life, aiming, you might think, for some simplified one-celled form of entertainment, and ultimately merciful oblivion.

The show began, historians insist, as *commedia dell'arte,* with Pierrot, Columbine, and Harlequin doing their three-way satirical *ménage* for libertines and proles alike. Soon, following some process of reverse evolution, *commedia dell'arte* turned tail and slithered back into ancestral swampland, there to wind up squatting in the mangroves and limelight as pantomime, the lowest of the low arts. The performance equivalent of atavistic reversal.

The word itself was coined in 1717 for an ad in *The Daily Courant,* I looked it up. But it wasn't until 1860 that anything we'd recognize as a traditional "pantomime" came along—that brash, shambling steam engine of profanity, song, and gender meltdown that runs year in, year out. Summer seasons in the resort towns, winter in the cities.

I was thirty-six when I did my first one. At a time when I needed something new in my so-called life, I spotted a *niche*.

You could say I identified a neglected area of the Arts where no one seemed to be experimenting or innovating. After the success I'd scored being the prettiest one in the Troupe—as we'd decided to call ourselves in that search for a post-ironic sweet spot between Warhol's Factory, the Manson Family, and Monty Python—I could see my face becoming more angular and, quite frankly, more Cubist with every passing month.

Fresh creases put my red lips in double brackets every time I smiled. A murder of crow's-feet trampled through the sooty ovals gathered round my eyes. These signs of time's creepy crawl were not so much as to ruin the effect, especially when I was done with my kit, just enough to remind me of mortality and the no-longer-Romantic brevity of youth and beauty. As if anyone needs reminding.

Am I right?

I needed a new frame for this changing face; if TV's hi-fidelity microscopic scrutiny was guaranteed to reveal way too much in the close-ups, I'd stage a retreat to the theatre, where everything happened in longshot. I belonged in a house of ill repute where the men were girls and the girls were boys 24/7 and no one called the authorities.

Pantomime fit the bill.

Little did I know I was entering my prime, like Miss Jean Brodie. Pantomime was the crown and I was the jewels. I'd found my vocation.

Prime, it goes without saying, comes before a Fall.

My first big splash came with the Prague Millennium production of *Cinderella*. I'd decided to play both Ugly Sisters at the same time as a "schizophrenic" having surreal, obscene conversations between her contending dual personae, or whatever it is they've got going on. We didn't do a lot of research into the issues around neurodiversity, I'm ashamed to say.

I'd designed a costume split down the middle with one sister on the left wearing shredded punk vinyl, all chains and razors, and her twin on the right wrapped in trashy clinging Lycra Day-Glo bimbo Flamingo sugar-pinks and acid-drop yellows; a death-dealing lollipop in the shape of a person.

It looked fantastic on stage, but I can imagine how offensive it might come across these days so it's the kind of experimentation I tend to shy away from.

I prefer to trigger laughter not PTSD.

Those were different days, a raw-meat decade sandwiched between transient periods of political correctness, so it's no surprise the audience went feral for my Ugly Sisters.

Playing my own comedy foil meant I could time each joke to perfection, something that's not always the case when your straight man is some half-witted clot of hair and spray tan off a soap, or a reality show.

My toes roll up like witches' slippers when I think about the parade of boy-band rejects or popular bloggers I've had to witness—hauled blinking into the footlights as Buttons, or Wishee-Washee, effortlessly translating their lack of talent in one area of the arts to a fresh platform of humiliation.

I've watched more naturally gifted entertainers at a chimpanzees' tea party, pelting one another with faeces and fairy cakes.

Forget it, Jake, I used to say—it's *pantomime*.

Which brings me right back here to where it started. Dragged high-kicking and screaming in falsetto towards the black-hole spiral sink of the world-famous Vallhambra Theatre. Downtown Gasglow. Down and down am I dragged.

And re-dragged.

Fortunately for us all, I'm something of an expert when it comes to drag.

The so-called Grand Duchess of Gasglow Music Halls, the Vallhambra was designed, by visionary architect and spectacular suicide Murdo McCloudie, in that amazing Deco-coco style that reminds me of cover paintings on old science-fiction paperbacks, yellowing into nostalgia in the windows of used bookstores, back when used bookstores and books were a thing.

After a suspicious blaze that left it hollowed, all façade and nothing behind, like a Hollywood stage set, or a pop star, the building ascended Phoenix-like, shaking cinders from its gilded plumage.

During the ten years that followed, the Vallhambra was lovingly and painstakingly restored—if by "lovingly restored" you mean glammed up like a resurrected temple whore from ancient Egypt.

A bit like myself in that regard: struggling to stay sexy, remain relevant, and cheat the wrecker's balls long past the glory days.

West of Circle Station and north of the River Dare, you'll find the happening part of town they call Gasglow's Broadway, a mile and a half of strip and glitter and trashy, flashing come-ons.

The theatre's situated near the intersection of Gargoyle and Charity in the guts of the city of Gasglow, opposite the Sugar Shack pole-dance club, sandwiched in a vile spit-roast between the Emperor, catering to devotees of big musical productions like *Nixon! The Satanic Bible* and *Papa Zombi!* and the Pandromo, which specializes in stand-up comedy tours and variety shows.

Gasglow, where the rain it raineth 330 days of the year, and horizontal sleet accounts for the days when even rain is too dispirited to fall. Gasglow, where eight months of perpetual gloom incubate monstrous genre mashups.

Supernatural romance. Sex *noir*. Comedy Gothic. It's all on the menu.

The high priests of meteorology have predicted a near-hurricane for tonight, the third "named storm" in the last month. This one christened Storm Ingmar for sins yet to be announced.

I wouldn't blame Ingmar for lashing out. Who'd want to be called "Ingmar?" The competition's too fierce. With Ingmar on the rampage, the Vallhambra offered its patrons sanctuary from the tyranny of Nordic Fimbul-weather.

We could be relied upon for shelter and community. We dispensed firelit visions of the Middle East and far Cathay. Manmade magic hours. Indoor summer. Sunshine and laughter guaranteed.

We had no time for stuffy ballet or strident opera on bright West Gee. You could get all that any day of the week at the top end of town—the Dramakademie doing *Euripides* or the *Oresteia*. Down on Gargoyle, the fun cathedrals offered light entertainment for the masses: dancing men and hot clever girls who knew how to make you laugh. Jokes. Songs. Sing-alongs. Spectacle and breathtaking illusion assured.

Once through the revolving doors of the Vall, it was Aladdin's cave inside. And I should know—I've been in and out of Aladdin's cave every night for the last six months.

I wish, listeners! Stay tuned for more on *those* headlines!

Which brings us back to where I am right now. In front of a mirror, with my face in its own bulb-edged comic-book panel, preparing to put my makeup on . . .

Don't fret, I can tell the whole story while I'm getting done up.

For tonight, ladies and gentlemen, boys and girls, and all the rest, I intend to vanish behind the florid features of wily Chinese washerwoman Widow Twankey, the comedy "Dame" role in a production of *Aladdin,* itself framed within a larger—let's give the thing more respect than it deserves and call it "post-modern"—narrative driven by bloody revenge, black magic, and dodgy philosophy, then titled *The Phantom of the Pantomime,* which is, to all intents and purposes, the plot of *The Phantom of the Opera* drugged, kidnapped, and rehoused in the ghetto of Irony.

The Phantom of the Pantomime tells the story of a theatre company rehearsing a production of *Aladdin* that's struck by a series of inexplicable accidents and deaths.

Inexplicable that is until the introduction of the titular Phantom—a disfigured actor who's been orchestrating the production's misfortunes.

As the cast numbers diminish, it falls to the remaining players to assume the roles vacated by their unfortunate colleagues.

Until eventually only one actor remains playing *all* the roles.

According to Dominick Float, our gifted, dangerously overweight director, the descent of culture that informs *The Phantom*'s subtext is implied right there in the title's biblical plummet from the high-flown operatics of the *bourgeoisie* to the proletarian troughs of panto sing-along. This structure finds itself reiterated in the tragic story of our histrionic lead, who, if I can lower the tone for the moment, effortlessly puts the "tit" into "titular character."

Now, I can already hear voices raised in protest all the way across the People's Republic, from Andong to Gorno-Badakhshan, from Xing'an to Haina—what's the story with a non-Chinese actor playing a Chinese character?

When faced with panto's melting boundaries and blurred identities, race is no more stable than gender, as you'll discover. Men transform into women, girls blossom into boys, and the poor get the chance to roll in vulgar wealth as class itself deliquesces to tasty bone stock in the bacchanalian broth.

The thing is, and here's where it gets complicated: *Aladdin* is from the Middle East—the story originated as one of the *Thousand and One Nights* tales that helped spare Scheherazade's swanlike neck from the butcher's blade—but dig deeper: the pantomime *Aladdin*? It's not set in Scheherazade's Arabia; it takes place in China. On the stage, Aladdin is a Chinese boy, son of the washerwoman Widow Twankey.

DNA was spliced from mythic and modern-day China with rogue sequence from the Middle East to create a single imaginary sprawl of hybrid cultures that fused a Bedouin Sahara with the paddy fields of the Cultural Revolution and its rubbish heaps of broken spectacles.

The pantomime's anachronistic collision of places and times suggested a dreamlike half world where familiar stories played out in endlessly retied knots through a confused congestion of half-real cities and times, embedded in nested narratives handed down through generations.

Widow Twankey's a textbook example of the confusion; when she was born to the boards in 1788, Twankey was Ching Mustapha, an unlikely cross-pollination of cultural signifiers that suggests an exotic variant of cocaine and reminds us how surprisingly widespread was the Chinese Muslim population of London in those days.

Now I'd like you to picture the most offensive stereotype of a sex-starved gossip—and you'll have me down to a T.

You'll also have Widow Twankey, who's all about flashy gutter comedy. Outrageous peacock costumes, fake tits and upholstered arse, winks and asides to the audience, double entendres. You know the kind of thing:

She's eagerly looking forward to a big hand on her entrance. Mug to the back row. *You can see she's got big things ahead of her.* Out-thrust chest. *44DDs by the looks of them.*

Twankey is outrageous, vulgar, and grotesque. And that's just her earrings. It gets worse the more you pay attention. Don't come looking for subtlety or nuance, you won't be disappointed.

The Widow is a flouncing, indomitable monster. A brash and trashy caricature even the goggle-eyed toddlers and the special-needs adults they wrangle to the matinees can recognize and identify. But she's no more Chinese than the people of Tibet.

Which brings me back to my point that casting a bona fide Chinese actor might be a way to double or triple the offence. Really, it's up to our hypothetical Chinese individual to draw his or her own conclusions before getting snarled up in what can be a heartrending, demoralizing audition process.

As far as I know, the role's open to anyone, regardless of ethnic origin or political creed, so why not have a Chinese man take a swing at Widow Twankey? I know I'd pay to watch that.

Anyway, enough chat about 19 percent of our planet's entire human population. Let's steer this back to me.

Although you might never have guessed from my present radiant demeanour, I'd found myself in a desperate tailspin after turning forty and breaking up with Luci. For a while I even considered suicide, until finally I went through with it, only to discover I'd guzzled an overdose of placebos.

You know how they work; I'd already convinced myself my organs were shutting down one by one, so that's exactly what I experienced. In excruciating detail. The placebo effect they call it. And while it was happening, I had quite a big sort of revelation.

I realized I'd been split in two. I'd been separated out, curds-and-whey-style, then subtracted from myself. In some black and backward act of alchemy, Mercurius, the androgynous spirit of wholeness, had suffered a near-fatal sundering somewhere down the line. One half abandoned, stumbling and flabby, with his neuroses hanging out like guts, the other banished to the Twilight Zone, leaving only traces and spoor: the cobby husks of her dresses, her empty coats and vacant shoes; drained bugs dangling on their hangers in a spider's web of wire.

Matter and spirit, formerly mingled as one in ecstatic harmony, felt like awkward strangers now, reduced at best to strained small talk over a dispiriting brunch. My spark-haired

Ariel was gone, exorcised. Only doughy Caliban remained, weighed down with his mud and mortality, cultivating a life belt of lard that kept me afloat in the featureless ocean of Nowhere.

Without Luci, I'd become a hollow man, a creepy *piñata* packed with nothing you'd want. Six years had passed since I put her away, since that separation. That primordial error.

I prayed. I prayed to triple-faced Mercurius to release me from the downward Coriolis suction. I prayed like a mother-fucker for deliverance. I prayed so hard that, three days later, the phone rang as if to shut me up. Even then, I had "Two Ladies" from *Cabaret* as my ringtone. I still remember it.

The caller was a forty-three-year-old neurotic genius named Dominick Float, then weighing about as much as one of his thumbs does now, who demanded I audition for his new musi-cal. The production company had bigger names topping their want lists, he explained; screen stars, established comics, he said, but he'd seen me chewing up the boards with my Ugly Sisters in Prague, he remembered me from the Troupe shows on Channel 6 and felt I could bring an edge to his "vision" for this thing called *The Phantom of the Pantomime.*

I'll admit I was flattered, but at that point the confidence I once imagined I'd have forever had evaporated like a fertile green Saharan oasis in the haze between the endless dunes. I couldn't recall the taste or shape or texture of confidence, to tell the truth, so I told Float I hadn't considered anything in the performance vein for a long time. I didn't say it in so many words, but I left him in no doubt: I considered myself more than a little bit past the lipstick, lace, and lingerie stage.

Float, unwilling to surrender even a single pixel of his per-sonal "vision," wouldn't take no for an answer. Where Twankey was concerned there could be no "past it."

Sir Ian McKellen had smashed the role at the Old Vic when he was sixty-five, a newly minted pensioner qualifying for a bus pass. I was an *ingénue* by comparison, Float assured me. Such flattery was music.

What else could I do? I prayed like the penitent Mother Superior of the Order of Ravens to Mercurius, who had, in infinite mercy and cruelty, tossed this raw and shiny bone for me to gnaw upon. I surrendered myself to the grace of my patroness and the Odyssean tides of the Glamour. The choice was clear: accumulate more misery until I sagged beneath the damp cold agglomeration of years and regrets or—

Or summon up the bright snake-eyed demoness I'd banished on my drunken stagger into middle age. While I became the stomach-turning portrait in the attic, she'd stayed young, flash-frozen, immaculate, waiting for her time to come around again. Waiting for me to summon her back into my evacuated life, trusting that the fire of her incendiary aura would shine so much brighter than the putrid phosphorescent glow of my personal decay.

Drag had been with me almost my whole life up till I separated from myself aged thirty-eight.

From the days when I was waist-high to that monstrous department store mannequin, the one I'll tell you about later, I've been attracted to the power of fashion, deception, illusion, trickery. The fake, the synthetic, the scary boundary where Artifice becomes the Uncanny.

Possibly, Doctor Freud, if my mother hadn't been overprotective, if circumstances and lack of closet space hadn't compelled her to leave a tempting chest of drawers in my bedroom with her stockings and bras inside, I'd never have made the choices I did, it's true. Mum's drawers had it all. And she was a very stylish good-looking woman, my mother, so I didn't get my start dressing in twinsets like some of these old-school CDs you used to see in cheaply printed contact rags; the ones who looked like ghosts showing up bored at séances, or mediums possessed by their own elderly relatives.

I didn't identify with any of that and I never felt trapped in the wrong body. I was more than satisfied with the slender-limbed form I'd grown to inhabit. I didn't need boobs or a womb to complete me, only flamboyant clothes and cosmetics. All I wanted was to look fabulous, breakfast, lunch, and dinner, like the photographs of those eternal fashion models I grew up admiring.

For me it was always about the drag.

What am I? Where do I fit on the scale, or the spectrum? How would I know? I'm sure I don't have time to be a narcissist—I'm too busy checking my makeup in the mirror.

My head was, still is, a half-built haunted arcade of shifting selves and liquid identities, voice impressions, disguises and shadows, reflections and lightning among the rafters.

Either there's nobody there at all, or dozens of us share the one skull, passed like the ball in a very strenuous game of Rugby Union. I was chosen to join the unseen throng on the day I saw the door in the Horus-inked eyes of the mannequin.

In truth, at the secret heart of me dwells something attenuated and alien, a long-limbed genderless flame if I had to be precise. Existing so close to the boundary with nothing at all, it could pass for anything. Shakespearean, an alien, a Puck perhaps, its general gas-jet attitude easily summed up in the trickster's famous quote: ". . . what fools these mortals be!"

I'd been branded on that steamy August afternoon all those years ago by the cosmetic runes of the Glamour, its hieroglyphic alphabets sketched in Egyptian kohl, Nefertiti's death mask illuminated with bold lip-pencil outlines. I was drawn through the shimmering cut-price veil, the glittering bead curtain, the tinsel portal that opened onto sorcery and to Luci.

In the beginning, I had no separate stage name for what I became when I was dressed and made up; as I said, there was no inner division. It was only later, when we started up the Troupe, that I christened myself at the font of Mercurius:

I became Luci LaBang, a *nom de plume* dripping with steaming pearls of meaning.

But after a great many adventures, I'd given up Luci. I'd made my tearful farewells. Her dresses haunted the closet, unworn, sulking spooks. Being honest, I was scared to call her back, certain she'd never allow my face, that pocked and dimpled canvas retrieved from a carpet-bombed museum, to distort her beauty. I was frightened of what I might find when I dug her up, smelling of mothballs and accusation.

But I knew there was no backing down; Widow Twankey, avatar of the Three-Times-Perfected, had delivered the perfect excuse. I was being presented with the opportunity to surrender to something stronger, faster, more real than anything I'd been for so long. I would light my old lamp and dust off my wand, my rusty dagger, my cup, and my books. My Louboutins and *Agents Provocateurs*.

I would summon the Glamour one last time and let it burn me to chemical incandescence in its blue occult flame.

A couple of pills started me down the Yellow Brick Road. Vodka tonic, double. What's the worst that can happen? I thought. I'll shit myself and choke on my own vomit in the back of a taxi or onstage. At least I'll die with dignity.

I always start with the music—my personal theme tune is Thomas Tallis's *Spem in Alium,* which is Latin for "Hope in Any Other," as if you didn't know. I can't tell you how upset I was when they used this music for a shoddy sex scene in a terrible film based off an even worse book. It almost but not quite ruined it for me. Nothing can spoil the impact of forty voices rising, up and up, all sparks and chimes and the bright glory of God.

I raised my vivid lipstick aloft, my crimson wand, and called her name—*Luci Luci Luci*—three times and there were ripple flickers on the still pool of the mirror, and there beneath the surface, the afterimage of a remembered face arose—the Lady of the Lake preserved in the green tank of her frozen millpond, waiting for the looking glass to thaw . . .

I drained a tall flute of pink champagne—which is exactly what I'm doing right now—if you'll excuse me . . .

Think of it as the sacrament. The Cup of the Blood of the Moon. The cannibal Grail of the were-woman. Call it what you like, if it gets you in the mood for transformation.

Mercurius, brother-sister, dark and light, up and down, Hermes Aphrodite. Bride and groom wedded as one.

So unfolded the celestial ascending spirals of *Spem in Alium* hand in hand to Heaven with increasingly pleasurable pharmaceutical rushes, that came on as fresh and childhood-scented Easter breezes blowing away those last leftover autumn leaves of crispy fear, shame, and doubt.

I was invincible. I was morning incarnate rising over the jagged peaks of Kanchenjunga. Where tumbling unfinished thoughts and cycling jingles had ruled the inner airwaves, where private critics formerly jostled to judge every move and condemn every word, there was only air-blue silence and what you might describe as limitless magnificent transparency.

The muscles of my face relaxed, becoming slack and pliable to the touch. I pushed and pulled, and carefully reset each learned configuration of zygomatic arch and risorius, levator labii superioris, masseter. Tweaking and palping, I sculpted a new expression into place.

The ritual progressed—these were white hours with no time—I couldn't remember how her fabulous smile wound up on my face, but I supposed I must have put it there. Her Babalon scarlet rising in satanic counterpoint against the heavenly silver choiring of King's College, Cambridge.

Angels and the devil in a tango, complementary partners arranged as tessellated black-and-white tiles in one of those ever-so-clever M. C. Escher drawings.

There I was, with all this joined-up thinking going on,

absentmindedly scooping homemade lentils-in-stockings tits into my bra before I realized the music had come to an end.

In that hush profound there was only the *Sangreal* glow of the face in the mirror.

Fairest of them all.

Her familiar, forgiving smile making its way through the wrinkles and slap, a beloved song surfacing out of static on the radio.

Hey you.

The wig goes on last, an exclamation mark to complete and emphasize the statement. That's when I find the tuning—and become the receiver for a force of nature I'm calling Mercurius.

I know it sounds a bit weird, but I'll explain later, and you'll see that it's bigger than just weird.

The hair was new, and smelled of plastic, packing, and processing—sacred in its box-fresh connection to eternity.

I set it in place, her crown and diadem. The Empress Twankey.

Destroya!

I looked a bit like Luci's mother might look if she'd had one.

As it turned out, Mum looked quite hot in the full-length; a MILF Widow vamping like Cruella de Vil and Elizabeth Báthory sharing a double exposure.

Luci LaBang shaking her ass in the noonday blaze of an indoor sun, in a *por favor* where forty-four was just a bingo number. Magnum Force! Forty-four. *And she looks*—I grinned at the time—*not six months past her second bitter divorce.* The blood in my veins ran with alternating current, so it felt like the resurrection by thunderbolts of the Bride of Frankenstein.

Like bacon, Luci LaBang was back, sizzling on the world's hob.

The Luci LaBang Twankey would reinvent pantomime tradition. How could I settle for anything less?

Except—except—my heels, as I recall, had become twin

Rubik's Cubes of fidgety strap and nano-buckle. Imagine two unfeasible and maddeningly intricate puzzle machines at the end of your legs, and those were my Azzedine Alaïas. I persevered, huffing and squealing with the frustration of a monkey made to do a jigsaw puzzle by scientists with electric prods, until I worked them into place and was back in stilettos where I belonged after those years flat-out in the desert.

My immense and shaggy neon *faux*-leopard coat swung like a bell across bare, oiled shoulders, perfume moving ahead of me as a bow wave. Pausing to let the mirror snap an unsaved selfie, I raised my faceted tumbler with a leer and a Venus flytrap wink.

Was I seriously planning on going out like this? After all these years? At my age? Forty-four.

Open the door. I tipped back the vodka tonic and a great and special quiet brought its sudden blunt calm upon the world, answering all my silly questions with an articulate silence.

Just the right side of wasted, as I hope my description conveys, I found myself descending the staircase to Cinderfella's waiting pumpkin carriage, Duchamp afterimages stitching together as a shaggy leopard-striped bridal train at my back, head tilted all imperious, Her Majesty the Queen of the Madhouse in a drag production of *Marat/Sade*.

The cabdriver gawped in the cameo brooch of his mirror. The brute's semi-disorganized features twitched like gloves and I could tell I'd violated his safe space in more ways than one.

My perfume, Twankey's perfume, was Tabu, with its overwhelming allergenic waves of suffocating patchouli, its blindingly acidic citrus squalls—less delicate fragrance, more full-scale climactic upheaval.

You like my perfume? It's Tabu—I managed to say without laughing.

I knew what he was thinking: Tabu, as in incest, cannibalism, and bestiality.

The Vallhambra, driver, I remember instructing the by now

half-Cubist cabbie. *I'm auditioning for Aladdin, the panto. Widow Twankey.*

His expression relaxed in the *niqab* eye-slit of the rearview. Now the inexplicable moment made sense. But he still rolled down the window, eyes watering. Tabu, yahoo.

The ecstasy was cresting in a calm blue-and-white Hokusai breaker, all Mount Fuji azure Zen as I tipped my charioteer with a generosity born of intoxication and clambered out, all legs and leather, strutting through the gawping throng, submerged in profound aquarium light down my old pal, Gargoyle Street, basking in the silky pedestrian airflow.

Oh look! There's me!

The Vallhambra's endlessly revolving doors cycled a familiar face into view, this face leaving the spacious lobby as I came in. As it did, a shuffle of random features superimposed themselves over my reflection in a briefly disturbing kinetic overlap. My delighted brain assembled the jumble of ghost-pig eyes, juicy nose, and raw-kidney lips into the image of a "formerly"-alcoholic host of a weekly quiz show based on some old board game.

For the life of me I couldn't recall a name. Still, that punctured party-balloon complexion deserved a witchy wink and a grin if nothing else. As our paths crossed briefly, I'd swear the ghost of a distillery followed close on his heels. Then he was gone; Tam O'Shanter pursued to his waiting limo by unquiet ninety-proof spirits and tender minders.

He looked smug, at first, all self-satisfied, certain he'd scored the gig; his Twankey, honed over years of rote performance, was the gold standard traditionalist's take. If the production was trawling for the precise qualities this metastasizing human tumour had to offer, I was fucked up the far end of the spectrum, infra-dig to his UV. He seemed to know he was the bookie's favorite; as far as anyone was concerned, he was the most famous, the funniest: the most special. Department of Foregone Conclusions. The deal was dealt.

Until he saw me swing in.

He scanned me up and down with a personal radar and I could almost feel the burn marks on my butt cheeks where those laser-guided brown-hot peepers finally anchored themselves. I was way too high to grasp the threat he represented. I knew I had my work cut out, but I trusted my next half hour to that hopeless look in his eyes. The one that said he'd recognized me straightaway, Nemesis to his Hubris.

All I had to do was live up to the myth.

I swung my skinny protruding hips, proudly extended the shelf of my *ersatz* tits, and certain I'd never see the quizmaster again—

—I certainly didn't expect to see his coffin lowered into a six-feet-deep, three-minute-long slot on the evening news two months later—

—I toppled into the audition on six-inch platform heels, made regal and ridiculous in a towering bleached-blond wig. A shaggy petrol-blue and fluoro-pink leopard-print coat. Vinyl miniskirt. Gasping for breath after a drag on Twankey's vaper, I tripped into my routine.

Aladdin! Where is that boy of mine? There are sheets to be washed and I don't want to get ANY MORE behind—a backward glance. *MY BEHIND'S BIG ENOUGH AS IT IS!*

I didn't stop for the laugh. I was on the express train of thought, riding First Class, aware that the blast radius of Tabu had reached my audience, bringing on the first symptoms of hay fever and shock.

They would never forget this audition.

I'm very nervous—I say. *But everyone tells me it'll be all right on the night . . . I just hope I can remember my lines.*

A half beat for the rhythm.

It's all too easy to get my tongue twisted around a REALLY LONG HARD ONE.

I'd crafted the makeup to look like Twankey had hit the

menopause at high speed, careered out of control across the midlife junction, and failed to slow down. I'd made the best of my sagging skin, the droopy jowls, the interlabial drapes, and laden eye hammocks.

Mine was a Twankey who binged on celebrity gossip. A Twankey martyring herself to Botox injections and lip fillers, as if to hold back the inevitable depredations of a washerwoman's life on the bustling narrow alleys of her make-believe Peking.

Rubber tits, augmented arse, monstrously sexual, eternally unsatisfied, driven to live or die trying; I was the Bride of Frankenstein with a Gorgon eye for the cable guy. Strutting and puffing, I found myself out of rehearsed material, improvising a Restoration Twankey, sneering down her nose and flipping her thumb in the direction of a saucy next-door neighbour's condo.

When fortnightly to the rigs doth fly her man,
That Mrs. Egg Fu Not so Yung next door is wont to call the builders in—
To have enwhitewash'd both her porches, front and back!
Where best they're pleased to park the van's a guess I dare not make.
But day and night she doth extravagant deliv'ries take!

There's no real suspense, so I won't do the whole twenty minutes I eventually gave them. I got the part. Of course I did. I wouldn't be here otherwise. There would be no story. No mystery.

No crime.

Float told me later, they were swithering between me and the quizmaster, but I think it's important to make it clear that, contrary to some people's opinion, I didn't *only* get the part because my one rival was diagnosed with early-onset Alzheimer's before his unlikely and suspicious death. A dementia brought on by the steady replacement of all the liquid in his body with a transfusion of alcohol, let's face it—not by some doll I stuck pins in!

Believe that and magic's real. And then, where are you? Anything can happen.

The inaugural production of *The Phantom,* as I've explained, opened here in the Vallhambra Theatre on Gargoyle Street in Gasglow, declared that year the nation's Culture Capital—the gesture was ironic; our meta-burlesque would open in the home of some of the most fondly remembered and spectacular productions of the Golden Age, like *Cinderella* or *Aladdin,* when they'd have enchanted carpets zipping overhead on wires and fleets of haunted pirate ships sinking on stage.

And it worked in our favour; the first reviews came in as a storm of love letters from unknown admirers.

". . . it's scary, it's fun, it's a treat for kids and their parents on seven different levels."

The *Daily Monitor:*
"The jokes are superb, topical and near-the-knuckle with a potentially offensive edge that sails over the heads of the young audience to keep their parents in stitches while the disturbing backstory plays out . . ."

The *Evening Banner:*
"The cast is superb but special mention goes to drag comedienne Luci LaBang as Widow Twankey, and Gwen Skillicorn as pitch-perfect straight man Aladdin . . ."

The *Gasglow Messenger:*
"Sublime, frighteningly self-aware nonsense . . ."

Float's gamble paid off with a hit show. Next, we lit up London's West End. Then came the off-Broadway offer. We were sold out every night. The Tony Award seemed an unlikely prospect, but it still sits there today in Float's office gathering particulate matter between a photograph of his estranged wife, his strange children, and his honorary doctorate from Gasglow University. God knows, I've waited long enough for mine! There were parties and limousines. Even both halves of Buttercup the pantomime cow got laid, in what must have looked like Damien Hirst directing an orgy on Sesame Street.

And I *became* her.

I lived Luci's life, with beautiful people, shallow unreal people just like Luci. And through it all, I rekindled a love affair with myself. I felt reunited with my long-lost twin in a fabulous, mercurial *ménage à moi* that mended the holes in my soul.

That's the thing about holes, though: Fill one, another one opens. Whack-A-Mole!

Now here we all are, back to where the show began, back in Gasglow for a victory-lap season that opens tonight, would you believe?

That's why I'm here, in front of the mirror, applying my slap for what might be the last time.

You'll know better than me how it all turned out, though I have my suspicions.

There's one more thing about pantomime before I take it for granted you're up to speed and can pick up the rest as we race along to the point of this monologue . . .

The key to a successful pantomime lies in audience participation. No other live dramatic narrative format relies on such close, immediate interaction with its audience. You might find a bit of that with one of those radical performance collectives where they haul paying customers onstage to embarrass them with dangling rubber cocks and blood bags but that's a more aggressive, invasive kind of interaction, to my mind.

The trick in panto is for performers to establish an intimate, confessional relationship with the audience while at the same time wrapping them into the performance as a kind of omniscient chorus. There's a dialogue between stage and stalls. We use a call-and-response style to build rapport, breaking down the barriers between the action onstage and whatever they're up to in the back rows.

He's behind you!—they'd shout, early-warning guardian angels when the villains were creeping around in the shadows up to no good. *He's behind you!*

It's the job of the Dame to get the crowd warmed up; when Widow Twankey glides onstage in full sail, the first thing she'll do is turn to the howling mob, with less than a minute to engage their sympathy.

I'd get going, explaining how I sometimes forgot my name for all kinds of reasons, and how I'd need their help to remind me periodically. Then I'd have them shout out *WIDOW TWANKEY!*

What's that? I can't hear a thing.

WIDOW TWANKEY!

I'd shake my head. *I must be going deaf. Me, at the age of thirty-five! Who did you say I was again?*

WIDOW TWANKEY!

Three is the magic number. The tentative murmuring swelling to a Colosseum roar.

WIDOW TWANKEY!!!

A summoning that ran down every vein and nerve and wire and neuron as pure platinum lightning.

Well, you seem to have figured it out, even though it's written RIGHT HERE on the sign for my Chinese laundry! Next time I forget, you'd be doing me a big favour to remind me if I ask you . . .

Every time I came onstage, I'd play the same gag—*It must be my Alzheimer's. What's my name again?* Wobbling on three-storey spikes. Laundry basket under one arm, the other hand cupped to my ear. That was the cue for every kid in the audience to yell *Widow Twankey!* in a jet-plane takeoff of synchronized voices.

In the end I'd pay off the gag with a reveal; every time I'd talked the audience into yelling my name, they'd been advertising my bespoke Chinese launderette. Thanks to their hard PR work, business was finally booming!

I've got a few layers of foundation down now and I'm about to erase my eyebrows with wax and glue.

I say layers, they're more like geological strata. Dig down through this, and you wouldn't be surprised to unearth a few old strollers, dinosaur bones, and the remains of once fertile river valleys.

Five years makes a major difference. "You look young for your age," they'll all tell you, but I'm older than I've ever been before, younger than I'll ever be again, and it shows.

Thinking like that brings the ugly old pressure drop inside. The bleak bath-bomb of depression, dissolving into grey fallout flakes of regret and fizzing existential terror. There comes the sure and certain knowledge that it won't get better, so cover it over, paint it out, three coats deep.

In times like these, drag is camouflage. Concealed for a little while longer from the fangs of time, the troubling face in the mirror evaporates into a jungle foliage of cosmetics and colours, becomes invisible as the patterns drawn on its skin—arched brows, glittering lids, the glossy plastic sheen of outlined cherry lips—replace what lies beneath the surface with a hard, new veneer. The enamel visor lowered into place for my hopeless battle with the clock.

I can see her the way a medium might catch a glimpse of the first faint fog where ectoplasmic tendrils spill and coil together, spinning a death-mask of vapour and fag-ash above an urn. No one else could detect what I can. Not yet. The image might as well be transparent, a distillation so dilute, she's hardly there at all. A trace element. A homeopathic dose of Luci.

I can taste her. Bitter lemon and chocolate.

Then, from that faint, profound impression, I bring her in

through the brushstrokes, the tints and glosses, the moondust sparkles.

I can do it now without all the abraca-jumbo I resorted to in the old days. All it takes is her signal, the transmission. The fizzing static from the Big Bang condensed in a receiver. She's the Cosmic Background Radiation and I'm the radio telescope cupped like a listening ear.

I know you're listening carefully too. I have that of which every performer must surely dream, a captive audience.

You're listening because the law requires your attention. You're obliged to put up with my horrible jokes. You're required to deal with my florid descriptions and long-winded digressions. You're duty-bound to play along and join in, and applaud, when I ask you to.

Audience participation. That's how it works.

You're listening because this, what I'm about to tell you, is evidence.

They'll be on their way now—kids tugging mums and dads like reluctant parent-shaped balloons, student couples delighting in the clever irony we have on offer, professional theatregoers alerted to the trendy legitimizing of a proletarian artform by Sunday supplement reviews, lovers of novelty and extravaganza. They'll come in all shapes and shoe sizes, all ages and Pantone shades. For four hours, including the interval, they'll park their worries and their differences at home.

The world in here, our little kingdom in a bottle, all dreamy gold in the luminous fumes of the dry-ice cannon, promised life with the boring bits trimmed out to fit the story's formulaic requirements.

Framed in its cabinet, TV before its time, ours was a world where life came fully choreographed and scored, and no one forgot their lines. Here, conversations were comedy routines. Good people were rewarded, and the bad ones faced punishment according to their natures.

At the pantomime, every story ended with a kiss and a promise and a twinkle in someone's eye.

Even our meta-story, the tragic musical tale of the Phantom, had an unexpected conclusion. A nod to the power of pretend to change the world, ambiguous enough to appeal to everyone and send them home swapping theories.

Out there in the narrow Tic-Tac-Toe grid-streets of Gasglow under cloud lid and Storm Ingmar's sullen Scandi seethe, the arctic rain came sleeting off the broad bare back of a Siberian wind.

In here, boilers and generators and the power of make-believe, the potency of the Glamour, brought to life the dust and heat of evil Abanazar's desert citadel.

The hurly-burly of a market in Peking. The vibrant, lively backstreets where Widow Twankey ran her Chinese laundry. The multicoloured majesty of the Cave of Jewels.

Where would you rather be on a freezer-cabinet-cold night in November?

The doors open soon. They'll be climbing into cabs, packing the kids into people carriers. Slipping in a last round or two after work, or lectures.

They'll come to laugh out loud and hold their breath and most of all they'll come to join in. They'll cheer the heroes and boo the villains.

They'll roar—*Widow Twankey!* And—*SHE'S BEHIND YOU! Oh no, they're not!* And—*Oh yes, she is!*

They'll come to take a step across the subtle line dividing real life from show business, where the glamorous funny people onstage are talking directly to them, eliciting their advice and support. They'll be hypnotized into a fantastic waking dream, swept along in the rapids of the action. Wrapped up in a world of such artificial grandeur, such feigned luxury, it becomes more real than any real world.

They will enter, with me, into the eternal Glamour.

And when the curtain falls, they'll scatter from the theatre into Gasglow's unrelenting rainscape, trailing pixie sprinkles.

Some will hail taxis. Some will disperse, drawn by the warm bellows-breaths huffed through stalled traffic on Gargoyle Street every time a punter opens the door of the Karachi Kebabatorium.

In Gasglow, the night comes smoked and seasoned with fragrant frying oils, its irresistible animal aromas released by the measured rotation of a sizzling barrel of compressed halal lamb. Seduced to the dark side by the promise of hot, salty junk food best savoured outdoors when the weather's foul; that's how it played out night after night.

I had one or two surprises planned.

I know some dames who claim they can do their slap in fifteen minutes flat. I say, you're not even trying. I prefer to approach my transformation into Twankey as a work of art, taking my sweet time.

It takes at least nine minutes nineteen seconds for the best choirs in the world to sing *Spem in Alium,* but I'll have it on a loop until I'm done. After the last shimmering chord, I usually finish off with a bracing blast of "Pretty Vacant" until the pristine Buddhist condition of *shunyata* is achieved.

That's when I know it's time to go on.

The music is a vital part of the ritual. The one you're helping me with.

Did I mention this was a ritual?

Did I make it clear we would stop at nothing?

Never mind. Once I've explained about the Glamour, you'll understand what I mean by that.

You'll see what happens when witches go to war.

Nearby, from the dressing room along the corridor, I'm sure I can hear her music starting up in competition. I taught her. Our Principal Boy. Our Aladdin who let the genie out of the lamp.

And although I haven't mentioned her yet—this is Luda's story.

Everything that happened, everything that's about to happen, is because of Luda.

There.

Now we've all gotten to know one another, let's move on to Luda.

C*an we try that over again?*
How many times had those six words tramped in formation across the windswept parade ground of my mind?

In the quotidian world, you get one chance and one alone. Rattle the dice in the cup, pray for the half dozen, and go for it; the moment will never come again. We pass this way but once. All the things you never did will haunt you in that hospital bed at the end. *Mektoub.*

In the theatre it's different, we have *rehearsal.*

Can we try that over again?

That rolling fruity voice, all too easy to imitate, was the primary weapon in the impressive dramatic arsenal of Dominick Float, director of *The Phantom of the Pantomime,* and those were his favourite words in all the dictionary.

Can we try that over again?

By smouldering wet June, rehearsals for the triumphant Gasglow return of *The Phantom of the Pantomime* had already deteriorated into guerrilla warfare, skirmishes in the undergrowth of ever-changing script pages, rewritten scenes, and personal grievances.

Pantomime rehearsal times are the shortest in the business; sometimes the cast, the chorus, and the musicians have a two-week window to tighten up a two-hour show. In our privileged case, the framing device that elevated the show at least halfway in the direction of dramatic art conferred upon us the prestige of legitimate theatre with a five-month rehearsal window that gave Float leave to make us repeat every scene, every gag, every kinked eyebrow and knitted lip until it became instinctual, unconscious.

Having lost our original Aladdin, the "radiant" Gwen Skillicorn, to "schedule clashes" with higher-profile gigs than this extravagant labour of self-loathing in a perpetually drizzling post-industrial scab of a city, we had three months left to master the art of pantomime with several new and rubbery-raw cast members.

Otherwise, we'd assembled most of the original cast the way you'd summon relatives to a family funeral, and they'd responded with much the same enthusiasm.

You'll have to excuse me: I've some touching up to do— talking too much. Giving it all away.

Rules of the Glamour: The face I put on is more real than the one I conceal.

Which brings me back to—

Can we try that over again?

The first four hundred times I heard Dominick (with a *k*) Float repeat his go-to mantra, I had Herr Float diagnosed as one of those addictive types you see on TV—*can we do it again and again, and again and again?* OCD. A packed and organized fridge of a man. I imagined him bringing this one simple directive to every area of his married life, especially after watching him tackle a full English breakfast by inhaling it.

Cuckoos cuckoo, pigeons coo, parrots they parrot; and so too Dominick Float, singing his own individual, reliable song.

Can we try that over again?

Please reset to the end of the last scene—Float's production manager interpreted for him.

In the early days of our production, Float could squeeze between the tines of a dessert fork, but that was before success off Broadway, translated into doughnuts and five-course dinners, encouraged him to triple his mass, like the lead character in a remake of *The Fly,* where, instead of a loathsome insect, the scientist is turning into a hot-air balloon. I know I shouldn't go on about his weight the way I do, but I saw it as my duty to stand in the way of a potential cardiac extinction event.

Now, I realize I'm painting a less-than-flattering picture of a man I've often seen described as a genius, but first impressions are important. You'll get to know him better as I go on and try as you might to judge him harshly, you'll wind up like the rest of us, forgiving Float his idiosyncrasies.

Think of this as your last chance to hate him at first sight.

Can we try that over again?

"That" was our first clumsy stagger-through of an early scene in Twankey's Laundry where Abanazar insinuates himself into the Widow's confidence by pretending to be a long-lost brother-in-law.

She's naturally suspicious until the wizard rattles his purse.

Then again, I do have a terrible memory!—I repeated the line for the fifth time. *Why don't you ask the boys and girls?*

Then came the reply:

Is there time for a toilet break first? My prostate's ringing like the bells of St. Peter's.

And with that, Gofannon Rhys enters the picture, our slumming Royal Shakespearean television star, sick of a TV sideline playing trustworthy avuncular types, detectives with personal problems, essentially decent widowed ex-soldiers or eccentric magical uncles. By "toilet break" he meant "booze and pills interlude."

Rhys had a history of alarming racist outbursts but was given more leeway than the average extremist on the basis that the brunt of his intolerance and blind hatred was borne by the Mundugumor tribe of what he called "giant pygmies" in equatorial New Guinea. Allegedly some ancestors of the current indigenous population had once casseroled and consumed an intrepid nineteenth-century Rhys forebear and the actor found it impossible to forgive their successors. For this reason, fellow thesps tended to yield the man more rope than he deserved, regarding him less as a bigot and more an out-and-out madman with a CBE.

His role, like all our roles, was dual: called upon to represent the wizard Abanazar and to bring to life the tormented actor playing the sorcerer in a doomed quest for career redemption.

I know it's complicated but it's not that difficult. I'm asking you to pay attention to what's being said, that's all. Stop looking at your reflections on phone screens and listen. You'll be expected to make a big decision after I'm done. It's important to concentrate on the details.

God is in the details, as they say. Funnily enough, the Devil is too.

It almost makes you think.

You'll recall Abanazar; he's our slimy villain responsible for getting things up and running in the prologue to act 1, and it all starts when he raises a stiffie for a certain Magic Lamp in far Cathay, and no wonder: Possession of this Lamp will guarantee Abanazar the absolute eternal power he's craved since he stopped being a baby.

Thing is, Abanazar has a major problem; being altogether too evil and way too lazy to hunt for the wonder Lamp himself, the self-appointed wizard's obliged to trick a resourceful and, it must be said, very naïve Chinese Muslim boy named Aladdin into doing his dirty work for him. In this way, the vile sorcerer contributes motivation and provocation, providing the inciting incident that supplies our transcultural urchin with his heroic prince makeover.

The first table read was a dress-down event; my days of turning up for rehearsals in full drag were, in true pantomime tradition, behind me. There's medical evidence to suggest I should have stopped wearing tight jeans that year, when I realized to my horror I was a fifty-year-old man with the sperm count of a mummified pharaoh, but you know how it is; self-identifying as an artist means you can dress any way you want, especially when you're too old to be serious. And who needs children?

Go bold when you're old—I always say. I feel it's vital to give youngsters some positive role models for their own disgraceful, inevitable dotage.

When I decide to clamber aboard the number 36 bus looking like Marie Antoinette has risen from the grave dressed as a three-ring vampire monkey circus, that's my prerogative. It's performance art. That's what I tell myself over and over. You could say it's my mantra, my personal "Can we try that over again?" My plea. My excuse.

The car-crash shambles taking place at the table read that day *might* have eventually, conceivably succumbed to identification by police pathologists as a clumsy stab in the vague direction of performance but only an expert could tell.

As to art, the killer had made off with it, leaving only a crude chalk outline.

You know we can try all of it again from the start, Dom—I said. *We've just proved that fourteen times already!*

My hydrochloric *bon-mot* triggered a nervous laugh from the rest of the cast, including the aforementioned Gofannon Rhys, stand-up comedian Dez Blue as the Genie, pretty, self-obsessed soap star Dayanita Jayashankar as Jasmine, and our sweet Molly Stocking playing Aladdin himself as a rabbit flash-frozen in the headlights of an oncoming eighteen-wheeler.

Bringing up the rear we'd found gainful employment for musical theatre and panto veteran May Tang-Taylor and on-line lip-syncing "influencer" Aiysha Dyce as, respectively, the Empress, mother to Jasmine, and the Slave of the Ring, the wizard Abanazar's sassy, body-positive sidekick . . .

There will come a time, after you've settled in, when you'll ask yourself why the wizard's so eager to get hold of the Lamp when he already has a magical being at his beck. Honestly, your guess is as good as mine. I suppose it's the difference between a roller skate and a Rolls-Royce, or a gecko and Godzilla.

We began again, reincarnating spirits spooled and looped backwards up the page where every line is delivered as *déjà vu*.

As far as I was concerned, it was all about getting away with it. I still had my extravagantly long legs to see me through. Otherwise, the utility belt I'd accumulated around the midriff would quickly succumb first to the corset maker's art, thereafter to a punishing diet of vodka tonics, hot rocket, and sulph.

Where the Dame role is traditionally played by an older man in drag, Principal Boy is a part reserved for young women masquerading as handsome princes. It's best not to question the arbitrary rules, I've found. Just play along; it's more rewarding, and truer to life.

The dyed blonde, whose idea of dress-down was a paparazzi-baiting ensemble crafted from yellow neon rubber and murdered marmosets, was the previously mentioned Molly Stocking, one of five alleged entertainers in a manufactured girl group called Pussyfever.

When I say "manufactured," I'm talking unskilled labour struggling under punishing conditions to construct a band using human flotsam and hair extensions. They'd visited a string of hits on the unsuspecting world five or six years back, or so she kept reminding us.

How many hits could the poor world take before it staggered and fell clutching a burst and bloody nose, begging for mercy? I asked her.

She smiled, no idea what I was talking about.

Ever since the quintet's semi-acrimonious, alarmingly amoebic division into five individually talentless cells eighteen months previously, our Molly had doggedly slogged across a hit-free wasteland that seemed to stretch, or so she confided in me, all the way downstream to an inevitable reunion tour occurring just in time for the band to look as if their mothers had replaced them onstage.

Molly was a good-looking girl of twenty-five, proud possessor of a face so swollen with chemicals and fillers it should have belonged to a matronly MILF trying and failing by a whisker to resemble a twenty-eight-year-old porno star. Much of the work had been performed free of charge by unqualified doctors and nurses at a clinic in Turkey, in exchange for aggressive social media promotion, but honestly the project looked most likely to crash with gruesome results against the rocks of Molly's early thirties.

It seems like so many of the young girls these days have that identikit face bolted on: filtered self-denying "selfie" cheekbones and fish lips. A "rich girl" mask you can't remove without specialist tools and years of PTSD.

Deny it if you can: Everybody's in drag, nowadays, especially the girls.

No surprise then, given her pedigree, that Molly's true talent lay in an unerring superpower, a bat-sonar that guided her directly to the flat troughs or sharp peaks surrounding every note she aimed towards.

As for Molly's dancing, let's just say it was Seven Veils short of Salome and leave it at that.

I'm working as hard as I can not to be mean. This is me trying, honestly, and to be fair, no one could deny Molly rocked the part after they nailed her into that streetwise Aladdin outfit, all gilded turban and Day-Glo-enamelled Nikes.

I was there for the fitting; she looked fantastic. She'd aced the audition. We knew she could handle it.

Now here she was, losing her figurative handbag in rehearsal. Some performers are like that: Take away the audience feedback, they can't remember why they clambered out of bed in the first place.

At the time of the table read, Molly was between two men,

and not for the first or last time, I shouldn't wonder. Her current beau, Olympic triathlon bronze medallist Vladimir Orbit, was too tame, or so she explained; too clean and too sober. Orbit, a paragon of decency and athletic accomplishment, was bad for Molly's new image as a wild and dangerous party girl on the rebound.

With that story line in mind, Molly's publicists lined her up with fellow pop casualty Joss Weill, the proto-human, third-favourite vocalist of Boystalking, swaying and blinking like Piltdown Man in the orts of his solo career.

They'd shack up together, that was the idea. They'd plan a wedding, then she'd catch him red-handed with a trans pole dancer, or some rival pop cast-off. Preferably younger. Another love rat exposed. Named, shamed, and binned.

It's not worth the energy it takes to stay in the drag race. The same showbiz shock stories play out with different names, like actors doing Sherlock Holmes, James Bond, or Hamlet. I should know.

Molly's representation was keen to get her back "on top," as she put it. They might as well have put her on top of a bonfire like what's his name, Guy Fawkes, or Joan of Arc.

Where's that boy? Aladdin?

I floated the line a second time, setting it free to roam the otherwise empty stage, butterfly in October.

As I lingered in vain for Molly's response, I could hear papers shuffled and throats cleared, thinking how that was probably the precise sound of things right before the Big Bang and the beginning of the Universe.

Aladdin?—there's me lobbing the cue back, the ball in a game of solo tennis.

The Principal Boy is the lynchpin of the pantomime, they say— we rely on the audience to buy wholeheartedly into the young hero's simple story, allowing us to drape our theatrical razzmatazz over a time-honoured clotheshorse of narrative familiarity.

I'd seen Molly on the front page of one of the gossip rags that morning on my way to work—*Hey You!* or *Scorch* or *Close Enough!* or whatever they're called. A glum-looking photograph of the girl, whey-faced with minimal makeup and three double chins, on the phone. The headline:

WHY DOES EVERYONE WANT ME TO FAIL?

Float, raised and educated by cynical sophisticates, instructed us all to draw upon those bottomless wells of self-deception and *hubris* we actors bring to the stage. Naturalism *ist verboten*—artifice, fakery, illusion, decadence: These are our watchwords.

Float had already anticipated the delicious layers of irony he might peel back by casting an untrained actress in a pivotal, leading role.

When we lost our first-run Aladdin, the talented, insufferable Gwen Skillicorn, to Hollywood, Float worked hard to convince himself that Molly's coquettish naïveté or, as I saw it, her superhuman lack of charm and talent, would win the day. Her tabloid fame, he reasoned, would be sufficient to lure a new "hip" under-thirty audience to our revival of *The Phantom*.

He was both right and wrong in every way.

I took Molly aside.

I don't know why it's not working—she said.

You're letting them discourage you. You beat off lots of young women to secure this role—I told her—and I know!

Try as I might, it's hard to stem the tidal bore of innuendo released by my inner Twankey.

I am a tiger!—I growled. *Let's see you snarlin', darlin'! Remember? You'd come on in tiger-print vinyl outfits. I'm sure it was about tigers. It went to number three in the charts, right?*

"Tigress"—she reminded me, with a pointed emphasis on the final syllable that conjured up the hissing asp that did for Cleopatra.

I didn't think they let you say that nowadays—I cautioned.

I've been on the sharp end of political correctness often enough! *Nobody says "actress" anymore, and it's the same thing.*

It was a song about feminism—argued Molly, putting her foot down.

Even better—I assured her, refusing to take the bait. *Now do what I do, and you won't ever forget your lines again.*

So began the eye-to-eye transmission of simple folk wisdom. *Here's the plan*—I said. *When I read the lines, I'm already wearing my costume. Think about the turban, the waistcoat, and the pantaloons—you're wearing them right now. The curly slippers. Not the sort of outfit pop star Molly Stocking would wear, am I right? More like something Aladdin would wear.*

She nodded, baffled into wonder.

When you're in costume, you stop being you; you become Aladdin. Aladdin has problems of his own, but they never change, night after night, and he turns them all into opportunities. You can do the same.

I sensed the beginnings of what you might call a paradigm shift, a shuffle of mental plate tectonics capable of rearranging the conceptual ground beneath her feet. I thought back to the magazine headlines I'd read earlier that grim Tuesday.

You know why everyone wants you to fail, babes?

Because they hate me!—she wailed.

They're evil, jealous bastards!—I explained, patiently. *You're young and beautiful and they're old or ugly and unsatisfied with their lives or they want to take your place. They think you have everything they wish for. They think you don't know how to be sad like they do! What else did you think it was? Why you'd want to put your self-esteem in the hands of evil jealous bastards is a problem for you to tackle with the help of a qualified professional.*

You saw that? Her eyes took on the bright, cracked glaze of eyes in a Dutch oil painting.

You're Principal Boy! You're brave and good, even if no one knows it yet. You're a superhero! Show them what you're made of! Slap your thigh! Aladdin can't fail.

Molly Stocking smacked the meat at the top of her leg with an intensity that crossed the line into self-harm. Then she smiled, snatching at me with a cat-clawing motion accompanied by a halfhearted growl of defiance.

Anytime you forget who you are onstage, just slap your thigh and summon Aladdin—I told her. *It's not you saying the lines, it's Aladdin. Aladdin wouldn't forget his own words, right? He's expressing himself. Everything that's you—push it away when you're onstage; it's a simpler world. In that world—you're Aladdin.*

Gears in motion ratcheted behind Molly's luminous eyes. I pictured cogwheels cranking a woodcut sun of understanding over the painted hilly horizon of the backlot of her mind.

I had just enlightened Molly Stocking to one of the basic tenets of prancing on stage and playing a role. Something no one had bothered to teach her.

The harder you pretend, the more real it becomes.

Rules of the Glamour.

I heard you do magic—she stopped, shyly. She'd been reading about me on her phone obviously. In my past, I'd said too much.

That's Abanazar . . . he's the wizard!—I joked, with my smile locking into place like a visor on a crash helmet. *Don't get me mixed up with him!*

I read about you. Magic. Like angels and the occult.

That was it. Time to shut this down.

It doesn't take magic to put a smile back on your face—I said. *Look at you!*

I think you're special—she insisted. *There's something about you. A light. My nan sees angels. I'd love to know more about magic. My nana read tea leaves.*

It's not what you think—I told her honestly.

Meanwhile, I was thinking—*the last thing I need is a disciple!*
Funny how things work out.
I should have taken my own advice.
Glamour, babes. They want us to shine!—I insisted, sure it
was true.
Back in rehearsal, Twankey's first lines came pirouetting
along my tongue to trip like hosts of seraphim taking flight.
What's my name?
My posture relaxed into Twankey's hobble-skirted stagger. I
walked as if I were in heels, as if to show Molly what I'd been
talking about. The hip swing and tipsy teeter coming from my
gut not the shoes.
And you all shout "Widow Twankey!"
Dressed down, I could still feel the furry weight of Twankey's
rare, imaginary animal-pelt coats in fluorescent pinks and baby
blues, the tanned hides of infant unicorns and endangered
teddy bears. In comfortable jeans and a hoodie, I made myself
recall the drape and the weight and the texture of every clattering, restrictive item of the costume I'd be wearing onstage.
I mentally outfitted myself in phantom drag before tumbling
from the wings, choking on an imaginary vaper.
*Now, if you catch me puffing on my vape, stop me. I've given
it up for my health but I sometimes forget—*
You'll remember how it's important to establish my forget-
fulness to the audience.
The next big scene is a two-hander: Me and Aladdin.
Aladdin and me.
And there was Molly's wan face, crumpled with worry to
look like one of those first-draft pages a dissatisfied writer
chucks in the bin. A pang of maternal responsibility gripped
me, and I was reminded of how it felt to be a volunteer on the
suicide hotline, encouraging this fragile lovely young woman to
embrace life.
Help me call out for him!

The dialogue prompt was launched with all the precision of a rocket strike across the stage to where, in the wings, our Aladdin intoned a prayer, apparently struggling in the white-hot talons of demonic possession. Her eyeballs rolled back as if to sneak a peek at her brain in full spate as she dragged what seemed to be words in great rusty chains from the haunted cellars of her derelict memory palace, with an effort not only visible but audible.

Then imagine lightning hitting a tree! That was Molly as she flared up and sprang into motion, electric with narcotics, exploding sap and toxic overconfidence!

He's behind you!—the imagined audience screamed as one.

As rehearsed, I'd spin around, and so would Aladdin, and we'd miss each other by fractions of seconds, like two ninjas each inadvertently shadowing the other's movements, each disappearing into the corner of the other's eye.

Aladdin! I know he's here somewhere . . . I can even smell his sweaty trainers!

He's behind you—they yell, and this goes on until we *freeze.*

No one moves. The audience reactions subside to murmurs. Silence.

The Phantom is revealed, watching it all from his elevated perspective.

The puppet-strings that hold us up are seen to reach into the lighting rig, where the fingers of our mysterious overseer manipulate the story.

This always gets a gasp from the audience, even when they've read the reviews and they think they know what's going to happen.

It was clever, *The Phantom of the Pantomime,* but it was simple, and funny, and easy to follow. You could take it and read it any way you wanted, and still get something out of it, whether you were bright and eight years old or a strutting twenty-six, or elegantly eighty on the way out.

The Phantom descends from the rafters, riding on a chandelier no less, to wander through the set, among us. No one moves but the Phantom in his weird mask, adjusting our limbs in preparation for the next scene before his departure into the overheads, leaving only blue smoke and grey questions.

It's what drew me to *The Phantom* in the first place. That scene where we're reminded nothing is real.

You know the story already: The Phantom kills the cast off one by one and the absurdity revolves around the production's attempts to do *Aladdin* with a diminishing number of performers, until only one remains onstage, playing all the parts before the killer shows his face at last—

Twankey and the Phantom are one and the same!

As it turns out, the Phantom only believes he's disfigured. When they take off the mask before the big finale, the whole audience can see they're remarkably good-looking, if I do say so myself.

That's when we understand: What the Phantom finds horrifying is the sight of their own ageing face in the mirror! They wear the greasepaint mask of Widow Twankey to hide the unbearable disfigurement of simply growing older.

And that's not even the big twist! To get that, you'll have to keep listening.

I told you it was clever in its own way. Even knowing how it plays out makes it more ridiculous and ordinary and human— Aladdin meets Beckett if you like.

Dream on.

Molly was more than delighted with that idea. More than anything, she wanted to be taken seriously. I'd been harsh, and I shouldn't have wished bad luck on her.

I made up my mind to think only pleasant thoughts. From this moment on, I told myself, I would live to encourage and inspire.

Molly sidled up at the end of rehearsal, to tell me I'd been really, really helpful. When she smiled, you'd swear the petals had opened on a lovely Botoxed sunflower.

Only two reallys?—I shot back but I did it with a grin, so she'd know I was being facetious.

Really, really, really!—she repeated, all radiant and full of herself now.

I gave her a big smile and a bigger hug. She'd be insufferable soon enough.

When she slapped her thigh again on her way out, the brutal crack of the impact told me this was the sort of thing that could easily progress from a pleasurable habit to a lifetime problem, but I let it go.

We all know what happened next.

The sets were coming on slowly; the role of a street in China was played by an enormous plywood tableau where painted Han-dynasty pagodas shared a skyline with the Burj Khalifa, Hong Kong's Lippo Centre and Gasglow's Skyview Tower.

Before starting on *Phantom,* we'd researched every performance of *Aladdin* since its opening night in 1852 at the Drury Lane Theatre. Some of those Jack-the-Ripper-time shows were epic blockbusters relying on cutting-edge stagecraft: semi-silvered Pepper's ghosts, and other cryptic tricks of light, seeming somehow, in hindsight, like real magic.

Float wanted to bring that back. He was obsessed with ideas of deception, simulation, artifice. The haunted music hall.

Or as I knew it, the Glamour.

By the time of the first dress rehearsal, Molly had raised her game by leaps and bounds. Not the most appropriate choice of words, I'd agree, bearing in mind the poor girl's impending exit, stage door left on a gurney.

I effervesced onstage in my finery, wrapped for Christmas and the New Year in shiny PVC and candy-coloured *faux* fur.

The look was post-makeover Glamorous Gran in slapper

shoes. It's easy to imagine the Widow blowing her late husband's life insurance payout on cosmetic surgery and trashy
outfits, wheezing for a puff as she stalks the streets of a paint-
and-plywood *papier-mâché* Peking; a stop-motion glam ty-
rannosaur on HRT from one of those old Ray Harryhausen
pictures.

Where's that boy? Aladdin?

Triggered by her cue, Pavlov's Pooch drooling into action,
Molly sprang out, all radioactive overconfidence like when
they've mastered their yellow belt in karate and there's a gang
of tooled-up bastards huddled round what only looks like an
old lady at the ATM.

Like they do when they've learned four chords on the guitar and the big time is smiling and saying *come on—take that
next step—no one will laugh when they realize you can't sing* or
play . . .

Like they do on ching.

He's behind you!

Molly Stocking aka Aladdin flashed a grin, tossed back her
head with gay abandon, and slapped her thigh like I'd taught
her. When her right knee jerked up, she lost her balance and
was gone.

We were all of us onstage treated to a singular sound like
brittle bone snapping as the heel of Molly's shoe cracked.

This was followed by an equally unrepeatable shriek as her
ankle shattered in sympathy and her left leg telescoped, pitch-
ing Molly face-first, all turban, pantaloons, and nerve-shredding
cries of anguish, into the prop basket outside Widow Twankey's
Laundry.

The ambulance arrived forty minutes later, using the traffic
on the Ringway at Dundare as an excuse. Molly was stretchered offstage left, still sparkling in her Aladdin costume, a gift-
wrapped accident loaded into the back of an ambulance as an
early Xmas present for emergency room staff.

A rambling message arrived later that day, thanking her fans, her mum and dad, me, her management and publicist, her ex-bandmates, ex-boyfriends, and her "best friend" labradoodle Villanelle, before the morphine accomplished its merciful labour and silenced her for the night.

Experts offered vague assurances they couldn't possibly back up; she might be able to dance by opening night. We would be wrong to count her out. Miracles had happened apparently. They were in the Bible.

Reason suggested otherwise; even if Molly could learn to regrow her limbs like a salamander, she'd miss out on months of essential rehearsal for a very demanding part.

The understudy—a can-do smiler with a Neanderthal matriarch lurking somewhere in her DNA—wouldn't last the week. Float was already talking auditions. Thirteen weeks to opening night.

I've said it before and will again: The role of the Principal Boy is the lynchpin of any pantomime production. Except for the Dame, of course.

Principal Boys are all cut from the same marketplace cloth: diamonds in the rough, losers from the lower classes who turn out to be winners, like Dick Whittington, Aladdin, and Hansel, with the odd Prince Charming or two from the upper crust seasoned into the recipe.

Float, incapable of deviating from his single-minded, scorched-earth approach to every problem, decided all at once that what we needed was an unknown for the role of Aladdin. The search was on for a star yet to be born, a heavenly body undiscovered by terrestrial telescopes, an as-yet-significant gap in the map of the sky.

Like some fabulous new continent—I suggested wearily. *Unexplored.*

Like that. Yeah. Someone special—the gaze of the genius was medicated, dissociated. *Someone fresh.*

So, we're looking for the complete opposite of Molly Stocking?—I said.

He stuck his thumb up. Farted spectacularly. Another magic moment in the company of *der* dictator Dominick Float.

Indistinct auditions smeared by; neither of us could remember any but the last few minutes of those endless indeterminate afternoon hours. Time slowly crystallized, as if nothing could ever happen differently and this was the way things were engineered to be.

It began with a restless prowling apprehension; we both knew if we failed to find our perfect Aladdin before sundown or its equivalent, the pressure would cause the walls around us to inflate and burst, along with our heads and hearts.

And we both knew. In the future it had already happened, one way or the other. There had to be an Aladdin on opening night or there was no *Aladdin,* no *Phantom.*

The question became: When would our Aladdin arrive to set us free from waiting?

We found ourselves willing an unspecified moment, wishing a notional being into existence, wringing the immensity of possibility down into a single Aladdin-shaped container made to hold precisely the right candidate.

Our accidental invocation was—and now we come to it— answered by a gunshot-ricochet annunciation from the corridor beyond.

As I sit here sponging shallow moons of Kryo white under my eyes, going back to that last minute before the arrival of Luda, I remember Dominick signaling, with every scintilla of accumulated nonverbal passive aggression at his disposal, how the time had come to give up and go back to re-appraising the best of the also-rans.

Float was hungry. He had not fed since lunchtime when he'd swallowed the entire contents of a farm and left the restaurant unsatisfied. His dad-gut snarled at me, and stomachs have their own brain cells apparently. Gut feelings are as real as ravenous tigers.

That's when he said—*It's going nowhere. I'm out.*

Already on his feet, shrugging his jacket on, and fingering his car keys like pocket wind chimes. I had a feeling, a gut feeling you could say, that we should stay a moment longer. The static electricity in the room felt satanic and sexy, casting scalloped batwing shadows across stained glass portraits of saints.

Wait—I said. *Just. Wait.*

Is that when I noticed the clock had stopped?

Float seemed to acknowledge the moment. He listened to his watch. He frowned. He shimmied his wrist as if to fix the problem then listened a second time.

I was equally surprised by how much time had passed since time ceased to matter. I looked once more, to be certain, at the motionless clock face and the hummingbird hover of the second hand.

Only one thing counted: that abrupt, repeated rifle-shot ricochet of heel on tile approaching down the hall. Metronymic— *click kit-kick click k-tik*—striking the floor tiles. Multiple possibilities were measured and discarded in precise jeweller's hammer strokes, chipping and flaking the one singular, inevitable moment into place.

We both felt it happen, Float and I; our wishes converged and took form as an undeniable future, upon us like an approaching, mysterious tsunami, an aquamarine tidal surge of the uncanny headed our way, leaving us powerless in the undertow.

Kick click click k-tik went the syncopated snare-drum strike and counterstrike of spiked stilettos in Pop Art SF/x staccato.

Think of the dreadful *tick-tick* of the timer on a bomb whose countdown, growing louder, suddenly stops into the roaring silence when a firing squad receives its order.

And Luda was there at the door.

Luda was there.

You must understand: In that eclipse everything gave off a lacquered numinous glow, a superlative holy gloss and polish, where each detail, each lambent light and Rembrandt shadow, came burnished to the profundity of precious stone.

Am I high now?

Looking back, I'm certain the temperature fell at least ten degrees when Luda entered the room. Crucifixes spun on their axes. Outside, the hearts of birds stopped, and they crashed dead from the sky. A distant sun was slaughtered by a new black star.

And somehow, we missed every warning, seeing only the answer to our prayers.

Oddly enough, in all our efforts to remember what happened, we had no memory of Luda's arrival. The one thing of which we could be certain was that she was there, in front of us, as if she'd always been there, waiting for this moment.

How to describe Luda? Where do I begin?

Do we start with Luda's impossible eyes? Do we end there?

Do we proceed from the outside in, like a pathologist, commencing with her white vinyl coat, concluding in the black tar pits she keeps where others have souls?

I hope I'm not too late—she said.

We're still clinging to life, if that's what you mean—I deadpanned. *How's your first aid?*

Float sat down to consult his schedule. *I don't think we were expecting anyone else*—he said. *Do you have a name?*

Luda—she said. And that was that.

First impressions first: Glacial. Tall. Hair in an iridescent copper-violet bob. Under the white coat, she dressed head-to-toe in Vantablack. Spray-on black leather pants, black Oakley boots, a rhinestone spider spinning its glittering web across her black T-shirt. I remember every detail. The studded collar she wore. The voice, educated, measured, and too precise.

You don't look much like Aladdin—I went on.

Thinking that was enough to put her off guard, I threw her a few daft lines from the Haunted Bedroom scene to see how she'd react.

I've heard there's ghosts in here—I said, accessing Twankey mode. *I hope you're all right sharing a bedroom with a ghost or two, Aladdin!*

My attempt to knock her off balance had the opposite effect of propelling Luda into character. Light of foot, quick of wit, Luda became Aladdin peering nervously beneath an imaginary bed as we flew off book.

As long as the ghost's paying his share of the bill—she shot back.

With what?—I said. *Ghost money?*

Luda pulled out her empty pockets, cartoonishly glum.

It's more money than what we've got—she said, wide-eyed. *Anyway, I don't believe in ghosts. Do you?*

I'm more likely to see a ghost than I am money! It's money I don't believe in!

Then suspicious.

How did you pay for this room anyway?

I promised him a free fluff 'n' fold—I winked.

Is that what they're calling it nowadays?

Float settled back in his seat as we ping-ponged surreal improv, pooching up his lower lip as the signal he was taking mental notes while nodding intermittently, like my dad had done eighteen months into his Parkinson's diagnosis.

Can we try that over again?

Float was fooled by Luda. I wasn't.

Anyway, I don't believe in ghosts! And as for money . . .

And that's how it went until Float, quivering with an intensity I'd last seen in a kitten chattering after a blue tit on a twig, clapped his Michelin mitts together.

Let's have your best eight—ah, Luda—said Dom, and we settled back to enjoy a hard-hitting, uncompromising interpretation of "To Sir with Love" that made up for in ambition and sheer volume whatever it lacked in finesse.

As the last keening note splintered against the ceiling beams, Dom pretended to take a tough line.

We really appreciate you turning up like this but you're not on the list and we weren't expecting you. We just need a minute, love.

Luda nodded, smiled like the sun coming up, and skipped off, swinging a Goodbye Kitty! satchel across her shoulder, each inevitable Muybridge moment of her exit enshrined in my memory.

The only thing I can say in my defence is how I was aware of something odd about her heel-spin and the afterimage she left behind. A faint double exposure seemed to follow her, a Kirlian aura trail, an ectoplasmic smear on the backdrop of reality.

What are you so scared of, Lu?—said Float, turning to look at me, cutting to the chase.

He was right. What *was* I scared of? Competition? I couldn't compete with Luda for youth, or for beauty.

Why *was* I afraid of her?

Did I fear my fragile heart would break if I was made to face her every day and dream about her every night?

She'd have a muscular, open-minded boyfriend with a well-paid job in the arts. Girls like her always did. A bisexual photographer probably, or a radical digital artist with a six-pack, a vision of tomorrow, and rampant bipolar symptoms.

That flawless Fibonacci sequence symmetry. Her youth and her potential. All her numbers adding up to the Golden Ratio.

I excused myself and followed Luda to the facilities where I fussed at the bathroom mirror, making sure I was close enough to hear her toneless humming and the sound of her youthful, exuberant piss sluicing the porcelain. From the reverberations, it was easy to calculate the angle of arc, the spray trajectory, plop, and splash.

Put it like this: There are some things you just can't hide.

I heard the latch slide back and out she strode from the cubicle, a film star resurrected from an upright golden coffin. Big generous smile. Cheekbones of a sexbot. A fuckdroid. Skin smooth and dusted with a pearlescent haze I can't explain. And then the eyes: South Sea island lagoon water. The turquoise impossible eyes of a deadly ghost fox woman from a Japanese folktale.

I hope I didn't hold you both up.

Luda met her reflection with a bold grin of pillar-box red, checking the minutiae of her slap for errors no one but me would ever notice.

Both of us? It would take the world's strongest man to hold up Dominick Float for thirty seconds, love—I said, making a *moue*.

She looked indestructible; my cue to drop the bomb I'd been saving since her audition.

Pee sounds different when you're standing up, babes.

Luda only smiled, all glossy red lips and white teeth as regular and even as the headstones in a military cemetery, unleashing the pitiless light of an exploding hydrogen bomb from those Pacific atoll eyes.

You think I'm over-egging it? Just wait.

My future is in your hands—she shrugged, handing me the scrunched rose of a paper towel she'd used to dab scarlet gloss from her top lip. That was the worst of it in the end. She felt nothing at all. She didn't have to feel anything because she knew how it would go. She knew exactly what move I would pull next.

As I later discovered, Luda's strategy was to stay five moves ahead in the game, and it *was* a game, darlings, with Luda laughing at the rest of us as we flapped to catch up, still in denial we were already glued to the strands of her web.

The name of the game was Golden Dames.

Like I said, it wasn't jealousy that set me on edge. Well, truth to tell, it's always been jealousy with me, but this was something beyond all that.

Something about Luda was so familiar I wanted to scream and put my face right through that mirror. She was my dream girl, my fantasy Jungian *anima*. She was everything I'd wanted and wanted to be. The girl I hung out with in dreams, who knew me best of all, looked exactly like Luda.

That was probably the best audition we've seen—Float said, as if we'd watched Luda take off, fly around the room on gilded angel wings, and shit rainbow tinsel fireworks.

Which, to all intents and purposes, we had.

Is it a good idea to let a complete unknown sashay in off the street and do Molly Stocking's job? That's what I thought about saying and—

How come nobody seems to have seen her CV? What else has she done? Who's her agent? Where's her portfolio?

—but I knew it sounded ridiculous. Luda had rendered Molly obsolete.

Maybe she has no representation at all—he mused. *You must admit, she was good. Raw but good. There's work to be done . . .*

Isn't it funny she just turned up and was that good? I said, suspiciously. *Out of nowhere?*

And he was like—*Isn't it lucky for us she did?*

You don't think she was a bit masculine?

He peered at me.

Aladdin's a boy!

That was it. I couldn't hold back any longer . . .

She is *a boy!*

I don't know why I blurted it out like that, but I did. I was guilty of misgenderment in the first degree. I knew I looked bad.

Luda! That's a drag name!—I blundered on, fumbling the ball over the goal line. *We don't know if she identifies as female twenty-four seven, do we?*

Float only shrugged.

I don't care. I'm asking her back—he said. *We got lucky here. It feels supernatural. I need to go home, pour myself an enormous Old-Fashioned, and contemplate the loving grace of God.*

Float lifted his banyan-trunk arms in surrender or supplication. A Space Invader waving the white flag to cover for his buddies dropping bombs on the digital skyline of planet Earth.

I want her to come back on Friday. I want to see you do the Mangle scene with her.

She's a boy playing a girl playing a boy.

I love it—he said. And he meant it. *I love that.*

He was right, but I'd witnessed doom in Luda's luxury swimming-pool eyes, and I was right too. There was a skull-and-crossbones rippling beneath Luda's generous smile.

We agreed with a sparkling, eagerly nodding Luda to meet again to talk through the general challenges ahead, and the specific intricacies of the Mangle scene.

Delighted, Luda flashed me several sidelong conspiratorial glances, as though we were already accomplices in a crime, then spun on her heel and was gone, trailing a scented wake.

I see what you mean now—Float said. *Up close. Doesn't matter.*

The second hand was on the move once more.

I couldn't wait for the torn-off calendar pages to bring us together again.

I'm already starting to look better: Contouring for the stage is its own discipline and I like to take my time; the audience must be able to read your expressions from the back stalls and the gods. The joy, the surprise, the pain, the sadness, and the victory should be visible from near Earth orbit.

Sometimes, as in now, as I attempt to plaster over the incremental damage time seems to pride itself on inflicting, I imagine myself a specialist mortician, called in at the last minute to renovate the corpse of Luci LaBang.

How to make the dear old queen palatable to a future she'll never inhabit?

Looks to me like the grand old dame's been down there for a while, Sergeant, partially preserved by peat and compost.

That explains the leathery countenance, Constable. Observe the cracks and folds. The withered landscape of her once strikingly beautiful face. Filled in with mud and goat droppings.

They've done their best to tart her up on the slab but there's only so far artifice can stretch, and even the mortician's commitment to her art can only ever apologize for the ravages of nature.

I know that face.

This is her story, not mine. I can only watch through laced fingers.

The death clown is here, seeking retribution.

Widow Twankey takes the stage.

Can we try that over again?

11
THE SQUARE ROOT OF 5

E very now and then, you'll be invited to consider the truth of a "true story" that stretches the bounds of possibility so far "possibility" might as well mean "alligator" or "pencil case," or just about anything else you want it to mean.

That was me.

The way things have a way of going, what with this, that, and the other, I wound up ten minutes late at the "world famous" Café Rendezvous, where I'd arranged to meet Luda.

Here, I'd been promised with a wicked twinkle, she'd explain to me whatever it was that had happened between us following Friday's rehearsals.

We're on the South Side now, three miles out from the Left Bank of the River Dare, among the magic-carpet-coloured stalls and storefront barrows of the Asian Quarter where pyramids of precariously stacked melons and plantains share space with spiky bouquets of Day-Glo flowers cut from cardboard, bargain prices sketched in Sharpie ink strokes.

Me, I'd traded up to the trendy West End almost twenty-five years ago, after the Troupe's first big splash on TV. Before all that commotion, I'd whiled away my late teens and early twenties here, working hard to build a normal life for myself and for Rose and the baby that never was. I'd moved into Rose's rented ground floor apartment on a row of architecturally noteworthy red-brick tenement houses carefully wrapped by its designers in an orbit plan around the hub of Spiral Park, or Tit Acres as the beauty spot was known to locals and tourists alike, a result of its distinctive mammary silhouette.

Unchanging like the Sphinx or the moon, evergreen with decay, miraculously self-renewing as the centuries come and go, the Café Rendezvous abides, cryogenically frozen in that world-famous Sci-Fi Deco Gasglow style while generations prosper and wilt, leaving their cries for help or attention in etched ballpoint tabletop graffiti. All those risible promises of eternal devotion, vows of success, now fading and overwritten; names of former showbiz hopefuls with no one left alive even to forget them. Those initials scratched patiently would outlast their owners, embedded in Formica time capsules, to be puzzled over by caffeinated, wild-eyed amateur historians of the twenty-fifth century.

All those lovers married now to people they hate, each other more than likely. All the boasts, the flags and manifestos, the abandoned street plans for teenage Utopias. Pop songs gone stale, lyrics scribbled over, lives remixed like landfill under the latest layer of the palimpsest, promising a new flyover with a more direct route to the cemetery.

On the smoked-ham glaze of the walls hung framed, signed photographs of visiting entertainment stars, the radioactive half-life of their fame decaying to black-and-white afterburn—a cooling silver fizz that persists when the light goes out and the stellar halo loses its heat—this parade of now-unidentifiable mugshots and cancelled TV specials. Who remains to nod in recognition at the names? Rickie Blend? Zita Vermouth? Mr. Biceps? Lou Coil? Saxy Berzerk? The Perfect Men?

Do I have to go on?

But you do remember the Rendezvous. Everybody remembers the Rendezvous or somewhere like it, where you and your friends "hung out" in the uneasy years between Happy Meals and awards ceremonies.

Here I'd met girlfriends and boyfriends, all of us crying and

laughing, elevated and wide-eyed on drugs or raw love or simply being young and so wet behind the ears you could bathe
in it. Here I'd huddled with homegrown visionaries devising
elaborate blueprints for life, with accompanying charts and cal-
endars; two of which came to fruition at least.

Think of the Rendezvous as a nexus, a plexus, a Bohemian
Ground Zero; haunt of freeze-dried poets, pop ghouls, resting
actors, and the dregs of the dreaming classes since 1933!

Since exiting the driverless taxi that brought me back to my
gnarly roots, I'd made numerous rapid consultations with every
available reflective surface to arrive at the angle that best flattered my features.

Ever since that day, somewhere around age eleven, when I'd
first taken quite seriously the lifetime suspicion that I was the
star turn in some invisible observer's dodgy entertainment—
somewhere in a parallel universe or distant galaxy—every move
I made was a self-conscious nod to this unseen audience; each
gesture and joke, every shed tear designed to be appreciated
and applauded.

Mine was a calculated slow-motion vogue through life. If I
kept it interesting, I reasoned out, Scheherazade-style, maybe
they'd keep watching, or listening. Maybe they wouldn't pull
the "early death; unfulfilled potential" lever before I'd been
given my singular opportunity to show how diverting I could
be. Maybe they'd be willing me to get through it all unscathed.

Now, I'm sorry if these admittedly toxic levels of ultra-vanity
can be hard to process; think of it as my personal response to a
crawling permanent sensation of being scrutinized and judged
by a concealed audience. Call it madness or call it self-affirma-
tion but if I can't convince myself I'm great, how will I persuade
the Spectators?

It's been an inexhaustible theme in therapy for me going
back decades. I'm not saying everyone's like this, but I think a
lot of us are.

That June afternoon, on my way to meet Luda, the sun showed up watery and diffuse, losing its circumference to white haze in a way that reminded me of how an effervescent pain-killer froths at the edges when you drop it in a glass of water on the morning after a self-sabotaging bender.

Which, coincidentally, this was. Just fifteen hours previously I'd ruthlessly annihilated half a bottle of Watchtower vodka, before vaping a quarter of hash and settling down to half of a *Game of Games* season 6 box set, which everyone was watching, that year. I checked out when they brought zombie mammoths into it.

I shared a dressing room with genies and evil wizards every day at work; what use did I have for gnomes, man-eating cockatrices, cock-eating manatrices, or whatever they were meant to be? You have to draw the line somewhere.

I beelined across the gum-pocked sidewalk, focused on my immediate goals, which waited in the opaque interiors beyond the Rendezvous's ziggurat-etched glass—too preoccupied to register the optimistic shuffle and nod of a whippety-looking youth punting this month's issue of *Homeless Times* in the toothless socket of an adjacent doorway that now stood as a memorial to the final resting place of one recently deceased branch of the Bite Me! sandwich franchise.

Why don't the top 1 percent just give a bit to everybody and we'd *all* be rich?

I wondered if Luda was the sort who'd give money to a desperate boy like this one as I passed him with an apologetic grunt. The bell on its spring above the door rattled a familiar welcome.

Her generation came from a different place. Luda. I had no idea how her morality might work. She had a bad attempt at a finishing school accent. Was she rich? I wondered extravagantly. Luda.

Ten minutes later, I found myself reduced to wondering what Luda would do if she ever showed up.

Seen through glass, framed by etched Aztec borders, the *Homeless Times* boy appeared stuffed; a specimen in a museum case, with a shamefaced admission revealing how people once died in the Middle Ages. People like us forced to live without penicillin, Marvel Comics, or TV. Our tour guide would apologize for any upset, explaining how they'd once roamed the land looking like this. Getting away with it.

Seventeen, or thereabouts, all poxy, snottery, and viral—three of the Seven Dwarves of Poverty. I could make out speckled glue blisters under his Queen of the Nile nose along with the scintillant beauty crusts at the corners of his lips that signalled the presence of freshly scabbed cold sores. A junkie more than likely. Rent boy.

I decided there and then to think of him as Rentboy, an Irvine Welsh character, fluent in demotic. Poet of the commonplace.

Herpes simplex notwithstanding, he had lovely lips. Hunting-bow lips.

Rentboy was hot, to tell the truth, if you like the heroin-chic thing, and these days I can't be sure what I do or don't like. After seven years of enforced and unwelcome celibacy, all I'm willing to confirm is this: Left to its own devices in the cesspit of abstinence, the imagination trends dirtier not cleaner.

In a world where every existing thing has commodity value, I wondered how much Rentboy would charge for a blow job.

In a world like that one, of course, there was only one question: How much would I be willing to pay?

I planted my arse cheeks in a welcoming crater of deflated foam and cracked bull's-blood *faux* leather, worn by bums of the ages into the all-purpose glute socket of a chair designer's fever dreams. The same effect was reproduced, with an artisanal level of detail, on each of the premises' chairs as a mass-manufactured Pop Art decay. The fractured laminate foldout menu hadn't changed since 1933 except to add a vegan "V" option. In a giant leap for humankind, it was now possible to order vegan bacon and vegan sausage rolls, along with vegan onions.

My choice of seating was premeditated, sited a little too close to the gender-neutral "restrooms" that came complete with their own micro-climate of cheap antiseptic and urine, this test of my olfactory tolerance received its intended reward in a decent view of Rentboy's dorsal architecture.

Nice legs. Tight butt. Skinny. The rest, it was hard to tell. He'd scrub up well, that was for sure. That other thing, the nasty spicy yearning I tried and tried to blank with a homemade mantra, was simple envy.

He wasn't the sort of sensitive hard man I tended to swoon over. The potential I saw in Rentboy was something else.

I spot a boy like that, all emaciated and waiflike with cheek-bones to kill for, the first thing I think about is: How much better would he look in drag? I'm sorry, I do. I dress people up in my head. What was it about this one's derelict life that couldn't be sorted with a wig and a boa? Unseen, unnoticed as a spotty boy, he'd stride spotlit through the world in wigs and heels, an object of desire, not disregard.

Just then, I caught a glimpse of a disgusting old pervert in the next booth; his sly, twisted grin and greedy gaze spoke of debauch and rot that ate down to the soul's marrow . . .

I remembered why I hated the Rendezvous. The creepy old cunt was me.

There were mirrors all around the booths, compelling me to confront my sagging chops from every angle. Long ago, when I was twenty-one, those mirrors offered an agreeably Warholian mass reproduction of my image. On that wilted day in damp summer, two-thirds of the way through my fiftieth year, the traitorous *roués* in the etched panes convened as the mocking members of a heartless, elderly, and unforgettably corrupt jury.

I wasn't sure if I'd react with horror or relief when Luda finally appeared, if she ever did.

I don't know why I had this odd presentiment—there was something about her that was all fate and doom and Greek Drama. Even the name.

Luda.

It all comes back to Luda. Luda. Luda.

I was enraptured by the spectacular artificiality of how she went about her business. Like Supergirl's evil duplicate, her laser-blue eyes could cook a steak with a single withering stare. Her spookiness offered a real opportunity to understand something not made to be known.

The Uncanny Valley, they call it: when the simulation's real, but not real enough to be comfortable.

What else could I do but circle back to Rentboy?

I ordered a double espresso for my nerves, knowing it would only amplify my everyday anxiety. I stood, legs akimbo, at some terrible crossroads where devils swap skills and youth and other mortal perishable things for lightly soiled souls. One false move meant damnation.

Rentboy shuffled uncomfortably, arranging those heroin cheeks and hairline lips into an aristocratic pout. I saw for a moment the mouth of a mosquito. A bloodsucker proboscis extending in a predatory air kiss. I tore my eyes away, even though I knew how much it would hurt to stop looking at him.

Excuse me—are you?

I supposed I was. Even I had to admit it. The waitress, wearing her selfie face, beamed brighter than a star's dying farewell. My eyes made a swift sideways saccade to make sure Rentboy was keeping tabs on this power exchange. If he suspected I was semi-famous, it could switch the whole dynamic; I was being handed an opportunity to morph, with a single signed autograph, from creepy uncle to bachelor playboy daddy.

I thought it was you! I hope you don't mind. I just started in here—can I have a selfie?

Of course, I obliged with a flustered—*Hope you don't mind.*

I'm supposed to be meeting someone. Tall, legs right up to here, bit boyish, looks like a model, copper hair like Cleopatra . . .

The waitress started to shake her head halfway through that second sentence.

Nobody who looked like a model had come within nautical miles of this dump for an age. The models had moved on, to NorWest, and the reclaimed working-class ghetto *chic* of Charliesburn and Agnesland, on a languid prowl for successful online influencers now the musicians and boy poets had lost their lustre and their earning capacity.

Did I want, did I need, another espresso?

Luda was fifteen minutes late, so why not? Why not accelerate my already pounding heart to a Dutch techno blur of arrhythmic beats?

The clock hands juggled scythe blades in smooth, indifferent arcs through the waving, grainlike hours and minutes. My reflection, in the relentless mirror walls of the Rendezvous, displayed a field of brow furrows, ploughed ever deeper, yielding ever less in the way of fresh produce I might add.

I don't know about you but that's the way I find my mind working after sinking three espressos, which I had, leaving bitter sparks on my lips and prophetic slops on the mug's interior. For a moment, something there on the brim looked like death wearing a top hat.

My career as a fairground fortune-teller foundered in that moment, abbreviated by a looming shadow, deliberately obscuring the sun's halfhearted attempt to rise above the plucked trees of early spring and drain its solar dilution into my coffee mug.

He sat opposite me, as if I'd invited him, blocking my undead reflection with his own face as precisely as moon eclipses sun.

Rentboy?

WTF?

I looked around in a panic. I felt certain he planned to threaten and extort me right there, in broad daylight. I'd been caught staring at his ass . . .

What age was he? Could I get in trouble?

Can I get you something?

The waitress had every right to be suspicious now. I couldn't blame her for frowning and tensing up. The Rendezvous encouraged a bohemian clientele of guitarists, rappers, and painters, but there was an unspoken understanding that the café's hospitality drew a line at homeless, possibly infectious junkies wearing "Open Grave" by Calvin Klein.

He's not with me—I started to say but, I was wrong about that.

Red velvet cake, eh! It was Rentboy's voice, but it was Luda who unleashed the first strike devastator of her confident, generous smile. The teeth so straight and white only a millionaire or a classical god could hope to look that *finished.*

Rentboy straightened his spine, raising an imperious delicate-fingered hand, all white trash in Elysium! I looked on, appalled at first, until Rentboy's features melted, rearranged, and repositioned the social frame.

I'm so sorry—we just finished shooting over at the ice rink and we're both desperate for a quick one.

Her diction was nearly flawless; the crystal-cut consonants and elastic vowels of Gasglow's upper middle class squeezed through a vocal apparatus more accustomed to whining glottal stops. What could I do but relax and enjoy the show? She was determined to prove she could handle everything.

I play a violent ruffian, as you can see. My colleague here, whom you probably recognize, is a ruthless, unrepentant killer and we'd both kill for a couple of drinks—

We don't do alcohol until after six—she said.

He winked at me, then at her.

Just this once. Go on. We'll swap two drinks for a selfie! And a couple of slices of that red velvet cake you're famous for.

Just one—I said, pursing my lips.

He ordered vodka Red Bull as I remember. I had Watchtower and tonic. Luda was already best friends with the waitress.

I'm not famous yet—Luda confided in the awestruck girl. *She is.*

I'd taken years to learn how to master those facial muscles. She was a natural. Thin lips seemed to unroll and inflate. Luda's eyes, nose, and mouth emerged from Rentboy's underfed sulk as an optical illusion at first, one of those *trompe l'oeil* pictures; a moulded mask that goes from convex to concave as the light changes and the shadows shift; a clever how the fuck can *that* be *this*? . . . as if a puzzle worked itself out in flesh.

The waitress, stunned, walked away. She looked back, confused.

Red velvet cake?

Rentboy smiled, reading me like a beer mat, then lowered his face to his hands, rolling the left eyelid back to squeeze and flip a brown contact onto the tip of one finger.

I registered a flash of halcyon blue that took my breath.

Rentboy repeated the procedure with his right eye, there was no one else he could possibly be.

Luda used Rentboy's face to look at me.

Hey you—she said.

I suppose I should have guessed, but there I was, paralysed again in the lagoon clarity of Luda's turquoise eyes.

I know who you are—she said.

Who was I? I had to think of something fast.

I'd like to think you do. We only met on Wednesday and I haven't forgotten who you are. They say early-onset Alzheimer's gets earlier all the time. I'd have that looked at if I were you.

His only reaction was to roll out a red-carpet introduction.

I read your online diary when I was thirteen—he said earnestly. *You changed my life you did . . . and this. This is where*

*you and the Troupe used to meet. Your old place is just across the
street through the park. You started here all those years ago. It
seemed like a good place to start something.*

How could I fail to be seduced? He'd done her research.

Go on then—I said. And that was the end of me. *Go on.*

You know things. Secrets no one else knows.

A moist slice of red velvet cake glided in to land. Rentboy,
his eyes cooled back to brown again, wasted no time forking it
into his head as if supplying a garbage disposal chute. I swear I
blinked twice, and the cake was no more.

Gone like Luda's smoky, seductive self-possession, replaced
by a needy, aggressive whine that brought bad news of poverty,
illness, and a hastily-abandoned state education.

Yet as she shimmied back in her seat, I could see Luda's big
super-red and white smile glowing, as an X-ray trace through
Rentboy's sallow parchment skin. I could see her luscious ghost
playing peek-a-boo behind his mask of frail mortality.

I don't know how you can eat like that and keep your figure—I
said. Of course I did know; twenty-five years ago, I could gorge
myself like a *pasha* on chocolate, chips, and Charlie, and still
limbo into a size 10 skintight rubber dress for a night out.

You don't look so bad yourself.

Flattery gets you a first-class ticket to everywhere, I thought.

. . . If my dad did drag!—he shaded me.

*You've come to the wrong place if you're on the hunt for
Daddy*—I shot back. *But play your cards right, you might have
found yourself a fairy godmother, babes.*

Looking back, it wasn't a bad improv, in trying circumstances. The whole Dad thing's a sore spot for me, as you'll
discover soon enough.

We should go back to your house—he said.

If I could live it, over and over, again. More than the sex and
the drugs. More than the delicious horror. It would have been
worth it for that moment when I felt viable again!

I swear I saw what I understood to be a whole new appreciation for me, rising like dawn over the beaches of Tahiti, done double in those boundless ocean eyes.

In hindsight, all I saw was the blinding, terrifying come-on the red squirrel sees in the headlights before life is smashed into roadkill.

I won't say a word—I promised. *I don't think Dominick would care anyway. He loves you.*

The truth is I was all over him and it was all over by then and he knew it. I sensed in him the purpose I'd been seeking. A focus at my time of life. I had knowledge I could pass on. I missed the next bit when he spoke and said—

I want to learn how to disappear into someone else . . .

I missed it.

So, what's the going rate for a hot little homeless boy these days? I asked, all worldly.

Blow job for the price of a cup of coffee—Luda said with a contemptuous sneer. *For you, darling.*

I waggled a finger to attract the check. Reflexively, I was signalling for a taxi, calling for a doctor—anything to escape this pauper's coffin of a booth, this stale crypt where the dead and the living rendezvous.

My mum didn't want me. Dad didn't want me—Luda was saying. *No one did, so they left me outside that place where the girls go to get their abortions over by the convent . . .*

He was talking about Mercy Mansions, making me sweat.

I said—*I need a proper drink. You're welcome to join me.*

I was homeless—he said. *Like this for real. They found me.*

I shook my head—*The police?*

The Marvells!—he insisted. *I have to tell you about the Marvells*—he said. Like the poet, not the superheroes. The Marvells. What else could I do?

You must!—I insisted.

I don't remember much about the taxi ride home. I have a fond recollection of his hand gripping mine. We had a bag of booze we'd bought.

There was something about an intricate close-up on a worn, buffed Yale key unlocking the door onto my narrow hallway at the top of the stone stairs—the bedroom to the left—opposite my private dressing room.

The living room, the open-plan kitchen, and the working toilet are to the left, which is where I brought him. All of it new again and bright. Showing him around the valued things I'd accumulated, I got to know my dear possessions afresh and loved them so much more for steadfastly sticking by me all these years, through the bad times and the loneliness.

The pert, self-conscious three-legged phone table with its red, yellow, and blue arrangement of Toot-A-Loop vintage bangle-radios. The umbrella stand, in the shape of a pelican, or a toucan, or some other bird of paradise, bristling with brightly-patterned umbrellas. The elephant grass fronds. The sunburst mirrors. The transgender barometer from a novelty store in Berlin's Schöneberg. A collage poster for the Troupe's Edinburgh Festival debut hung next to a bus-shelter ad for our final TV special.

I poured Rentboy a long glass of Watchtower vodka spritzed with a haze of soda and garnished with a lime slice. I imagined me as some sun-hatted, sunstruck, field-tilling mortal in a Greek tale, entertaining an incarnate divinity in fleshy guise, hoping I could get him and her mortal, as they say.

I spectated all agog as my boy drained the cocktail with a flapper flip of her wrist.

Do Luda again—I begged, hoping it didn't sound like begging. *It's amazing.*

You don't like me this way?—Rentboy pouted.

I think boys generally look better in makeup and heels. But no—I just think it's amazing what you do. I'd like to see . . .

His body language softened, heralding let's call it a fantastic translation from the harsh glottal stops of Rentboy's physicality to the liquid silver trumpet syntax that announced Luda's imperial entrance.

As I watched, impressed, muscle memory eased out the hunched shoulders, melting into a sinuous stripper flex of spine and arm, so that Luda seemed to be shaking herself loose from Rentboy's cramped whipped-dog posture.

I understood now why she needed me to get her to the next level of the Simulation.

There was something deeply fake, unnatural, and artificial about her performance. Decadent, like the art movement.

Tell me more—I said, settled with my drink on the sofa beside her. *You said something about the Marvells.*

I drank Watchtower neat as she talked, perched on the silvery rim of drunkenness with the best seat in the house. I poured more. Sat back among newly-familiar cushions, simply dazzled, intoxicated, overwhelmed, by Luda's presence in my room. This boy, Luda in disguise with diamonds, or the other way around, had entered me like a drug.

Charles Marvell was fifty-five, Luda explained. I struggled to reorient myself. How much had we smoked? Why were numbers such a struggle?

Who the fuck was Charles Marvell?

In Luda's description of this mysterious mister, Charles Marvell appears as handsome, predatory, hawkish, with hair like abundant tides of steel wire, immaculately turned out in Brioni, Patek Philippe, and Louboutin. Body by Peloton. Mind by de Sade and Machiavelli.

It was easy to picture the fiend, I assured her. I'd seen his type in action movies and comics. The unlikelihood of him existing in the real world almost made it more convincing.

What age were you?—I pried.

He counted backward in his head until I told him to stop.

Wait. There's this pair of sexy millionaire perverts trolling for homeless jailbait and God help us—you were there—I said, clutching my handbag.

It's not funny to me—he said.

I assured him I wouldn't crack a smile before, during, or after his recital.

I won't utter a titter—I promised. *Let alone the guffaw I had planned. Chuckles are off the menu.*

I drew an imaginary zip across my lips. Looking back, I maybe was being a little glib. I get like that when I'm drunk; I don't want to hear bad news.

To tell the truth, I'm of the opinion that everything's funny when the curtain comes down. Our lives are rock hard candy with one word—*Irony*—written in sour sugar icing all the way down to the hole in the centre of everything. And if it doesn't feel even slightly funny to you, it'll be downright hysterical to someone watching from a safe distance.

But I'm far from heartless. Split me from gizzard to gills if you must; you'll see a big pink squidgy Valentine beating below these convincing fake breasts, based entirely on my own design and costing less than a pair of tights and a couple of bags of lentils, I should add. Compare that with the prices they charge for silicon and latex, and you're looking at an unbeatable bargain.

Luda painted a vivid, arousing picture of squalor and exploitation as she asked me to visualize him, as I ask you now—in Rentboy camo, malnourished, starving, shivering outside St. Jude's subway station, downtown Gasglow. His inner compass spinning like a comedy bow tie, unable to find polar north. His future sitting on the end of his nose with the off switch in its hand.

You can see how they'd film it—picture the strobe effect of legs scissoring past in quick time. December crowds blur into a picket fence of multiple overlapping limbs while the poor destitute teenager remains unmoving at his pitch, and the light changes; the cinematic equivalent of a statue placed in an alcove to commemorate the unholy martyrdom of some unlucky saint.

He is overlooked, unseen. Any last traces of uniqueness, of individuality worn down to anonymity by the oblivious slipstream friction of all these passersby. In a crowd of warm-blooded mammals, he is slowly dying of the cold.

Our heartstrings are plucked, our sympathies aroused! Here, at the poor orphan's lowest ebb, comes a tinkling voice. The chimes of a Christmas angel with devilish intent.

Hello? Are you all right, child? Oh dear God, the little darling is half dead!

As I listened, I understood: Luda was mad. The best cocktail mix of all: beautiful and crazy. In a tall glass with a slice of low self-esteem and daddy issues, please. Predatory instincts I've tried hard to suppress were given provocative bloody rags to snout at, I'm sorry to say.

Weed?—I offered.

When Charles Marvell physically hefted him up from his pitch, the boy who would be Luda could barely walk. He'd been sat in the same position for three days. It was Christmas Eve and the boy had stage 2 hypothermia, which explained the missing toe he showed me later.

The boy had forgotten his name. It may have started with a *K,* like some existential hero teetering on the edge of the Abyss of modernity. Or maybe just Kevin. Or Ken. Kieran?

Charles Marvell offered to help him out, taking his temperature as a prelude to taking everything else, barely able to believe his luck as he swaddled the homeless waif in a blanket and stowed him in the back seat of the Marvells' people carrier. This lost boy. No friends. No family. No trace.

No longer a cast-off rag of human refuse, his earthly lead was sublimated, elevated to become the Marvells' gold. Their Fleece. Their Holy Grail. The ideal subject for an experiment they'd until now only dreamed was possible.

Did they?—I half said. *Was it some sex thing?*

As I recall, the pause was nigh-on Vedic, with a span that extended endlessly, engrossing fathoms deep, while the duration of the whole conversation was brief. Three seconds. Tops.

Their daughter was that girl. The one they thought was kidnapped, remember? Nobody found out what happened.

It's not something I like to think about. My sense of humour's twisted like a noose, I'm the first to admit—but I don't like hearing about real-life cruelty or crime. I'd rather create a world of my own where nothing like that gets in.

It was her eyes. They were quite unusual—he said, holding the moment, underlining it even, by pausing his tumbler in freeze frame on its way to his pneumatic lips. *Remember?* I knew he would only go on saying "remember" until I did, so I remembered.

There had been a case. Sobriety and I had agreed to a trial separation around the time frame in question, but what he said about the *unheimlich* eyes of the missing kid seemed oddly relevant.

Intense, like those colours you only see in animated movies and videogames. Like a computer-generated saturated primary shade, a laser beam slicing through dry ice.

Like your eyes—I think I said, not certain what was real and what I dreamed later or just made up.

That shade, that hue, the hyper-blue of Luda's eyes has been my favorite colour since I could spell "turquoise." My mother preferred green, though, and she spent her life trying to indoctrinate me into agreeing with her.

Personally, if pressed, I'd have to point to Yves Klein International Blue, chosen for distinctly nonpartisan reasons. It's more of a glow than a colour. "The Azure" of Artaud. Feeling guilty over my lifelong noncompliance with Mama's aesthetic diktat, I made a heroic effort to synthesize her first choice with my own preference, with aquamarine the only plausible compromise.

A colour in the sweet spot between green and blue. Like Pacific Ocean water. Naturally, Mum loved the idea, dying much later into a blue-green submarine Heaven on morphine in a hospital ward.

Turquoise. Aquamarine. A wavelength of 495.08 nanometers. The colour of *Phi*. That's what Mrs. Marvell said. She was a behavioural scientist. A lecturer. He was a surgeon.

I'm finding this very hard to believe—I admitted. *But I could listen to you talking all night.*

Luda's cartoon-kitten-skulled Goodbye Kitty! satchel lay open on its side, spilling its Caesarean booty of intrigue. I caught a glimpse of a single shoe. There was something familiar about the blocky heel but at the time I had no idea how momentous this detail might become.

What else have you got in there?—I said, reaching down.

If you don't believe me—Luda began, racked by sudden gulps and shudders as she broke down and tears streamed down his hurt, pretty face.

I'm not stupid; I had a hard time convincing myself his feelings were real, but not so hard I didn't fall for it. Through a supreme act of kindness and self-delusion, I made myself believe the tough little homeless boy gone spineless in my arms was truly weak and fragile. A sobbing helpless niece for Widow Twankey. I held her and stroked his head until Luda stopped jolting and the sobs softened to whimpers and snuffles.

We can talk more about this another time.

So, I chose not to smuggle a peek in his satchel. It's funny to think how much of what happened proceeded from that decision, although maybe "funny" is the wrong word.

She'd finished his drink, so I helped him tidy up and poured her another. Maybe I could tip my guest off guard and get to the bottom of something before the night was through.

I only expected a meet-and-greet—I drawled, nibbling on another mint Matchmaker. *It doesn't have to be therapy.*

Now pacified, Rentboy, or Luda, or whatever the name was of that intoxicating apparition, passed me the plump and smouldering jay. A radiant red *détente*. We'd smoked it down to the candlewick and all the vodka was gone. It seemed so wrong. I had no recollection of what we talked about except how to destroy the straight world . . . and save the tiger. Black cats. Familiars. Jaguars and panthers and Harry Harlow's Barbed Wire Mother experiments. The buying and selling of souls. We had so much in common!

He upended his glass to reach the remnant dribbles before getting to his feet—pacing the room to create lurching German Expressionist shadows all over the fixtures and fittings. All flickers and fritzes, his wiring seemed amiss—a fireworks display of random, brief fixations.

I like your house—he said admiringly, fingering the window sash where it screamed for repointing. *I may have burgled a few like this in my time.*

I followed him, just in case he'd gotten his beady eye on my threadbare erotic DVD collection.

You won't find much that's worth anything in here—I said. *TV's ancient. Sound system runs on coal. Smoke?*

He accepted the spliff, inhaled at the door to my dressing room, and blew breakers of unrolling vapour into my dimly-lit *sanctum sanctorum*.

You don't owe me anything. You can just go home if you want. I don't need the whole story. You've got raw talent. We can work with that.

Calmer now, with four vodkas and two spliffs of Bhangistan Indica in his personal rearview, he asked if he could show me something in my mirror.

At least I think he asked, although when I look back now, I don't remember his lips moving. And I'll never forget his lips.

My "altar." That's what he called the dressing table, which set off clanging alarm gongs right away. He'd done his research.

He said he'd be honoured to sit where I did my face. I let it go. I couldn't say no. I'd have paid a week's wages to have him sit *on* my face. I instructed my suspiciously-muttering inner parliament to fuck off just this once.

Rentboy arranged an immaculately-grooved arse in my chair as though ascending to the royal throne of who knows what Elizabethan fairy queendom; the peacock-tailed throne was from *Superstar Survival,* and I'd demanded to have it included as part of my prize when I came first in the season 3 final.

There was a plump pink Valentine-heart cushion contrived for the perching of dainty bottoms. The sumptuous red-gold upholstered wooden backrest was draped with strings of pearls and feather boas slung like trophies, pelts of feral plushies I'd hunted and skinned through neon-pink-and-blue jungles. And, as I mentioned, a lavish fan of iridescent quills formed a dandy halo, a Kirlian aura of petrol colours that could turn anyone into an avatar of the Glamour.

Luda was right to acknowledge that seat of power. She knew exactly what she was doing when she composed herself to tell her tale to the mirror.

It's easy to see what's ahead when it's behind you.

He leaned forward, as if to dip his face in its own reflection, beauty magnetized to its own symmetry, cancelling out like two waves. I suggested he try it with the lights on to get a proper picture.

Framed in that suddenly blazing rectangle, his face was mathematically symmetrical. I could almost see the Fibonacci watch spring tightening towards his cheekbone. He brought a finger to Rorschach-blot lips and gently, with a pearl-lacquered nail I hadn't clocked as quite so long and feminine until that moment, he gently scraped away what I'd taken to be cold sores.

Brown sugar and Vaseline, he revealed, proud of his invention. He was still Rentboy, stuttering and whingeing through the details of his barely-plausible adventure, but, as he kept on, his voice underwent subtle shifts and startling modulations.

His vocabulary expanded, as if some heavenly engineer had turned up the volume on his intellect. His voice softened, shed an octave.

I could see all the mistakes now, but it was an impressive effort for a young pretender.

You know the way tyrants roll out their tanks and missiles on May Day parades? That's how he carefully laid out the pageant procession of his kit, the military precision of his pencils, brushes, liner, rouge. Like that. They made a circuit diagram of tubes and horsehairs, compacts open like mirrored oyster shells, a deconstructed Luda, spread there in abstract.

Buzzing with fresh possibility, I felt mesospherically high, flirting with cartoon satellites in low Earth orbit. The luxury-swimming-pool eyes of my guest appeared to outgrow his skull to flood the whole horizon as he did something very precise and very particular with liner.

I came to call this cosmetic operation the Luda Swoop—a shorthand sketch of mismatched gull wings in flight—and vowed to correct it.

There—said Luda with a Hollywood grin.

The Marvells, Luda told me, felt sure they'd never survive the loss of their beloved little girl. The grief was devastating enough on its own, without the attendant relentless allegations of collaboration and cover-up that placed full responsibility on their collapsed shoulders. They drew up a suicide pact then reneged at the last minute after convincing each other that their Penelope might yet return and concluding she'd likely be dismayed to find her parents replaced by date-stamped headstones. There was nowhere left for them to go, so they went mad. That's all. Pain sent them round the bend, until at last they convinced themselves they could do something impossible, something as thoroughly against nature as a Big Mac. They'd find a way to bring her back, from scratch, from a rag, a bone, and a hank of wig.

I was already racing impatiently to next base. *They didn't . . .*—I said, holding his gaze. I felt sure he was making it all up and zoomed in on minute tremors of his eyes and the dimpled corners of his lovely mouth.

I'm looking these people up—I said. So, I did, expecting to catch him out with facts.

But no. There they were. Charles and Victoria Marvell. Educated. Successful. Patrons of the *avant garde.* She looked haunted, vacated. Whatever it was that moved out when her daughter vanished had made space for something else to take up residence. You could see it peering out from her attic-window eyes. A thing made of nothing.

As for him, Charles, his scrutiny turned you into a specimen; evaluated, classified, measured up for a microscope slide.

Saying that, the lion's share of the pictures dated from the raw aftermath of the disappearance of their daughter, so it's hard to imagine what would be acceptably normal facial expressions under those circumstances.

The couple had now separated, according to reports; Charles last glimpsed with a beard and an entourage at a Bangkok *katoi* bar, Victoria flaring in a brief public supernova as she waged all-out war against online trolls before her absolute withdrawal, her *tzimtzum* retreat into anonymity, into hearsay and conspiracy theory.

That's what I'm telling you—Luda said. *Charles Marvell was a surgeon. His wife was a behavioural scientist. Victoria.*

As the application of his makeup grew ever more elaborate, so did Rentboy's story.

Kids nowadays, they have it all worked out. Online makeup tutorials are a wonder of the Age of Information. I had to learn it all myself. Trial and error. Lipsticks worn down to stubs to get it right just once. I admired his elegant fingers working the base onto his skin, zeroing in on the bitten, broken nails as he expanded on his theme, teasing out the salacious details, the unlikely wonders. Those would have to go.

I was half dead, a smackhead. I could easily disappear. I could become someone else and no one would care. That's the reality.

Legs crossed, leaning forward with her neck extended to face the mirror, painting in the final details.

I want to know how to do it my own way—Luda said.

I can see you've got talent. I could help you develop that—*but what's in it for me?*

In Rentboy's place sat Luda, fully grown. Dew-damp and bejewelled. She ran her tongue across her plastic upper lip. Should I have noticed it was forked?

I am—she said, conjuring a whole new universe of possibilities with those tried-and-tested words.

As Luda's attention snapped around, and her eyes ignited, I took a step back, shot through the soul with a yearning arrow, curare-tipped and fletched with hummingbird feathers.

She had my wig on. The big-haired Op Art Twankey wig I wore for act 2's sing-along. She looked phenomenal as me. She could play me in the film, if the film showed me with all my flaws corrected. I wanted her to play me.

Play me! I screamed inside.

I can take it off if you want.

I knew a caustic envy, burning me as she blazed on oblivious.

I wish I looked as good as you. I did once. Never take it for granted.

I'm not Widow Twankey—she said simply, taking the wig off and putting it back carefully on the dummy head. *That's you. I am Aladdin. I'm the Principal Boy. We'll be rehearsing scenes together soon enough.*

But I wasn't paying attention. I wasn't listening. I was

dealing with a riptide of unreality sucking the carpet and the floorboards out from under my feet. The lights got brighter.

When you said "I am" just now . . .

She'd gotten down on her knees where, all the while maintaining eye contact, she deftly opened my flies, saying—*I am Aladdin. I can make anything happen.*

She had my cock in her hands. Those long birch-twig witch fingers, dipped in crimson lacquer, closing around a sudden exclamation mark.

All I need to do is rub the Magic Lamp—she said.

I couldn't believe it. When was the last time?

It came to me how long I'd been waiting, tensed in a knot.

There, in the oak frames, enclosed in the mirror's triple geometry with me, was Luda.

Her head bobbing came with a wet hot sound of suction and chewing gum. She looked like me when I was her and she'd be me someday and the feedback was deafening.

She looked up at me with those big round swimming-pool eyes, her wet red mouth shining and slack. The tongue again, split. Reptilian. Or so I thought.

Try not to cum—she said. *What do you do to stop yourself cumming?*

I go through a list of the gangs—I explained in a matter-of-fact voice, sputtering now at the edges. I'd discovered over many years of practice how to postpone orgasm using my own idiosyncratic method. The old Gasglow gangs from the Razor Years. Alphabetically.

Tell me—Luda insisted then left me to counter the sound of primal gobbling with intelligible speech for as long as I was able. With each metronomic bob up and dip down of her head, my house became increasingly enchanted, inflamed, engorged with all the wonder and the glory of the Genie's cave.

Dull familiarity lifted its face dripping and bedazzled from immersion in wonder and shone as if electroplated with the true and impossible colours staining the heart of everything. Common things caught fire and were remade as lights at a carnival.

I could go on.

Turquoise fire in a flux over every surface. The ceiling moulding began to dribble ultraviolet pearls all down the wall into the carpet.

I found myself thinking of Heaven going on forever, tangled in infinity. It was that all over again, like when I was little. Falling backward into the crushing gravitational pinprick of the Big Bang before there was me.

LaBang.

I know I'm practically acting the whole thing out with voices here, but that night is very vivid in my memory. It was one of those epiphanies you sometimes hear about. From some unforeseen and sacred recess of my innermost Self I salvaged the names of the Holy of Holies.

The Boigey!

My voice shivered, finding a natural comedy vibrato.

The Fanto! The Fekka!

The veil between what was happening now and what was moments ago shimmered and was rent asunder, so that everything seemed as likely as two flying saucers landing on a café table and pledging matrimony. Buying their first apartment together—starting a family of UFOs—

The Gombo! The Mini-Team! The Teamo!

Every time I warbled out the name of a fresh squad of violent young offenders, Luda swallowed me whole, drained me out, and again and again and again like that.

The Troye!

Desperate to elongate this moment to its ultimate elastic extension *in excelsis,* I'd run out of my supply of hooligan teams and moved on to pantomime stars in a doomed effort to dam the pressurized reservoir of backed-up jazz.

DAN LENO!
Famous dames of history.
ALASTAIR SIM!
The Great Twankeys of pantomimes past.
BIGGINS! CHRISTOPHER BIGGINS! FUCK!! FUCK!
It was as if I melted through my chair, headfirst.
STANLEY BAXTER! DANNY LA RUE!
The walls rippled as though painted onto fluttering prayer flags.
DANNY LA FUCKING RUE!
My stale apartment where I'd been lonely, where I'd been manless in Moloch for so long a time, underwent a spectacular metamorphic process, turning itself inside out like a glove to reveal the holy hidden firebird soul I'd first discerned in that Timorous Beasties wallpaper when I bought it before it was taken for granted for years.

Just by being the same, everything was new.

And—stay with me now—because here's me in the mirror. And she's here with me. In triplicate.

By this point in what was a very professional blow job, all I had left were words for "nothing"—how many could I recall—
Nought.
Zilch.
Nil. Nada. Zero.
Holy zero.
The world's wet paint backcloth surrendered to liquid inferno and a pulsing insistent kick from my balls where Luda was slow-juggling them into her face.
ZERO! ZERO! ZERO FUCK!

When I was done and dazed, flopping and staring, beached and newborn, Luda lifted from her knees in a single wave-like motion to lick my mortal salts and alkali from her immaculate lips with a dismissive gesture.

Tell me the secrets of the Glamour.

I hesitated, but Luda was already taking off her clothes.

Teach me the magic—she persevered.

Why is it so important to you?

I told you—she said with an ardent yearning made to soften hearts—*I want to become someone else; to disappear.*

I know! I couldn't have put it better myself. The Devil has only to tell the truth once, at the start. The rest takes care of itself, if only in the way a gangrenous wound can be said to take care of itself.

I want—she said with eyes the colour and intensity of the eldritch gas jet that gave Ursula Andress her immortality in that film—*I want there to be nothing left for them to find*—

She-who-must-be-obeyed. Ayesha!

How far do you want to take it?—I inquired. *Are you talking about transition? Surgery?*

But she wasn't.

Of course. I could see no other way. I ignored the mysterious "them." I would educate Luda in the refinements of the Glamour. It had to happen. I owed her a debt of kindness at the very least. Whatever Luda wished to learn, I would bend over backward, possibly literally, to teach her. The fruits of my life as a drag *artiste* and shapeshifting witch would be hers to gorge upon until the juice ran down her chin onto her plastic tits.

I vowed to take this opportunity to instruct the holy fuck out of my disciple.

She's BEHIND YOU I heard the audience cry, spiralling into the suction.

Oh no he isn't—

Oh yes, she is

Oh no

Oh

O

Afterward, I had Chinese delivered. Salt & Chilli Chicken.

She ordered Turkish—ours the combination of spices and cultures that was Aladdin.

Not what you'd call an authentic dish. A hybrid, a crossbreed.

The doorbell did its thing, making me jump to my feet. She nodded to my crotch and said—*Zip*—with a big red smile.

The doorbell was still buzzing but I got there just in time to accept the delivery, zipper sealed.

We can't do that again—I said. *It was amazing*—I admitted. *I'm flattered—but we have a play to rehearse. I think you could be fantastic.*

Egg Fu Kebabs! Luda grinned, crunching her prawn crackers to grit and dust between movie-star teeth. *Chicken Chow Tikka!*

I watched the crumbs accumulate in her lap, a light snow of savoury debris and hallucination. We didn't talk any more about the Marvells. That came later.

That Chinese was the best I've ever tasted. Rentboy never left my apartment, Luda did. Luda cross-legged in a taxi home, wide awake at 5 A.M., with the next day's lights reflecting in her marvellous eyes.

The Sorcerer's Apprentice.

As you put on years, you start to think about how best to pass on what you've learned during your tour of duty. How to be useful. You can't take it with you, can you? All the precious memories, the lessons learned, the nuggets of wisdom polished by years to an exclusive shine. What's the point if it's not rolled up and passed on?

In my view, it would be perverse to visit my curse on another generation. There are too many fucking people as it is, if you can excuse my rare use of the word "fucking" to make a literal point.

We shouldn't celebrate the birth of yet another mouth to feed. In lieu of children, I vowed to encourage disciples, acolytes, apostles so enamoured of me, they'd compose undying scripture preserving my every fascinating deed and flippant *bon mot* in a book of golden parables for *Life and How to Live It in the Glamour.*

Which is to say, the thought had crossed my mind more than once—in the event of a young *ingénue* in need of a new messiah, I was right to be on the lookout for mean, keen recruits to my cult of extravagance.

The truth was more complicated: I'd always been wary of *protégés,* fans, and followers; I knew from bitter experience that what started as devotion all too soon curdled into envy, then anger, before boiling over into an all-consuming desire for positively Jacobean revenge.

Why then did I leap at the chance to coach Luda? How did

it go from a few singing and dancing lessons to full disclosure of my personal, private cosmology?

I've read the beautiful, savage King James Old Testament and its pacifist Jesus-led Sequel. I've struggled across the desert of pedestrian prose that is the Quran and boned up on the sci-fi sales manual known as the Book of Mormon. I've been dazzled by the Diamond Sutras and the *Bhagavad Ghita,* I've swallowed whole the *Book of Shadows,* the *Satanic Bible, Liber Null,* and *Nihil Unbound*—I've done all the Holy Tomes, so I like to believe I've given it all a big think.

While my interest in the subject was genuine and scholarly, I played up the whole "devotee of the occult" thing during Luci LaBang's nervous breakdown years—forty to forty-three—to cover for a precipitous decline in my mojo, where "mojo" in the equation equals "grip on reality."

Mine was an arcane system of symbol and correspondence, a DIY grimoire so personal as to be inimitable, an Outsider Art School take on the systematic colour-coded maps of Qabalah or the etched Tablets of Enoch. The rudiments of the Glamour.

Like a highly-developed musical or artistic talent, like the mongoose speed and focused power of a tenth-*dan* black belt, the Glamour can look like sorcery from a distance, but these human miracles are the result of practice, repetition, and motivation.

There was only one way to enter the otherworld and return intact, only one method guaranteed to cross the eyes and reveal the fused image, the stereoscopic faerie realm where two worlds overlapped, and that was to reject duality.

The Glamour provided the means to blend the real and the imagined, smoothing out the divisions between the physical and the not, subject and object, the masculine and feminine, God and Devil. The Glamour encouraged new relationships between seeming binaries that folded all polar opposites together into multifaceted wholes.

I was delighted by the idea of spirit being dual and one. I imagined milk and plain chocolate in the same delicious bar, coffee and cream, one and zero, man and woman, alchemical Adam and Eve and all of us in between . . .

The Glamour as endless creativity, perpetual transformation.

The best of it came front-loaded, lined up at the start in those first few days and nights; I woke from a validating dream where I was the witty, confident centre of attention at a fantastic nonstop party.

It must have been 4:20 A.M. judging by the footlights glow of dawn at the horizon above the shaggy treetops of Prospero Park.

Luda lay asleep in the deep, her head and left hand heavy on my chest where she'd passed out in my arms.

Three of her press-on nails had come loose, carmine plastic petals spilled across my rib cage. Faded to black, she was a deadweight. Her schemes undone. Her destiny briefly abandoned, her head rising and falling in oblivion with the expansion and contraction of my lungs. Her wig shifting independently, yanked askew where the weave had snagged on my bra clasp.

Me?

I spun adrift on a shoreless ocean of expansive unconditional peace. Mine was the kind of tranquillity you'd finally achieve on the last day of a long and tedious Buddhist retreat where they won't allow phones, pens, or off-colour jokes.

It was still dark; feral car lights, drivers up past bedtime, raked through the half-open blinds to throw travelling bars of slatted beam and shadow that lengthened, slanting into long oblique italics before the changing angles were bent and folded across the ceiling and the far wall while tyres sizzled on the rain-rinsed streets three floors below the bedroom window.

Luda with tight skin pulled snugly over tighter flesh, taut muscle, and springy sapling bone. Her steady hot heartbeat, first syncopating, then pulse by strong pulse more steadily synchronizing with mine; her flinches, her inevitable blockbuster champagne farts. Her measured inhale and exhale. Tension and relax. My arm losing its boundaries to a fizz of pins and needles.

Even then, in the flattering ashen light of an early-summer morning still unbroken, Luda was a long way from the polished sculpture I'd gazed upon with awe-blistered peepers when we first met in the rehearsal room.

Close up, her scuffed foundation exposed the yellow pinheads of a shaving rash. Bristles breaking through the porcelain laminate along her jawline robbed her of perfection. Yet Luda's flaws made her more perfect. She was real, tangible, physical in my arms, and in my bed. I felt I'd won a prize at the Wheel of Fortune and kissed her head, and caught my breath, and thanked my lucky constellations.

All you care about is the sex, I bet. The sex magic. What we got up to. Details will be craved. Top-shelf tittle-tattle. Red-top exposés. Gossip-site headlines. What was it like?

Yes, she sucked my cock until it popped pearls again and again. Yes, I licked the rim of the bright sour midnight singularity of her arsehole. Yes, and we French-kissed with the lube still bitter on our lips. Yes, to all of whatever you imagine went on between us, between the sheets, among the stretched-out shimmering hours in the Cave of Jewels.

And no. None of that happened.

There was no sex. After that first night and the blow job, I had to take sex off the menu. Sex ruins everything I told myself. Ensuring sex was kept at a safe distance from our budding guru/student relationship was my only hope of retaining any dignity and holding on to my treasured status as sage of the stage. Not that I didn't think about it every hour of every day, but I couldn't afford to be another of her slobbering admirers.

It was my job to be different and special. My job to draw the lines accurately.

I opened my eyes to be sure I was still asleep. The red traffic lights hadn't changed for what felt like hours, making me wonder if I'd been granted my wish by Aladdin's Genie and hung suspended between now and forever, crucified on the eternally-motionless clock face, pierced by the second hand, the minute hand, the hour hand, as I posed for Salvador Dalí doing Saint Sebastian!

Be careful what you wish for. What had greeted the day as a reliable and efficient left arm was nerveless now, at best a novelty paperweight, "gone to sleep" and enduring a nightmare of amputation. I thought of the sadhus in India. Mortification of the flesh.

Barcode stripes steadied and stood still on the wallpaper, stalled in the stark diagonals a convict chalks on the walls of his cell, counting the days like sheaves of corn, or the years, and the sound of the rain became a static hiss, a radio wavelength broadcasting nothing but the solid-state buzz of indecipherable Buddha conversations on car radios or hands-free sets. Murmurs of the Cosmic Microwave Background Radiation. Cars dreaming, snoring insomniac at the red end of the spectrum.

Diagonal slashes of brake light and blind shadow divided Luda's face, marking there a "forbidden / no entry" bar that put her off-limits.

Then the cars moved off the line, casting outsized I Ching yarrow stalks across the film poster for Claude Miller's *La Petite Voleuse* I'd framed above the fireplace twenty-five years ago. Hexagram 51—

The superior man sets his life in order
And examines himself.

I won't even go there! It's always a man with the I Ching. Where's the superior woman?

I remembered I couldn't sleep. I'd lain awake, too wired for REM until that gauzy flush grading up from the windowsill reminded me time would restart and dawn would arrive sooner than I wanted it to.

Smelling the nape of Luda's neck, its faint vapour of warm, fresh cake mix and new cosmetics, I wanted this moment to never end but inevitably it did just that, leaving me beached on the sheets, with no idea how I'd arrived at this point in my life, or when time had restarted its one-second-per-second progress.

Moving with stealthy purpose, shadows sloped across the ceiling, and this time I made myself ignore some faraway warning bell as I imagined a row of tall thin detectives in narrow overcoats, fine-tooth-combing the ceiling for evidence. To make them go away I had to stop looking.

Five minutes later, I'd surrendered to delta-wave activity and deep sleep. Dreaming department stores where I was lost.

All things must pass, as they say. Excuse me while I refresh my flute . . .

By remarkable coincidence, the poignant brevity of human experience as exemplified by my inability to snooze became a theme of the next day's rehearsals.

Time started up again and tipped both Luda and me bleary and glowing faintly out of bed—via coffee and taxis—onto the stage where it was up to me to set an example, as Float muttered menacingly.

It's up to you to set an example.

Luda was struggling through her Cave of Jewels meeting with the Genie, as portrayed by an irate Dez Blue, who kept breaking character to complain about this one particular aspect of Luda's performance.

You do know Aladdin's supposed to be a boy?—I could hear him snark incredulously. *A lad! It's in the fucking name. You're playing a BOY!*

I expected better from her—said Float gravely. *You promised you'd get her up to scratch.*

Suddenly it was all my fault and there was worse to come.

Luda stalled again, motor sputtering to a halt, while Dom prompted from the script bible, his tone increasingly impatient.

She's not concentrating—Float grimaced as I joined him at the production desk, where he turned to face me with a disenchanted wobble of that cannonball head atop its plush and fleshy ruff of neck. *I hope you're not back to the drink and drugs and late nights . . . I hope you're keeping it professional.*

I stared at him, hand on chest, making a big stage O with my mouth.

What age d'you think I am, Dom? I enquired, affronted.

They stop counting after a while—he said. *Sort this. Tell her not to go off-book unless she can back it up with solid improv.*

We were dry-rehearsing the Cave of Jewels, a key scene where Aladdin discovers the Magic Lamp—the source of all his supernatural superpowers. No costumes, no songs. By this point in the show, end of act 1, the audience has been waiting impatiently for the Genie to finally show up. Their tolerance will only last so long; everyone knows the story doesn't really get off the ground until the Genie arrives.

Most audiences are familiar with the Slave of the Lamp from Hollywood films—and whether it's as a shapeshifting mercurial Robin Williams on cocaine, or a weird patrician boyfriend who looks like Will Smith, he's always *blue*.

Our Genie enjoyed a bit of both worlds; sprayed gold, he was summoned to life with an eye towards cultural sensitivity as a near-the-knuckle Islamic *afrit* by malignant TV comedian "Dez" Blue.

Blue, his *nom de theatre,* traded in a confrontational, aggressive style that was reinforced by his towering frame and wrestler's build.

He'd chosen to introduce the newest member of our cast to his unique performing style. Method cunt, you might call it, in the Gasglow vernacular.

I'll say it again. Aladdin's a boy—he's in love with a hot princess—he's not some simpering—there was a dot dot dot moment where Dez bodypopped into a grotesque and leering *I'm a Little Teapot!* posture.

Then *AAARGGH!* His cartoon roar was loud enough to be visible, his gilded hands wringing the neck of the firmament as Dez "the Genie" Blue left the stage to call his agent. No one could be sure if he was expressing real feelings or testing an unrehearsed routine.

Our director drifted towards me during a break, resembling, I must be honest, a crashing dirigible. The *Hindenburg* listing ominously towards the high-tension wires—played in this ghoulish reenactment by me.

What's your take on this?—Float barked. Less genuine enquiry, more how-to manual on the training of an unruly mastiff using voice commands.

My take seemed obvious but who's listening to me, not our portly "genius" director.

Luda—he said, as if I hadn't noticed. *She needs to hold her own with these people. They smell blood and they're like pajama fish, as my youngest calls them.*

Naturally, I was responsible for Luda.

Why can't she hit her marks?—he flapped, a turkey kicking up dust in the yard. *Going off-book with the improv is one thing but everybody has to hit their marks.*

He's giving her a hard time, Dom, I said. *You need to step in, or I will.*

Said the Domster—*I don't think she's levelling up, Lu. I thought she could take him, honestly. I was certain she had what it took to put these fuckers in their places. That's how it happens in the* Phantom*! I've taken a big chance here on your recommendation . . .*

My recommendation? I thought. Luda was his idea! As I've put all of you through great pains to make clear already, it was

Dom Float himself, our director, who insisted, against *my initial reservations,* on offering Luda her shot at the big time.

I couldn't be bothered setting him right. He was too busy flapping his annotated bible in Blue's direction.

Skating close to thin ice, Dez!—he said. *Give the girl a chance to recover.*

Look, I tell it like it is—Blue bellowed back. *People like me have been silenced for too long.*

So, I said—*What, genies? Or arseholes?*

Like Solomon judging the baby case, our Dom looked from Luda to Dez Blue and back again.

I know you can knock it out the park, Lu. Let's take five.

I'm sure none of you could miss that "Lu" he tossed in. I know I didn't.

I asked Luda what was wrong, but she couldn't explain.

They're just old-school arseholes—I found myself opining, *vis-à-vis* Dez Blue and his geriatric partner in crime. *A pair of pricks. He won't pull any of that like that when the lights go up on opening night.*

On the way back from the Ladies with a steaming coffee, I interrupted a conspiratorial huddle that might as well have been two bashful male lovers, planning some assignation with childish titters and snorted whispers.

The shifty two-man tether unravelled to let me through, lifting my coffee cup both to avoid spillage and to threaten it at the same time. I'm not ashamed to admit I enjoyed making those bastards cringe and retreat as I slopped scalding cappuccino mere inches from their faces.

Get a room, boys!—I said breezily. *A love like yours is nothing to be ashamed of.*

We were discussing the modernity and daring of casting a transgender rent boy Aladdin—Rhys drawled.

Don't get your hopes up—I smiled. *They'll be able to see them from the back row!*

Coming in at the top of the Cave of Jewels scene, Abanazar is offstage, yelling instructions to Aladdin, his pet thief, now deep in the gloomy cavern interior.

The murk down there is so dense and absolute there appears no way Aladdin will ever find the Lamp. Given his notoriously short temper, it's hardly a shock when the formerly avuncular wizard Abanazar grows increasingly agitated in his demands, driven to ever-more-hyperbolic extremes of frustration until he's ready to go off like Krakatoa, West of Thailand.

For Gofannon Rhys, this scene afforded a Licence to Kill.

I think I've found the light switch!—Luda said flatly, her voice weak and lacking presence.

In performance, when the lights came up, the audience would see the fabled Cave of Jewels for the first time: a dazzling storehouse of treasure blazing with flavours beyond measure; rainbow trash heaps of precious stones, every faceted gumdrop colour you ever imagined, landslides of gold coins of different sizes, heaped under the watchful jade and cobalt eyes of profile portraits where unknown emperors and empresses were rendered in mosaics made of rubies, sapphires, emeralds, and diamond. Or their paste and painted equivalents, endowed, by theatrical sleight of hand, with a majesty and magic that was entirely deceptive.

If you hung around, some of the bejewelled stalagmites would even come to life at the end of the scene and dance around like an episode of DTs during the big act 1 closer.

Now then!—came the voice of Abanazar. *Can you see a fucking Lamp!*

I'd made a point of warning Luda about the old man's tendency to lace every line in rehearsal with profanity. Opening nights, he'd switch to the clean version without apology or explanation—other than a brisk sniffy *Tourette's darling*—

Armed with this detailed intel Luda was able to keep her cool as the sluice gates of filth and abuse were ratcheted open.

Dazzled by the gem-light, Luda, as Aladdin, cleared away a rubbish spill of priceless coins to expose beneath a battered old oil lamp with a spout—it can't be this cast-off, surely?

There's only some old piece of junk!—Luda called back, with a double-edged defiance in her deviance from script. She turned the lamp upside-down. *Long past its sell-by date! Full of nothing but dust and air!*

Why—why that's the very object I seek, you tragic fucking twat!—cried Abanazar, tripping nervously on his tongue. *B-buhbring it to me now, Aladdin, you brain-dead shitwit!*

As the story goes, Aladdin's very reluctant; he's thinking, why waste the precious storage space in his pockets on an awkwardly shaped, worthless lamp? Not when the floor is carpeted wall-to-wall in jewellery of every description, where stalactites are strung like diamond icicles dripping melted gold, and the walls glint with starlike super-precious minerals.

What do you want a useless old lamp for?—says Aladdin. He's too young to see the signature glint of the holy in the broken and profane.

I've had enough!—Rhys howled with the reverb turned up. *If you won't do as you're fucking told, you can stay here for ALL PISSING ETERNITY, you atrocious little spunkstain!*

A bass-heavy sound-effects rumble through the hall would cue the audience to an offstage rockslide sealing the cave and trapping Aladdin inside with no hope of escape!

Unless—

The lamp!

Luda glanced over at me, eyes as wide as a frog's in the terrible headlights of an SUV driven by a toad-hating sociopath who's stayed awake all night on crystal meth and can't tell the difference.

Dodging between one obliterating wheel and the next, she stroked the lamp, three times in a furtive manner, a conjurer hiding a trick in a gesture. She knew what was coming and she was right—

Is that it?—Dez Blue protested, sputtering with exaspera-tion as he waited to manifest. *If you think that's going to get the Genie aroused, you're not even trying!* Sensing another golden opportunity to road-test his stand-up act, he kept on going—*Is it in yet? This is what I mean! It's like she's comforting a chin-chilla with PTSD! Rub the fucking thing!*

And here he turned to Luda, towering over her slight frame like Goliath—*Use your cock, if you've got one!*

You can't deny this is bullying—I said to Float. *You can get reported. You know how they feel about hate speech! We all sat through the seminar.*

Float held me back. He was waiting for some epiphany, some primal confrontation to spontaneously develop into art, releasing Luda from her freeze.

The last thing we want is for Molly to rally—he said in a heartless manner that suggested the smooth running of a pro-tection racket. Molly Stocking, as it happened, was recovering from her injuries with a courage and a speed that no one had dared suspect. She'll return to our story soon enough in a star-tling new role, but this was Dom's sly way of weaponizing her against me. *I know she can do it*—he said, meaning Luda, laying all responsibility at my back door.

With a flash and a chip-bag bang, Aladdin faced the Genie, drawing himself up on tiptoe to look the creature in the Adam's apple.

And who might you *be?* Luda peered at the Genie's nipples. *I've seen those eyes before—were you in a fight?*

My eyes are up here, puny mortal! For I am no less than the Genie of the Lamp! Your wish is my command!—said Blue with a smirk. *Well, up to a point, love. I'm nonbinary but I won't do anal!*

I sensed the presence of Death in the room.

How about you?—the Genie leered.

She didn't seem to know what to say, so I said it for her.

There's no need to be a cunt, Dez, I said flatly.

Float's disapproving expression made me wish I hadn't just brought up the penalties for hate speech. He dragged a finger across his throat . . .

I don't imagine you get up to much—said Luda. *Being a eunuch.*

Who says I'm a fucking eunuch?—Dez protested as she hit a nerve and drilled down through the pulp with a killer smile.

I've got their names and addresses but we don't have all day—she said, watching the retort fall to bits on the tip of his tongue and waiting . . .

There came a moment, an unscripted unrehearsed split second, pregnant with inexplicable significance. It was as if we all knew we were part of an interlocking sequence of events, where we were each waiting for the same thing to happen next, all fully aware there was no way to avoid any of it. As if all the things likely to take place were being rapidly sifted and discarded in favour of what was certainly about to occur . . .

And BANG!

Then followed a splintering, wrenching, rotten noise from the rigging—swallowed up by a whomping, whirling whiplash; the sound of death in the form of an owl or some new kind of spinning bomb; by the time you hear it you're already gone.

Trailing a rat's tail of unravelled rope and cable, one of the overhead scoop lights exploded into component parts, dismantling violently upstage right, just three feet from where Dez was standing—he tilted his video-ready face up to the complicated scaffolding of pipe grids and rope, then leaped with a howl into the orchestra pit, as if that would save him.

Instead, Blue's reward for his rash escape strategy was a broken hip.

A thin drizzle of coil chain, turnbuckle, and rivets sprinkled onto the still-fuming potpourri of metal, glass, and sparking element that was formerly the scoop.

Maybe wait until opening night before we bring the house down—I suggested in an unwelcome attempt to lighten the mood as handymen ran around like cockroaches released from a tin can and Dez Blue screamed from the pit, a farmyard animal mid-slaughter.

We each craned our individual necks to peer at the loading galleries high above our heads, where height became darkness. Were there signs of furtive movement there among the track and rigging?

What about those ambiguous shifting shadows slanting against the rafters?

Well—said Float, as if nothing had happened—*might be a good idea to stop there.*

That was when we attended to Dez Blue, the all-powerful Genie of the Lamp, squealing like a butchered trombone in the pit.

Pain seemed to bring out the best in Dez. The paramedics could hardly stow him in the back of the ambulance for laughing. He posed for mad-eyed selfies, with the tears still drying on his florid cheeks. He improvised a barnstormer of a routine as they juggled him into restraints, laughing at his own jokes before going out like a trouper, stage left, or bastard side as we call it in the biz.

Morphine's a miracle—Luda said, sounding more like me every day.

Later, over free booze at McCloudie's, the Vall bar, tense table talk took a turn towards the paranormal. We'd all seen what had happened. There was no rational explanation for it, Dee Jayashankar assured us, even though I could think of more than one.

Luckily for the superstitious among us, the Vallhambra had no shortage of ghosts, including the unquiet afterglow of Ronnie "Ritz" Fervour, a popular television and stage impressionist from a few decades back. He'd quite literally died onstage when a massive stroke felled the massive entertainer like an overweight sequoia halfway through the middle eight section of an inadvisably rigorous performance of his signature tune, "I'll Probably Die Laughing!"

Wormy rumours persisted of a forgotten plague well beneath the theatre, one of those subterranean sinks where diseased *revenants* still squirm and squirrel through the dirt in rotten smocks, a seething shoal of pale and lambent maggots with rancid human features.

If we've offended the spirits here—and here Dee shook her head disconsolately—*We may have to expect reprisals.*

I couldn't shift the cast away from the inevitable as the talk took its unavoidable turn to the Vallhambra Curse. The Halloween jinx laid on us by the theatre's ghost of ghosts. The prime postmortem suspect in our rigging misadventure was the man who'd started it all. The damned Romantic architect set in Eternity's amber, shackled forever to his deformed creation.

Who would deny the weird coincidences, the circumstantial boundary posts marking out some otherwise-imperceptible karmic county line where the revenge plot of the *Phantom of the Pantomime* and our few scant misfortunes so far could be persuaded to overlap to spine-chilling storytelling effect?

If we could lay blame for our near-death experience on any of the Vall's many ghostly inhabitants, it was surely, reasoned the aforementioned Dayanita Jayashankar—in a proclamation to be cosigned by the morbidly superstitious Gofannon Rhys, eager-to-please Aiysha Dyce, and both halves of Buttercup, the pantomime cow—*surely* the work of the unquiet spirit of mad Murdo McCloudie.

Dayanita, "Dee," basked in the attention; she'd previously secured for herself a key role as the witchy one among the cast. Comfortable in this strange territory, her stature as our resident paranormal expert was elevated immediately. She'd had her cards done, and her bumps read, and she'd gleaned the ins and outs of the spirit world from extensive online investigation and a life-changing fortnight's detox at some old *ashram* or other.

Luci's very into magic and the occult . . .—May Tang-Taylor drawled. *So I've heard.*

Not really—I lied and waved my hand dismissively.

If you've been keeping up, you'll remember Murdo McCloudie as the architect who designed the Vallhambra Theatre, in whose mock-Deco-coco bar we now huddled, survivors of what was rapidly becoming "the Curse."

Dee regaled us with the often-told story of how, feverish, fuelled by laudanum and a corrosive phobia of failure, McCloudie had taken his own life only three days after his first trip to the location of his masterwork.

It had taken several gangs of workmen three and a half years to erect the three-thousand-seater auditorium and during all that time, or so went the story, the architect had neglected to pay even a single site visit, saving his moment of revelation until the opening ceremony.

That explains why, when Murdo McCloudie stepped out of his carriage, anticipating the avalanche of rapturous applause he'd surely earned for his revolutionary, picturesque addition to Gasglow's iconic lack of a skyline, there was no applause, no fanfare!

Instead, into that claustrophobic silence came a porcine snort of laughter! First one voice, then two, then dozens, until the entire crowd was laughing. Laughing at him, in fact, and poor McCloudie only understood what was so funny when at last he raised his eyes to the magnificent façade of his greatest creation to discover that, somehow, the carriage had dumped him at the back entrance! The very arsehole of the building.

And all the while the jeers, the whistles, and the insults grew in intolerable volume!

As it turned out, the project's foreman, a notorious imbecile, had crafted his magic from carefully-drafted plans turned upside-down. As a result, he'd organized a squad of unhesitating labourers to erect the Vallhambra the *wrong way round*!

Instead of a south-facing portico, as intended to overlook the River Dare like a pagan queen on her throne, the theatre's showy frontage opened north onto narrow Gargoyle Street, presiding over the strip-show red lights of the city's sleazy entertainment quarter, the boho latitudes of Andersburn and Collegehill.

As Sabbath bells of mocking hilarity pealed out, summoning the faithful to witness his public humiliation, McCloudie shrivelled backwards into the split leather of his carriage seat, they say, as though struggling to reverse time back to the womb.

The architect's wonderful day, the crowning pinnacle of a glittering career, now faced its own monumental demolition into raspberries and catcalls, boos and hisses, cries of *stupid cunt!* and *arsehole!* as he became the first of many pantomime villains to call the Vall their home, the first of many pompous snobs to be humbled, heckled, and hissed offstage.

The way I look at it, he was lucky they didn't have some steampunk telegraph variation of the internet back then; it wouldn't have taken him three whole days and seven bottles of absinthe to come to his decision if he could have read what everyone was livestreaming about him. Not these days. He'd scan the comments section and it would all be over in minutes!

The public disgrace was all too much for a sensitive young dandy draughtsman. Imagine! McCloudie, now completely broken and undone by the relentless ridicule of what should have been his greatest accomplishment, brought a coil of stout rope to the top of the North—originally South—Tower three days after the grand opening of the Vallhambra.

Knotting it securely over one of the crossbeams, then in a loop around his bulging, shuttling Adam's apple, Murdo McCloudie took a few moments to recite a self-penned sonnet titled "Why Me, Jesus?" before walking calmly into thin air ninety-four feet above the stage, "*as if setting out on a gay May Sunday promenade,*" according to witnesses.

One small step for a man, followed by a thirty-yard plummet brought to its abrupt conclusion with a sound very much like God cracking a bullwhip made of human vertebrae.

If I'm reading the room, we're seriously considering a Phantom of The Phantom of the Pantomime!—I drawled. What had seemed almost funny suggested a nauseating infinite regress that did nothing to quell the bilious insurrections of my gut microbiome.

Get me out of here—I said as I scrambled to my feet, reaching for my jacket. We were taking the rest of the afternoon off to think about what had just happened, so I'd decided to have an early night and put the commotion of the day behind me.

When Luda got up to follow me, Float caught her arm.

You sure you won't stay for a few more drinks, Lu?—he said emphatically. What's the "Lu" about, I thought. That's his name for me. And I know! It's twice now I've had to mention it.

Luci's been looking after me for a few nights. Until I get my own place back from the cockroaches . . .

Arched eyebrows all round like a sighting of the Loch Ness monster, that line of humps.

I'll stay, though—she agreed. *I've barely gotten started.*

Luda kissed my cheek. *See you later, babes*—she said adding a zesty relish of implication to each syllable.

"Babes!"

She swung back a couple of hours later, more sober than when we'd started, to find me rolling a jay.

I made friends with them—was all she had to say before curling on my sofa, beneath the Miller poster, with the dog-eared, stapled pages of *The Phantom* in her hand. As she methodically, silently, mouthed her lines, Luda seemed determined to prove the doubters wrong.

I dragged on my penny whistle of smouldering weed.

They're miserable old showbiz cunts—I said, popping smoke rings. *You're new and fresh. That's always a threat.*

She looked over the top of her script—*I felt like* him *standing there. Him who I was before. They saw who I really was—they taught me a lesson.*

I sat beside her and took her hand.

They saw what you could be. That's why they were scared. That's why they reacted. I was sincere. I really was. I knew exactly how she felt, and I knew the only way to get over it was to *shimmer.*

I placed the blunt between her incredible lips and she sucked.

How about we rehearse your duet?—I offered and received a shy little smile by return of post.

Dom said they're paying your wages into an account in the name of Luda Marvell—I ventured, hoping she'd take the bait and tell me more about her mysterious background. How much of it was real? How much was a game she played? *He said you don't have representation—*

I'm self-taught—said Luda, scanning the pages, flipping them like a robot learning lines at high speed. *Self-motivated. If I do a good job as Aladdin, I suppose I'll have to think about getting an agent. You can help me.*

I'll help you right now; steer well clear of my agent, whatever you do!—I warned her with a histrionic shudder. *Unless you've set sights on a life of reality TV and summer seasons in decomposing seaside resorts.*

From now on, I'll do whatever you tell me—Luda, clear-eyed, lied.

Well then—I said, retrieving my personal copy of the *Phantom* script before adjusting glasses I've only had to wear since I was forty-four and leafing to page 5, scene 3. *You be Aladdin*—I said archly. *I'll do Princess Jasmine.*

Aladdin wanders lonely as a clown—I said to set the scene.

Yearning, besotted, weighed down by a hard-on the size of the Burj El Arab.

We both had a laugh at that, a spoonful of sugar to sweeten the sting of instruction.

I know you can carry a tune—I said. *But this is different. It's not a pop song where you can just sing*—I love you—*over and over until fade. You're living out a story people will believe. I know you've worked hard to be a girl, but*—and believe me I hated to admit I agreed to any degree with Dez Blue's evaluation—*Aladdin's a boy. You're playing a boy who's in love with a princess. Find a way to hold yourself that makes you feel the way a boy in love with a princess might feel.*

I demonstrated with a stiffening action-ready posture, a broadening of chest and shoulders that signalled a sanctioned annexation of the surrounding personal space.

What if she's out of the boy's league? Luda objected. *What if the boy can't have what he wants? What if it's all bullshit?*

Do I have to explain the difference between real life and made-up stories?—I said. *Now let's have the line*—

Shaking Aladdin into place, Luda breathed deeply and spread out the first-line melody as smoothly as peanut butter on toast.

If only I could find her—*the special one I've waited for*—*I'd tell her now I know what dreams can do*—delivered with an anguished tug at the fabric of her T-shirt, her arms spreading wide as if to give the whole horizon a manly embrace. A fist dashed against her downcast brow.

You don't have to act out the entire Kübler-Ross scale in the first line—I said. *We'll call that a good strong start. You can imagine a voice like that summoning the faithful.*

She had no idea what I was talking about, but you'll be more experienced and more educated people, I hope.

All Luda had to say was—*I can't wait to hear your sexy princess voice.*

Imagine the sound of a rubber sex doll with a leak—I shot back. *I'm a trained professional, babes!* Hand on her knee, girls confidential. *You don't do Jasmine all "Happy Birthday, Mr. President"*—I said, lifting and liquefying into the breathy cartoon Marilyn impression I'd refined years ago to creep guys out when they realized it was making them horny.

She nodded slowly, eyes like a cat's triangulating lunch.

You've seen Dee belting them out—I went on. *Princess Jasmine is "feisty."*

If only I could find him—the prince that I've been dreaming of—the boy who knows my heart is warm and true—

Aladdin hears the song, this moony ballad of pubescent infatuation, wafting fragrant and irresistible on the Peking night wind and sets off in search of the singer, imagining how lovely she'd have to be to come complete with a voice like that; if not strictly the voice of an angel, at least on a par with a semi-talented stage-school brat.

Separated by clever moving scenery, Aladdin and the princess trade increasingly passionate verses, but even though their voices cross-blend and harmonize, they can't find each other in a shifting maze of streets and hallways conjured by Abanazar's sorcery.

I stood behind Luda, matched my body to hers exactly, and lifted her off the floor so she was standing on my feet, two dominoes back-to-front in a box.

Feel what I do—I said. *I'm the princess—now I'm going to become Aladdin and you're going to copy what I do—*

And sometimes for a moment I feel certain that he's near me—

Luda matched my movements. I raised my arms and hers with them, puppeteering her. I took control of her posture, guiding her limbs into place like a life-sized articulated drawing model.

I straightened my spine, shifting my pelvis to imitate Aladdin's adventure-hero bearing. As I walked with a hipshot urchin swagger, I piloted Luda, an exoskeleton.

I'm sure she's walking somewhere close at hand!

Overlapping synchronizing vocals drag us kicking and screaming towards the final chorus. The neighbours beat down on the ceiling, causing us to redouble our volume.

But those are only feelings, as fleeting as a love heart drawn in sand!

"Feisty" was Aladdin and Jasmine pumping up the drama until one last strident high note was all it might take to burst the walls of the theatre like a balloon.

Luda spun me to face her, taking charge. We linked fervent fingers and stared into each other's eyes. For a moment she seemed almost threatening, and it struck me that her portrayal of maleness came with an edge of intimidation.

Someone—and somewhere where we two could be two TO-GEH-THER!

In the heart-wrenching full-throated crescendo of this ear-splitting mating call, the young lovers come within moments of meeting face-to-face at last. The final barrier slides away. Nothing can prevent this meeting of souls until . . .

A terrible grandfather clock strikes in the attic. The cast of *Aladdin* freezes in place as, once again, a lurid spotlight picks out the Phantom of the Pantomime himself descending on the Versace spider of his favourite chandelier to a tidal chorus of hisses and boos.

With the dire unnervingly deliberate rhythm of the bells of mortal doom as his soundtrack, the masked Phantom sets to work rearranging the scenery to separate the couple before they can meet.

The song plays out, the outro breaking into lonely fading sighs—

A place of our own—

Where we could be alone—

Their pining set to haunting strings, Aladdin and Jasmine drift apart once more, lost in the ever-changing maze of walls and doors unopened.

Alone the way we always are—TO-GEH-THER!

As the thumping on the ceiling ceased, as the harmonies rang into oblivion, I hugged Luda close.

More of THAT!—I said. *And hit your marks—that's all Dom cares about!*

You don't believe in ghosts, do you? Luda said out of the blue. *You believe in gods and angels but not ghosts.*

I said it was complicated, which it was.

Will you show me some magic?

Who am I? David Copperfield?—I said, and she said—*Who?* which was fair.

I mean real magic—the Glamour—she said.

It's all the Glamour—I said, putting on my best guru. *Finding the fabulous in the ordinary and bringing it out, making it real, is the Glamour.*

I'm talking about magic spells—said Luda, and I said—*So am I.*

She said—*I want to learn to disappear.*

The track skipped on my player—a garbled backward masking warning I ignored.

How do you know I'm not teaching you right now?—I asked. *If I can make you vanish into Aladdin, who knows what's possible?*

We've been invited to a party—Luda said, changing tack. *One of the pair from the pantomime cow. Or maybe it was both of them.*

She passed me a flyer depicting a juicy Edenic apple dripping black liquid latex onto a red-gloved hand with the words GARDEN OF SIN in petrol-blue Gothic lettering.

A sex party!—I squealed. *A swingers party in the suburbs like you read about! We've been invited to a sex party by a pantomime cow! Think about it!*

The key role of Buttercup, the 'skin part', or pantomime cow in *Aladdin,* was shared by a young couple of indeterminate and ambiguous sexuality. There was a rumour they were brother and sister, or brothers, or sisters. However they contrived to work their magic, as soon as this remarkable duo were zipped into their cow suit, they ceased to be two independent entities and merged instead into one cartoonish creature driven by its simple desire for grass and laughs.

We dress like this at home—they'd told me one time over a drunken card game of Happy Families on the tour bus. *The cow's the least of what we can do.*

Tell me more—I said, eyeing the exit sign.

You should see us doing a giraffe or a camel—said the one on the left. *We specialize in land animals, ungulates, mostly. Plant-eaters.*

We're vegans—the other one had said, not looking up from their phone on the M4 to Bristol.

They never asked me—I observed with a sulk that Luda ignored. *It's you they want now, not me.* A Star Is Born*!*

I turned over the flyer. DOORS OPEN SATURDAY. NINE O'CLOCK. LOSE YOUR INNOCENCE!

It's been aeons since I've had any—I said—*and aeons since I was invited to one of these*—I babbled on, excited despite my affected pose. *Geologic eras have been and gone! My last invite was back in the Cretaceous. Do come! it said. We're all getting together at Chixclub to watch the asteroid flying overhead!*

I rambled away like that a lot now I'd installed someone around the house to put up with my endless *non-sequitur* monologues. I loved the sound of my own voice, the daft rippling texture of my stream of consciousness flowing down the rapids. You'll have some idea what I'm like by now. When I'm happy, it's like they turned up the volume and the brightness. I'm so busy entertaining myself I forget it's an acquired taste.

But Luda laughed at everything I said, as if I were dishing

out bright comedy gold ingots from the inexhaustible vaults of Widow Twankey's personal Fort Knox.

In truth, and like everyone else, Luda had learned to switch off when it got too much. Most of the time, she had no idea what I was talking about and just laughed because it was easier that way, and because she found me funny, not necessarily my banter.

Let's do the song again—I said, riding a clear high wave of rare distilled elation. *I think I heard the neighbours go to bed.*

We opened our mouths as one, inflated our lungs to capacity—

We two could be two TO-GEH-THER!

I should pause here; all I remember of that strange sex-party Saturday are mysteriously edited clips. TikTok skits. Speculative wedges of bright, concentrated experience with no connecting tissue. Fantastical Mardi Gras stations on a line with no rails to link them. Animated Tarot cards, crackling with symbolism.

Some of the clips, arranged in the correct chronological sequence, almost add up to a story. As for the others?

Listen without prejudice if you think you can.

I'll do your makeup three times—I told her, imparting the strict rules of a fairy tale. *Three looks. Each time you can think of it as an initiation. Secrets of the Glamour as applied to cosmetics. After that you'll be able to do your own . . .*

Luda sat in my chair, reflected three times in my oak-panelled triptych mirror. Her back was as straight as the left-hand column of a graph showing her progress over the last few months.

You still need to work on your voice—I said. *Here*—and I took her hand in mine, setting her fingertips against her Adam's apple, which fortunately for her wasn't one of those prominent ones that look like a snake's swallowed a fridge. *Feel where it sits?*

She nodded, and she gulped, so I felt Luda's little throat knuckle shuttle up and down.

Now lift it above where my fingers are and say—And she said it—*the rain in Spain falls mainly on the very plain . . .*

And I said—*Raise the pitch—can you feel your Adam's apple? Lift your voice.*

I saw the midsummer 4 A.M. rapture of understanding light up her face as she spoke in a fluttering teenage falsetto.

Nearly there—I said. *Go any higher than that you'll be having conversations only bats can hear. Lower it just a little bit more*—

How is this the Glamour?—inquired Luda, boosting her timbre to mimic an excitable preteen until finally settling into a register that sounded like mine.

Shapeshifting—I said—*literally—it's why it's so easy on molly when everything relaxes . . .*

I peeled the copper bob off her head, baring a pale scalp razored to stubble and purple. I kissed the bristling bruised and wounded skin.

Now—think of yourself as a screen. A silver screen—I said. *You can project any film you want onto a blank screen.*

I felt her body unwind and release muscle tension. She conceded with a sigh of surrender.

Are you paying attention?—I said.

And Luda said—*Yes*—though I barely saw her pretty lips move. The drugs were softening her edges, dissolving her defences. She felt like clay on a wheel. Fingers stroking foundation smears along the vectors of her cheekbones, limning tight bilateral proportions that were made to be highlighted, defined, embellished.

Moving muscles around like putty—emphasizing or minimizing them with painted shadows and impossible light sources made of powder and gloss.

Glamour—I told Luda, much as I'm telling you now to spare you some research time that might be better used watching the latest shit on TV, *is an old word.*

It began as *grammar* in the sense of reading and writing.

Scholars were seen as possessing real magic; to a largely illiterate population, books were inexplicable—that someone could open a collection of parchment leaves disfigured by intricate ink illuminations unintelligible to you, the average peasant, and from those pages conjure the actual words of a dead king, or Jesus himself, was the very source of wonder. Think about it. The written word itself was magic. It could make you hear the voices in your head of people who weren't there.

Next, I blended, tapping not swiping with the sponge. That's critical to getting the finish right and preventing a clash of Fauvist streaks.

In Scotland, early in the eighteenth century, *grammar* spread its academic crow cloak to become *grammarye* with that *why ee* exhalation at the end.

Then it slurred and melted into *glamour* and as the meaning itself shifted shape in some inspired attempt to pin a label on that elusive, almost supernatural quality of allure, where something ordinary could become truly extraordinary just by pretending, the wereword shed its scholar's gown and mortar, slipping into Hollywood heels and silk stockings to sip from a cigarette holder by candlelight.

I pulled feathered strokes of concealer back towards her hairline to emphasize Luda's already-prodigious cheekbones.

The essence of glamour became defined as a heightened, artificial characteristic; exaggerated to seem more real than real, it attempted to bottle the captured dazzle of a dream world. A world more professionally lit and tastefully arranged than the thrown-together sets where the drama of everyday experience plays out like amateur hour in a draughty community hall. Like the contouring strokes I apply to mimic Golden Age Hollywood lighting, like the haunted holy shine of the face I summon in the vanity glass, the light of the Glamour is directed from an unseen source, defining and separating the remarkable and the individual from the all-comprising context.

I brightened her brow, her nose, her chin with highlights then went to work on her eyes—stroking concealer over the creases of her lids and under her sockets to sculpt the huge oncoming headlights of a manga character bearing down on her hypnotized admirers like a haulage truck doing porno.

Spem in Alium unfurled its sonic brocade as I applied a glossy candy-frosting to Luda's lush pink lips until they glistened like confectionery.

The power of the Glamour could rearrange figure and ground so that the unnoticed was unexpectedly accentuated, while foreground dissolved and disappeared into its surroundings.

So you could disappear?—she asked eagerly. *You could be totally someone else . . .*

You can change your face. You can change how you move. You can change how you speak, and people will react to you as if you are what you pretend to be—I explained, rolling the snipped-off end of a used stocking over her skull, an improvised cap, so I could fix her spectacular wig in place with an elaborate snakes and ladders of bobby pins.

Dress like a rock star, behave like a rock star, you'll be treated like a rock star . . . act like a supermodel superwitch . . .

With a last finger-flounce of ribbons and silver strands, I said—*You can open your eyes.*

I directed her gaze at the flawless, dew-damp vision of powder-pink wide-eyed teenage innocence we'd evoked together. Platinum-blond bimbo bunches gathered up in ribbon scrunchies.

Funny—she said as I worked her look. *You've made me look like YOU.*

There are worse things to look like, darling . . .—I said, but the barb stuck. I adjusted her head, aiming her eyes at the mirror, immersing her in her own beauty.

You put that picture online—I said, lapsing into Twankey to take the edge off—*the boys will be falling over themselves to get the cocks out their boxers—*

You think?—she said quizzically, lost in herself, drunk on being Luda.

Mother knows best—I said and tweaked her wig to make her silhouette sublime.

I'm not doing it for boys or anyone else—she snarled. *I don't care about them! This is for me!*

Let's ask the Glamour to take us deeper—I said, becoming high and ignoring who she was.

I expected we could anticipate some meaningful synchronicities later that night. Now that we'd committed, we could surely look forward to a symbolic encounter with the hypothetical power of pretend in its purest form.

As I've done to my cost before, I was miscalculating the dose, misjudging the settings, and in the process exposing us to the unadulterated hot-pink voltage of the Glamour.

Thunderbolts of desire and madness came arcing our way!

W e'll start with Clip 1 to make it easy: Clip 1 is vivid and colourful, bright with magic and melody. Compared with everything else that went on that evening, it still comes across as something that could potentially happen to real people in a real world.

Unlike most of the rest of what I'm about to tell you.

In Clip 1, we're all dolled up, Luda and I, awaiting our ride. Me dressed as headmistress of a respected fetish school, in patent platform peep-toe sandals from the Little Shoe Box, a polished black leather hobble dress, red bob wig, mortarboard, and gown; an evil Disney stepmother leading her innocent blond victim on a jingling leash. Luda in this story was a soon-to-be-debauched disco dolly, in her pink latex gymslip, white socks, and Pleaser lace-up platforms colour-coded to match the glossy plastic flamingo sheen of her lips. A budding starlet hoodwinked into a life of booze and drugs and porn parties in the canyons.

You look gorgeous—I sighed with jealousy and pride. *Nobody ever did you up like that before, did they?*

She shook her head, mesmerized by her own reflection. In the mirror a freakish double exposure revealed a "before" and "after" of the same person, the distance between them measured in decades of unanticipated experience.

I squeezed Luda's candy cobweb lace-gloved hand.

You're perfect—I told her. She was.

We'd decided it would be even funnier if I secured a studded pink collar round her elegant neck and buckled it and clipped a pink leather leash into place so I could lead her around and keep her out of trouble.

Delirious. Disquieting. The mirror never failed to fill my head with the same old ideas.

As Clip 1 stutters a few frames into the future, we're punching the air and howling along with "Two Ladies" in a lip-sync mirror meltdown. Glam Goddesses Gone Wild.

I should put you on the streets—I shrieked in Twankey register, waving my magic wand so the plastic star on the end began to flash its maddeningly repetitive mind-control patterns. *I'm your fairy godmother; I know what's best for a nasty little truant like you!*

We hooted and tumbled our way in a tangle into the back seats of our taxi, riding the first raunchy boost of the evening as the MDMA came on, and there we were at last staring into each other's souls before the car pulled away from the kerb, before we settled back in the plush with slashed burgundy-and-rose grins on our faces to watch the light show.

Clip 2—we're making minor adjustments to our makeup for the third time. Luda looks flawless, like a creation of CGI. The trip out to the suburbs has been going on for the last twenty minutes or twenty thousand years of playacting, giggles, and obscene improv in the back of a taxi, with the drugs scrambling all incoming sensory input to abstract impressionism and where inexplicable coalitions of leaves and light were immediately, disappointingly I have to say, reclassified into sudden trees; where the inexplicable wondrous bellowing of shining metal walls clarified into buses filled with gawping aquarium faces as the lights went to green and laughing we were gone.

Luda's fingers fit the gaps between mine so naturally my heart liquefied to molten gold.

This!—I said earnestly, returning her grip.

Turn that one up!—we shrieked, and the driver complied, enjoying the show. It was "Run the World (Girls)," if you must know. Beyoncé.

We added what sounded to us like tight if ambitious harmonies. The driver was nice and kept his opinions to himself as the town gave way to semi-detached post-war bungalows, then unlit parkland, sprawling cemeteries shoulder-to-shoulder with bowling greens, rows of shuttered shops and the interlocking darknesses between.

Clip 3. And here's me, paying the driver—we're already here where it's noisy and bright and I'm apologizing for our singing as I sweeten the sour with a generous tip. Trading double entendres.

What kind of party is it?—he says, clocking the flash cars, the tipsy guests in fancy dress as nuns and bikers, schoolgirls, octopi and coral pollutants.

I don't think it's the party we all voted for!

He seemed to think we were quite good—I told Luda as the cab pulled away in a bloody swipe of taillights. *Asked if we were a couple of pros . . .*

I heard him say I was your daughter—

My daughter . . . YOU WISH!

Luda laughing.

Poor you—she said.

I checked my reflection in the slope of a car window. Tigress unbound.

I could be your daughter—she said and stuck out her tongue. I tugged on her leash to pull her close, which cued the Pop Art BANG! of an expensive firework.

As missile light drew fiery chalk rocket scrawls over the ornamental gardens, we almost kissed for real.

Until a second gunpowder boom blew the moment to smithereens and nanoseconds, coming as a self-important divine fart that made us laugh together at the same unspoken thought while a flower head of whistling sparks opened into an umbrella made of dandelion galaxies above the specimen trees.

A soft genie released from its bottle towered overhead, looming momentarily in a gust of mauve smoke. I could hear its rumbling laughter echoing through the sound of the gathering crowd. Expensive tyres bit gravel. Pounding EDM. The chortling of the Djinn.

Make a wish—I said, mesmerized, before making mine, which in the end failed to come true.

Luda was mashing the crunchy grit into particulate dust with her princess heels, her pink platforms, gawping up at the façade of the mansion, where falling firework embers were reproduced across every reflective surface in a slow shower of lights.

Don't do that! You'll ruin those shoes!—I said and as I did, I had a warning of something that hadn't happened yet.

Broken heels.

Now we'd reached our destination, I expected to relax into the chemical slipstream. I could lazily drift upriver to when I was thirty in the Troupe, and beautiful. Luda's lace-gloved hand in mine, like a sweet love letter folded into a sinister leather envelope. Best girlfriends!

I told myself I couldn't be the oldest one here.

Password!

He's behind you!—we said in unison, laughing madly at our rapport, our precious telepathy, while the door swung open with a smooth electronic tongue-click of approbation to divulge a sour-faced dwarf standing on an antique chair dressed as Louis Quatorze, if Louis had neglected his trousers. The jaded doorman had accepted this lucrative gig before being notified of a requirement to spend the night in voluminous diapers, the sort you'll need when a lifetime's anal sex catches up . . .

It was all a bit try-hard, I thought, ashamed of my cynicism when I saw the lights bursting in Luda's wide-open eyes.

As we tumbled inside cackling madly, caroming off the wood panelling, clutching each other's marvellous handbags for support, we immediately found ourselves component parts in a gear mesh of interlocking beautiful bodies all in restless motion and set to Industrial Techno. They were playing a mix of "Venus in Furs" by the Velvet Underground, although this was a girl-band cover I think I preferred to the original.

The beat made us feel like domme queens striding into the arachnodelic web of swirling lights in search of bizarre adventure and unlikely victims among the hustle and bustle of flesh and vinyl, feathers and fur.

We kissed and flirted our way through a crowd of masks, and leers, through gurning gorgeous pill monkeys. A muscle girl with a shaved head and her Clark Kent boyfriend. A cluster of football stars and their pop-eyed girlfriends dressed for this year's *Love Island* season.

There's an oddly-angled, elongated moment where Luda's leash gets tangled around a grotesque sculpture—a reverse of Epstein's *St. Michael's Victory Over the Devil* from Coventry Cathedral, where a priapic leering Lucifer is shivving the Archangel to death in a prison toilet.

Clip 4. Commences as a *tableau porno* of the rich, the famous, and the deviant in masks and devil wings, where everything is lit up from the inside like a Halloween lantern or a Hollywood soundstage and where it feels we've been here for ages, orbiting the light like moths. Warm burnt orange. Wrought-iron banister. Polished wood. Modern art.

It's like a film—Luda said, and it was the first time I'd seen that awestruck expression. Luda reduced to a child opening her eyes in Santa's Grotto, gawping at the Christmas lights flashing off cheap baubles, tinsel, and bubble wrap as if they were miracles.

I loved her so much. The kind of love that made the world

go round; the love that was the drug; that was all you need; that was the sweetest thing. That kind of love.

What film? Pinocchio?

We necked vodka from a three-litre bottle—two rough-cut crown jewels of ice on top, an unrepeatable double chime of light on mass-produced rim, and we were off to the races, with another pill-chaser each.

Plastic tumblers—I said. *Cheapskates!*

Luda and I swaggering on our slipstream of strong, long legs in high, high heels through the panelled hallway in search of familiar faces. There were quite a few that night: television stars, a celebrity judge, an MP, him from that band. The girl and her teacher from Balthus's scandalous painting of *The Guitar Lesson.* Our own faces startled and fascinating in the profusion of mirrors.

The art collection skewed towards the *erotique gothique très chic* as I recall—twisted bronzes of souls having sex with centipedes in Hell. Bondage scenes with Peter Pan and Darth Vader. Inflatable guillotines, blow-up electric chairs. Massive silk-screen prints of famous ghost photographs. A life-sized Picture of Dorian Gray quite naked and wholly corrupt.

I don't fancy yours much—I said.

Clip 5. In this one, an hour or so must have passed since we arrived—a crawling unease stalks our perimeters. We're planing down off the first rush, descending the plateau before the second and the third waves crash in and sobriety's last flotsam is swept away by medicinal tides.

I know this place—Luda said more than once but that kind of disjointed *déjà voodoo* is common enough on the lucky dip of mindbenders we'd guzzled so I let it pass without much consideration.

I know we talked to people and put on silly voices to tell lie after lie about who we were or weren't.

I was Lady Prospero, named for my address, and Luda my lollipop-licking niece, the Duchess Lizzi LaDitz, whose jangling tether I tugged sharply as I introduced her and explained about her medical need for restriction.

She's wild. Captured alive in the PVC jungles of Venus—I busked excitedly, loving the barrel ride down my stream of quicksilver consciousness.

But the white shine was coming off, and the second pill had barely ignited. A disquieting conviction decided to grow: We were failing to live up to the tits-and-tinsel promise of the event.

We were missing out.

I'd brought Luda here to dive headfirst into the shallow waters of illusion, where I could begin to explain the Glamour: How it works. What it is. Where it comes from.

All we'd done so far was get wasted and laugh at people.

They can get a bit cringey in real life, these things—it would look better in a film. I stopped short, to snatch another glass of champagne from a passing topless waiter.

I raised my glass to the guests all around—*To the Glamour! May it show up fashionably late!*

As I caught my balance and sipped at the slopping lip of my glass, I caught sight of Luda showing all the warning signs of what I recognized as a *Break on Through* . . . episode.

Teeth grinding mad-eyed, she stared over my shoulder, asking—*You said something about familiars.*

I might have done. I just didn't know why it was relevant.

What the fuck's a familiar?—Luda pressed. *Like a witch's cat?*

In answer, there came from the corridor a hallucinatory clip-clop sound on parquet and marble; a lopsided double gait that signalled a freakish arrival from beyond the frame.

Luda thrust out a definitive pointing finger, the kind of gesture you'd use to single out the witch in the local crone community.

Is it like that?

With these words, I turned to face the strange.

Jostling through a knot of semi-naked furred and feathered dancers, as if intent on making its presence known, felt, experienced to the full, a nodding, glassy-eyed refugee from the madhouse of the collective unconscious now thrust its remarkable snout. Polka-dotted, rag-tongued, it careened towards us, striking sparks of multicoloured stardust from polished hooves. It was a pantomime cow cackling on cocaine, sweeping us aside in its galloping rush to place first in the Bedlam Sweepstakes.

Backs to the walls, staring into each other's eyes across the corridor's abruptly uncanny gulf, we let the Devil-horned beast rampage past, praying it wouldn't notice us.

None of the other guests seemed particularly surprised. Instead, they appeared to think it was funny. Lofting glasses overhead to avoid spillage, they cheered the night-mare's antic gallop or slapped its upholstered rump with encouraging whoops.

If it's Buttercup—I reasoned. *They'll be heading for the secret room where all the really weird and dirty stuff goes on. We should follow them.*

They're quite hot—Luda mused. *I wouldn't mind.*

I felt a twinge of jealousy there; more than a twinge, this was a twin-bore tsunami of doubt that called for immediate course correction.

You could always watch—she leered.

Let's stick to what we know—I said firmly slamming the brakes on that train of thought. *I'll have the front end, the back's all yours.*

But Luda was uneasy, and for good reason. Her lacy-white fingers gripped my black-opera-gloved wrist as she directed my attention to a troubling tableau: The boys or were they something else who should have been piloting Buttercup the cow could be seen in the adjoining smoking room partially woven into a complicated reef knot of naked limbs. Stripped of the cow suit, they wore matching angel and devil wings from Victoria's Secret and expressions of ecstatic surrender.

Reeling at the implications, I spun, gyroscopic on my five-inch heel, to catch a glimpse of flywhisk tail departing around the corner with a flirty twitch.

It's telling us to follow it! I felt certain of this.

Is that a good idea?—the cautious student inquired.

The Glamour always sends an emissary to open the path—I went on. *You've heard of familiars?*

As far as I knew it was the first time I'd mentioned them, but all the same, she had.

An emissary. Luda repeated the word, each time with a deeper sense of portent until no further *gravitas* was possible and a dirty laugh came bubbling up.

Think of it as a sign—I said earnestly. *The path is open. The catwalk awaits.*

A pantomime cow is our familiar—she said as if I'd told her my uncle Bob was an octopus. God knows he might as well have been, Bob's hands were everywhere.

Well, what did you expect?—I said. *A pair of pantomime cows like us!*

She had no answer to that.

This was the Glamour in action, I told her. The Glamour in the shiny surface of things, in the moment, always deceptive, seductive.

What was the cow trying to say to us?—I asked Luda. *Use your imagination!*

It was trying to say . . . follow the cow—she said so very seriously we couldn't stop laughing as we clattered, all heels, in the wake of the heifer, chasing its receding footfalls, tracking the hand-stitched spirit creature's spoor through what might have been an underground laundry room as it made its ungainly clip-clopping way back to whatever cellar of the Abyss had calved it.

The mood was mock-Arthurian. The Questing Beast. The Unicorn. The White Hart. Sacred and heraldic beasts cantering through a profane Cumalot. We both knew we were honour-bound to follow the lowing cry all the way to the shadiest of Hades if need be.

This bovine entreaty led us to strange stone stairs that gave access to an unexpected basement level, a Playboy Santa's Grotto lit green and red; we could both agree on that in hindsight. And we both recalled a misshapen four-footed shadow splashed back across the whitewashed wall.

They're an endangered species! People hunt them you know—I disclosed. *It's terrible—parties like this! They arm themselves with popguns and water pistols—it's the only thing that can kill a pantomime animal!*

Is it just horses and cows?

I don't see why it has to be—I whispered, theorizing a whole panto-zoo; hand-stitched mockeries of nature pacing in traumatized circles behind imaginary bars, or swinging on tyres with a knitted dick in one hand and a lump of *papier-mâché* shit in the other.

We should have stopped but we didn't, even when the idling engine turnover of conversation receded to a faraway grumble of departing motorboat noise stranding us far from shore.

Luda wanted to know about the other pantomime animals, a cladogram of cloth and glass, a bestiary of rags and cast-offs.

Pantomime lions. Pantomime Komodo dragons—I said then slipped into a minor fall. *Extinct soon.*

We should have reconsidered our course when the music became a subliminal bass pulse so soft it might as well have been our watches ticking for all the sound it made.

Luda joined in—*Pantomime unicorns!*

Cackling, we rolled halfway down the stairs. Going down's

always easier than trying to get back up, as we'd find out soon enough.

Only a true virgin can tame a pantomime unicorn—I dead-panned with an exaggerated Twankey eyebrow raise. *Which puts you out of the running, I'm sorry to say.*

There were Roman candles in her eyes when she laughed at my stupid jokes with toothpaste-advert tiers of teeth a dentist in her Marvell days had made for her.

The radiant moment lasted less than a second before her laughter was stopped dead by the most spine-chilling screech anyone could imagine. A slaughterhouse yodel, an abattoir so-prano . . . it could only be the inhuman death-screech of a cloth-and-canvas cow with a tail made of rope and bristle.

In a nerve-racking aftermath, clots of silence thickened to a fog that clogged our ears as we sank into its deaf and dumb acoustics.

Maybe we should go back—I heard her say. I should have listened, but I never do. In my own defence, I wasn't ready to listen to one more sound at that exact moment.

As to where we'd found ourselves, knock-kneed and cling-ing to each other like a kooky fashion shoot in the Bates Motel basement, it might have been a wine cellar except for a distinct lack of bottles on the conjectured racks. It was too dark to tell. It was too dark to think.

Did you hear that?—I whispered, reaction delayed by the pause button of shock. I had no idea how much of anything she'd heard; or how much meaning she'd extracted from the marrow-freezing sequence of catgut squeal and slobber. The pallid horror on her sweet rag-doll face told me it must have been enough and as she gave in to an enchanting and vulnera-ble moment of ripped-back panic, Luda's fingers gripped mine so fiercely it felt like we'd been stapled together by a sexual-ly-repressed bank clerk.

Oww—I said. She was sorry, wide-eyed. I was her only

protection against the capering, demented Unseelie Court that might at any moment charge loose from the wallpaper and the mouldings, inflating with life and menace in a tidal surge of collapsing perspective and ill intentions.

I think it needs help. The cow—Luda whispered, as if afraid to draw attention to herself.

By the sound of that spastic scrabbling for purchase, those in-drawn bellows for breath, the artificial Holstein had blundered into a well, straw hat floating on quicksand or tar as the head went under, the glassy goggle eyes rolling in four directions at once, the tongue a dishcloth lolling from a grinning face that would be comical but for the death throes.

I think we're in the spirit world—Luda said in that discon-certing way she had of making things creepier.

I nodded slowly.

Something at the foot of the stairs stopped us short. The plunge from a boast to a scream as they say.

Luda had found something to stare at on the floor and I followed her gaze to where several variously-proportioned amoebic asterisks on the wooden floor were splottered in bright comic-book red.

Fresh BLOOD!—Luda said hoarsely, and for one horrible moment I took it as a request.

I thought of that poor pantomime cow, an endangered spe-cies, wounded and dripping the lurid red carnations of its life-blood as it grew weaker, swaying in the limelight. Brought to four human knees it never knew it had, wearing lace-up sneak-ers beneath patent-leather cloven hooves.

Prey of the vampire!

Clip 6. And this is where what happened becomes inextri-cable in hindsight from the range of severely-distorted impres-sions and disassembled episodes provided by the drugs we'd taken.

Two "Skyfall" ecstasy tablets. Two or three drops from an eyewash bottle of liquid LSD my dealer Paddy sourced ten years ago.

The Byzantine sport of chemicals combining with subconscious emotions—occurring in the expansive cathedral ambience of minds whose incessant running commentary had been stunned into a prayer-like hush by MDMA. Anything can happen.

Except we both remembered it the same way.

I know, I said it before, we should have gone back upstairs, we should have forgotten about the stricken pantomime cow, but they never do, do they? In spooky stories, they never do the sensible thing. A stolen glimpse of the Underworld's too much of a temptation.

When the Glamour calls, when the power of the strange and forbidden comes into your boring old life, it's hard to resist at first. It wouldn't be the Glamour if it didn't seduce with a promise of sin.

After a few experiments in conceptual lighting design, Luda succeeding in directing her phone at the sudden darkness. The beam from the screen clipped out a giddy trapezoidal section of corridor and I thought about H. P. Lovecraft and what a strange life he'd had. We seemed, you and I, to be fastened inside a black-and-white movie reel where the edges on everything caught in the projector beam were dissolving into those fizzing feathered spectra on the blue end.

It's a bit spooky . . .

Shadows congregated from every corner as we tiptoed on down some nonfigurative representation of a hall; vague spectres magnetized to our iPhone light, to our crown chakras radiant on molly and mandy, their separate forms condensing around that elongated lozenge of visibility, suggestive of a gathering crowd, a gas of intimidating shapes discovering their common cause as one all-engulfing life-hating darkness made of who knows how many lost and pissed-off individuals. Their edges mingling, running together into a fused mulch of rage, turmoil, and self-hatred.

I decided it was time to pop the expanding bubble of fear in my chest and seized my chance to show off.

Disregard the air of menace—I said. I knew these shades of old and I told her so. And with all my meridians opened wide, I felt only a profound compassion for these tattered wraiths. They gave me an unexpected chance to impress Luda.

Electing myself Afterlife Agony Aunt, I reached for that kindly, *I know you've taken something but there's still hope . . .* voice I'd taught to everyone in the office when I did six months on the suicide hotline, and I addressed any attendant bad spirits.

I made what I thought was quite a generous offer to listen very carefully to their otherworldly grievances and promised frank and sincere counselling.

That seemed to do the trick; the looming swarm of shadow-people was suddenly dispersed, obliterated as if in some bright *Fiat Lux!* accompanying my voice. If you don't know what that means, some say it was the car God drove to get there in time for chapter 1, line 3 of the Book of Genesis.

In this instance, I'm talking supernova. Big Bang. The triumph of Light Supreme over Eternal Darkness, accompanied by a flat metallic *tick,* a sound effect sublime in its straightforward, secondhand annunciation of the Kingdom of Heaven.

The shadows had utterly dispersed, banished to the corners at precisely the same instant as the primal click I'd experienced! If nothing else, here was a sturdy basis for religions of Gnostic binary austerity, I reasoned, imagining Sherlock Holmes doing clever diagrams in his head. The 1:2:3:4 rhythmic finger-pop that started so many songs.

In the thumb-and-forefinger snap of awakening, the *pabitra mudra* became a bebop count-in that made the house lights blaze.

At the heart of this cascading muddle of effect and cause and mystical speculation lay a simple reality: Luda had found an antique light switch—one of those round Bakelite domes with a lollipop-shaped metal toggle—which cunningly and with much consideration she'd then manoeuvred to the "on" position so that we stood in a drably-illumined hallway painted leaf green and pale mustard yellow.

It occurred to me that we hadn't moved an inch since Christmas or last Saturday, stopped dead at the door of what I took at first to be an abandoned school classroom beyond the frosted pane.

Tiled walls. That's usually a bad sign—was the best I could come up with. *Makes you think of mad butchers, serial killers, torture camps . . .*

Don't say that!—she said, too late to stop me.

My recollections of that night remain as rapidly-edited shaky cam footage of piled-up newspapers from decades gone by. Elections lost and won. Wars and weddings. Discarded headlines wrapped in bundles at the bottom of a long flight of stairs, stacked in the alcoves that lined a short corridor with a green door at the end, like in the song.

This incredible pileup of incident and detail happened to someone but surely not me?

It occurred to me again that we hadn't moved since Christmas or last Saturday.

Are you seeing this?

It occurred to me again.

Clip 7. I was witnessing green gloss paint, decaying over decades, throbbing with significance and portent. Not the faerie jade of the Celtic Otherworld—this was a 1950s hospital spinach.

What remained, what intensified to an in-held breath that went on too long, was a terrible impulse to *hide* from forces beyond all control.

It's like in Equus—*where the boy goes mad and mutilates the horses*—I observed, lost in pop culture.

Luda shuddered. Frying on the egg-pan of her mind were frenzied collages of disfigurement and animal sacrifice, enacted by stripped puppets in Hell. The last thing she could use was nihilistic humour. I kept on, secure in my conviction that a gallows grin was the best medicine..

It's that—but with a pantomime cow. That's my pitch, Mr. Spielberg!—I screeched. I was only trying to make her laugh, but I think I came over a bit demented.

Don't open it—said Luda as I reached for the distempered brass knob.

Beyond the green door, though I don't remember it opening, we found a pea-green and custard room; big, vacant. A lecture theatre. Mission control.

The room had the feeling of somewhere you shouldn't be but not scary—the second pill had lifted us above mere human concerns—we felt clear, hyper-aware, experiencing every subatomic nuance of this remarkable experience.

Imagine a schoolroom in summer's limbo months. There's that evocative thrill of trespass, but you wouldn't want to be found at your desk by a prowling janitor; or think of when you were little and there was that recently-vacated house, the kind that only pretends to be abandoned to lure you in. Hollow rooms without furniture except upright pianos, a scrawling impending apprehension that, any moment now, a door would open, and it would be too late to escape—it was all of that—as if we'd descended through memories into the world of dreams itself.

Is this like a film set?—Luda ventured.

Imagine a crime scene. To move at all is to disturb the dusts and the tape—*and soon they'll return.*

The atmosphere thickened through Goth into positively primeval where our unnatural presence seemed to insinuate a crouched hidden intent, as though a leopard-thing from the ancestral dark had its greedy eyes on us, coiled to spring from cover behind the antiseptic mint gloss paint when we least expected it.

There was a worry that we might never find the door we'd come through. A worry we might never be sane again. I reassured her. *What about Alice in Wonderland? This is like that but with rubber! She came back sane, didn't she?* I couldn't put any money on that last bit and tried to dispel the sudden squall of seamy sexual feelings; me the degenerate headmistress leading another innocent unhinged child to the basement . . .

It's a museum—I said. *It's like Churchill's Bunker. It must be something from the War*—I said.

And that sparked something. *What if it's his dungeon?*—Luda theorized.

Sex dungeon—I nodded, clinging anxiously to the splintering driftwood of rationality. *What else could it be? This is where he gets up to all sorts. High Court Judge. Top legal mind. It would be exactly like this, wouldn't it?*

Then I had a better idea; *I think it's just more of the art like upstairs. A creepy art installation.*

Looking back, these were all good enough guesses. The place didn't seem fixed. Depending on the angle, it could be one thing or another.

I mean, why would you have that in a dungeon? Are there people who get off on gradients and river valleys?

It was a question that made no sense even to me until I became aware that Luda was examining a map hanging on the wall.

Is this the spirit world?

I nodded.

I say hanging on the wall, but the map *was* the wall; six feet tall by twenty-five feet wide, it depicted a sprawling city not unlike Gasglow as an immense unfolded urban nervous system, pinned like hide on the walls of a municipal premises store-room in the Underworld, with its coloured wiring for streets and flyovers, its capillaries and tributaries in the form of roads branching off into avenues, crescents, circuses. Its rivers and ponds opened up, outstretched and nailed down as a freaky anatomy lesson.

The detail, crystal clear in the magnifying lens of memory, was extraordinary, and there was even a bas-relief effect—with the little hills standing up from the surface as proud scar tissue. The rivers fingering forth from Mother Dare's splashy roots thirty miles upriver cut tiny trenches no deeper than the grooves on a vinyl record.

You'd think a master jeweller made this—look at the little bits all moving . . .—I said, wandering in wonder.

And there, that master-jeweller thing again, which is why I bring it back up. The map was something you'd see in display windows in the Arcade—wedding-ring worlds of glittering diamond separating the light into planes.

I first extended my leather-gloved fingers to touch the map then withdrew, suddenly afraid that if I made contact whole city blocks would collapse in the real world, as a force unknown toppled the flyovers, snapped the bridges, and let the floods charge in.

Thereafter, I thought, I'd surely be hauled before a jury comprised of history's most sadistic and inhumane fiends.

Charged with *Reckless Apocalypse,* I'd pay the inevitable price for prompting wide-scale havoc and loss of life with a flippant flick of my false nails. I couldn't take anything seriously. That was my problem. That was where I'd gone wrong.

The leering, lascivious, downright homicidal jury mocked me, as if I was some new arrival, thrown into the weird offenders' wing.

It's Gasglow—but it's NOT.

Luda was correct: The map showed Gasglow but not; bigger,

sprawling past the city's recognized boundaries, to spread its mycelial threads in directions only sleepers recognize from dreams they've had . . .

Seen from a few steps back, I swear I saw what Jim Morrison was on about. The snake that was long, and old, hooded and tensed to strike as it writhed through the Dare Valley to the sea.

The blue, winding River Dare divided the city into north and south; widening to the cobra-fan of its head where it dislocated immense jaws as if to swallow the ocean whole. The river's natural course was embroidered upon by more recent human interventions; abandoned docks and shipyards left traces chiselled out in deft right angles from the curving mother current.

How do they get it to move like that?

I couldn't answer.

Here upon this dull wall was pinned the ninth wonder of the world.

A sapphire viper festooned with branching aerial adornments from belly to throat where industries had grown and died and left these cryptic prosthetic scabs, incisions, excavations for future archaeologists to find and fail to identify, in a world without heavy industry and no need for ships.

Up close, these odd additions suggested unreadable letters in a secret oneiric alphabet—the italic lowercase *e* of the Magdalena Docks, the truncated *f* of Turner's Yard where my granddad lost his footing and plummeted forty-five feet from the riveter's platform where he worked into a scrap heap of jumbled clinker that disassembled his vertebrae.

Each individually-crafted hieroglyph came with a talismanic singularity, gold-leaf characters in some occult or religious script.

This is what it's really like—they don't want us to know how big it really is—Luda said, with eyes far brighter than could be good for her.

Who's they?—I said. *The Mayor's Office? The Parents' Group?*

In this way we arrived, step by faltering madcap step, at the obvious conclusion that we'd uncovered an operations room where plans were made concerning the secret policing of Gasglow. We could agree on that momentarily at least.

Why would the police set up down here?—I said, casting reasonable doubt on this latest of an increasingly provisional series of homegrown conspiracy theories we'd inflated to working cosmologies, then debunked in the last few minutes.

It made sense that it would be much easier for them to police the real city, we reasoned, if ordinary people were permitted to experience only a limited cross-section of its entirety in our waking world while law enforcement had access to the whole map; all the corners we never look around, the lanes we pass each day on our way to work and never choose to venture down, the overgrown brownfield sites we're too preoccupied to explore. All the rabbit holes, and snow-filled wardrobes, the phantom tollbooths and freestanding doors we ignore in favour of the ordinary were marked here on the wall chart.

There was a note of urgent alarm in her voice that I wasn't ready for. We'd been having fun and now things were trending creepy as though the shadow of something invisible was drawn across the light.

Perhaps even more horrible to contemplate was the implication that our habitually-prescribed routes, the regularly-reinforced boundaries of our daily round, those snug spaces and accustomed faces, demarcated the limits of our cramped prison-cell experience, while the map of Gasglow brought to life the true extent of the penitentiary's pageant sprawl; its escape tunnels and unlocked gates barred by an unvoiced consensus, its exits blocked with the dusty rubble of doubt.

I had no idea where we were or how to get back to where we'd been before this. Our adventure was surely my fault and she'd hate me forever if it went wrong, I reasoned, unable to look her in the eye now . . . until I did, firmly . . .

It's the Glamour—I assured her. *We followed the familiar into the Glamour.* I took a deep breath. Reality swam and bulged and settled as a jelly congealing. *Everything's meant to be.*

It's all moving around a fixed point—Luda said, confounded. *There's a hole through everything.*

She leaned in close. Her voice seemed to drop an octave, but I was probably just imagining it.

This is damnation and we are the damned.

Even though I didn't want to, I tried to see what she was seeing.

What you're describing is a classic migraine—I cooed, too sure of myself for anyone's health.

The map seethed uneasily—a queasy sifting of the granular component particles of reality was taking place, triggering a memory of hundreds-and-thousands shaken onto icing, where imperceptible sudden pixelations sprinkled together into new sand-painting configurations of almost familiar roads and place-names, where Amberwood Street dissolved into Broomeward Lane, as if to foil the monthly meeting of the Residents' Association! Stumbling home in a dream where your keys won't fit the locks on a worryingly alien front door. And Drewboard Terrace was already rethinking its whole approach to urban planning before resetting as Wonderbra Mews; I surveyed entire postal districts squirming and rearranging themselves like a bathtub of cartographic maggots. Except these wiggling words were more well-behaved than larvae.

They moved as if *to order.* Finely calibrated, tracking tectonic shifts in the Dreamtime Deserts where we'd kicked up the sequins and thunder of the Glamour. Needles nodding, accelerating to a frenzied pecking crescendo as unknown energies were released, or contained.

It won't stay still—Luda said. *I don't think I want to keep looking at it. Maybe we shouldn't have come here.*

Don't touch it—I said, but the warning came too late. Or was that another helping of *déjà vu?*

Luda swiped away a film of dust to reveal the letters on the stuffy brass nameplate set into the map's painted wooden frame. MYSTERY CITY it read.

Or maybe it was MISERY CITY. Or MISTER TITTY. Or MISTRESSITY.

How can it do that?—Luda wanted to know. I worried she was losing control of her emotions: angry, scared, angry . . .

Letters were shuffled restlessly, scrabbling from one half-formed thought to another thought that still somehow suggested a single concept viewed from multiple directions at the same time.

The concept as I came to understand it was Luda, reflected in a music-box arrangement of five full-length mirrors, omnifold.

It's the spirit world—she said again with a chime of awe in her soft little Disneyland voice.

It was, and it wasn't. Just before you write this off as some unlikely and unconvincing ghost story, *The Shining* in six-inch heels, I should step in with an assurance: The Glamour doesn't go in for the supernatural.

What's natural and known is quite spectacular and peculiar enough for anyone when you learn to see it all from the best seat in the Dress Circle. Or the Pit, which is where Luda was at that moment, peeking round the edge of things into the gulf, gey grim, that bubbled below the worm-eaten timbers we'd been using to fix the holes in everyday reality.

Determined to respawn and remotivate our intrepid videogame character sprites, I tried to remind her how not so very long ago those wild-eyed witches, those extravagant partners-in-crime, Luci and Luda had deliberately, indeed ritually, consumed industrial quantities of hallucinogenic sacrament.

Bearing this in mind, I explained to her, our present

deconstructed perceptions, this ongoing exotic spectrum of moods, suspicions, certainties, and puzzles with no names—ranging from bass-note infra-terrors to the bright hypersonic frequencies of ultra-bliss—could be expected to come with the territory. I emphasized this with the sincere authority of a professor defining a solemn mathematical proof, but the information failed to connect with my student's immediate concerns.

By the time I'd got all this worked out to my own satisfaction and felt comfortable saying it to Luda, we'd become separated by a wall of transparent, rotating shutters whose interminable operations were only made visible to a lucky few and for a mercifully short time period. Echoes of their ceaseless rotation could be experienced in the revolving doors of big hotels and department stores. You've been with me this far along the winding dirt track through Deep Dark Woods so you'll have to take my word for it and don't let go of my hand when I tell you these shutters offered a rarely-glimpsed representation of Time the nightclub bouncer's tendency to huckle us along the uglier we became, the farmer threshing every last one of us into the future, fed as laundry through an invisible mangle called life; creasing, drying out . . . the metaphors accumulated as spray-can snow on a window ledge in Santa's buried grotto.

And all I had to offer in return for this synaptic cascade of spark-spitting dendrites and axons was—*Where's that Aladdin?*—half aware that I'd taken refuge in Twankey's rudimentary personality yet again as a substitute for my own, presently-misplaced Self.

Where indeed? Aladdin had wandered off into a folding-napkin Narnia made of unfinished notions and temporary spaces bound for the bin. Otherwise known as the room we'd come into only minutes earlier.

I'd brought Luda into this sunken hypogeum—this tomb of the Unknown Man from the Ministry. This revolving Pharaoh's

Antechamber—and I couldn't for the life of me remember why it had seemed like any kind of idea, let alone a sensible one.

We shouldn't have done this—was the last thing she'd said, echoing the cries of my own inner demons. I couldn't understand why I'd led her into this obscure and intimidating space.

What were we thinking?

When I turned to reassure her that everything was proceeding to plan, I had to concede the Devil might have plans of his own. Luda was frozen in place, Lot's wife immobile on the Plain, caught looking the wrong way and reimagined as a five-foot-one tower of sodium chloride when the Angel of the Lord enacted the spiteful wrath of the Almighty on the sex-positive hedonists of Sodom and Gomorrah.

Oh fuck—she said, staring at the floor. *There's been a murder!*

I could hear the exclamation mark at the end of her sentence. I'd hoped I could steer her away from misinterpreting quite ordinary sensory input, but this was different.

Unnerving chalk lines were drawn around a creased heap of shed skin on the floor, nauseatingly reminiscent of a spider's empty carapace it's shrugged off on your carpet in favour of some roomier nightmare form.

Except this was no spider or snake husk: Before us lay a massive broken swastika of limbs and torso and grin—the crumpled, discarded skin of a dappled pantomime cow.

It's just a cave painting—I tried to reassure her as the shrieking paralysis in Luda's nerves became almost audible, wind in the wires on the wrong side of night. *Remember? When they need good luck on the pantomime aurochs hunt, the shaman does one of these sketches* . . . I thought she'd laugh at that, but she'd gone too far for giggles.

What happened to its head?—emerged as a wuthering moan. *It hasn't got a head* . . .

And if I wasn't wearing a wig, I swear the hairs on my head would have stood up like Jesus's halo on a Byzantine fresco.

Hanging from a nail above the transom was the empty head of Buttercup the pantomime cow. The goggle orbs were still, fixed by gravity and death in a cross-eyed pathos. With those outsized piano-key teeth bared in one final oracular rictus, it knew now what the dead know and was eager to impart the terrible secrets of Dante's barnyard in what I imagined would be a marrow-chilling sequence of reproachful moos out of Hell accompanied by the skeletal *gamelan* clacking of the bell she'd worn in life.

The accumulating palpable aura of the paranormal was too much to tolerate. I'd brought Luda into this world of shifting scenery, this borderland zone, where tremors shook the foundations of the soul and where the planks of reality, rotted through with the acid drip of leaking, overflowing bad inclinations, now splintered into rotten pulp beneath our heels.

I've seen this—she said in strangled tones

I experienced a Hitchcock focus-pull, a vertiginous horizontal fall towards a telescoping background wall. Unsure how we'd gotten to here from there. We'd set out in high spirits to party among beautiful perverts. Instead, we'd wound up, Luda and I, trapped in a basement going mad and neither of us could locate the exit. We were too terribly high and there was a simmering extravagance of spirits crowding that lost basement room, caught in the unceasing, cycling press of time.

How long had we been here? Hours? I was the responsible one in this situation, which I have to say was an unusual experience for me. I was the Jedi Master; it would be unthinkable to stand by as my young Padawan succumbed to the dark side of the Force—otherwise known as the Police Force if we couldn't explain what we were doing down here, trespassers in the Twilight Zone.

Luda, spaced out, her tether to the command module severed, seemed to rotate in her own personal anti-gravity, beyond any hope of rescue.

I've seen all this before—she repeated.

We might still be there if I hadn't heard what I knew to be very real footsteps coming closer. Sensible shoes on a concrete floor would sound that way. Three, maybe four men. Brogues. Lace tips as yet unfrayed.

Luda swayed on her heels and staggered backwards with hands thrown out ahead, an evil hypnotist's victim, or old-school movie zombie. I caught her wrists on the edge of a precipice you didn't see but felt in your heart. An existential edge shelved away at her back, a bottomless psychic crash, a black suction presided over by the severed head of a mad cow.

It's not the first time. It's not the first time—she told me again and again, as if the words were unknown tastes and textures in her mouth.

The resulting expression on Luda's face was so beautiful, so defenceless, and vulnerable, so fragile and impermanent, I wanted to protect her somehow, from the multiple-tracked clock beats of the footsteps approaching down the corridor on the far side of that never-more-extraordinary door; the inevitable calculated pace that rose in volume; from time, to time, unhurried, taking all the time in the world.

Luda—I said. *Look at me, sweetheart.*

The void revolved at her back as she surrendered to the singularity. Only me gripping her two hands prevented a fatal backward stagger; one step, two, then toppling, shrinking, smaller and smaller, draining of colour until Luda was a fading dot, a blinking cursor on a screen. Then nothing at all.

We need to get you out of here.

Her hands were locked to mine, so I felt it like a candy-floss landslip when her entire body started to shake uncontrollably, from her painted toenails to her matching "She's a Bad Muffuletta" OPI neon-pink fingernails.

I had to admit something was especially wrong when I realized her pupils had expanded to eclipse her blue-green eyes.

Around then was when Luda began to resonate, you'd have to call it, the way a tuning fork, struck on the edge of a kitchen table, then touched lightly against the hollow belly of an acoustic guitar, transmits its pure tone into the wood and the plucked string.

Struck like a bell, Luda rang in unison—no pure G or E, this was a sick tone, a semi-demi-quaver out of sync with the natural world and all the wholesome laws of the universe. The flounces hemming her party dress moved like seismographs tracking the tremor and, as far as I could tell, it was demolishing bonds down at the molecular level, clanging her to pieces, along with everything else in her vicinity that had pretensions to material existence, a classification that still included yours truly.

I was shaking too, in sympathy, until it felt as if my skeleton was dismantling into kit pieces, discreetly, behind the modesty screen of my skin.

First, she'd caused the Birth of the Universe with the light switch, now she was ringing it to its End.

Don't let go of me—she tried to say and right there, at the exact moment I opened my mouth to scream—*I need to let go, or it'll kill me*—it was as if she'd been hit by bespoke lightning.

Her face went white and her oil-spill eyes popped bright as lightbulbs obliterated in a power surge. Voltage divided down her veins. Her jaw seemed on the verge of dislocating, prepping to swallow a whole gazelle.

You're all right. It's all right—I knew I was well wide of the mark there, but I didn't know what else to say as Luda was cracked like a bullwhip—so that I swear I saw a blue sine wave working its way from head to toe and flexing her every muscle to its limit.

When you're with someone who looks to be on the edge of either grand mal seizure or demonic possession, the best thing to do is keep it light. Don't scream or tell them they've turned green. Don't mention the sweat, the drool, the rolling whites of the eyes. Whatever you do, don't bring up the vomit laced with razor blades and crusty fishhooks. I mean that bit didn't happen in this case, but I don't doubt we'd have got there if my last vestigial link to common sense hadn't worked to our advantage.

I'd forgotten about the approaching footsteps of doom during this razor-sliced tissue-thin fragment of what was turning out to be a disordered sticky substitute for the calm progress of the conventional seconds and the minutes and the hours I was used to.

The voices were louder now. Then they stopped, outside the Operations Room, where the map still seethed on its wall. Words were muttered in some understated European accent. Government business. The Bureau and the Department. Keys jangled like charm bracelets, or maybe handcuffs. It's all joined together in my head. There were a lot of handcuffs at the party. Enough keys, and locks, and chains to account for the clinking shuffle we could hear but not for the mounting panic we felt.

It occurred to me, at last, that this might be some category of courtroom.

In the pointillist scramble of the pebble-glass window, dot-matrix shadows skewed in parade across the wall. The voices switched to ominous mutterings. The locks rattled impatiently.

What if we were to be placed on trial in a dreary Kafkaesque purgatory while a sex party went on overhead? What would happen if we stayed long enough for the magistrate to park his fat arse in his seat in front of that demonic wall map? Would he condemn us for shocking violations of rules we didn't even know had made the statute books?

Anything could happen.

Trust Luda then to make it worse with a Sibylline whisper that augured inexplicable fate, obscure judgment . . . while hinting at a nameless price we'd have to pay for desecrating the ritual chamber, thereby invoking its implacable flat-packed guardians.

Flat Police—Luda confirmed through grinding teeth. Teetering over the rim of pure pandemonium, I picked her up in my arms and manhandled her out of the self-dismantling room through the door I'd somehow found again exactly where I'd left it—*Flat Police*—

You there! STOP! Stop right there!

I'm not sure who said that, but I'm certain somebody did. As it was, we chose *not* to comply.

Clip 8. Here all I can offer are smashed-plate recollections of narrow Cubist stairs that played havoc on our heels; flashing squad-car lights ahead and behind us; the witch-whooping of burglar alarms and approaching banshee sirens attending our getaway.

Far-off voices and music hastily assembled in our scrapbook awareness as if to suggest a narrative of relative sanity at the top of the stairwell.

I half dragged my semi-conscious Sorcerer's Apprentice, clattering upstairs on a halting, tumbling trajectory that seemed much longer than when we'd come down. If I hadn't had sturdy ankle straps, if Luda's platforms hadn't been secured by tightly-fastened cerise laces, we'd have lost our footwear down there along with our wits—as it was, I twisted my ankle badly enough to need an elastic bandage. My Little Shoe Box heels would never recover, and I loved them.

There's always a sacrifice, isn't there?

Jesus coughed his last on the cross to redeem us all in our personal stalled clocks of torment at the end, Odin hung by one leg from the Tree of Life for three days and nights and lost an eye to gain mastery of the runes for all humankind.

There are no free lunches. Well, not unless you count the pigswill the catering staff dishes up during rehearsal.

And Luda?

Luda kicked and writhed in my arms. From the bubble-gum

gloss of her doll-smooth lips, there effervesced a starry froth of Celtic knotwork, or so it seemed to me all lit up like a sky-scraper. She sprayed a bardic foam of words that couldn't be spoken, only interpreted by druids as they dripped sizzling in silver from her chin.

Gasping, squealing, praying to Mercurius and any other listening deity with an ounce of providence to spare, I followed the thudding heart of all music, all defiance against death and restriction, closer to its source!

Top of the stairs. Opening out again into colours and people, like those pop-up books you'd get as a kid where entire cardboard cities would spring from the pages with little stiffened paper levers to work the moving parts.

Following our Underworld adventure, the onrushing sensory excess seemed to immerse us completely in a welcoming warm wave; all naked bodies, rubber, strap-ons, gas masks, sweat, and scent, unfettered life.

I rejoiced in the pulsing party light, the humanity, here in this room with its *déjà vu* reproduction of *The Guitar Lesson*.

We'd made it. Here in the upstairs world, my body felt pleasantly cold in the heat and the body weather, the climatic sultry gusts of lube and pussy, ass and poppers, PVC and rubber, *hors d'oeuvres*. Goosed by a blade of air I could tell that I'd split my dress down the back, but it seemed a small price to pay for safe passage up from Tartarus. The noises, the shrieks and laughter, the grunts and glissandos of orgasm and desire, the commonplace lights of familiarity's blessed shores. I was very, very, high, I realized. Something big had just happened, something inexplicably lifechanging. No one seemed to realize any of this. Something had to be done about these closed-minded, hedonistic narcissists! Or so I thought.

Someone began to yell, panicked, shrill, and theatrical. It turned out to be me.

Is there a doctor?

Picture me waving my arms like a chicken struggling to outrun the butcher's wife.

Luda shuddered and thrashed in my arms in sputtering black-and-silver flashes, her film spooling in chequered ribbons off its mortal reel. I have to say she made even a seizure look hot.

Please—I heard myself shrieking. *Is there someone?*

I knew there had to be *someone.* There's usually more than one qualified medical professional at these sorts of parties. I don't know what it is about doctors and fetish, but you can generally count on that.

Or at least you'll get a dentist. Rarely a vet, I've found. I think they're just too busy.

That's when the scenery flipped. What had been a bejewelled Versailles populated by some fantastic celestial and polyamorous elite turned squalid and flickering, a vintage dirty movie sputtering towards climax on an antique projector. I saw myself staggering through a post-nuclear flea market, lost among creaky splintered trestle tables laden with joke-shop novelties of cardboard, tin, and enamel, threadbare soft toys, tattered books fresh from someone's deathbed. The treasures of civilization. I had become nakedly aware. All at once came a razor-edged raw immediacy—a cold-water baptism in the abrupt indecent squalor of the real, unmediated by chemicals and self-deception.

I was unexpectedly sober in what some Buddhists call *shunyata.*

The woman bent over Luda's quaking body—a doctor I deduced—wore a mask like a raven's head, beak and all, and nothing much else aside from a black hooded cape and a pair of Terry de Havilland boots to die for.

I thought she was possessed!—I tried to explain. *Your boots are incredible!*

It's grand mal—the fabulous, feathered hybrid assured me in withering tones I felt were quite unnecessary. *She's having an epileptic fit. Tonic-clonic seizure.*

Often mistaken for demonic possession in the Dark Ages—I pointed out, so as not to seem completely gullible. *Those are Terry de Havilland, right? Your boots.*

You must get her onto her side—she said but she'd already managed that, and she'd loosened Luda's buckled collar, leaving me with nothing to do but helicopter nervously as the bird-lady placed a nearby cushion beneath Luda's head and curtly monitored her watch.

Shouldn't we put something in her mouth to stop her biting her tongue?—I suggested, looking around for a suitable example, finding only dildos and vibrators.

Only if you want to break her teeth or jaw—came the snippy reply. *Am I using the right pronoun?*

To stay in the game, I nodded a series of fervent agreements. In my distraught and absented state of mind, I was certain I recognized this carrion Florence Nightingale as the Morrigan, battlefield goddess of the Celts, and I certainly didn't want to find myself on her shit list.

She'll be all right—quoth the Raven as the jagged ferocity of Luda's jerks and whiplashes began to ease off. *That's two minutes.*

The beaked head snapped round to confront me. I felt as though I'd done something to aggravate Batman.

What were you doing? What did she take?

We were looking for something—I confessed, cowering in the beady-eyed glare of justice. *Something happened.*

Not all dialogue's worth repeating. It went on like that for a minute or two while a whimsical crowd gathered, as if assembling to witness an accident in a circus brothel.

I was handed what appeared to be a dead cartoon snake. It was the leash I'd buckled onto Luda's collar. *This almost strangled her*—said the Morrigan gravely, as if the whole debacle was somehow my fault!

I sat back awkwardly on my wonky heels as the miraculous

lady doctor, this vision plucked nude and feathered from a Max Ernst canvas, cantilevered Luda into the recovery position where she rolled her eyes and ground her jaws as though intent on chewing through masonry.

Clip 9. I knelt beside Luda holding her hand as she recuperated in a quiet wood-panelled library decorated as Tutankhamun's Tomb. Looking back, that must have been when I took my glove off. No one had been keen to call the emergency services. Not to a party like this. There were too many well-known faces—celebrities, sportsmen, dentists to the rich and famous—to risk involving the authorities.

Luda lay back in a decadent spill of Versace velvet cushions, obsessed with a tinkling music box, another of the fabulous château's morbid art pieces, as it toiled its way through Cliff Richard's "Devil Woman," simplifying the Peter Pan of Pop's 1976 chart hit to serial cracked chimes while a black-painted, pipistrelle-winged ballerina spun like a tiny toxic kebab in a tutu.

Enthralled by the plinking, struggling music a grinning Luda extended her arms languorously, pantheresque! I had a suspicion, immediately to be confirmed, that she'd learned absolutely nothing from our recent brush with danger.

I feel amazing—she said, proving me right. *I'm so horny!*

You just had a fit—I tried to explain but she didn't care.

It's not the first time—she said breezily. *I'm used to it. It feels amazing when it stops. I'm just a bit tired.*

Chopping up coke some flunky had delivered on a silver saucer, she asked if I wanted to join her.

I'm going home!—I said stunned. *And you are too!* I stood up briskly. I held out my hand as if to a reluctant child. Luda wasn't interested.

You just had an epileptic fit—I said. *You need to take it easy after that.*

No, I don't. Who the fuck are YOU?—she spat. *You're not my fucking mother!*

I wouldn't have had you on a free offer, sweetheart—I said, keeping my cool as best I could in the face of chemical cues urging me to do otherwise. *You look demonic. You shouldn't be doing that . . .*

She bent across the bedside table to snuff a waiting tramline, then jerked up to face me. Her eyes shot blue-hot bullets.

I understand now. About the Glamour.

What?—I said. *That's just the drugs . . . I haven't told you anything yet.* But she wasn't having it, directing her blowtorch glare as if by staring hard enough she could melt my contacts into glue.

How it's all changing all the time. How one thing can change into another! How one place can be all places! Like you, changing me into you—

It was one way of putting it, I suppose. Maybe she had picked up some of the basics.

You're just mad because it's taking me and not you—she announced, suddenly on her feet and in my face. *You're jealous it had a message for me and not YOU!*

Message? What message?—I sneered.

You'll find out—said Luda.

I dismissed her with a condescending wave; watched her disappear, turned on her side, then rolled back into the throng, into the swollen throbbing beat, where a statuesque nude with the black marble-eyed head of a bird beckoned, waiting to take Luda by the hand and lure her into the churning quicksand of bare flesh, vinyl, buckles, and hot-pink rubber to be engulfed, squeezed flat as laundry. Alice in Wonderland somnambulant, squashed to her psychedelic pulp in the pulsing mass of those moist carnal multitudes.

She'll be all right—with me—I heard the Crow Doctor chuckle.

I imagined Luda's individual self, her own unique signal, absorbed to a final dwindling crackle in the synchronizing frequencies of the Party Pod People.

With a nauseating lurch into present tense, I'm breathing loud and hard on the cold glaring steps outside the mansion. It's morning and the sun is up. My shoulders heave. I do believe I've been sick, and it seems I've been crying too. *I'm much better now, babes*—I try to explain to the young men helping me into a taxi. *Being sick felt fantastic. No really*—

I've lost a glove. I've lost Luda. Everything is hot and cruel, fizzing on a Catherine Wheel roundabout. Didn't I just get here? Wasn't I different then?

The boys were nice. I remember them being lovely and kind. I'd dropped my purse and one of them found it for me on a chair near the stairs to the basement. Another of the lads slipped me his personal details written on one of those lurid flyers for the event I had now elected to flee.

At least that's what I thought until I called a few days later and got the Samaritans hotline!

Thanks for that!

Still. You never know when it might come in handy.

Clip 10. How did I find my way home? Muscle memory. Instinct. A salmon-like sense of direction kicked in that knew to follow pre-ordained migratory routes whenever higher brain functions were obliterated. Nothing remains of the taxi ride, except for a savage stumble to the sidewalk at the end. Staggering against the wall, betrayed again and again by my treasured peep-toe plats, each ungainly step of the way to the third floor, the front door.

I struggled to recall why I was carrying a towel.

The impossible keys, the symbolic lock, the merciless light, with the hall carpet coming up to meet me. The mistress brought to her knees, with torn stockings and dribbling mascara in the third act of a comeuppance story from one of those old Stanton bondage comics.

I looked like a hag in the mirror. A wretched, painted crone. A stupid, vain old bitch. The imprint of a kiss on the brutal glass reminded me of when I'd mistaken myself for beautiful not so long ago.

I don't fancy yours much—I had to laugh as I closed the front floor behind me, a bed-seeking hag missile.

My broken left boot-heel flapped loose from the sole on a tongue of leather. My ankle, swollen and throbbing, would recover but the beautiful shoes were toast. In a glint of recall I remembered when it had happened, on that frantic scramble up the stairs from the cellar, filling in another odd and amorphous jigsaw hole in the night's puzzle.

The cellar. It didn't seem real. What happened in the cellar to ruin everything?

I lay still under the duvet, counting the clips from 1 through 10. *Savasana.* Yogic corpse posture. Feeling the bruises. Shivering and wounded in the flaking emotional comedown, I was Icarus singed and practically hospitalized, repeating my personal mantra as I struggled to repel the foul fiends gibbering and gnawing at the fringes of consciousness where impending sobriety reared its misshapen bulk up from the primal ooze of intoxication.

My left knee hurt badly where I'd cracked down on it, and there on my gloveless right forearm, the blue-black and yellow map of an alien continent could be seen, pictured as if from near Earth orbit, an undiscovered country fading into view in the style of a photograph developed in a tray.

As I unzipped my hitherto skintight skirt, now bulging like sails in a Force 11, as it fell open in segments, I was rewarded with some crumbling morsels of poorly-preserved incident; a thuggish good-looking Croatian boy is bringing a towel to (a) protect me from embarrassment and (b) spare guests the nauseating horror of my exposed back end, while a smirking dwarf looks on, a sleazy Yule Lad chugging on a cigar bigger than his forearm.

By 6 A.M., adrift among starlit ashes, I was almost recognizable to myself again as I took up position for a gentle parachute reentry; I was troubled only by a small, infinitely concerned voice that advised me against drinking too much while still encouraging my drug consumption.

I was glad to be alone. Scared that Luda would never show her face again. Dreading her inevitable return.

Cars rolled as red flashed to green and their headlights across the wall threw narrow angular shadows—but this time they were the leaning shapes of tall thin men marching in single file. Searching the room, shadowy detectives with hands stuffed deep in trench-coat pockets, on the hunt for clues, inclined against a wind only they could feel.

She would have to leave, I told myself; Luda was a magnet for danger and derangement. The sinister aura of criminality, corruption, and carnage that attended her was heady nectar to Flat Policemen. Her very existence was an invitation to the forces of depravity. I should have known when we met; her cockroach problem only underscored my suspicions. They were night creatures scuttling in her shadow. She'd be telling me next about her problems with snakes, vampire bats, centipedes . . .

So passed the untethered hours, locked in my cage at the glitter zoo by those travelling bars that striped the walls and ceiling on repeat. Those shapes that were not Flat Policemen. And on repeat, compulsively, I replayed the random clips compiled in my threadbare album of recollections.

From Clip 1 to Clip 10, backwards, forwards, retrieving a few seconds of detail and incident on each anxious rerun, still cautiously pacing out the edge of a ragged lunatic hole at the centre, where that basement room had plumbed deep foundations in my memory, sucking in light and sense; leaving nothing behind but an excreta of old newspaper scraps, torn headlines that only made sense as Surrealist poetry, and a restless unreliable map of the city of dreams. That bleeding vision of a contorted, hidden geography of Gasglow laid out in nauseating bas-relief, dissected on an autopsy slab for all to see.

The entire sublime yet inconsequential psychodrama enacted beneath the uninflected gaze of a sacrificial pantomime cow, slaughtered in accordance with who knew what sacred screed or taboo.

Of the ten hours since we'd left as a human storm of giggles, peacock shimmer, and flapping flamingo wings to the sound of "Two Ladies," I had succeeded in pinning down perhaps fifteen minutes' worth of reliably-unfolding episodes.

I cringed as if stung by a venomous swarm of hunter-killer memories; sobbing in the forecourt—promising blow jobs— the suicide hotline—oh fuck!

I stayed awake, thinking she'd turn up and curl into my embrace before too long. Fantasies were entertained of what might come next in an ideal world.

Unwilling to stay spiked beneath tombstone clouds, the sun had risen from the grave like Dracula, sick ghost of itself in a grey shroud on that pale and rainy vampire dawn in late August.

Teach her nothing more about the Glamour—my Guardian Angel cried like a blue, red, and yellow parrot gone mad in a gilded cage. *TELL HER NOTHING!*

Let Luda make her own mistakes. Hadn't she hurt me enough?

You'll regret it!—my protector squawked more raucously until I shook with a last rattle of fury before lights-out.

Why should I tell the ungrateful cunt anything?

She'd only use it against me.

You've met her now; what do *you* think?

Me, I think I must have been eleven years old.

We've all been eleven, let's face it, unless the law's relaxed its rules and allowed some inquisitive ten-year-olds in the jury box. Stranger things have happened.

It's the next frontier, isn't it? Votes for children. I'm all over it. They couldn't do a worse job.

Being eleven is a condition of being twelve, or twenty, or thirty-five. Or fifty. You can't have it any other way. There are no forty-year-olds who missed out on being eleven.

And yet, scientists tell us, and they sometimes know what they're talking about, they tell us how every seven years we exchange every single molecule, or maybe it's every atom of our bodies for new ones, that get recycled from the restless particle churn that's been going around and around since the Big Bang or whatever creation myth you'd prefer to argue in favour of.

There's that ship in Greek mythology, the ship of Theseus—where they start out replacing the worm-eaten mast, then they find they need to refit the rotten planks on deck, before they're on to rebuilding the damaged hull and casting a new anchor chain, while the gunwales and the fo'c'sle, or whatever it is they call it, receive their own makeover, chucked on a skip, and replaced by newer, stronger parts.

The existential question being: It's got the same name on the prow, the ship of Theseus, and it's freshly painted in the old-fashioned style with the inevitable glaring mystic eye at the front—but can it really be called the same ship?

What makes it the ship of Theseus, other than consensus?

With people, there's the same lifelong exchange of particles but instead of making us look box-fresh, these new incoming atoms know to make us look older. They're programmed to build us a personal ship of Theseus that gets leakier, less seaworthy with each new influx of spare parts.

With us, it's the whole human race that's the ship; we're the nails that get rusty and need to be replaced by shiny new pins that look the same and do the same job but aren't "us" any more.

As I always say when I want to shut down a boring conversation, if you filmed a whole human lifetime, from birth until death, and sped the playback up to last an hour, you'd witness a transformation to outdo the most shocking effects sequence ever seen in any horror movie; this bouncing bundle of newly born wrinkled fat unfurls and inflates from its explosive hospital arrival into a bright, inquisitive child—then it's honed by time into a handsome man or beautiful long-legged woman striding vigorously through the world until piece by piece it wizens and goes grey, evaporated by the friction burn of time, until the knees turn brittle, the eyes go out, the stripper's in a wheelchair, the hero's a dotard, and the gorgeous paragon of forty minutes previously collapses to dust, shrieking like a noonday leech on soiled hospital sheets.

These are the futile voyages of the Ship of Theseus from port to faraway port, on its three-score-and-ten-year mission to seek out new life. Lose a bit here, gain a bit there. No one will ever know the difference.

I don't mean for it to sound so grim. If you'd never been eleven, you wouldn't be here, would you? As adults we're all balanced on the frail shoulders of the infants and tweens we once were, wobbling on their epaulettes to reach the lofty vantage points of middle age, blinking above the tree line as we wonder if the physical effort was worth it for the cheerless panorama.

Chipper as Victorian chimney sweeps, our younger selves earnestly support us, bearing the grim load of their own future histories with uncomprehending smiles on their fervent little faces.

So, where's eleven? I know I spent a whole twelve months there, so why can't I stroll back down those old tarry streets in summer, smell the air-freshener scent of wildflowers in that time-lost garden in July, see Dad riding his bike, Mum when she suited a bikini rather than a coffin's plush?

Why can't I visit? I remember being there through a sort of fog, I'm sure you do too, and I'm positive things like Mum and Dad and the door and the couch were real and solid, so where did all of that go? Why can't I walk to it? Why can't I point to it?

Why can't any of us stroll back to the days of being eleven and shake paws with our not-yet-threadbare teddy bear, Boggles?

Time's tricky. Invisible, never satisfied, time holds us fast as it tracks us through the waving elephant grass of our imagined days, our estimated hours. Time's fangs coming closer, always there, camouflaged in the momentary stalks, its steady approach detected first by the older or the weaker members of the herd, the outliers who need to stay alert to stay alive . . . whom no one listens to any more . . .

I do get morbid sometimes. Tonight, on opening night, especially. There comes an awareness of darkness and purple, the webs of spiders and Fates, and what might be stuck there.

Eleven's a funny age.

I was eleven when my mother brought me into Gasglow city centre on the number 36 bus on a rainy school holiday in summer to buy a special dress.

Not for me, I hasten to add, but after what happened that day in Levitz's department store it might as well have been.

So, there I was, and from our privileged viewpoint thirty-nine years later I invite you to progress along my timeline, ladies, gentlemen, et cetera, to a point several hours after the remarkable incident that was to occur on third-floor ladies' wear in Levitz Bros. department store; here's little me curled in on myself, a living comma, water swirling round my own drain, on the fat, familiar, punchdrunk couch in our living room, paging through a Batman comic, while Mum and Dad yelled at one another in the kitchen. Again.

Like me, reading through his adventure, Batman could only move in one direction, from the start of the story to its end. Left to right towards a prearranged destiny.

Where I was from, as seen in relation to Batman's existence on the page—and you'd be right to imagine I'm no Caped Crusader, although we both share a common enthusiasm for tights and boys in panties—what made me exceptional was a talent for moving backwards and forwards through Batman's life as it was paced out in boxy ruled panels across the pages from the foggy dockside wharf on page 1 to the sinking schooner at the end—

I found I could pause on page 12 then go back to page 5, to study clues the artist had left. I could skip from an inescapable death trap on page 15, to the Batman's triumphant defeat of the disfigured, mentally-ill "villain" without any of the intervening *sturm* and attendant *drang*.

These thoughts—entertained as Mum and Dad volleyed shrieks and accusations—were not entirely welcome, it must be said.

As I've hinted earlier, something unprecedented had happened to me that day in August. The profound meditations on cosmic geometry that now troubled my prepubescent skull even as crockery shattered inevitably next door were only side effects.

A cymbal crash of commemorative GASGLOW 1938 WORLD EXPO plate shards accompanied Dad's throbbing aggressive bass line and paved the way for Mom's shrieking solo vocal, whose nerve-shredding treble and tremolo I recognized as performance, not real feeling. Her litany of indictments and disappointments a shrill libretto she'd mastered by copying the actors in films and soap operas.

Back in the safety of my comic, Batman was hot on the trail of a new opponent I hadn't heard of, Spook-Man. I flipped listlessly through the pages and back, settling on the ads, then searching for the missing ingredient that had once brought these crude pen-and-ink drawings to life. Something was wrong. The story felt lacking in some essential vitality. Viewed through the arse-end of the captain's telescope, these were simply unsophisticated scratchings made by artists who knew they could be better, if only they were given more time or more money, or more respect.

A terrible thought rang its bell in my mind: My hero was a loser! Batman was a wank!

Looking back at that strange day from here, maybe it had something to do with the steady drip of pre-adolescent hormones—perhaps it was the loss of some focused attention that grants us complete immersion in play and picture stories, where we consciously dissolve the boundary between reality and illusion and toys turn real.

I don't know. I'm not Sigmund Freud. Look at me. I'm barely done up. Too much talking, not enough slap. And I'm onstage in two hours!

It wasn't long before we found ourselves, the Caped Crusader and me, his boy partner, approaching the end of the story where Batman had, true to form, gotten the better of Spook-Man by exposing him as an embittered, probably disfigured Hollywood stuntman.

I flinched as another precious kitchen thing broke into bits. More jagged fragments added to family life's accumulated rubbish heap, for Dad to painstakingly glue back into place as if completing a grim jigsaw portrait of his increasingly fruitless marriage to Mum.

Through the crack between the peach-painted kitchen door and its frame, I caught a strobe-flash slice of time where Dad was a snarling monster. All man, all teeth and fire and pain.

Clutched in his fist, a sparkly evening dress. He seemed to throttle it in his grip, and shaking it like maracas in my mum's face, Dad roared his wounded vocal accompaniment.

The bull-bellow contained a simple request broadcast at 120 decibels: He wanted to know where the fucking dress had come from.

I could tell him that! If he'd asked me first, all of this might have been avoided. It was, as usual, *my* fault they were fighting.

It was none of his fucking business, Mum screamed. What did it matter to him? When was the last time?

Usually when they fought, it was over money, or the lack of money but recently the tenour of the exchanges had taken on a new flavour of poison.

Only I knew she didn't have a lover. Not yet. That came later. She'd bought the dress herself, *to make Dad jealous.*

I know that because I was with her when she bought it.

That day, as I started out explaining, we'd hopped the 36 bus into Gasglow city centre from our house on Stonepark Street, part of what they called a post-war housing project on the South Side. It was raining, so I'm thinking it was probably oh—any month of the year in Gasglow, but most likely August. Low pressure on the barometer. Warm and wet.

The 36 was my preferred bus journey, with an absorbing, wide-ranging route that wound lazily through the rich enclaves of Breckridge and Prospect Gardens with their cranky turreted mansions and gated entrances. They looked like the haunted houses you saw on TV and in the comics, so that's what they were to me: haunted houses, old and rich in character, where lonely young women were glimpsed at the windows in pale shifts. Then past the ice rink and the transport museum whose vaulted hangars were strung with World War I biplanes frozen in victory formation above cold grand halls showcasing out-to-pasture steam locomotives, tractors through the ages, and the decline of the tram.

Past the Brutalist mall complex where despairing trees grew in the yards. Where there were cinemas, fast-food outlets, and pharmacies, there was the 36, its unwavering course plotted through the tangled railway yards and bus depots on the South Side of the Dare, before crossing the Bridge Street Bridge into Gasglow city centre, past the theatre district, up Charity to Saxonhall, on its halting progress via Calvinside and Nethersdale, to the leafy West End's churches and tennis courts; its patisseries, wine bars, and outsized porticoed townhouses.

Lost in the shuttling, interlacing paths of raindrops racing on the window, and unwilling to get wetter, I'd have happily stayed with the 36 all the way to its terminus, where Newtonsburn's bowling greens, its spacious heights, surveyed the mysterious northwest sprawl of the city, with the blue-hazed outline of the Duncairn Hills beyond, but Mother was on a mission. Only the big stores on the busy shopping grid of Gasglow central could fulfil her special requirements.

In the rain, keeping up the halting, hiccuping pace of a three-legged horse just to stay inside the protection radius of Mum's umbrella, I dodged among jostling wet strangers.

Outdoors felt like indoors, that day when I was eleven, as if we'd all crowded into a sauna still wearing our clothes in prudish awkwardness. People steamed like kettle spouts and brought with them the smell of damp Labradors, rubber, soaked carpets, reeking the way rolled-up towels do carried home in plastic bags from the swimming baths.

By the time we'd segmented ourselves through the spinning doors of Levitz's department store—five floors where all the treasures of civilization were spread out for sale, or so it seemed to me although at that age I was only interested in the toy department and, for some reason, the electrical goods section—the intervening floors, specializing in shoes and underwear, held the same attraction for me as the adult news bulletins on TV.

Rain ran from the tips of umbrella ferrules to form puddles on floors, until nothing was dry. The escalator repurposed as a mechanical waterfall feature.

When we reached the third floor with its fashion concessions, Mum swept and spun through rack after rack with a brisk professional eye that allowed her to appraise and reject items for sale with a glance.

She'd always been fashion-conscious, my mum. I think I've mentioned that. Her tabloid-sized paperback copy of *Vogue from the 30s to Now* had been a bible of mine during my teenage years. The other Holy Books and Grimoires of the Glamour that Mum bequeathed were *Hollywood's Golden Age* and *Marilyn,* with poolside pictures of Monroe by Bert Stern to accompany Norman Mailer's nigh-on ecclesiastical devotions.

While Mum went to work, I scanned the photographs of models on the hosiery packaging. It looked like an enviable life: stretching out your long legs in nice tights, or racy stockings and suspender belts, or even better clad in the sleek and futuristic compromise that were hold-ups, while photographers bottled you in their lenses at your best, looking willowy and vague, livening up the shelves among the other three-inch-high Cottingley Fairy photos.

I liked pictures of beautiful things, like the model girls and cars in *Vogue*. Clara Bow. Veruschka. Kate Moss. The shape of the '20s, the '60s, or the '90s. Attenuated, stretched-out, and frankly boyish. I was confused back then; I thought I found women like that sexually attractive, when the truth is, I was just envious. It doesn't bear thinking about.

There you are—I heard Mum say, but she wasn't talking in

my direction or about me. She already knew where I was, stuck on the end of her hand.

Mum was addressing an elegant store dummy, wrapped in a short and black spangly cocktail dress. Not the sort of thing a married woman in her late thirties might instinctively choose.

This dress had been designed for cocktails at the casino in Monaco, or Ferrari rides at dawn through twinkling party cities on the Riviera.

It was sewn to be unzipped and emptied of its gently-perspiring contents into an apartment with French windows letting onto a shallow wrought-iron balcony overlooking Montmartre.

It was lovingly cut to be cast in a heap of stardust beside scattered Safrano roses and empty bottles of Clicquot on the Persian carpet next to a four-poster bed in Nice . . . and Mum *knew* it.

So, while she was preoccupied by the alarming price tag, I performed a subtle Houdini-twist I knew would loosen my fingers from her handcuffs grip. A free agent, I went for a wander among the aisles like Mini Odysseus on a budget. Leaving me to drift, Mum made a beeline for the sales desk where I, from the corner of my eye, could see her pointing out the dummy to one of the cashiers. She was asking if they had a size 10.

I thought she was talking about me, but as I said, I was eleven, not ten, so I don't know where I got that from and right about then was when the overhead lights intensified to create the same hyper-real effect you get onstage when the house lights are being tested all at once and everything from the studs on the cheap seats to that crack in the trapdoor seems to be screaming for immediate attention at the same time.

The cut-glass clarity of brilliant stage-level lighting exposed in a frank appraisal the obvious artificiality of the big store backdrop I seemed to have come unstuck from. Solid walls were cardboard sets, flimsy and wobbling, that threatened to fall flat any moment, exposing the stark mind-bending machinery of time and space behind their painted scenery.

This loss of reality or volume came with a corresponding drop in temperature. I understood I was flat too, projected on the same backcloth, sketched on the same stretched paper with no more thickness than a shadow and, now that I think about it, I knew that paranormal chill again when Luda walked into the audition and again much later in the story, as you'll find out . . .

So, here we've reached the point—if we didn't get here already—where what I tell you next could easily prejudice your outlook on my glossy fingernail-grip on sanity.

I know what you'll think, but when you sit down together and the decision-making hinges on "what about that bit when she talked about hearing voices . . ." please take the following into consideration.

Remember I'm eleven years old. I'm foot fancy, loose, and free on the third floor of Levitz's lingerie, fashion, and ladies' wear, my mum nearby, still gassing with the till girl. It doesn't matter; she might as well be a million miles away. None of it matters.

So, let me tell you about this voice—it came from inside my skull, but it wasn't my voice, and it wasn't any of the voices and characters I knew intimately from what I liked to think of as my inner Committee—the Bully, the Loser, the Leader, the Joker, the Judge, the Lover, the Artist. The Arsehole.

It said—*What are you looking at?*

As I came closer, the overhead lights oscillated on the dress, so that each careful step caused sequins to turn on and off in random configurations. There was something welcoming, even comforting about the dress winking its Christmas-tree semaphore. It was sending me messages.

All I had to do was learn its party vernacular of tinsel and twinkle.

I was fine with the dress itself, fascinated even. It was the inexplicable plaster-and-paint figurine wearing the dress I couldn't be too sure about. The heightened reality, the searing fretted edge on everything, was so overwhelming I felt no fear, only surprise. Shining gift-wrapped surprise after surprise like all my birthdays combined—firework displays of surprise too bright for fear or reflection.

That all this could be *all this*!

Heavy with a burden of unavoidable destiny, I faced the mannequin.

Starting with the feet, which the doll-maker had moulded into the shape of elegant shoes, with pointed toes and three-inch heels, I gradually raised my eyes in an old-time camera move, the kind that pans up to reveal the face of the *femme fatale* as she sashays downstairs to the speakeasy.

I noted how this outsized Barbie doll had done away with ugly awkward feet altogether and replaced them with sleek stilettos. I was so jealous. I hated feet.

Gaining the resolve to face the Incarnation, I allowed my gaze to creep up the shins, the knees, the thighs of those endless model-girl legs—where plaster flesh met the starfield horizon that was the hem of the dress, before a voluptuous satin blackness spilled out into hips and waist and hourglass contours spangled with aluminium constellations. The gravitational swell of galactic breasts. The swanlike neck emerging above the *décolletage,* an Elizabethan barge emerging from Pre-Raphaelite star fog and river foam.

The sculpted chin, the hard and generous lips, the symmetrical planes of the airbrushed rosy cheekbones as the features assembled into their traditional arrangement.

There was nowhere left to go except to stare into the painted eyes of the mannequin. Those coolly preoccupied eyes outlined with thick lenticular slashes of black, aerodynamic wing-tipped flourishes. Cleopatra. Horus. Egyptian. The green glass pupils reproduced in miniature the blinding light of the fluorescents overhead.

What do you want?—I said, immediately regretting the attempt to sound tough.

I knew something was about to happen in my life that had never happened before, and when it did—it was accompanied by a brittle *clack* sound, when the painted eye *winked*—and as it did, it was. Just like that.

It took a moment to frame what I was looking at. At first, I had it down as one of those life-like killer robots I'd seen on TV, but this theory couldn't support the sense of intelligent presence and self-determination the dummy possessed. Whatever I was facing was very much alive. The voice I'd heard before now returned. Clear and calm, it was the voice of a confident young woman with an accent impossible to place.

Stop looking!

The voice could now be heard booming from the store loudspeakers, arriving somewhere in the centre of my skull—where it gathered like a storm cloud—where it said—

We do any looking that needs to be done round here!

There was a prickling sensation at the back of my neck that made me want to turn around; but I knew that would be a mistake on a par with Orpheus.

Honestly, I swear it felt as if something was standing behind me, fixing my collar or touching me somewhere I couldn't point to on a social services dolly. Because it was inside me, that was it. Turning around wouldn't have helped. I'd have to turn inside-out to find the source of the voice I heard and the contact I felt.

We've been watching you. Do you know why?

The voice spoke those words, then the tannoy followed with its delay, an overdub, a reverberating feedback loop of five or six voices speaking together, with micro-second intervals between each word to add a staggered "Frère Jacques." Now it was more like twelve confident young women. Then a forty-voice choir talking in hypnotic layered harmonies.

Why me?—I asked.

Is there someone else we should be watching?—they asked.

I wasn't sure how to respond. I'd never had to wonder whether I might be special or not. I suppose I'd taken it for granted that I was *especially* interesting because I was *me;* and everyone I knew seemed to agree with me on that score. Now that the whole edifice of my being was called into question, I felt unprepared to argue my case with any confidence.

Something about the way the question was phrased came across as threatening, insinuating. Each syllable doled out with its own distinctive lip-smacking leer that suggested a shadow-choir of chuckling middle-aged deviants concealed in the subsonics below the soaring tremolo.

Immediately, I thought of Mum, convinced I was all that stood between her frail reason and a mixed-voice choir from beyond the beyond.

Mum was in danger. And as much as I understood danger from TV dramas, I was familiar with a special brand of peril that came served with a side of sleazy sex.

I knew it was my job to keep this pervy searchlight attention from finding her.

As a child I could handle these eruptions into the real but Mum, I felt sure, would be defenceless against this gathered murder of angels.

So, I said—*No, there's just me.* Then—*Tell me who you are first.*

Now I know I'm making it sound all Alice in Wonderland— *oh, it's ever-so-queer said Alice—well that's just the way it is dear, the Queen of Hearts replied . . . we're all queer round here . . .*— but it was a bit like that.

The real thing, my contact experience if you like, was all over me as an unrehearsed free-for-all of roaming feelings, crayon-coloured pictograms—*If you tell me who you are, I'll tell you everything!*

You know the mannie-queen—the voices replied, with a note of triumph.

That's how I heard it. The "mannie-queen." A dream word, seeping like serum out of some dreaming outsider's ears onto a soggy pillow. It wasn't a name at all. Not even a Rumpelfuckingstiltskin.

Names have power and they knew it. Rules of the Glamour. Always travel under an alias.

I knew I shouldn't take my eyes off the mannie-queen, but I had to make a sharp, nervous little saccade to check the aisles either side. On Levitz Bros. third-floor ladies' wear, the store dummies outnumbered the people by three to one at least, I calculated. If they were an army, we were fucked!

My furtive peek confirmed one thing: The other store mannequins were different from the specimen in the spangly black dress standing in front of me; their posed flash-frozen attitudes lacked the essential quality of sly, smirking plastic life possessed by the wearer of the sexy black cocktail number, where nebula dust scintillated hypnotically on a tailored section of void cut to the egg-timer shape of a woman, a personified cosmic sex goddess in a Marvel comic drawn by Steve Ditko or Gene Colan.

The mannie-queen was as real as everything else, which is to say not very real at all on that sultry damp afternoon in late summer.

Is this real?—I asked.

We're real. Not sure about you yet.

What do you look like?—I asked. Eleven years old, remember? You don't think you're being rude at that age. You'd never think twice about asking an embittered lathe operator why his sleeve was flapping from the elbow.

What do you see?

Secretive by nature, my new friends preferred to avoid showing up naked but since I'd been so inquisitive, they decided to honour my childish request. I was a brattish native of the third dimension; I think they wanted to teach me a lesson in brilliant geometry.

The lesson I learned: The world wears a mask too; a clever cosmetic job conceals beneath its smooth and flawless veneer of lacquered light a different, more terrifying face of reality. Look hard enough and the *Mona Lisa* starts unwrapping into Picasso's *Weeping Woman.* A face with more angles, more wrinkles, more unfathomable creases and fissures than you want to have to think about or give names to. The face of experience and disillusion plated over with an android cosmetic glaze. The light arranged, just so, to hide the joins, conceal the ragged edges where the scars of existence bleed through.

Once you get over the shock, that understanding gives you an edge that used to be called Magic. The Glamour.

What do you really look like?—I persisted in my line of questioning.

As I watched, the fashion doll's newly Cubist head revolved lazily, leaving a solid arc of smeary, waxy faces in its wake as it spoke . . .

You asked for it.

The mannie-queen's arms unlatched generously, like the archaic, specialized gadgets on a Swiss Army knife, multiplying into a spectacular fan of elbows, forearms, and scissor fingers, with branching fractal nails lacquered red.

We come from the Glamour.

The mannie-queen did something in a Vegas-y showbizzy manner suggestive of a lunatic TV quizmaster shuffling Thematic Apperception Test cards right before my soft brown eyes. It was manipulating elaborate origami folds of such complexity as to transform it from a spinning carousel of articulated doll limbs into something like a Christmas tree bauble hatching into a lipgloss constellation.

Looking back, I also recall a Hans Bellmer sculpture undertaking a disconcerting but vigorously-choreographed four-dimensional cancan. I'll swear to a chorus line of dismembered puppet-girls unfurling petal displays of legs and faces, while deep in the lewd, botanical heart of the spectacle were piercing peepshow glimpses of an exposed, heartbreakingly expressive kaleidoscope of living polychromatic crystal. This shrunken Cave of Jewels, this precious, shielded interior dimension, looked for all the world like the Koh-i-Noor diamond melting and re-forming in cascades of never-to-be-repeated colour combinations, each of which represented a new art movement, a new axiom, a new philosophy.

We're watching you . . .

Those were the last words as that divine wink descended once again, a sexy thunderclack of lid on lid.

Give us a show.

All the horsehair eyelashes on all the glass eyes snapped down then up, all at the same time on all the dummies on third-floor ladies' wear, standing around in their weekend best, nonchalant under strip lighting in their underwear.

The intense illumination of the overhead bulbs increased—an indrawn breath—until every outline of each existing thing came with a chromatic peacock trim where it seemed the unfinished edges of reality were visible to the naked eye, crosshatched into sketchy electrifying, schematics . . .

. . . then it dimmed on the out-breath until the dull, beloved disappointment of things as they are most days was completely restored. Time. Place. Everything put back in the box where it belonged.

Everything except me.

Into the pressurized silence that followed my takeoff and landing bloomed an old record-scratchy voice saying—*This is definitely THE ONE!*

I only had a few panicked moments to act normal, as I hastily, clumsily reassembled the red and blue and yellow lettered building blocks of still-cooling sensory input that required me to identify the approach of what I understood to be an older lady. She was talking about something important. Me perhaps.

Is this your daughter? She has great taste!

My son—Mum gently corrected.

I'm sorry—the shop assistant apologized. *He has great taste.*

Mum found me "transfixed"—which was an interesting choice of words on her part, I've always thought—in front of the elegant dummy in her spangly LBD.

She had no idea I'd stood in the afterburn, at the crossroads, in the intersection of rhomboid dimensions, breathing a cosmic overspill of sequin spatter galaxies embedded in a sexy primordial darkness curved like the mum of all space and time. Some Greek primordial Titan on the mother of all nights out. The Dress.

I was locked in gunfighter stance, immobile, fixated, speechless, she said. Her words. She told me she was sorry for what happened to me that day.

Why was she sorry?

She told me I wasn't scared or threatened. I couldn't put it into words. I looked like I'd survived a lightning strike, Mum told me later. She said I was resplendent with shock. Transfixed.

You like this one?—Mum said, trying to bring me back down to earth. I suppose I must have liked it and nodded slowly. *I did too!*—she said. *As soon as I saw it, I knew this was the one!*

Then I said—*It's like space!*

On the number 8 bus, a faster, more direct, more utilitarian route home from town, I was jumpy, or so I've been told. Checking over my shoulder, frowning at the vacant seats.

Back home, snorting with frustration, I selected a turquoise felt-tipped pen from its see-through plastic pack and tried to draw the next dimension beyond a cube, only to fall like Icarus banging off a glass ceiling.

It was just a power surge—Mum reassured me much later. *When the lights got so bright. That's all it was.*

I knew she suspected I'd suffered a form of electrocution unknown to conventional science, but my bland, edited version of the Levitz Bros. incident could offer no reasonable corroboration for that theory.

You may want to consider, as I've done myself, the possibility that this and subsequent visionary episodes were nothing more than evidence of temporal-lobe seizures or some rare species of schizophrenia.

That's the thing. As you'll learn, when it comes to the Glamour, it all shakes out the same in the end.

After that day in the big store, I became acutely self-conscious, catching sight of my reflection in windows and car mirrors. Correcting my posture. Angling my head. Painfully hyper-aware.

I couldn't tell Mum what had happened in Levitz Bros.; knowing what I knew would place her in spiritual danger. I entertained a suspicion that I'd made a pact with shiny demons and it was now my job to protect Mum and perhaps all of humanity! I knew now there were things that could come at you from inside as well as outside . . .

The impulse purchase of Detective Comics from the kiosk at Circle Station, with its stuffed-to-bursting magazine dockets, was a bribe to shut me up, that's obvious now.

Don't tell your father where we've been—she coached me as she pressed the rolled-up mag into my hands. *Don't say what we've been doing. We just went for a wander round the shops and you got a Batman comic.*

That was fine by me; I don't believe I had the vocabulary at that age to tell Dad where I'd been or what I'd seen that day. I'd have had to resort to the medium of modern interpretative dance, and I know that wouldn't have gone down too well.

Dad was a practical man.

Compared with what I'd witnessed on third-floor ladies'

wear, lingerie, and footwear, the three-dimensional assembly of floors, walls, and ceilings I'd grown up inside now seemed flatter than panto scenery, my world a crudely-rendered tableau of half-remembered streets and little old-fashioned passersby, some with the features left undone where the painter couldn't be bothered to give them a rudimentary personality.

These were playing-card people with smudged thumbprints for expressions, cranked from the printing press for no other reason than to fill out the crowd scenes.

I was afraid of joining that world of shades, with its dismal, endless Sunday afternoons in various convalescent wards.

If real life had become as flat as a sheet of paper, imagine the diminished state of the Batman book I tried to read that unfinished August evening with light still Batman blue in the sky at nine o'clock; the comic, with its odd locations and outlandish characters pressed down like petals in a book.

It looked as crude and cheap as it was. A crappy souvenir from a smelly stall specializing in garish and diabolical mockeries of the Glory of God's Kingdom. I held in both hands a cack-handed attempt to secure a dream on paper rendered with a rushed ineptitude that made the promised wonders tawdry. Here was some pure artistic impulse rendered down to its ugliest unskilled expression.

A faithful scale model of the world itself and the Good Lord's failure to live up to his promise.

Dad yelling.

The door slammed with a bang so hard it cracked the wood. Dad knowing he was using his strength in the wrong way.

Maybe it was all a dream. Maybe I would inevitably wake up and be some different number of years old, dreaming my future or my past.

Performers need to dig deep, to snare those phosphorescent primary emotions that swim in the deepest reaches of the self, don't you think?

The flatness of things persisted; the screen-printed surface of this world I lived in, had always lived in, before I was made to confront the unsettling actuality of its odd compacted edges, its crude folds and corners that only ever trembled on the edge of achieving solidity and reassurance; I imagined if I could just shift my perspective a little, I'd see the edges of Mum and Dad, like cardboard standees of film stars, inflated with life from the front, diminished to paper-thin lines of flimsy minimum existence seen side-on.

Flat pages became flatter in my hands, bleeding dimensions into the ink that came off on my clammy palms.

Dad shouting at mum in a negative anti-matter world. Their cosmic Boss Battle going on for a while, but far away, as if contained in faded speech balloons, drifted loose from the panels of a lost comic strip. Jagged edges and bold type to signify raised voices. A Pop Art argument played out on a gallery wall in ten-thousand-point type Lichtenstein WHA-AAMs and POWs, carrying no more weight than the clouds pumped up with urgent internal monologue above the superhero's head.

That's how I tried to explain my desperate, phantasmagoric childhood—and some of my present-day eccentricities—to Luda as we lay in bed together at the end of the awful day I want to tell you about next.

The Glamour was a way of seeing, I told Luda that night. The Glamour was a method whereby we could put makeup on the dullest moment, transforming it into its own best self.

The Glamour—the original name for magic, for spells made of words and intent—was the dazzling cloak we threw over the ordinary world to make it shine and dance and live up to its potential.

That was the Glamour.

Here's me, as one of those desperate bastards on the tilting, sinking deck of the wreck, Luda the raft of the *Medusa* I clung to, knowing I would drown anyway. Knowing the rescue ship would arrive too late. My voice lulling her into unconsciousness.

Ten hours earlier, I'd crawled mechanically from my pit engulfed in a numb elysian light that informed me I was still drunk and shortly to pay the price.

I glugged my way through four bottles of springwater in the driverless on the way to the Vall, while lugubrious clouds hung heavy with rain all the way.

As too often happened after a rough night, i.e. any time in the last few years, my soul cultivated its own special hive of horrible itching doubts and apprehensions. Being observed by unknown forces was the least of my troubles. I had been called to the witness stand at a hostile cosmic court and failed to arrive on time, necessitating my own trial.

I had no idea what I'd done that was so terribly wrong, I only knew with a soul-shaking certainty that my misdeeds were up there with Lucifer's Mutiny and the Fall of the Rebel Angels. My disobedience and my shame equalled those of Adam and Eve.

I'd offended existence itself; that's how it felt.

I swear I couldn't have suffered any more guilt if I'd deliberately taken a shit on the mother-of-pearl throne of the Almighty.

As if the Fall weren't enough—here, while I lay twitching

and disassembled, too weak to defend myself, came the awful bells and whistles of Last Judgment. A ruthless lunchtime audit of a lifetime's bad karma lay ahead. I vowed to take it easy. I promised to look after myself and never have to go through this ordeal again.

Farewell the ever-spinning wheel of karma!

When I arrived and dumped my bag of blues on one of the folding chairs by the door, Luda was already there. Luda wore hot-pink leggings and a loose T-shirt with a retro RELAX slogan as she lounged against the wall. She had adopted the purposely-unstudied Paris-collection poise of a fashion doll, feigning the kind of absolute un-self-awareness that always conceals a heightened brittle self-consciousness.

Being watched, she was watching all of us. Watching everything. Not just watching, *observing,* like a scientist, or a specialist trained to record details so fine no one else would know they existed. I read once that cats can hear molecular motion. Luda could see it. I swear she could detect angels dancing the Gay Gordon with atoms on the head of a pin.

I caught her zooming in on micro-movements of the performances, sampling and repeating a florid hand gesture she could imitate and use again. She wasn't subtle, and I knew all that arch posturing was something she'd need siphoned out of her repertoire.

Self-consciousness made her look like a boy doing a girl doing a boy, although I think she enjoyed the disorientation, encouraged it.

But there was something else, as a more disturbing thought came to mind; there are plants, bee orchids, that mimic the shape of sexually-available insects to attract pollinators.

What if Luda was a mimic, an imitator, a synthesizer sampling, filing, and replaying a representative assortment of natural human behaviours for her own ends?

In her inventory of gestures, I now recognized some of my own—that sort of thing happens, doesn't it? We find ourselves imitating traits we admire in the people we like enough to spend time with. We rub off on one another, it's only to be expected, but somehow this felt intrusive, intimate, unsettling.

Float interrupted—*We're running through this big scene with the Two Ells for a few reasons. One, we don't have our Abanazar today! The good news is he might be out of the oxygen tent by the weekend.*

When he said the words "oxygen tent" Luda snorted.

The atmosphere was glacial; you could have raised money to build a sanctuary for polar bears in the space between us as we turned the rehearsal into a war zone.

You'll have to help me, Aladdin—I've gotten a little behind!

That's wishful thinking—said Luda. *Don't flatter yourself!*

I served up a look loaded with menace.

You can help me with the laundry—I'm doing the wizard's underpants today!

But I need your help!—Aladdin wailed. *I need somewhere to hide!*

There was a genuine urgency in her voice. A heartfelt note of jeopardy. Her delivery was terrific, as if she'd blazed her way through a dozen colour-coded karate belts in a weekend's training. As I saw it, Luda was clearly bringing her A-game as a deliberate challenge. Taunting me to rise to the occasion against my inclination.

It was too bad I had to wreck her moment by rolling out a pair of gold-embroidered Y-fronts big enough for a family of three to sit out the apocalypse.

I said the wizard's underpants! Talk about big jobs! I bet these have seen a few of those!

Oh no! Ma, they're coming!—Luda shrieked before I had a chance to finish my lines. *They're here! You have to hide me, Ma!* Then she dived through the scaled-up underpants into a laundry basket the size of a rowing boat.

Hot on Aladdin's heels, two "comedy" policemen, idiot heirs to the Keystone Kops / Police Academy genre, barrelled onto the scene, stage left, waving outsized truncheons. Released from the innards of Buttercup the comedy cow like Romulus and Remus springing forth from that she-wolf, or whatever they did, the twins were completely unrecognizable.

As Twankey, I'm so preoccupied jamming my head through the leg-holes of the wizard's prize underpants in search of Aladdin that I don't see the Law creeping up. As usual, I'm relying on audience participation to keep me up to date as I flap around like a chicken, caught up in the sorcerer's gusset.

They're behind you!—they'd shout from rows and balconies.

You just won't leave my behind alone, will you?—I huffed with exasperation in return as I draped the pants carefully over the ironing board. *Can't you see I've got very important work to do for my brother-in-law the wizard?*

This last line came out like air seeping from an inflatable chair. I had nothing to give.

How can he be your brother-in-law?—Aladdin pointed out. *You're an only child!*

I supposed I was. That explained everything!

With the insurance company insisting on a stringent safety review before anyone else was allowed on stage at the Vall, on-site rehearsals stuttered to a halt. There was Evil afoot. In our new cramped performance space, I endured glances of recrimination from Dominick Float and the cast, as if I were somehow to blame.

There followed more wearisome talk of ghosts. An ill wind blowing. A flapping sheet haunting the production. Unassailable excuse for every lapse of concentration, every mistimed joke, every yawn.

I don't smoke, not tobacco anyway, and I needed no

legitimate reason to hang around street corners in high heels, but it was the best way to get the gossip.

That morning's puff break brought confident talk of a full-blown Curse as the unsettled ghost of Murdo McCloudie extended his spectral pall over our production. Even though he'd died peacefully in his bed a long, long time ago, in a Gasglow far, far away, the architect still somehow walked among us, determined to ruin everything for reasons no one could arrange into a string of sensible words.

By this stage in the sultry grind of the season, I'd developed an admiration for the great McCloudie and his remarkable postmortem reach. I can guarantee I won't be remembered in ten years' time, let alone two centuries; not for all or any of my personal achievements while living, let alone as a ghost doing sweet fuck-all in the *après-vie* lounge.

After what for me was a purely symbolic lunch, where I made too emphatic a point of avoiding Luda at every opportunity, Float felt compelled to stage a second intervention, wearing his memorable "disappointed dad" expression.

So, what's all this about an oxygen tent?—I asked, in an all-too-palpable attempt to divert him.

Some fish sauce found its way into Goff's vegetarian Tom Yum—Float said with such solemnity I had to stifle more than a chortle. *Anaphylactic shock apparently. Quite severe.*

Life imitates Art, I thought; the parallels to the meta-plot of *The Phantom of the Pantomime* were too faithful to simply sweep under the Axminster.

That's not what I want to talk about—Float went on, all ominous. *There's something going on here.*

It might help if we stop blaming ghosts whenever things go wrong!—I pointed out reasonably.

It's not ghosts. Spirits, though, well that's another thing—he said, visibly pleased with his own rabbit-pellet of a quip, an exploratory jab as the bell rang on Round 1. Little did my opponent suspect that I'd studied his every mechanical, unspontaneous, and downright routine strategy over the many years of our association; I knew exactly what would happen next.

The drink. The drugs. She's half your age at least—think of that as Big Dom's trademark upfront emotional sucker punch.

Traditionally, he comes in hard then bounces back on the balls of his feet, permitting his foe a moment to shake out the shock of stars they're swimming in, covering the precision of his moves with slapstick attempts to sidestep into kindness that in this case came off slippery and unctuous—*I need you to look after yourself, Lu.*

I'd been here before, relaxing my guard the first two times he ran this script instead of tensing in preparation for the inevitable blow, which wasn't long in coming—

Since Luda came along you've lost focus, Lu. Twankey's at the heart of Aladdin *but you*—and here he paused for a sorry shake of that wrecking-ball head. *Your heart and soul's in fucking Fairyland and I need you here. Understand? Let your hair down when it's over.*

I bristled at that. *Fairyland?*—I said. *If it wasn't for fucking Fairyland, we'd all be out of a job!* Sick of all the post-party wretchedness that was the world I'd been condemned to inhabit, I snarled in Float's face. *I'm not her keeper! She's a free agent! I haven't even seen her since Saturday night.*

That was all he needed to hear; my flushed face, my shrill injured tone and teary defensiveness told the whole sad story.

After what happened to Molly. Then the thing with the light. Now Goff's out of the picture for who knows how long—Float said, composing an expression that made me think of a boy in a film, watching a beloved dog die of rabies in the barn. With his opponent staggering and confused, he was strategically positioned to deliver the killer wallop, the slobberknocker—*It's not Luda we're worried about, Lu.*

Oof!

Morale is low right now—he rumbled on. *I need you leading the troops. I need Twankey on point.*

I executed what I felt was an openly contemptuous ballet turn.

Can we try that over again? Top of the page—Float instructed his unenthusiastic, ever-shrinking band of actors after an unappetizing lunch. *Where we left off with the policemen.*

Even the understudies had begun to sense the possibilities offered by the sinister undercurrents of the McCloudie Curse; its immediate effect, as far as I could tell, was to induce various minor accidents or viral infections necessitating bed rest, sympathy, and exemption from work.

As an imagined audience struggled to attract my attention to the stealthy progress of the boys in blue at my back, I the Widow Twankey laid the iron flat on the wizard's elephant pants before wandering round the stage in search of Aladdin, driving the anticipated crowd nuts every time I reliably failed to pick up on the movements of the crafty policemen shadowing my every move.

You what?—I cupped my hand to my ear, trying to imagine the response through the sneer storm of inner voices telling me I'd been born a cunt.

They're BEHIND you!

Finally convinced, I'd turn to face the Law and utter a guilty shriek. Today it came out as world-weary grunt of resignation in the face of a higher, crueller prerogative.

Looking for Aladdin, are you?—said Ping.

That's good—said Pong—*because so are* we*! And we know he's here somewhere!*

That was my cue to flap my skirts and snap my apron, shooing the snoops away from the basket of clean clothes as I'd chime in—*I haven't seen Aladdin for, oh, it must be since the last time! He only comes here to borrow money and since we haven't got any we don't see much of him—do we ladies and gentlemen boys and girls and others!*

Before the audience could offer their wholehearted support for my blatant lie, the cops took the opportunity to muscle in.

Liar!—said Ping.

Liar!—said Pong.

And in unison, *Liar! Liar!* Cuing up audience reaction to make them point and scream . . .

Pants on fire!

Aladdin was inches away from capture by deranged authorities, but there was something they hadn't spotted yet. That iron I'd forgotten to retrieve from the wizard's barrage balloon underpants now began to smoulder, distracting Ping and Pong from the suspicious laundry basket with Aladdin hidden inside.

Shrieking, I emptied a full basin of water over the iron and standing amid the rolling steam clouds I flapped out a pair of soaking Y-fronts big enough to make a sail for a skiff. There, for all to see right through, was a smoking Gothic arch of a hole where the iron had reduced the satin and gold trim to ash.

Goggle-eyed, I peered through the munitions-shell stencil outline all the way back to the empty seats receding in perspective where shadows gobbled up the back-row stalls.

OOOPS! I know.

My lines dropped dead.

We'll call them hot pants and charge him half price!

My voice emerged as a ramshackle cackle, stumbling from my lips like a meth head exiting a wooden outhouse privy.

If I was flat that day—and I was flat *squared* at least—it showed up as a steam-ironed depression reducing me to a film, a membrane.

Under the scrutiny of a malicious unseen court and its ever-impending apocalyptic verdict, my whole universe, the one I'd been left in charge of and asked to look after, felt damned, irreparable, condemned to suffer and burn for sins too numerous to list, too toxic to describe, too awful for redemption.

I sincerely wish I could drink and take drugs then spend the next day recovering gently, all spectral and illuminated like I used to. Nowadays I wake up mangled, bent double on the twisted, sweat-soaked, cum-stained sheets of my dissolute life. I can feel the pinholes where a new strain of vampires has gathered to feast on my depleted serotonin. I am that concave space that's left when the sparkle has gone elsewhere. I am as I feel, and I feel like dirty laundry.

Which brings us by a *commodious vicus* to the Mangle scene! A mainstay of *Aladdin*—a knockabout set piece scripted to run with all the precision and pageantry of a mechanical clock in Prague except with real people. You can see how it might go wrong.

As we return to the action, grabbing our seats, we find Twankey twitching and flipping the wizard's smouldering Y-fronts like a matador's cape but there's nothing she can do to make the smoking church-window shape go away. And to make matters worse, the wizard's servants are already on the way to pick up his laundry!

Think fast, Widow Twankey!

We'll have to tell him it's the new fashion to have a massive hole in your underpants! Aladdin! Here—and here I thrust the flat of the iron against Aladdin's , exuberantly enough that Luda gave a genuine yelp.

See—all the hip young people are doing it! In a frenzy of invention, I scurried around burning neat rowing-boat-shaped holes in every pair of underpants I could find. *Everybody's doing it!*

Ma! I've got something I need to tell you!

That day was a prop rehearsal, and it might make things easier to picture if I explain the stage setup.

Before I get down to it, I will have another! Thank fuck

above for small mercies, Float knows I do my best work on more than a bottle. And I'm pleased to report they've left more than one bottle.

Slainte!

Now, I expect you'll have seen the incriminating photographic evidence; all I can add to the picture in your head is that Widow Twankey's Chinese laundry was conjured into vivid life by a rough-and-tumble squad of rude mechanicals who brought to their labours a self-effacing desire to achieve the impossible on a budget that wouldn't stretch to the possible.

Giving them credit where it's due doesn't mean health and safety considerations played a part in any of their decisions.

For this scene, they'd worked like cave trolls to hammer together an outsized mangle, comprising two immense rollers in a sturdy wooden frame painted to look like wrought iron and operated by a giant, side-mounted wheel-crank. They'd done the frame as the I Ching character 36, which signifies "Darkening of Light" or so I've been told by the prop manager. It's probably not true.

Right up close to the mangle, they'd fashioned an impressive working model of a clanking, hissing boiler with a sweaty oily precipitate of liquid copper rolling down its robot hide.

This frankly mediaeval apparatus was commonplace in any typical laundry room before some genius came up with washing machines and dryers. Seen from the balcony seats of the twenty-first century, it might as well be a devilish instrument of torture from Torquemada's Dungeon but somehow the audience, even the youngest ones, seem to know what a mangle is and what it does in a working-laundry context.

The clothes were hefted from the copper boiler using a big stick called a washing dolly; transferred, steaming and saturated, to the mangle, where the wheel was hand-cranked and the wash water squeezed out like pulp from an orange until the laundry, pressed flat and wrung dry, could be hung wrinkle-free on the line.

Nearby we had an ironing board complete with that outsized prop steam iron perched like a Bondi Beach surfer all golden and rigid at the business end.

Here's me: *So, tell me what you have to tell me from the laundry basket, why don't you!*

Prior to this scene, which opens act 2, we've seen Aladdin escape from the Cave of Jewels carrying the Magic Lamp he's found for Abanazar.

Here he comes tumbling out of the laundry basket, flapping around like a ghost until they shake him loose from a sheet.

Now he's on the run from the police, with the flower of Peking's constabulary represented by Sergeant Ping and Officer Pong. I know!

I'm sorry. I'm only telling the story; I didn't make up the names.

The idea is for these two to chase Aladdin around the stage—with strobe lights lending a delirious silent-movie clatter to the proceedings—until he tricks them into thinking he's absconded between the rollers of the mangle so they have to dive in after him. Which they do without a single thought for their own safety.

During this bit of biz, the first cop, Ping to give him his dignity, dropped behind the prop and crouched there to be replaced by his stand-in.

In the early days of the pantomime, they'd rely on a midget to play the part of the now shrunken lawman—and apologies if I've resorted to a word that's passed into infamy. *Lawman* that is, not *midget*.

The trouble is, the safe option of *little person* could just as easily apply to a child as a four-foot, six-inch-tall adult and, in this case, it actually does.

In our production, the part of the micro Sergeant Ping was

reserved for a little boy named Ales Margin. This preening twig had an online following of two thousand witless tweens lined up to help delude their tiny hero at a moment's notice into a belief that one brief appearance onstage as a miniaturized law enforcement officer was nothing less than the first rung on a golden ladder leading all the way to an Oscar nomination.

Margin rolled out from a hidden compartment under the mangle wearing a tiny helmet, tumbling gracelessly across the stage in a high-pitched voice yelping—*You're under arrest! Where is that Aladdin?* This was guaranteed to have the audience in stitches, but even the voice wasn't his own; we had the odious Dez Blue huffing on helium balloons to provide comedy falsetto from backstage.

The second policeman, Officer Pong as I'm sure you recall, tried to steer clear of potential outrage by emphasizing the aromatic implications of his name—so that when he chased Aladdin into the mangle and was horribly trapped there like his fellow constable, while Twankey and Aladdin worked the wheel frantically to free him, it was to the accompaniment of a fruity farting cannonade that never failed to bring the house down.

Ping's partner emerged from the mangle played by a roll of wallpaper with an elongated drawing of Pong printed there and suspended on strings to simulate movement.

In my infernal exile from mental and physical health, laboriously turning the mangle wheel backwards in some hopeless effort to rewind the doomed plods, it struck me there was something queasy and gut-curdling about the flimsy policeman bending and flopping his way across the stage. His serpentine peristalsis evoked the invertebrate inchworm crawl of a soul broken for fun in Hell.

I knew I was losing it. The wheel in my hands endlessly rotating. *Samsara.* Ixion. Saint Catherine. *Wheel of Fortune!*

All I could do was face her down, communicating all

my disappointment, all my fear and suspicion in one lethal death-dealing killer line.

I faced Luda at last. I was supposed to say—*Now what have you done to me, Aladdin?* I knew that much.

I took a deep breath and began to belt out my lines, which emerged, not entirely surprisingly, in the form of sick. With all the gusto of a top-flight tenor exploding into "Nessun Dorma," I projected both my voice and the partially-digested ingredients of the lunch I'd hardly eaten towards the rear wall of the theatre.

You'd better take Luci home—said Float to Luda, who nodded gravely.

We sat silent in the taxi. I couldn't look at her. I couldn't do much except stare straight ahead without triggering a cold sweat and an up-thrust fist and forearm of waiting bile in my clenched oesophagus. It went on like this for more than half the journey before she played the first move.

You're not supposed to get jealous—she said, as if the game came with a rule book and she was finally having to explain the basics to a tyro.

Who says I'm jealous?—I said. And of whom? Was I jealous of them? Or of Luda?

You are—she said. *You shouldn't be but you are.* Interlude. She took my hand, enfolded me in that liquid blue gaze, and progressed to her next move.

Can I stay tonight?—she said. *The cockroach problem at my place got worse . . .*

I had a nasty reply kept in reserve, but my tongue stayed tucked in its holster, which was just as well, and I sighed instead, laying my head back on the seat, exhausted by life in the material universe and the length of this sentence.

I'm really sorry. I didn't mean to hurt you—Luda said with a catch in her voice that recalled Rentboy's apologetic nasal register. *You've been really nice.*

She looked so sincere, so convincing a life-like portrait of someone caught in the act of being sincere that it hurt.

I put a chicken in to roast and left Luda to take care of the bread while I had a smoke and a sweltering bath. Gliding a razor delicately round the base of my balls, my smooth perineum, the threat of cosmic justice diminished, as the great mass of anxiety broke apart into smaller clouds of nebulous apprehension, wispy puffs of disquiet that disintegrated into condensation. By the time I turned up in the kitchen, freshly shaved from the bath and swaddled in a plump duvet, I found her draining *schmaltz* from the baking tray into a chipped Pyrex bowl I'd kept for decades.

Is there anything you can't undo?—I asked, running a jaded eye over the scorched, carbonized sweet potato she'd failed to rescue from the crematorium oven.

We can do chicken soup tomorrow.

Together we selected out the few edible potatoes into a side bowl and tossed the chicken breasts and legs on a pan to make fried chicken sandwiches, with jalapeños and salad.

Then she put me to bed and later she joined me, stroking my head as she asked me to explain my bizarre behaviour earlier.

I just felt sick—I told her honestly. *Nothing to do with ghosts or bad luck.*

None of it's real—she confirmed. *I looked it up. Murdo McCloudie died in his bed when he was seventy-four, singing "Jerusalem" in French translation so it says.*

I touched her Artemis-bow lips with my finger.

Who are you?—I said. *What are you, baby?*

I didn't mean to hurt you—she promised. *They were just boys—just people having sex. You're special. You're different—* and so it went.

Love bombing, that's what they call it. It's what I'd expect if I joined a cult like the Children of God. Hustlers for Christ,

Sex for Salvation. It's what comes before what happens next in the structured, calculated breaking-down and reprogramming of another human being, in a procedure perfected by Scottish mind-control maven Ewen Cameron, who makes his way back into the plot soon enough.

An intriguing fiction will always outlive a commonplace reality.

She and me, we're chemsex-loving gender rebels.

Then we're some late-married couple in the kitchen, like it's eighteen years after the honeymoon and they still get on. If it all seems too dirty-cosy, too good to be true, think of me raised up on clouds of glory so bright I couldn't see a thing around me.

I'll go back home if I have to—she told me. *I'm starting to quite like the cockroaches. I've given them names. There's Nero and Mike, Tug and Penny, and Gran. I've decided to capture and release my favourites before the exterminator comes for them.*

Nero and Mike, Tug and Penny and Gran. How could I fail to love Luda?

They're not welcome here—I said. *You'll have to find alternative accommodation for the cockroaches. But you can stay for as long as you need to, babes. You're always welcome* chez Luci . . .

Looking back, it was that scene in the movie where the idiots invite Count Dracula or the lesbian vampire Carmilla across the threshold and, given licence, the monster takes immediate advantage.

That night we watched *The Omen* on TV. Luda had never seen it, or so she claimed. I did notice she was more sympathetic towards the infant Antichrist than to any of his victims.

He's just a little boy—she insisted, burying the lede.

Murdo McCloudie's surrender of his rationality to the deadly gravity of myth and madness gave me the slick segue I was looking for to another of the lessons of the Glamour.

I sat her down in my chair in front of the mirror's double-hinged segments, folded open like a gatefold sleeve on an old LP record.

Today's lesson: Consider the Narrative. The Frame.

If you understand how to manipulate the context around anyone or anything, you can quickly reduce a complex and contradictory human life to a simple story—to hero or villain, Beauty or the Beast—and disarm them as completely as if they'd been hamstrung.

If you won't tell me I'll explode! Luda had whined through gritted teeth as if to release steam. *What about the secrets of the Glamour? It's taking forever!*

I hesitated—*I know what you want, babes, but what do you plan to do?*

She didn't answer the question, just said—*Teach me the magic!*—whining like a ten-year-old girl begging for a pony in the gap year before discovering boys or other girls. *We went to the spirit world together! You saved me from the spirit cow!*

She kissed me warmly, the way you would a relative, snuggling up close, supple and warm.

You're responsible for me!

Of course, she always knew what to say. She was made that way.

The ongoing first-person story you tell, the central role you imagine yourself playing needs to be strong, I explained to Luda, who nodded eyes round as a cartoon bunny. Whatever your character, it needs stable foundations, like a tree needs deep roots, to resist the storms that shape it. Even if you only see yourself as weak and shallow, you can stand strong in that conviction. But all it takes is one chink in your armour, an Achilles' heel; all it takes is for the right person to distract the audience with a story that's more powerful and plausible than your own; a true tidal wave of a tale so convincing and extraordinary that your love of dogs, or an innocent preference for lemon mousse, can easily get swept up in a chaotic flotsam of insinuations calculated to expose you as the villain, not the hero.

Suspecting nothing, I felt calm and collected after all the attention I'd received. My personal pedalo revolved afloat on a still and wine-dark sea. Aegean-night-blue ceiling overhead. The walls merging with the sky above the tenement conversions. The ski-jump shadows cut by the blinds.

Sex was always prowling on the perimeter, held at bay by the rules of mistress and pupil, an electric fence to curtail the impure impulse.

Luda pacing the room next door, rehearsing lines beneath her breath. Her breath.

Dazzling late-summer stars waltzed through the plane of the ecliptic, spitting light like the stitched sequins on that dress Mum bought to trigger Dad, launching intercontinental ballistic divorce proceedings. The dress that started a riot and atomized the family. Lost. Hidden. Forgotten.

Neither of them ever found out where the limp and blameless murder weapon wound up.

That rainy humid night when I was eleven, Mum took off to the movies with Aunt Rae, a routine they repeated every Wednesday no matter what was showing, while Dad embedded himself in the guilty semi-dark, the semi-silence, the flickering semi-shine of his private Plato's cave, draining a bottle of Victory Gin to ease his glide into jellied oblivion at the TV. Serenaded all the way by the mournful dying rasp of Johnny Cash.

While Dad splayed effortlessly in his plush recliner, allowing his bowels the time they needed to perfect a sequence of spectacular endangered elephant-herd impressions, I carefully unlatched the back door and slithered through the crack between latch stile and jamb into the panoramic sparkle and the brittle shiver of a winter night with its sky opened out as if to reveal the inside of a vast illuminated box, with countless hollow pinholes admitting only a fraction of the brilliance of a higher astronomical world that shone above the 3D crossword puzzles of the housing blocks. There was another, lordly world beyond this one where the mannie-queens revolved in all their stately, spinning-top majesty and fancy delicacy, observing a newly hatched child rebel creep to the bin shelters under a sequined roof.

There followed some distasteful rooting through cereal boxes, slimy squeezed-out sachets of cat chow, butchered sanitary towels, sticky packaging, and bubble wrap, but it didn't take me too much longer to retrieve the dress from the communal garbage. I swiped away lamb-and-turkey-flavoured nuggets of jelly and gravy before clumping the fabric underneath my coat and sweater with a giddy thrill of transgression. The treasure was mine now. The night belonged to me.

While Dad was asleep, and before Mum came home from the pictures and the traditional follow-up G&T in the Quo Vadis with Rae to gently unlock the door before padding on her stockinged feet to sleep on the foldout bed in the guest room, I pulled the dress over my head and posed in front of the tall mirror in the hallway at the top of the stairs outside my bedroom door. Naked legs, head cocked, hair brushed and sleeked into a bob, appraising the effect as I strove to imitate the models in Mum's fashion mags.

I looked, I decided . . . sexy.

Sexy!

And although the dress was longer and more modest on me than I'd hoped, it seemed in that moment as though I'd found the lock for a key I'd been hanging on to my whole life, the purse for my belongings, the pocket where I fit as snug as a warm hand on a winter's day.

I was finally worth watching.

The dress is still there in a suitcase. I kept it all these years. A trophy. A totem. Not even Luda knew about that.

When I was twenty-one, trying on the first pair of heels I bought for myself with my own money, I scissored four inches off the hem of the dress to make a pelmet mini, extending my slender boy legs to infinity.

It became the cassock of my secret order, my surplice, my chasuble, my glitter-spattered habit, and I kept it safe, worn only when ultimate Glamour is called for.

I'll tell you about that later.

But only if you're good!

1000
IRRATIONAL NUMBERS

*D*o *you think I'll look like you when I'm old?*—Luda mused, seemingly incapable of unfastening from her own mesmeric blue gaze in the mirror as she tallied up the figures and reckoned the arithmetical gulf that separated us.

You should be so lucky—I said, leaning over her shoulder so we were cheek-to-cheek. *How old do you think I am anyway? Go on. Have a guess.*

Must be about five hundred. She poked her tongue out. *At least!*

I pulled a mock sulk that barely hid a real one.

Five hundred's just a number—I breezed on, lifting the loose skin over my cheekbones with my fingertips. *They say five hundred is the new three hundred.*

During this brief interval in the proceedings, we can take a pause to remind ourselves that there is an end to all this in sight and we're almost halfway there. That doesn't mean you can stop paying attention. In fact, you'll have to try harder from here on in.

We're *only* almost halfway!

I'm being generous—she said.

I'd raised the subject of Botox again. I couldn't go on blaming defects in the glass for the pouchy signs of "tiredness," or the magnetic-field pattern of lines at the outer corners of each eye.

It occurred to me, and I know this might be hard to believe, that even with a very high bar to clear, I was becoming vainer and more dissatisfied with my appearance now that I had Luda for constant dispiriting comparison.

There's nothing wrong with how you look—she said, but she was looking at herself, tilting her head to enjoy each view as she rolled her eyes up and reran Aladdin's act 1 vow of love for the unattainable Princess Jasmine under her breath.

Can't you see the lines?—I muttered, pushing and pulling at loose skin.

I've got lines of my own to worry about—she protested, flapping her script.

There's a reason for it. Everything I've told you. Dropping pearls, leaving clues, hinting at intimations. Making a game out if it seemed appropriate under the circumstances.

After all, Luda, as her name practically yodels across the peaks of the Tyrol, was playing a game too. I don't mean that figuratively, in the modern sense, like emotional manipulation and gaslighting or whatever, although oodles of that were served up too.

I'm talking about a literal game no one suspected she was playing let alone winning. A board game with human lives as counters. A bagatelle with rules, moves, tokens, forfeits. It wasn't chess or Go or Monopoly or Risk. Not Snakes & Ladders, Scrabble, or backgammon.

The name of the game, fittingly enough, was Golden Dames, but we'll get to that soon enough.

Hang on a second till I have a sip . . .

It's top-drawer champagne at least. I always insist, only the very best on *my* opening!

Opening *night,* I should say! I wouldn't want you to get the wrong idea.

I'm fixing my lips now, inking the arc, but I can still talk. I'm a professional. Communication. Charisma. Gift of the Gab. They all come as side effects—*siddhis* of the Glamour.

I start by extending my lip line past its own natural contours to imply a pumped-up porno pout, glistening with gloss and wax. The collagen fillers make it easier.

And here's a tip: The colour goes on first. Then a coat of powder to fix the layer of gloss—do that a few times and you'll build up a shiny moulded-plastic finish that can't be shifted by anything less than a kiss from a stick of dynamite.

Who needs Botox when you have the Glamour?

Dom's choreographer, a formidable Romanian matron with the equally formidable name of Elena Marilena Mia Novac, came with a colourful background in experimental interpretative dance productions. She worked with the chorus at a big new studio by the old dry docks out past Dareport, developing *The Phantom*'s set-piece song-and-dance numbers.

She's getting better—Dom nodded, stroking the cinders-and-ash beard he'd allowed to accumulate, a furry *jabot* to discreetly obscure the union of neck and chins that was fast becoming one of his distinguishing features. *She might just be the genuine triple threat we talked about.*

I'm teaching her—I said, reminding him who was in charge.

She's getting better than you—he said, without any regard for my feelings. *Can you believe we've been so lucky?*

The dance went on, the staccato pterodactyl cries of Madame Novac shocking young limbs into robot lockstep. Stop. Start. Repeat. She brought to piano rehearsals the single-minded ruthlessness of a sadistic drill sergeant on a parade ground.

Following a spectacular all-singing, all-dancing opening scene depicting the hurly-burly of "The Market in Peking," we're introduced to Aladdin and Widow Twankey in full flood.

I've just arrived in a rainbow rickshaw drawn by Buttercup the frisky multipurpose pantomime cow, I should add. If I could arrive everywhere in a rickshaw I would. Descended on four-inch platform soles, I take a bow, fold down my parasol, and use it to whack the head of *my lazy good-for-nothing son, Aladdin*—as I introduce him, currently reclining among the laundry baskets preoccupied by passing clouds and idly polishing an old peanut-butter jar when he should be grafting.

Don't just lie around there dreaming!—Twankey urges. *There's work to be done, Aladdin!*

What's wrong with dreaming!—he yelps.

It's not the dreaming I'm bothered about—Twankey shoots back, flapping her apron. *It's the lying around! And what good's an empty jar! Get rid of it.*

He comes right back all indignant as if his killjoy mother just interrupted his discovery of electricity—*I've heard sometimes there's magic in ordinary things if you know how to unlock it!*

Never mind that! I say to trumpet accompaniment. *Can't you hear those trumpets?*

I thought that was you after a curry!—he says.

I grab a prop broom and swing it around wildly, shifting litter and rubbish from one spot to another.

The Royal Carriage has been shunted down our alley—I tell him with a rising rocket-fuelled whine of hysteria. *This place looks like a junkyard!*

That's because it's full of junk! Aladdin points out.

From offstage left come much louder Whoopee-Cushion trumpet voluntaries as the Royal Party trundles closer.

I have to look my best!—the Widow frets and fusses. *They might be on the lookout for a good washerwoman!*

They've come to the wrong place—says Aladdin.

Twankey lifts a palm, all set to clip the lad's ear, as the horns repeat their brazen annunciation, cueing the fussy arrival of the Vizier, unrolling a scroll.

By express order of her mother, the Empress herself, anyone caught gazing or otherwise sneaking an unsolicited peek in the direction of the young princess will face immediate execution without trial. It comes across as harsh I agree but you wouldn't be royalty if you couldn't abuse your authority now and again, would you?

Why can't we look at the princess?—Aladdin inquires. *Is there something wrong with her?*

I heard she's got cock eyes, a pig's snout, and a laugh like a horse—Twankey replies, struggling not to mix it up. *And that's before we get to the bits you won't see at the window!*

She's hoping this mental picture of a farmyard monstrosity might do the trick to discourage her son's potentially fatal curiosity, for it's all eyes down on pain of death, the Vizier assures us once again.

Naturally, Aladdin can't keep his eyes to himself.

As the Royal Carriage rattles across the stage, our young hero risks a furtive peek, anticipating at best a forbidden glimpse of spoiled fruit, a stolen gawp at the misshapen harvest of centuries of inbreeding.

Instead, he locks eyes with the radiant living playing card that is Jasmine Princess of Hearts, and as he does, Aladdin falls immediately and conclusively in love.

No more immune to the heart-seeking missiles of Cupid than her guppy-mouthed besotted admirer, Jasmine finds herself instantly, catastrophically smitten.

And in that searing instant of eye-to-eye contact the peanut-butter jar slips from Aladdin's fingers and smashes into sugar glass fragments.

Guards!—the Vizier cries out in horror, one bony finger targeting the boy.

Palace bully troops surround Aladdin, deadly numerals on a clock face counting down to checkout, the spokes of their spears aimed at the hub of his heart, awaiting the order to thrust and be done with this flagrant transgressor.

Here, Twankey utters an ululating cry and throws herself between the guards and her boy, only to be manhandled away.

Surrounded by piercing symbolic lances, the Principal Boy

is saved from certain death by the arrival of a familiar figure, a tall fastidious man we recognize from the prologue as the ambitious conjurer Abanazar.

I'm your uncle, Aladdin! Your long-lost uncle Abanazar—the wiry liar is quick to assure Aladdin and Twankey as he discombobulates the guards with a few mystic flaps and third-rate illusions courtesy of Aiysha Dyce's jaded, deadpan Slave of the Ring and the prop team.

I don't remember any long-lost brother! Then again, I do have a terrible memory! I repeated the line for the fifth time.

Come with me!—the Wizard cries while—*Come with who?*—says Twankey.

Abanazar!—he repeats.

Gesundheit!—Twankey replies, hauling from her cleavage a huge polka-dotted hankie she hands to the baffled conjurer as he hurries the Widow and her son to safety.

Back at the Vall on press day after another mostly abstract lunch, I couldn't help registering a new addition to the elaborate stage layout.

There was Dominick Float having his photograph taken next to a remarkable item of anti-spook technology he'd had installed and was keen to show off: a tall pole on a circular weighted base with a soft forty-watt bulb glowing on top, like a standard lamp missing its shade. I shuddered, shook my head, and sighed, in that order.

In the biz, we call this arrangement a Ghost Light, kept permanently lit onstage to provide illumination for benign spirits and a deterrent to any harmful unseen influences.

Was this your idea?—I said, confronting Float as photographer and newshounds dispersed with full bellies. *Why would you encourage this Curse thing?*

Float's eyes lit up like Hiroshima lanterns; his scruples took to the night air. *I don't want to say it*—he said, saying it—*but this is actual box-office gold.*

And I said—*You didn't actually say that*—but he had, and it was too late to stop him.

Indignation aside, it was easy to see what he meant.

We couldn't have asked for better publicity—he went on. *Ticket sales are through the roof! They're doing a whole feature—you need to talk to them!*

I made a mental note to stay out of it; I could see the snappers had an uneasy Luda posed in her Aladdin costume, vamping mock terror with a prop ghost on a wire for the morning edition. I observed that she was using her hand to obscure her face and break up its lines.

Won't be so funny if you're next, Dom—I pointed out, and his mouth formed a rueful tight smile I'd have cause to remember. *You're in a dangerous age bracket.* Which he was, and that's before you bring his weight into it!

Float stood firm. *The production needs all the help it can get. We play up the Curse, we pack the house every night! I guarantee it.*

It's hardly a Curse!—I pointed out reasonably. *No one's died, have they?*

And I was right, they hadn't.

Nevertheless, the doors to the Dancehall of Death would be opening soon enough.

I seasoned my recitation of the latest headlines with a camped-up Vampira sarcasm, bringing an arch and rolling horror-host tone intended to reduce the headlines to absurdity.

panto show curse!—I enunciated in a juicy dominatrix register. *top director calls on good spirits to save show!*

Below these words, next to a before-and-after shot of Dom goggling askance at the Ghost Light, was a portrait of the lead suspect in a haunting, looking his brooding best in daguerreotype from March 1900; the handsome, worried face of Murdo McCloudie, enigmatic and preoccupied, illustrating a sub-headline—

MCCLOUDIE—VENGEFUL? DID TROUBLED ARCHITECT JINX HIS GREATEST CREATION?

It went on in an unrestrained torrent of undulating, insinuating prose as cultivated by generations of tabloid reporters.

". . . fans of the creepy smash-hit musical were quick to point out how recent events closely mirror the onstage action . . ."— *and here's you scared out of your wits by a sheet on a string.*

Only partially listening, Luda clutched her scuffed script pages in one hand, opening and slamming drawers on the desk with the other, as she searched impatiently for a paper clip to hold her lines together—her brow corrugated, a certain sign she was struggling with a complex arrangement of doubts and uncertainties.

I'm trying to make sense of the end of the story—she said indignantly. *Is it that you go mad and we all come back as ghosts to haunt you?*

By "you," she meant the Phantom in the play, who as I like to think I explained earlier is the alter ego of Widow Twankey, as portrayed by yours truly, Your Humble Narrator and like droogie.

You can think of them as ghosts—I tried to explain. *Maybe he's gone mad, then killed himself, and now he's teaming up with them in the afterlife for the big closing number. He's a ghost himself! The Phantom.*

I thought it was something like that—she said, though the frown remained ruched in place. *So how come he's alive in the next scene?*

He's not—I pointed out. In response, Luda rattled the loose pages of the script like a *gris-gris* as if to magic me wrong.

In the show's bravura crescendo that seeks to combine surreal physical comedy with the horrors of one terrified human being's catastrophic cheerio to sanity, the Phantom aka Twankey is left alone spotlit onstage before attempting to play every part for a critical audience—making us cringe and beg for mercy as the fool exhausts the last of his dwindling energies across the entire stage to scoffs and taunts.

In a strobe-sliced nervous breakdown, the Phantom undergoes cellular division into his component parts, one role, one singular self at a time as the original actors return to dramatize the Phantom's dissociation.

The show closes with a fabulous upbeat song-and-dance number—the catchy chorus repeats, then repeats again then again, each time a little more ominous, to make the point before everyone freezes mid-line and whirling emergency lights of blue and red race around the walls of the auditorium. Then curtains, house lights, and music plays . . .

There I was, selflessly waltzing my pretty Padawan through the choreography for the Cave of Jewels one more time when Luda decided she'd been starved of fresh air and personal space, so I tucked some cash in her purse for wine and roll-up papers and aimed her at the local corner shop.

While she was out, I noticed she'd left the door to her room tantalizingly partly open. It took five seconds flat for me to wrestle my conscience to the mat, before swiping her tablet open and checking her search history, only to discover a representative selection of Pussyfever music videos.

Every chart hit on Luda's playlist was distinguished with a lead vocal by Molly Stocking, so keeping my mental health at the forefront, I fast-forwarded through Molly throwing shapes and lip-syncing "Tigress," "Boy Season," and "Queens in the Clone Age," the title track of their second album. I struggled to understand what Luda imagined she could learn from Molly's remorselessly predictable stage routines and warbling auto-tuned vocals that called to mind the painful struggle towards self-awareness of a Speak & Spell machine.

What's up?—said Luda, bursting into the living room

wearing the kind of scowl that only works on a boy as she caught sight of her kit in my hands.

Your tablet started singing—I said, covering with a lie followed by a swerve. *You won't learn much from watching Molly Stocking acting out symptoms of Saint Vitus's dance crossed with Saint Elmo's fire*—I said, throwing down the lace gauntlet.

Luda relaxed into a smile. It all made sense, which was all it needed to do.

I wanted to see how someone else does it, that's all—she explained. *I like how she dances even if you don't. It's modern. Audiences like that.*

I believed her but, when I looked back an hour later, she was running the footage again, leaning in close to study a freeze frame.

As she mapped the screen with her scanning eyes, Luda raised and rotated her left arm, locking it into an exact copy of Molly's paused gesture. Angling her chin just so to balance out the pose. I'm sure it must have occurred to me that this clip was different from the performances she'd been researching, and, unlike those, was picked out from a TV chat-show interview— but the thought didn't stay around long enough to register on a CAT scan.

I closed the door quietly so she wouldn't know I was there.

Luda was wired to the Sea of Tranquillity like a child counting down each second of the infinite seventy-two hours before Christmas. The days rattled by in chorus rehearsals and runthroughs. I could see Luda burning like Joan of Arc with anticipation for her public debut.

The brief Molly Stocking fixation had left no unsightly marks. To my great relief, none of what she'd learned from dissecting the dance routines in the "Sextin' with my Exes" promo had made its way into her own performance.

With Float's critique of her authenticity ringing in my ears, my mission was to teach Luda how to dredge real emotions up from her gut to load the first line of the song with feeling, and how to make the lyrics tell her personal story.

You have to connect what Aladdin's going through to your own emotions—I explained, as if sketching a broad outline of calculus meant for dogs.

How do you do it?—she wanted to know, as if there was a procedure, a reliable formula.

I try to imagine how someone might feel in that situation, based on things I've been through in my own life. If the character's sad, then I think about a time when I've been sad. It's not much more than that.

I made my best effort to demonstrate, and I won't deny that each time we rehearsed, she got better at sampling the nuances of gesture and expression that made it seem real. But she was only ever copying. It seemed to me her emotions were simulations of such high-fidelity exactitude, only an expert could tell them apart from the real thing.

Something happened to you—you don't talk about it—were you sad then?

The older you get, the more things "happen"—I said sagely. *You're trying to avoid work.*

Were you married?—she said. I had no idea where that came from.

It might as well have been marriage—I corrected her. *We were quite young.*

We're talking the war years then—she sneered. *The Trojan War years!* I let her get away with it; shade is one of the most devastating weapons in any queen's verbal-munitions stockpile. One of the martial arts of the Glamour, its mastery is to be encouraged.

Luda persisted; how, she asked, could anyone identify with the malignant Phantom, a masked supervillain with only evil on his mind.

Think about it this way—I said. *The Phantom's not a monster, he's an actor having a nervous breakdown.* Luda gave a vacant nod. *I was treated for mental-health problems after I left the Troupe*—I went on, baring my soul like a centrefold bares her bum for the cameraman. *That helps me as an actor to understand a little of where my character's coming from.*

Luda, frowning, unconvinced, consulted her script—*That's not what it says here*—she argued. *He kills everybody and they come back to life.*

Only if you want to take it literally—I stressed. *Everything you say might be in his head.*

So, it means a lot of different things at once—Luda said and I nodded, seduced by the rising dawn of an insight whose brilliance bleached out the scrunched exasperation from her expression—*I like that.*

I felt a rich encouraging throb beneath my ribs, knew the unselfish golden pride of a teacher illuminating a student, opening conceptual doors, uncovering new expanses of possibility.

The primary fairy-story plot with Aladdin and the princess is the sturdy cement that holds the narrative together for the kids; when the Phantom meets his nigh-on Faustian demise, youngsters can read it on a surface level as the moment the Aladdin/Genie tag team breaks the wizard's bad spell and everyone comes back to life, even Abanazar, all happily ever after singing and dancing in the endless finale.

If you were older, maybe a little bit religious, and inclined to read between the lines, I went on—and on—you might decide to observe the happy ending through biblical opera glasses as a story of judgment playing out; the vain murderer faces well-deserved punishment, where all his victims rise from the grave as ghosts and drag him to Hell, trapped in the final chorus for all eternity—redoing the big outro number forever, knowing he can never get it perfect because perfection doesn't exist anywhere except maybe in the form of everywhere and everything.

That's what I thought it was—said Luda, beginning to wane.

I had no intention of stopping then, and I haven't changed my mind tonight; let's say you'd found yourself sat in the audience and you didn't believe in ghosts or magic; you might decide you were witnessing a different kind of *dénouement.*

The Phantom's committed an unforgivable crime but what's he supposed to do? He's a tortured artist with self-esteem issues! He can't help the hand he was dealt! Everyone else seems to get what they want, except for him! He's only trying to express his pain, to make a story of his inner turmoil, instead somehow screwing everything up in the process. The Phantom's merely human. We forgive the special man his excesses, we permit the rock star to act out the compulsions of his id. We've come on what they like to call a journey with the Phantom, applauding his desperate attempts to keep it all together, to make it right, while he's getting it all wrong, sinking deeper into sin and psychosis.

We know how it works—the show must go on, after all—and so we watch, wincing, as he tries to keep the wheels of the production turning by taking on the traits of the actors he's killed, until he can't be everyone, he can't go on anymore, deafened by the clamour of competing voices, the carousel of contending recriminations in his head. He struggles to cope until his mind just squeezes down and flattens under the pressure, shattering along brittle fractures at the slightest stress, the least criticism.

Luda nodded slowly, beautifully, as if nodding had been invented to show off her graceful neck.

I thought that as well—she said.

In the final scene of *The Phantom of the Pantomime,* we're watching nothing more or less than a human personality flaking away. A silly old man dying in his own firework light. The Phantom is literally shedding scraps of himself, dissociating as he goes, leaving behind the husks of the people he's tried to imitate.

It might all be psychological—I said. *He literally loses his mind—but we see it as symbolic. The last bit where they're all singing together and it's the pantomime that's real?*

The Phantom can never escape the final chorus. He's doomed to fail to get it right at rehearsal yet, here in the spot, on opening night, his performance is flawless when it matters most—the farewell, the curtain call that's no more, no less than an idiot Old White Man, in the locked ward where he belongs at last, high on Thorazine or slumbering through a pointy ECG.

So, it's a fairy story—she said. *Then it's a ghost story. Then it's a detective story, then it's a serious drama about mental health. Fuck's sake!*

How I loved her, and how I loved having Luda around! Thinking about it now, I wish everything had been different.

More like all at once—I clarified. *It's a musical too. There's songs and dances and romance. A good story comes with a sprinkle of everything, like real life. I mean, doesn't it? We've always known it was this way. We're born understanding the rules. It's why we love camp and theatre. It's why we're drawn to the Glamour's candle flame. It's what turns a roll of Lycra into a starfield of a dress and makes hot-ass novae of even the dimmest, loneliest lights.*

I still don't understand how he can die and then come back—she said, gnawing like a bobcat on this major bone of contention. *Is he Jesus as well?*

Jesus?—I said. *Where did you get that from?* I took the script from her hand, swiftly flipping to the end pages to make sense of what she was on about.

You've got all the pages in the wrong place—a hundred and five comes before a hundred and ten—and I pointed to the page numbers to prove it, before reshuffling them into traditional numerical sequence and passing back the draft.

Doesn't matter—she said obstinately. *Is he dead?*—and I nodded emphatically, certain of that much.

He doesn't come back—I said. *Change the subject.*
That's when Luda pounced.
Tell me about them—she said quite innocuously, or so she thought. *Your group—the Troupe.*
I thought, if it gets her off my back about the Phantom . . .

The Troupe started out as a defiantly-idiosyncratic "indie" band playing upbeat angular electropop that sugared the pill of pungent lyrics inspired by Joe Orton plays, Alan Bennett, and Morrissey. I flattered myself as a hotter, younger, more alternative Danny La Rue, updating the Grand Dame's all-round entertainer appeal via family-friendly fetish wear and cultish outsider humour.

When I came out, aged twenty-eight, as nonbinary, gender-queer, or whatever they'd call my fraction of a degree, my slender wedge of the Gender Spectrum these days, the boys in the band simply accommodated my new look into our repertoire. With that unique newsworthy ingredient to establish our originality, we really took off. The surreal skits between the songs got longer, more elaborate, and more outrageous and we found ourselves ever more popular as a result.

Soon, as they say, fast-forwarding through the dismal early years of seclusion, experimentation, and disenchantment that we mined for fossil fuel to power the Troupe's success, soon we were selling out *and* selling out night after night at the Festival. Then, like eager bees to our sweet jangling pollen, came the TV offers. We chose Channel 6 because only they were willing to guarantee total creative and artistic freedom, which wasn't strictly true of course but sounded convincing enough at the time. Contracts were signed like post-modern masterpieces. Souls were never sold, I maintain, only rented. We traded in spiritual Airbnbs the Evil One could hire for orgies and black masses on condition the keys were returned, and the place was left relatively tidy at chucking-out time.

Luda handed me a steaming mug with NUMBER #1 DAUGH-TER printed on the side and perched beside me as I fired up the computer and googled "the Troupe," sitting back smugly to watch page after page appearing on-screen.

You did ask—I said, blaming her for this demoralizing plunge into my archive. I hate the past. I have no pangs of nostalgia for better days. I don't want to be young then, I want to be young now.

You were famous—she said, hoarse and lamplit, inching closer with the sharply-indrawn breath of a doubting nun perceiving Christ in the shadows of the convent rockery.

The ragged bitten edge on every word when Luda spoke was all I needed to hear; her vocal cords, protesting at their daily Olympian workout, cried out for the divine salve, the performer's friend that is the infusion of lemon, ginger, and honey in boiling water.

Is that you? Luda leaned in close to the screen, then turned to me incredulous—*You look HOT!*

I knew that. As I hope to have made clear, the fact that I'd once looked hot haunted my every waking hour, but to hear it said in present tense was very heaven. Tragically, the moment was blighted by the smell. I couldn't help but notice, now that her size 8 feet were planted on the cushion, how the soles of her tights gave off a rich and rank boys' gymnasium whiff.

We were a bit like the Monkees—I ventured. *The Goodies?* Luda waggled her head uncomprehendingly. *The Young Ones? The Mighty Boosh? Kids in the Hall?* Nothing registered. I'd discovered an immutable law of nature that stated any cultural reference prior to last Tuesday would be squandered on Luda.

We played ourselves as an unlucky boy band called the Troupe. I carried on, reducing our *shtick* to its molecular basics. There were five of us, a rock-and-roll kid gang playing out weekly surreal and satirical misadventures in a pop-culture fantasia populated by down-and-out vampires, alien cannibals, supermodel *succubae,* and ghosts with body issues.

The Orton-inflected running gag saw us so desperate to achieve success, we would try anything: cheat, steal, lie, betray one another, and even murder to get a shot at the ever-elusive big time, which led us into the kinds of bugged-out scenarios our show relied upon. It was all played for laughs, and we portrayed ourselves as relatable grotesques whose schemes tended to end in disaster, so no one went away hating us.

Luda had located a celebrated sketch we'd done as a parody of those blood donor commercials where eager volunteers rolled up their sleeves to do their bit.

PLEASE GIVE BLOOD—

Sad music scored poignant images of a group of underprivileged-looking men and women in capes and tuxedos, long white dresses, huddled in the cold around a brazier.

VAMPIRES ARE HUNGRY TOO THIS CHRISTMAS!

Falling foul of a new generation's changing fashions, our entire *oeuvre* was later reevaluated, possibly accurately, as tasteless unfunny dross.

As if conceived to add fuel to the critics' bonfire of condemnation, one of my regular characters was Fanny Bathory, a withdrawn Goth girl with the power to manipulate any conversation into the same frank and depressing discussion of which from a list of gruesome suicide techniques she should choose to end it all.

Fanny is surrounded by funny, optimistic, compassionate friends, but as the sketches progress and accumulate, every supportive comrade winds up driven by the nihilistic dreariness of Bathory's death-obsessed monologues to take their own precious lives, each time landing a different and more elaborately cruel punch line.

I can see how it might come across as tactless in hindsight. Different days. It doesn't even sound especially amusing when you say it back, but it went down a treat in a less sensitive time.

You had me in that same dress!—Luda exclaimed. *You can fit in it!*

She'd scrolled through pictures of me to settle on a publicity shot where I'm serving sexy schoolgirl pink vinyl realness, sucking on a massive rainbow-frosted spiral lollipop and corkscrewing my blond bunches around my index finger as Jennifer Freckles, a butter-wouldn't-melt-in-her-mouth sociopathic sweetie-pie. This drug-addled disco bimbo was responsible for the spiritual cannibalism of everyone drawn into her web; in a backstory we only ever hinted at, "Jennifer" would turn out to be an alien crab posing as human to attract and devour its prey.

With a yelp, Luda recognized the same neon-dawn-pink rubber gymslip she'd modelled for our ill-fated party night. Like her, I looked indecently good in it. Or I did, decades ago.

Boys had my posters on their wall—girls too—I said ruefully. I have to admit, it was something I'd heard rather than witnessed for myself, but we did a roaring trade in pinups, so at least let me fantasize about hordes of troubled youth pleasuring themselves to a self-interrogating climax with me forever blowing taboo bubble-gum kisses from their bedroom walls.

She wanted to know where, if I was so great, it had all gone wrong. Who or what, which one of us had sharply tapped the hammer, broken the safety glass, and ended the Troupe, and in what emergency, what last-ditch attempt to stop the gravy train shearing off the rails had our breakup occurred?

It's never any one thing—I told her. *It went to my head and my head couldn't handle the load.*

The media began to focus on Luci LaBang at the Troupe's expense, that's all it was. They were each brilliant in their different ways, but it soon became apparent I was doing the lioness's share of the interviews and the photo shoots.

It was Luci LaBang declaring war on fixed gender identity in French *Vogue,* vamping for *Vice* photo spreads on Alphabet City corners, sprawled in shredded PVC and black lipstick, in gritty SoHo loft conversion monochrome for the pages of *Iniquity*.

My rise to prominence especially upset our gifted lead guitarist, pretty-boy heartthrob and chief scriptwriter Jeremy Painter. We'd been friends from years before I came out and I have to say he was very supportive, especially after seeing me done up for the first time that night I turned up at his door with a bottle of pink champagne in my hand and pharmacological starbursts crazing my stare.

He'd been so kind and understanding as I released cataracts of upheaval and guilt and relief. All it took was that warm encouraging hug, that kiss on my forehead as he put me in a taxi home at 4 A.M., and I was tumbling down love's Alice well.

I'm surprised we managed to keep our hands off each other for as long as we did. We let the sexual tension squeeze down to a volatile explosive pressure for years as, alongside the other three, we fused into a single five-headed, twenty-limbed Voltron power suit to tirelessly build the act and conquer the world.

So it remained until I was nearly thirty-five, looking my very best if I may say so on account of sharpening up my drag to unheard-of levels of artistry. Straddling the divide between bimbo and MILF, lean and whetted like a greyhound, driven by jealousy, arrogance, and rosé bubbles, I couldn't wait a single second longer to push my luck with my best friend.

In the ensuing effervescent chaos of popping corks and popping pills, Jeremy and I were whisked into the whirlpool of a passionate affair during a weekend publicity trip to Berlin. Me in my insufferable *femme fatale* phase, single-mindedly scraping the moral barnacles from the newly-gleaming hull of my Ship of Theseus.

Since that wild night in Nollendorfplatz, we vowed we'd never repeat, I now had something to prove to myself and became obsessed with the idea of "stealing" Jeremy from his pretty girlfriend Chloe. I wanted him to renounce her like Peter renounced Christ, to disavow the straight world and join me in a shifting jet-set delusion of first nights, fashion shows, and international sex crime.

We talked of running away together, slipping the traces of fame and expectation. We would travel the world, agents of chaos, harbingers of a new world order of polysexual insurrection, drugs, and gender dysphoria!

Naturally, none of it went as smoothly as our well-oiled dreams do.

The weekend we spent together was spectacular I have to say. Jeremy, the Troupe's heartthrob, fed me strawberries dipped in champagne and in a crescendo of cheesy perversion that was my idea, I enacted a lap dance wearing lingerie I'd helped him choose that day as a gift for his girlfriend. On my knees between his thighs, tearing at the studs and the zip with both hands, tugging his boxers down to release his erection into my face with the force of a homicidal Jack-in-the-Box, I knelt at the gates of Heaven.

Am I better than her?—I repeated, until eventually, on a witches' brew of powders, lascivious disinhibition, and a touchingly genuine momentary desire to indulge my squalid fantasies, he admitted I was as he erupted down my throat and gasped—*yes, yes, yes!*

After that precious fifty-six hours of sexual betrayal, he wouldn't speak to me.

I turned up at his place the next weekend, mascara dribbling down my blushed and bronzed cheekbones as I used tears to draw a picture on my face of my helpless devotion.

He kicked me out, literally stuck his big army surplus boot in my red-vinyl-sheathed arse and thrust me back through the door onto the street—we were friends, he kept saying. We only worked as friends. This could never happen again.

It happened two more times after that—the last a scribbled

inspired sketch of what we might have been if he was less timid and I was less unbearable.

What might have been the once-upon-a-time of a fairy tale to end them all soon revealed its true nature as the opening dramatic hook in the Troupe's final chapter.

In the sizzling afterburn of our magnesium-flare liaison, the people who knew us were rendered blind and speechless. Chloe complained of Jeremy's increased aggression in bed. The weight of words unspoken began to throw the whole Troupe off balance; the act wobbling at first, correcting a so-far-reliable internal gyroscope to account for the extra baggage for at least as long as we could before the inevitable fatal tumble off our axis.

Chloe took Jeremy back on the same understanding that lips would remain forever zipped and although they never went through with the marriage, and she'd dumped him soon after for a shadow cabinet minister, I'd heard there were two bright, brilliant kids now, so at least one prong of our throuple's trident contrived to make a successful stab at a happy ending.

As we Troupers swaddled in layers of protective emotional armour to face the winter of our careers together, the light drained out of our days, and where warmth had been there came a creeping irreversible frost.

The Troupe played a few variations on the theme where I'd come on as a boy and the rest of the gang would be in drag, but it didn't stick. Our audience had made up its mind what it wanted from us; any deviation from the Platonic ideal was immediately rejected until nothing we did could ever match all the things we'd done.

Or so we told ourselves; the truth is that whatever Jeremy and I had incited, whatever chain reaction we'd set in motion, the effect was to undo the chemical bonds that held the Troupe together.

Which one is he?—said Luda scrolling through pictures from when we were young, while my mood darkened to indigo and beyond, into the infra-sombre ranges of the emotional spectrum.

Before I had a chance to point out Jeremy, she got there first—*I'd fuck him*—she said with confidence.

Well, I did—I said ruefully. *I took the hit, so you'd never have to.*

So, you don't speak to any of them now—Luda pressed, even though she could tell I'd had enough of this.

Fuck no—I said. By the end, Jeremy and the others were collaborating without my input on sketches that expressed everything they wouldn't say to my face, skits powered by the black residues of their pressurized anger that hinged on what a sly, devious, and manipulative bitch I'd always been. Starry-eyed and so full of myself I was no longer qualified to imagine how much these people I loved could hate me, I recited my caustic lines, oblivious to the burns.

When I realized what the Troupe's infamous "Your Immediate Attention" skit was about, I was mortified. The last thing I wanted was to provoke such negative feelings in people I cared about.

I took the opportunity to go my own way and never really spoke to any of them again after that.

You got famous and they didn't—Luda said presenting her own blank appraisal. *They were jealous*—reducing all those years of reproach and spoiled circumstance into a T-shirt slogan. I loved her for that too.

They went on without me. Times changed. Ryan and Ben kept working as a moderately successful comedy double act called Chocolate Robot. They had a weekly podcast now taking the place of a canned Channel 6 series that ended up developing a cult following on its second-to-last broadcast edition. They write for other comedians and do quite well, or so I've read.

Arlo, always more comfortable with the music than the comedy, went back to playing in psychedelic metal bands, entertaining increasingly modest, more intensely cultish crowds with his oblique lyrics in progressively more cramped venues, until finally swapping the uncertainty of show business for the trustworthy routines of school runs and extramarital online flings.

There were rumours of a Jeremy Painter comeback. He'd condemned in no uncertain terms my appearance on *Superstar Survival,* claiming to have turned down producers' entreaties several times and citing an unwavering self-respect, the likes of which, he insisted, I'd happily traded for attention to prop up my saggy chops.

From my *oubliette* of self-hating depression, I hit back by going public with details of our brief affair, complete with unflattering descriptions of his cock and his stamina in bed.

It wasn't quite Lennon *vs.* McCartney or Biggie *contra* Tupac, but the gossip sites and the tabloids had a bonfire party in the wreck of the Troupe clubhouse.

Jeremy never forgave me. Let's just leave it at that.

From what I gather, according to mutual friends, he's bald, divorced, bitter, disgraced, and alcoholic now but I'd still fuck him. Whether or not he'd end up fucking me in one way or another was a matter yet to be decided.

None of us kept in touch. I emphasized that. I hadn't talked to any of the others for over twenty years. Nostalgia has never appealed to me. Whenever I catch sight of myself in the rearview mirror, I think I look stupid, standing there all uncomprehending, facing tomorrow and seeing nothing but my reflection as usual.

You've been really lucky—was all she said in reply. *And you've never appreciated it.*

Where did that come from? I wondered—*I don't believe in luck, babes. And I know you don't either.*

You don't believe in luck and you don't believe in God—she said.

There's a big difference between their God and mine—I said. *I can show you the God of the Glamour any time.*

That got her interested.

I fetched from the shelf my dog-eared copy of *Alchemical Studies,* that blockbuster potboiler by C. G. Jung, shuffling through familiar pages until I located the relevant illustration, plate B2.

How about that?—I said.

With both hands I pressed the book flat on the table to display a sixteenth-century woodcut from the alchemical text *Rosarium Philosophorum.*

The plate presented a fusion of two human bodies, male and female, into one double-headed hybrid wearing a dress while balanced on a green dragon curling around itself and underfoot like a freshly-dumped turd courtesy of the Loch Ness monster. Not to be outdone by the flashy androgyne, the salamander sported three heads and a trio of hungry mouths with teeth like broken bottles tearing chunks from its own bleeding body in the desperate act of auto-cannibalism upon which it depended for survival.

In the left hand of the fused figure representing Mercurius, the philosophers' dream of androgynous unity, the image of spirit made whole, swung a commendably unflustered, rakishly crowned snake. In their right hand, Mercurius brandished a goblet from which three more charmed and charming serpents, one red, one white, the last black, rose writhing like ribbons of rainbow steam.

Close by, thirteen sunflowers bloomed from the emaciated branches of a vertical shrub, each with its own individual face. Completing the scene backstage on the flat emerald *field vert,* a formidable pelican pierced the white down of its plump feathery breast with a stabbing beak, treating two hungry chicks to the dripping stop signs of her own blood.

Some interpret the dragon as Christ, sacrificing the wine of his veins to nourish the world, and so too the pelican, selflessly giving up its life to succour its young.

What I see, as I tried and failed to get Luda to understand, is a symbolic image of biological fact, a literal picture of how it all works; the World Serpent being shorthand for the coiled sum of all life extended through time, one cellular source branching out into microbes, dinosaurs, giraffes and drag queens, growing ever more elaborate by repeating an elementary binary directive over and over through time. On/Off. Life/Death. Hunter/Prey. Empire/Rebels. M. C. Escher's *Angels and Devils*.

Mercurius—I said, delivering the name as the punch line to a joke I hadn't told her yet, as if cutting to the last line on the page of a book she hadn't read, the sardonic closing quip that finally explained what the story was all about. The endgame of alchemy and self-transformation. Man and woman undivided both and all.

Luda shook her head.

That's it? A picture in a book?—articulating her complete disappointment with a derisive snort. *I thought you were showing me God!*

This is so you know what to look for.

When?—she cried, driven to distraction by anticipation.

That's for me to decide—I said—*I'm curious.*

Bi-curious. Mercurius—Luda giggled, good-humoured and tipsy on weed.

Just curious—I said. *How did you choose your drag name? What made you decide on Luda?*

She wrinkled her nose. *Tell me yours first*—

The sting in her voice told me I'd picked a scab, so I gave her a moment to recover before pressing her on it.

Luci, right—I said with little to explain. *It's short for Lucifer and hallucinogens. Let there be Luci! Fiat Lux! La Bang*—I recited the spiel I'd committed to memory in the days when I did youth magazine questionnaires for teenage girls and boys.

LaBang is the Big Bang, the light and the thunderclap accompanying bright glamorous Lucifer's ejection from Heaven into Matter's muddy, agonizing splendour.

I was "LaBang," to counter the overtones of sexual aggression of the "Big Bang" metaphor.

I couldn't put it plainer than that.

Initiation into the Glamour, the drag, involves a re-baptizing, an induction into an unlikely tribe of mavericks. This early rite of passage we all go through is marked by the careful scraping away of some dated, outgrown label followed by the willed application of a new logo, new packaging, an on-brand name that sums up our personal individual core values and aspirations.

We assume new code names, superhero identities that describe who we are and what we do, instead of what our parents thought we'd grow up to be.

Val VaVoom. Lady LaDouche. Boi Georgia. Bambi Bo Peep. Pam Demonium.

You could have chosen any name for yourself—I said to Luda. *Why Luda?*

Luda made a show of being preoccupied with an attempt to project her mind through her gas-jet eyes into her phone.

It's the Latin word for "game"—I went on when she didn't look up. *Like Ludo, Cluedo,* Magister Ludi, *that book.*

Her answer when it came, came ironed flat.

Maybe I'm a piece in a game like the hat in Monopoly—said Luda, giving all her attention to whatever hypnotic scroll of text or images she'd found in the blue light of her screen.

Recognizing in her snail-like withdrawal an unaccustomed vulnerability, I struck as she retreated.

Are you playing a game with me?—I wanted to know, my confidence boosted by the champagne, the Purple Haze. *Are we playing a game now?*

I'd rather play than work—Luda said. And she turned her head to face me so that her smile was a searchlight, wide and red and blinding bright, rounding up her prisoners as they made a break for the perimeter fence.

If it's a picture of something—she said, steering the conversation back to the Mercurius woodcut. *I want to see what it's a picture of.*

Wednesday—I decided. *The French call it* Mercredi. *I'll show you what I'm talking about on Wednesday.*

Luda decided she was tired. She stretched up her tight fists on the end of wiry arms with skin softer than *chamois*. She intended to retire to her bed and read through the *Phantom* script now that the pages were re-collated in standard numerical order.

Aching down to the marrow, I watched Luda undress in the mirror through the tall narrow cleft between door and frame whose proportions made her look like an illustration on the spine of some erotic novel I'd selected from the library of the marquis. Golden Hours. I found myself vowing I'd do anything to keep this blazing seraph close, committing to any crime that might keep us tied together like Bonnie & Clyde even as I went down in a storm of ballistics and bad decisions.

She'd wound me up deliberately, poring over my pictures, encouraging me to talk about Jeremy. It was her fault I felt this way, I concluded to my own satisfaction.

I felt horny, edgy, reaching for Romance by picturing my mood as a heraldic rose secured with golden twine so its petals could never release to the sun.

As lightning unable to strike.

1001
WEDNESDAY'S CHILDREN

I'd chosen a Wednesday night, for reasons partially explained earlier, chief among them being the thematic appropriateness of that one-and-only day of the week. Wednesday promised a rare blood-moon event, when atmospheric conditions and short wavelengths would collaborate to shroud the moon in a fog of poppy breath and where ruby constellations, vermilion nets of night-jewellery, and attendant zodiacal mysteries would be revealed in the womb-glow of the lunar *menstruum*.

The auguries and the omens were irresistible. Wednesday was a red-letter werewolf day, an arc-lit Viking *Wotenstag*.

When I checked in on Luda, she was cross-legged on the bed in the fish-tank glow of her laptop.

I hope you're not still watching Pussyfever videos—I said. *It turns into a habit and by the time you realize, it's too late—they have people in clinics who'll never be right again . . .*

I've moved on to the Troupe—was all she said with a smirk and a shake of her head.

You're finally developing some taste—I fired back, enchanted and chary in equal measure, like a walk through the woods where Little Red Riding Hood was last seen by witnesses.

You're funny—she said, only turning her head in my direction when the Tennis Court Martial sketch, never a favourite, played out on its "Death by balls!" punch line—*Is God on his way?*

You mustn't misgender Mercurius—I tutted. *Hair and makeup. Come on!*

When it comes to the Glamour, you're stitching together anything you've got lying around that might help to anchor the desired sleight of mind in concrete reality, full moons, new moons, feast days, holidays, superstitions, talismans, and totems. It's vital to think on your feet, as imperative in my line of work as knowing how to put together an award-winning ball gown out of gift wrap, safety pins, and a shower curtain fit for the bin. You're looking to emphasize ideas of ritual, establish special days and hours for certain operations. Assembling a look, you want the elements to coordinate, to correspond. You want the drag to match the occasion and vice-versa.

My thoughts gathered pace, a dynamo cycling to capacity, a steam train shouldering out of its snail-shell shed. The combination of champagne and weed became my shovelled coal, and we were chuffing back to my place, where I was queen of the boundaries and frontiers.

Now I was ready to draw down Mercurius.

One of the first lessons we witches learn: The Glamour is best experienced in a state of intoxication. It's how the antlered shamans and druids and medicine dancers did it, and that's just the way it is. It's not that it doesn't work without booze or drugs. It works better with them, that's all. Otherwise, it can feel like going to a play and keeping your eyes closed until the end.

I mixed glitter and purple and applied it to her eyelids to darken down her gaze, to hood her extraordinary interrogating blue in the shade of massive lashes like awnings heavy with soot. A smoky perfect smudge to make the turquoise pop just so.

Three times—she reminded me as if I didn't know. *You said you'd do my makeup three times.*

That's because Mercurius has three faces, or phases—I explained, though I could never be sure when she was listening. Luda preferred the show to the tell. *You were the Virgin. Now you're the Mother.*

Mother?—she said, as if I'd accused her of sex crimes.

I assured her that the Mother in the Triad also referred to the sexually-experienced woman, the Priestess, Empress or Dominatrix. The third face belongs to the Crone, the Witch.

That'll be you. She grinned luscious and wicked. That face! So mobile and generous. So peerlessly proportioned! Delivering her sting with a giggle.

I applied the finishing touches to Luda's latest makeover, an airbrushed mist of glitter on the perfectly-emphasized letter-opener blade of her left cheekbone. Where previously I'd applied the pink-frosted, lip-glossed doll-sheen of a wide-eyed *ingénue* on the Bad Ship Lollipop, this time around I was serving the seductive, experienced mask of a bloodsucking, eternally young vampire countess with succulent midnight-blue lips. A three-hundred-year-old teenage black widow blinking in stripped-back starlight as I pinned her Louise Brooks copper bob in place.

And I said—*Where better to find God?* I said—*Look and you'll see.*

I wanted her to see what was always there. To twist her goggles and tilt her perspective so she could see ordinary overlooked things for the one-off heartbreaking wonders they were.

So, we drank wine and smoked until we felt as if the corners of the room were tucking inwards to cocoon us both in a dreamy lambent private space made of enfolding firelight and familiar things brought closer together to reveal new and undiscovered relationships.

Luda's sordid background wasn't mine; true, we were both products of the underprivileged working classes, but precisely where my mum and dad were supportive, self-educated, and open-minded, hers were kitchen-sink stereotypes from a dispiriting social realist play where everyone who should be a trusted figure of loving authority was replaced by a leering alcoholic junkie, groping child molester, or flailing fascistic bully.

Liquor and drugs and neglect were wound into her genetic line but still I saw in Luda what she wanted me to see: someone like me as I'd been when I needed someone like me in my life.

In this way I was able to convince myself she needed me, without understanding what that meant.

I'm saying parasitic fungi need ants, don't they? Ichneumon flies need living wasps to grow their larvae in. Vampires are hungry too this Christmas!

I experienced an overwhelming, seemingly instinctual need to take care of Luda, to make it my duty to ensure she'd never go off the rails or throw away her chances like so many gorgeous young things do all the time without realizing what they're relinquishing.

Cuckoos inspire nurturing reactions like these in the nests of smaller birds they commandeer, murdering the offspring of littler parents to take their place as they grow monstrous and demanding, too swollen for the humble nest. Exemplars of Mother Nature's bright cruelty!

Leafing through Luda's pages, I saw how I could correct my own first-draft errors, script-doctor my beginner's mistakes.

The Mirror's our doorway into the Glamour—I said. *Our window onto Heaven.*

I took her hands—two buoys, we bobbed in the beat, afloat together in a soul-nourishing soup of notes and horns and tidal strings. I took her soft white hands in mine. No raised veins, no visible armature of bones working like creaky Meccano wrapped in parchment. She angled her head, as if appraising a work of gallery art, lost in her own hi-fidelity re-creation in the mirror.

Baby witch!—I said, knowing it still sounded insincere. Luda had a way to go but she had me to point her in the right direction.

I led her to my bedroom, where, in no uncertain terms, I planned to introduce my apprentice to the irreproachable reality of the unbound godette Mercurius.

I pivoted Luda's slender body, a preserved copy of my own, if only I'd died and been tastefully embalmed at the age of twenty-five. I swivelled her face-to-face with her own immaculate inverted image, her flipped entangled counterpart. Convincingly life-like, except that the mirror girl's heart was on the right, not the left, and unlike normal hearts pumped blood in an anti-clockwise direction.

It's just a mirror—Luda said bitterly. *God's just a mirror?*

We live half our lives in the mirror—I explained. *We look to it for reassurance, or punishment. We stare into it for understanding. The mirror is so like God it might as well be God.*

I was superconductive, fuzzing and buzzing at the edges where vapour pouring off my skin frilled into almost visible fluid dynamics, where sweat clouds and perfume molecules converged mindlessly with individual scintillating skin flakes in a laser-show weave of interlacing rays. You must know what I'm talking about!

Be among us, my Mercurius!
Svelte quicksilver, bright, luxurious!
Black pink panther Lamborghini!
Super-shiny chrome bikini!
Triple-headed dry martini!

All the tall mirrors I'd arranged in that tightly-crimped room were angled into multi-cornered infinity so that everywhere she and I turned, through the four cardinal directions and beyond, we saw ourselves replicated in high definition, more real than real, like Dutch Masters. We saw mass-produced dolls rolling by on a conveyor belt. Cutouts made for dressing up.

You look gorgeous. Look at you, Luda babes—I said sincerely. *You can be anything—at your age—you already are anything—*

I was trying to repeat and reframe her disturbing vision of multiple selves.

Is it like gods or angels?—she said, and I said—*Well, yes and no . . . you shouldn't believe anything you've heard. Believe what you see and experience.*

Mercurius is the messenger, I told her. A metaphor. The gatekeeper, the key, and the gate, I intoned. Luda barely suppressed a snort of derision.

That doesn't even mean anything!—she said but it did, as I went on to elucidate.

Mercurius is of blended gender, remember. The gate is pussy. The key is cock. Two in one at the same time, mutually self-unlocking. Zero and one in quantum superposition. The binary notation, the on and off, the push and pull that builds a universe occurring all at once as a self-affirming self-negation . . .

Luda nodded slowly, amazed, enlightened.

Right—she whispered. *I get it.*

Shiny hotspots of reflected light glinted like pirate treasure beneath those impossible blue lakes of eyes as I raised the chant to freshly ecstatic euphoric peaks.

Inbetweenie! Mannie-queenie! Sisterbrothersupergenie!

A gasping invocation into resonant expanding space.

I am you are me are we Mercurius am he are she!

One is all and all is us!

My fingers made an arcing windscreen-wiper gesture and a stuttering, feathered trail of primary-coloured false nails spread and multiplied like fabulous red-enamelled wingtips from my fingers.

Three-faced we!

Mercurius!

A cool, pale lustre separated each movement into throwaway snapshots as we faced each other in the mirror glass, silvered and vaporous cigarette smoke holding brief human form.

It shows you what's real—and what's not—I said, seeing in the screen of the glass the Crone with the Mother wrapped in her jealous bony arms. There was a third Self missing between Luda and Me.

The Glamour.

Naturally I began to wonder if she'd faked the whole thing somehow, if the masquerade party that night was something we'd imagined together.

Now, I know what you're thinking, and it might seem irresponsible but not all forms of epilepsy can be triggered by flashing lights. I'd made myself a bit of an expert in the subject and as it turns out only around 3 percent of sufferers fall into the "photosensitive" bracket.

The category is—I said in a breathless dramatic MC voice—*higher-dimensional realness!*

I flipped up two arms to vogue a stark and hieratic *mudra,* and my fabulous reflection countered, like a statue of Kali unwrapping her lobster limbs to trail a cape fringed with fingernails, describing two wings of unfolding solid flesh that were suspended for an extended moment in our line of sight as the splintered afterimages stayed in place for ages.

Luda giggled.

Trails.

Laughing together, she and me, we flapped our arms in a vivid spectral smear of limbs, leaving snow-angel casts carved from spacetime's soft and yielding substance by our passage.

I said I'd show you my god—look!

In the choppy strobe flash, every movement had a silent-film stutter, a spastic flick with missing frames.

There's Mercurius—see? You and me, spun through the fifth dimension.

She had no idea what I was talking about, but the Flashy-Flickers flurry of multiple arms and myriad legs was its own best evidence. I subjected Luda to the multiplying visions of limbs blossoming freakishly in the hard, smooth glass of the bedroom mirror—imagining the sweet soft little cock between her shaved smooth thighs rendered impotent by wonder, drugs, and her determined refusal to be a boy ever again.

There's more to you than meets the eye. There are more dimensions than you can see. You've got length and breadth and then there's the inward direction, the infinite space we keep in our skulls—and I felt sure I was articulating all this with the concise eloquence of wisdom, but I don't think I opened my mouth once.

As she began to understand what was possible, I heard Luda moan involuntarily, so I had to hold her and channel her energy. I tried to resist the powerful erotic overtones of our embrace, resulting only in a throbbing hard-on gaffed painfully between my cheeks.

I held her gently as Luda, my young apprentice, lost control of her spine to the blue-violet Kundalini flash activating each individual chakra—*muladhara* to *sahasrara*—in explosive ascending sequence as far as I could tell. Rigid muscles liquefied in an unplanned, unrehearsed Salome slut drop until, succumbing exquisitely like Odette in *Swan Lake* to gravity and entropy, Luda needed my help to stand on two trained feet.

I made it back from the bathroom to find her gazing from the bowed window at the moon's made-up face smirking down on Gasglow. I did my best to bring her back from the splendour of the starlit firmament with a head massage.

My maternal instinct was still strong as the stubbled, scarred, and tattooed scalp beneath her luxurious red wig yielded to my fingers.

I bent to kiss her skull, impart my cherry lipstick's stamp of approval on her sealed fontanelle.

Somewhere in the white empty afterward, stars were born, and yesterday's babies died of old age. There were bees or doves or maybe moths in the room, tugging embroidered scraps of wings loose from the hearth rug and flittering around the overhead lampshade where they would burst into stained-glass fog against the bulbs or become trapped in the wallpaper all over again.

The kickback came almost immediately. The way so many spells can only be said to come true at the same time they backfire, bringing the inevitable reflex, the jolt of the rifle stock, the recoil—which in this case made its presence known that horrible following night, a subdued Saturday in early still-hot September.

On Saturn's day, with shite clogging the TV screen, our stern planetary granddad decided to stick his veiny nose into our lives, that lugubrious senior citizen of the Pantheon reflecting on the horrendous beauty and fatal equilibrium of time's arrow as it arcs in slow motion from left to right across Eternity's pages en route for his ancient pendulum heart.

I'd planned to impart to her one of the great secrets of the Glamour—never mind rabbits, here's how to make a cock disappear—but things took a different turn that night.

With far-reaching consequences, you might say, but we'll get to that soon enough.

Luda returned from dance rehearsal in a fluster of Muybridge motion. One sentence after another was chopped to incoherence by her rapid passage from kitchen to bathroom to lounge as she delivered a continuous data download.

I didn't really notice how quiet the place was without her, but it occurred to me quite suddenly how since she'd taken up residence, I hadn't slowed down, hadn't settled, hadn't meditated for long enough to get the benefits. I was always on my toes, waiting for her to erupt into the room like oxygen into a vacuum.

For so long it seemed, I hadn't been able to think for her noise, the jittery buzz and static of her company . . .

She demanded complete attention, occupying my total field of view. It was as if she represented some quantum event, a momentary lapse into being that might disappear if I wasn't constantly observing, reinforcing her existence.

The effort of staying alert for every spike on her EEG or

jagged tremor on her seismograph was making me agitated, edgy. I tried to remember when I'd last sat serene like a meditating monk at the centre of my own psychocosmos and drew a blank.

There was Before Luda and After Luda. Of the former Age, only folk memories were left, fading flavours of Eden, and its citrus mornings tingling on the tip of my tongue with all the other unspoken words, the forgotten names.

Could it be that her complete disregard for my needs, my routines, my possessions, had worked its way under my shell as an irritant, an itch I couldn't scratch even as it drove me mad with irrational frustration?

Was I really this prickly and guarded when I felt my space invaded and colonized?

I said—*You haven't seen my peep toes? I wore them at the party—*

What would I want with those?—she said. *There was nothing left of them!*

I was taking them in for repair—I insisted, wondering when the barometer would register the change in the weather, the hardening frost, the escalating chill.

They were horrible. Luda curled her lip in disgust. *I wouldn't wear them if you paid me!*

Luda, whose dirty tights lay draped over the sacred places of my home, the radiators and designer chairs, whose half-eaten dinners were stacking up in the watering hole where faucet gods had convened in my immaculately scrubbed stainless-steel sink.

Have you been using my razor? You shouldn't use all my stuff—what about infections—I said, unable to stem the incoming tide of irrational gibberish.

I don't have any infections—she spat back. *Is there something you want to tell me? Did you give me AIDS?*

DISEASES! You're the fucking disease!

I'm not a fucking thief! Stop treating me as if I'm HIM!

The door to the spare room slammed hard enough to bounce the brass doorknocker, the one shaped like a crow's skull, off its hook.

I'm going out—said Luda.

It was bad enough she'd disappeared for two hours after our *contretemps*. Now here she was framed in the doorway like Barbie in her cellophane display window, all stockings and heels, factory-fresh.

My response, when it came, came without words.

You can come if you want—she huffed, and I could tell she was praying I wouldn't say yes, yes, I will come actually.

She could see I was nowhere near dressed and even if I had been ready, I was in no mood to face another overlit, exhausting late-summer night out with the same gaggle of queens and wannabes in one of Gasglow's exactly three decent drag bars.

As if all that Saturnian, purple paternal solemnity had worked its way into the water supply, or more likely my vodka supply, I took one gander at Luda and—may God forgive me—uttered the phrase—

You can't go out—the words escaping from my lips like madmen from the asylum, like nitrous from a can—*not looking like that.*

I know! I prided myself on a lifelong *laissez-faire,* devil-may-care broad-mindedness, but as this petulant, self-pitying squeal came out like piss strained through a straw, I already knew it was fully deserving of Luda's merciless response.

Like you?—she said, supplying a brattish exclamation point with her stiff middle finger. *I thought that's what you wanted?*

How about this then?

She pulled the dress open down the middle and threw it at me.

Let's see how good you look in it!

Shrugging into a vinyl coat only accentuated the potential

for immodesty once she'd pulled the belt tight around her enviably trim waist, hiking the hem up her thighs to flash her stocking tops.

Your arse is hanging out! I can see your tape!—I told her, resorting to peeved teacher tones. *And that's not all. Have some fucking style!*

This is my style!—she spat. *This is how I want to look! You think I'm going out looking like you to meet people my OWN AGE?*

You're the one who said age didn't matter!—I reminded her, two rocks of ice in my tone.

Until you went ON AND FUCKING ON about it all the time!—she fired back.

And we were off at a gallop.

You're not my fucking mother—Luda volleyed, as if the word were a tainted cherry she had to spit out.

I wouldn't have you as a free gift in a raffle!—I struck back, conscious that I'd inflicted a wound much deeper than I expected.

*All you do is stare at me—and—mirrors and—*She went on and on like this, ramping up the disjointed abuse.

Until—*If you can't stand that you're an old bag, if you can't deal with it*—she snarled. *Do what all the other old bags do and get the fucking Botox you keep saying you don't need!*

You'll need it before I do if you stay out every night drinking and taking drugs!—I announced from my personal pulpit. *You can't hide party eyes!*

At least my face isn't hanging off my skull like a fucking waxwork in an oven!

That's enough!—I shrieked and that was the moment I finally cracked. *Have some fucking respect, bitch!*

She didn't expect the crowd-control-hose ferocity of my reaction and took a step back on her spikes.

Get out of my fucking house!—I thundered. As a performance, it was up there with Jehovah casting Adam and Eve starkers from their comfortable Garden hideaway and it was concluded with the coda Genesis forgot to record—*And give me my keys back!*

Take your fucking keys—she growled like a boy as she flung a frosty jingle of cut metal and Toytown-coloured plastic past my shoulder. *I don't need you or this shit tip you live in! You're an embarrassment when we go out! You're a fucking dinosaur that thinks it still rules the world!*

The keys struck the ironic barometer I'd impulse-purchased with Jeremy during that weekend in Berlin twenty-two years ago, shattering the brittle arch above the tiny cottage door on the left that said SHINE.

Your feet smell like a fucking locker room! That was my final flourish, and as final flourishes go, as shade is my witness, I knew I could throw so much better.

From the abject nadir of my despair, I found myself admiring Luda's brio; that insolent pause to correct her doomsday button lipstick with a pinkie dab in the mirror before the cannon-shot of slammed door, and subsequent fading reports, the crack-crackety-crack of her heels on the lobby flooring.

The space where Luda had stood preserved the brilliant absence seared into it, her afterimage still steaming on the wallpaper.

She'd seemed enormous only moments before, a storm cloud piling black on top of black, before evaporating into nothing like those spectral giants some oxygen-deprived climbers report, that turn out to be their own shadows magnified against fog banks at the summit.

I drank another half bottle of Chardonnay. Inhaled more grey-green weed clouds.

Tear tracks carved river-valley grooves through my makeup. I snorted great lines of air, shoulders heaving.

There's no point avoiding the elephant in the knicker drawer:

I knew Luda had to be fucking other men. I imagined it was how she made her money. She checked her phone more often than she checked her reflection, which was constantly. I suspected secret assignations. Independent income. Rich men. The kind girls like her were born to impress and fashioned to indulge. If there was any truth at all to the Marvell story, I presumed it was most likely the bit about Charles Marvell's voracious appetite for femboys and twinks. There was a class of older men like that, daddy types paying rent on bijou apartments near enough the office to expedite quick consultations.

"Cockroach problem!" I snorted.

She was probably on her knees right now—I told myself even though she'd only been gone twenty minutes. She'd be dressed in Victoria Marvell's white stockings and that boned, lace-trimmed summer-cloud-coloured wedding-night *basque* the Mrs. would never fit into again—how could I compete with that?

Building from this basic premise, I quickly and with a practiced routine scripted, directed, and shot an ever-more-elaborate cycle of self-loathing porno clips in my head; Oscar winners they were not, but the plots, direct and to the point, saw my leading lady, "Luda LaBang" according to the credits, progress from a sincere religious vow of chastity to threesomes, foursomes, and gang bangs with ageing sex offenders, until I was rigid at the notion of her depraved infidelities, imagining myself the sex-starved jealous stepmother gnashing her teeth—*Mirror, mirror on the wall . . .*—the Wicked Queen syringing a rosy apple with Soviet nerve agent.

That stupid old bitch Luci has no idea what she's missing—her handler, Charles Marvell, would gloat from a panting throne of living willing sex dolls where Luda writhed and cackled in his intimate lascivious grasp, just one more disposable plaything in the monster's twisted harem.

I'm Luda Marvell now!—she gasped as she underwent a

shattering orgasmic release. *My name is Luda Marvell! I belong to Charles Marvell! Charles Marvell!*

That did the trick. A bitter jet of spite and spunk pulled the plug on the lurid sizzle reel in my head. I lay, cooling factory steel, savouring the circulating steams of disgust and recrimination as they poured off my skin into a vaporous unhealthy darkness near the ceiling.

Jealousy can be unspeakably arousing if you give it a chance.

You need to try this on—I giggled and jiggled a bendy snow-white, lace-fringed leather *basque* that would never fit me again.

I used to come onstage with the Troupe as Virginia Plain, a super-horny virgin bride on her long-awaited honeymoon. The gag was her groom would do anything to avoid sex, having been diagnosed with a voracious STD the day before his expensive marriage ceremony.

I love it—Luda simpered. *If I can't be you who can I be?*

In that instant, as I began to suspect there was something entirely unlikely about this frothy kitsch scenario, something I couldn't put my finger on without bursting it like a bubble, the sound of sirens amplified to an insufferable volume.

I quickly came to the reasonable conclusion that the Apocalypse had been greenlit quite suddenly and without consultation, the way you always suspected it might.

They'd dropped the Bomb, all the Bombs if the all-inclusive roar was anything to go by. They'd unleashed Plagues and pandemics like genies from a thousand glowing radioactive test tubes. Frantic emergency lights were strobing out the last seconds of life on planet Earth and I had an unwanted ringside seat unless, unless, unless I could just—unless—I—

I woke up.

There's the call—"House is open!"—which means the audience is piling into the auditorium expecting to be entertained.

I've never been so terrified of those words before.

The end draws nigh.
"House is open!"

I woke up.

Put it this way, if the recommended softly-layered transition from deep sleep through drowsy reverie to eyes open, fully refreshed morning awareness might be compared to natural childbirth in a heated pool at a New Age retreat in Koh Samui, then my harrowing wake-up klaxon was closer in spirit to an impromptu C-section with a rusty can opener in an Ikea warehouse car park.

All at once was all the light, all the noise of everything happening at the same time. With me at the centre of it all, dazed and newly-delivered in the aftermath of an auto accident.

I sat up straight, jackknifing at the hips, to meet a roomful of uproar and orbiting lights. I flinched in shotgun blasts of incoherent impressions that cried out to be rapidly wrangled and arranged into any available convincing narrative. Ideally one with a dramatic arc more developed than—*it had to happen—the Gestapo has finally tracked you down!*

Fortunately, or not as upcoming events in this statement will serve to illustrate, what I'd taken to be a massed rock-drill assault on the fundamental concept of silence turned out to be nothing more than the door buzzer going on repeat, with a fierce and toneless insistence that implied a hapless game-show contestant, eager to attract the attention of an unresponsive quizmaster.

The combined forces of Gasglow's police and emergency services in full Armageddon formation I'd first inferred was scaled back to some flashing call alerts. Thankfully, I'd disabled the ringtone, preventing "Two Ladies" from adding its own shrill duet to the panic chorus.

Intent on piecing things together, I staggered from a tousled bed, tugging some vague woolly form of awareness down over my head. And as I draped a tiger-print robe around these bony shoulders, cinching the belt to hide my belly, I made sure to clothe myself as adroitly with my name, my phone number, and other essential details as might be required by the law. The intercom light flashed by the door, a distant lonely pulsar. Astronomical. Insistent. Hypnotic.

Hello?—I warbled, flicking the intercom switch to activate a between-the-dimensions crackle.

Don't turn the lights on! It was Luda's voice distorted, pleading through the unearthly acoustic space. *NO MATTER WHAT—don't turn the lights on, Luci!*

My stomach lurched. I'd just about prepared myself for the boys in blue, but I couldn't face Luda's Bunsen-jet eyes. Not after everything. This was further proof of her wayward energy, her disruptive power, her knack of disturbing what peace remained . . .

There was nothing to be gained by asking what had happened to her keys. I remembered them sailing past my shoulder to smash against the miniature rose-covered porch of the RAIN/SHINE barometer from Berlin with, in place of the customary bride and groom, two tiny plastic wives both wearing yellowing wedding dresses. I buzzed Luda in and waited as my stomach dropped for every floor she climbed.

Shamefully, I felt somehow vindicated, even triumphant. Mine was a bleak nasty victory, but it proved one sure thing: I didn't need her, Luda needed me.

Shadows shifted across the walls and ceiling, as if cast by tall thin spies, fine-tooth-combing the crime scene for evidence they could secure to convict the culprits.

My keys—she sobbed inexplicably, then toppled into the hallway and slammed the lights off with a flailing fist.

Flat Police!—she said. Her bulging eyes were empyrean cue balls and in the stripped, shredded pitch of her voice there shrilled an acidic chime of mania. *Flat Police!*

Flat Police—what was I getting myself into? I thought as I took her elbow and guided her into the dark living room. As I steered her round the footstool and cabinets, I felt a foolish pride at my ability to navigate this apartment blindfold if need be.

One after the next, the minutes clocked by until there were ten. The place lay still in shade, as Luda requested, relieved only by the dilute underglow of orange streetlamps and passing lemonade headlights, the cherry taillights receding.

You're shaking—I said, handing her a hot mug of tea with a big splash of brandy. I didn't mention the quarter Valium I'd added to the recipe. It was for her own good.

They had a whole room of me!—she said, staring into my eyes as if I'd understand immediately. *I went back!*

I had no idea how to make sense of what she was talking about until it dawned on me that everything Luda was saying that night had to be taken literally or taken not at all.

The Marvells kept backup copies of her, she assured me. She was disposable, dispensable, expendable. There were stacks of windup talking Ludas, she was certain of that, and she'd seen them inactive in their bubble wrap and polystyrene chip drifts, awaiting shipping to new owners. She was only the prototype for something that would one day be as ubiquitous as the phones we carry with us everywhere like colostomy bags.

To administer the inscrutable laws of a world where any of this made sense the rich employed Flat Police without form, without individuality, faces, or pasts.

Immune to the Glamour, it was the duty of these dimension-less dicks to ensure everything remained the same and things stayed as they were meant to be in old Gasglow.

The world we thought we knew was a matte painting, Luda seemed certain, a decorated backdrop against whose daubed unfinished horizons we played children's games while the harsh business of the adult world was enacted, tooth and claw, beyond the backwall vista.

The room in the Marvells' basement was their secret lair where secret policemen worked in secret guided by the map of a secret Gasglow, an unwrapped, expanded Gasglow, frequented by inebriates, *flâneurs,* restless sleepers, the deranged, the inspired.

This other Gasglow was a collage of shreds and patches; a precarious construction of associative clusters pinned like brooches along the meandering banks of a conjectured River Dare, in whose pious salts and waters saints still bathed and sinners bled.

This Gasglow was a city of songs half heard in raucous smoke-filled bars where the light was all the colours of a used Elastoplast.

This Gasglow was a mirage town hung suspended over the original's dour steeples and faithful chimneys, a grotesque awe-inducing shadow cast on the boiling fog rolls of the aether, projected across the dreaming sighs of the collective psyche as here precipitated into fat thunderhead fistfuls of drunken notion.

It took silhouette men, of necessity thinner than sheets of paper, to police these ethereal tenement blocks, these provisional alleyways made of conjecture and possibility.

A highly-trained division of Flat Police had long, long ago in the days of Gasglow's foundation established secret shortcuts through the real that took advantage of the squeezed-down geometry behind the printed façade. They had underground holding cells where the walls collapsed to an infinitely-curved plane surface that nothing could escape, not light, not even thought.

It's the plot for a horror movie, isn't it? Not the typical kind with creepy-crawlies from outer space, demons from Hell, or vampires from Eastern Europe.

This is more like one of those pictures where a fragile young woman begins to suspect something's gone badly awry, disturbing the OCD routines of her ordinary life, leading to the inevitable conclusion that she's possessed or under some otherwise elusive but palpably abnormal threat from the neighbours, her children, or, if newlywed, her beloved husband. That kind of horror. Psychological paranoid dread dramatizing all the different stages of a vulnerable person's catastrophic mental breakdown.

I said—*You have to think about it rationally.*

Rationality is a proven demon-repellent, one of the medicines used routinely by qualified practitioners of the Glamour, i.e., me. Demons falter I've found in the face of any convincingly expressed good reason why they cannot exist.

If you wondered why I made such a meal of the basement incident your own lack of imagination needn't hold you back any longer.

The basement exerted a black-hole tug our guttering Ghost Light was too bright to escape. The stars were going out in the auditorium until even the last cracked bulbs disintegrated, hurtling towards us as a razor-trimmed expulsion of death-glitter.

Rational?—she snorted derisively and flipped up some pictures on her phone screen—skewed close-ups on a raven mask, a slashing beak stained red, mad black eyes, reflecting other beaks, different faces.

The whole Marvell family would get together for costumed orgies of transgression, she told me, as if fondly recalling Yuletide celebrations. They'd made her take part in some ritual feast. Raw flesh was consumed of ambiguous origin. Offerings were made to the Great Flat Powers of the Constabulary in the basement.

I'm scared. I can't remember which of us said it first. When it came to rich and amoral people with powerful allies in the Establishment, I wasn't sure the Glamour would be enough to protect me from the vengeance of whatever nameless folk horror cultus they'd sworn allegiance to.

What happened last night?—I asked and I had to know.

My jaw's aching—said Luda.

Must be all the cock, babes—I said and wished I hadn't been so crass, while still congratulating myself on the comeback. *You had an epileptic fit. There was a doctor in a crow mask like this one . . .*

You don't understand—she said. *I went back! This happened when I went back to that house! I knew I'd been there!*

I held her as she bent into a corner at the waist, felt beneath my fingertips the thrill of her sculpted liquid muscles contracting, the soft gears grinding in her gut.

I remembered the house!—she choked and slobbered, until I finally twigged when she sobbed with round-eyed anguish—*I grew up in that house!*

That suburban mansion dragged up with rockets and balloons, that basement room where we'd stood at the Veil of the Threshold, belonged to Charles and Victoria Marvell.

The Marvells invited us to a sex party?

Luda's legs kicked and slid, flailing ungainly across the floor as a single strenuous retch and convulsion projected the contents of her stomach from the inside out. I imagined myself embracing a python as it regurgitated its deconstructed breakfast antelope in the form of stew shot from a hose.

Moments later with Luda groaning on the couch while I fastidiously separated the building blocks of her vomit from the carpet with paper towels and a sponge, it was hard to simply disregard the gobbets of undigested meat she'd expelled, the saw-toothed strips of flesh and fibre, the threads of fat in a *jus* of gastric bile and semi-liquidized mystery matter.

I envisaged her alone, isolated in that curious room tucked under things, with its squirmy wall map, the firing squad of mirrors, and the semi-circular auditorium.

Her surrogate parents joining her in that place, done up for a Halloween wedding in sleek feather masks, glutted on meats you cain't raise nor buy. That kind of horror movie, where the twist comes when we learn the victim deserves what's happening to them, as punishment for a crime ten times more horrendous.

I seized on the mirrors as doorways to Reason. It seemed so obvious! There had to be a way out of this claustrophobic *cul-de-sac* of nightmare logic and the obligations of *Grand Guignol*.

What you saw—I said, holding her hand while she sprawled on the couch, pale as the moon in the morning. *Think about it, sweetheart. What you saw were the mirrors—you were tripping when you walked out of here!* I was so sure of myself. *The copies were you. Reflections of you*—and my voice was as reassuring as I could pretend to be. Luckily, I'm a professional.

I saw calm wash over Luda's classically-proportioned features. Perhaps it had all been a misunderstanding, a trick of the perceptual shimmer. Perhaps there were no such things as—

BAM! BAM! BAM!

The police rap. Unmistakable. That heart-stopping triple thump meant only one thing. The thunderous descent of the gavel of justice as sentence is pronounced.

Fuck!—I hissed and clamped my palm across the lower half of Luda's tear-streaked face, so that she left a Surrealist lip-print in the hollow at the base of my thumb. It felt as though we were in a film, a weird modern thriller, and that was the sort of thing someone in a film would do.

Steadying Luda, I crawled along the skirting board, reaching up slowly, silently to finger the bolt into its bracket and flip the snib home.

In response, the door handle shook violently so we jerked back, flat against the corner, while bars of shadow wiped across ceiling and walls, scrutinizing, searching, analysing, then moving on . . .

They get in through the cracks—she whimpered. *Don't let them find a way in!*

What cracks?

Where they get in!

I threw a raincoat across the gap between the door and the floor, cancelling the light from the hall.

What's up? What's happened?—I said, trying to drag some sense out of her.

It's them—I think it's them—was all she could get out before it turned to glug-glug-glossolalia.

Shadows slouched across the walls, moving with horrible intent like tall thin men in single file, hunting for something . . .

. . . until, failing to locate their quarry, they paused, as if to confer in two uncompromising dimensions. I told myself not to anthropomorphize shadows on the walls, but it was difficult not to feel the probing intelligence, the roaming scrutiny as I crept on all fours across the carpet, until I was in position to pull the blinds, draw the curtains, and seal the room.

Flat Police—she whispered.

I wish I didn't have to admit it but what they did next was impossible; they'd never been able to stop then move in *reverse* across their charted course. They'd never been able to change direction.

Traffic flow meant there was no way for the slashes of light and shadow to converge the way I was seeing them do. Convening as if in rapid exchange of information, they huddled, a tepee frame of interlinked spars, then just as suddenly flew apart across the room and were gone.

The noise outside on the landing stopped. Crouching in breathless silence Luda and I listened to fading footfalls on the stairwell.

The sensation of imminent threat dissipated, as if a thundercloud had passed overhead and moved on, grousing into the distance.

I found Luda, face deep in the toilet, her wig a red-shifted spiral galaxy dashed on the linoleum, the sweaty slack elastic of her skullcap, her shaved head framed as in a cameo brooch by the porcelain rim.

I'm puking up ones and nothings—she moaned, or at least that's how it sounded. I'm not sure what was going on with her. *They've found me! They're coming for me*—she sobbed, wild-eyed and disconnected.

Who's coming?

I told you!—she spat, playacting the agonizing pauses between boot-heels on Anne Frank's floorboards. *The Marvells! We have to get out of here! Flat Police!*

What's the worst thing you've ever done?—I heard her say, gulping to steady her nerves. *What's the worst?*

It's not the time—you'd have to book a weekend to hear my mistakes, love—I said, then—*Why? What's yours? It can't be that bad . . .*

Well, it was. I discovered that a little later. I'll tell you about it then.

It would only prejudice you against her at this point in the story and I want this to be fair and balanced.

We're getting out of here—I said, because that's what people say in the sort of films I mentioned and I thought if I kept telling myself I was in a film then maybe it would turn out to have a happy ending.

So, we ran. We drained ourselves down the spiral stairs in a spin-cycle clatter of footfalls, decanted into the fizzing yellow rain of a September sunrise.

I was caught in Luda's story, inextricably gummed to the sticky flypaper of Luda's erratic plot dynamics.

As for the worst I'd ever done, that had yet to happen.

Luda and I flopped into one of many empty booths at the all-night Fastbucks they'd opened last year on the corner at

Stables and Carnduff. Aside from the two us, there were a few wrung-out clubbers, ashen in the fading light of chemical detonations.

I balanced a tray slithering with hot coffee mugs and saucers to our table, double espressos to keep us awake and alert. Two-inch-thick slices of iced ginger cake. Luda looked disarrayed and sexy in her belted coat and messy wig like a *film noir* heroine, *gamine* in a French film, on the run from *les flics*. This could only be her story, not mine.

After that night, she said, after the party she kept having flashes. During her seizure, she'd experienced a sizzling memory storm. Burning in a blue friction, she saw how she'd gotten here, telegraphed as isolated still pictures edged with lightning.

The trauma returned as a freeze-frame electrical squall of half-remembered fragments dating back to the time of her birth, some eight years previously. She'd been strapped down and zapped and was convinced the relentless ECT had triggered her epilepsy.

They used six rapid shocks each time, she said. She said imagine being machine-gunned with lightning.

And there was something about the clock on the wall; it told not time but lies. Sometimes it would run backwards. Sometimes it would stop for what felt like days. As Luda decelerated, I could tell the Valium was taking effect.

Then there was some other thing about being so hungry she'd scoop up every edible scrap they left on her plate, no matter how rancid. At first, she was starving, like she hadn't eaten for what could have been a weekend or more but then it was only ten minutes later until dinner arrived again for the third time and Luda felt sick.

And even though twenty-four hours must have passed, her stomach felt full and she couldn't get through what she knew might turn out to be her last meal for another three days.

Describing this to me, she made two thick cuts of iced gingerbread disappear in seconds, one of them mine.

This was her origin story, her "how I came to be"—a savage deconstruction by voltage and toxins.

The only way to explain any of it was to posit an overreaching global conspiracy of wealthy deviants. Luda was one element in the impossible jigsaw complexity of their conspiracies, as were we all. The scale of their reach was too much to think about, another hyper-object like weather or plastic.

That's not the worst!—she moaned, pawing at her phone.

She pushed the device into my face and there was a photograph of the crow mask, the same feathered headdress I'd last seen worn by the doctor who'd tended to Luda that night at the party.

Luda, what's happening?—I said.

Luda's eyes got rounder and bigger, inflating to cue-chalk-blue balloons. She seemed to be on the verge of a sublime hysteria that could not be denied, as if her red hair might combust and flare up like a struck match. I took her hands in mine and they were as chilly as rubber mitts.

They told me I'd never have to be cold, or sick again—she insisted. *They told me I'd never need money. I'd never need ever again.* All of this came drooling out of her face as saliva. *They told me they could change my life right there and then—and all I had to do—all I had to do was—*

Luda paused here. She seemed to evaluate me in that way she had, scrutinizing every micro-movement, each muscular tremor; judging by my tics and tells how far I might be inclined to follow her Pied-Piper-ish dance over the precipice. She had nothing to worry about. I was under her spell. There was no one in the whole world more riveted to Luda's every word and gesture than me in that moment. If she'd ordered me to storm the Capitol, I would have weighed up my options for five minutes before committing to an insurrection.

She let go of my hands, fell backwards into the fixed context of space and time where this would and had already occurred.

Charles and Victoria—she said. *The Marvells. The Marvells are coming to get me! I shouldn't have done it.*

Done what?—I shrilled. *What have you done?*

I did something wrong. I keep doing it wrong—she replied. *I stole something precious*—

That's when she produced an item from her bag, and I recognized with a drop in my gut the little music box, with its bat-winged ballerina, its hand-cranked note-by-note laboured stab in the direction of "Devil Woman," that buzzed and burned blue-black with bad luck. After a mental hiccup that felt like a failed attempt to reject the thought entirely, I forced myself to remember where I'd seen the trinket box before and, in that moment, dear long-suffering listeners, I climbed into a handcart bound for Hell.

You have to promise you won't let them get me!

How could I promise that? Except I had to. I told myself it was my sworn duty to commit. Luda was my student.

Luda.

Luda.

Even her name suggested some lost Delacorta thriller where Gorodish, played in my mind by Serge Gainsbourg, accompanied by a teenage Bardot as blonde *voleuse* Alba in her red thigh boots, would rock up at the château in his Citroën 11 Normale to solve the mystery of the wrongly-accused *chanteuse.*

They'll erase me—they'll wipe me out!—Luda wept. *I'll be nothing!*

I'll look after you—I vowed, gripping her hand in mine, barely suspecting the abyss that lay ahead as that handcart I just mentioned accelerated to where the rails ran out. *I won't let that happen.*

Promise!—she urged, her eyes filling with tears, to become

258 · GRANT MORRISON

otherworldly millponds of kingfisher blue. Highlights of indigo and viridian in those mermaid fathoms. Slave to beauty, I went under willingly.

I promise—I said, all too aware of an acrid gunpowder presentiment that made me wish I'd hesitated. I reminded myself the purity of my path was predicated on superhuman levels of self-denial and continued down the Yellow Brick Road to Yellow Brick Ruin.

In this way I convinced myself that Luda—and What Luda Did Next—was my responsibility.

Just when it seemed it was too early, too late for things to get any worse, the waitress dropped a bombshell.

Friend of yours?—she said.

I had no idea what she meant until I read the banner upside-down on her phone.

CHART STAR FOUND DEAD went the lead, while SINGER MOLLY SUSPECT rode shotgun.

Luda was online faster than me. Pictured, looking like one of those computer reconstructions they do of Neanderthal Man—was Joss Weill, the former singer of chart-topping Boystalking, found dead. There was conclusive video evidence that his girlfriend, Pussyfever singer Molly Stocking, had played a part in the apeman's demise. Crazed on drink, drugs, and irrelevance, he'd crossed the line and paid the price for his appetites.

Accompanying pap shots presented the arrest of a dazed and tearful Molly Stocking.

Molly says she wasn't there, it says here—I said, and what felt like a trickle of ice water ran all the way up my spine as I scryed the bedlam headlines laid flat on gouged Formica. *This wasn't you, was it?*—I said, reading an unwelcome answer in the blowtorch glow of those eyes.

Luda smiled, a red and deadly shallow crescent. Her tears had dried remarkably quickly.

Don't look at me—she said, well aware it was impossible not to.

Out in the Gasglow morning, early birds let it all hang out; *sans* conductor, their rousing orchestral arrangement of brass caws and woodwind trills, pizzicato peeps and fluting twitters brought order and organization to the morning as it did each and every day, asking no reward.

At least, I consoled myself, I could count on the language of birds.

I still had crows on the cortex fifteen minutes later in the waiting room at the clinic.

Fifteen minutes later from what?—I hear you cry. Have we missed something?

After that manic, panic night in early September, already receding into incredulity, there had been no more sightings of Flat Police. No reprisals, no follow-up calls. The coiled suspense we both felt, the hunched anticipation of a leather-knuckled knock at the door, a firm hand on the shoulder, slowly eased out of our busy days and nights as the year proceeded in an orderly fashion towards the exit.

Luda tried not to talk too much about what had happened. There were no more fights, but I made a note of the accumulating nano-aggressions, the cracks at the expense of my body or the progress of my bags and wrinkles. Sometimes it felt like the sleepy slap of subtle steady waves carving away at the chalk foundations in slow and patient tidal erosions of confidence. Otherwise, I pretended not to notice or care. And although no one said anything, there was an unspoken directive. My meditations at the mirror became ever more ruthless inspections.

Still, she had lost the snotty truant edge, dedicating herself to the craft of the triple threat. She was learning how to frame everything in terms of the Glamour; how to give her performances the power of ritual by adding meaning and intent.

I taught and she got better. Luda was a natural, everyone

said. In light of the subsequent revelations, it was an appraisal that couldn't be further from the truth.

But this is my story and it's down to me to control the fast-forward and rewind; it's for me to say we've reached mid-October where the days, visibly losing light from both ends, were bleeding heat in sympathy.

Wise trees knew from experience what was coming, tolerating the deepening chill in these declining days past the equinox. High and dry, on parade in the tatters of last summer's fashions, outmoded by the returning season's stark trend away from exuberant life-affirming emeralds to sullen blast-crater reds, the trees bore the approach of panto season with no detectable complaint.

Something silted in the corner of my right eye that might have been ash flakes swirling in the updraught of a cigarette but wasn't. That flurry of jet-black litter scraps swirling above the sprouting heads of oak and elm trees turned out to be a collective noun of crows bickering in the high branches.

Given their great multitude as they climbed in a jagged corkscrew whirl, the whole thing seemed more massacre than mere murder but that's just me.

A grating repetition characterized the apprehensive cries of one young bird with darts of white angel plumage showing through feathers otherwise scorched to black tar in the blast furnace of maturity.

The second bird in the drama was older, more cautious. Unlike her junior, no trace of hysteria attended the elder bird's monotonous reassuring caw. She stayed watchful, aware of every movement in every degree and quadrant, vigilant to every potential source of danger or distraction.

At first, I'd assumed they were squabbling over treetop turf, but now I could tell the older crow was teaching the younger one how to navigate the air currents. Bird school in session.

Between lines of a harsh vocalization that suggested a wrench shearing off an unwilling bolt head, I told myself I heard proud encouragement, the adult crow giving the raucous corvid equivalent of a thumbs-up with its pinfeathers.

Me? I needed all the encouragement I could get!

Now it was fifteen minutes later in the tense, formal silence of every grey-wallpapered waiting room ever, every transit lounge where no one ever came to relax, only to wait, as I tried to occupy my mind with trivialities.

The cracked vocabulary of crows dispensing wisdom. Well-thumbed general-interest magazines. Women's leisure. Bikini diets. Men holding up gasping fish for the approval, I could only venture, of other men just like them who shared the same taste for bullying defenceless river-dwellers. All the covers looked out of date, printed on the sun-faded presses of some adjacent, depleted universe.

The receptionist bobbed a nod in my direction—*Graeme Mott?*—she said. Inside, I died.

It should be pointed out, while I've got this one unlikely opportunity: They're highly intelligent birds, crows, and one of the few avian species to make tools as we understand them; as it turns out they have a special module in their brains that works like the crinkly crust-topping otherwise known as the human neocortex we have on ours, that crumpled crown of entangled neurons that gives us *carte blanche* to outperform and obliterate *en masse* all other animal species. Consider also the module in my brain that prevented me from seeing what Luda was up to until it was too late.

I thought of the photograph she'd shown me in the all-night café—that predatory mask. The scimitar beak oxidized with blood or maybe hot sauce. The flesh-eating gleam in the eye of obsidian.

As instructed, I did my best to make myself comfortable in an articulated chair whose design suggested a tentative branching-out by Ikea into the lucrative area of torture equipment, or "coercion furniture" as we prefer to call it.

In less time than it took to read the warning signs and disclaimers on the walls, Elspeth Beltane, my surely pseudonymous "aesthetic practitioner" as these needle queens prefer to be known, arrived, a Goth pinball flipped off the bumpers of her little consultation room. Spinning in contradiction, Elspeth's spherical weightlessness seemed grounded paradoxically in the loam of the earth, in the sedimentary foundations of Gasglow's glacier-slashed river valley, with coarse effusive dyed-black hair leaching minerals from the soil to nourish grey roots tinted metallic purple at the tips.

Then there was her mighty matronly landslide bosom, a black-upholstered bolster accounting for the lioness's share of her upper body, while the rest of Elspeth, her lower half, tapered away towards vestigial feet like tiny specialist chisels in child-sized Doc Martens, her fabulous midnight substance diminishing towards the floor as black sand sieved through the wasp waist of an egg timer.

You must be Luci—she said.

As ever in situations like these, I supposed I must. Like most people above a certain age (*shhh*—forty-six!), she recognized Luci LaBang aka "Graeme Mott" from the reality show, rather than the two ground-breaking, award-winning, Channel 6 series.

I'm Elspeth Beltane—she said—*we spoke on the phone*—

You might think we did, but that wasn't me—I corrected her, regretting the pedantry when she seemed so nice. *That was Luda.*

You sound very alike—Elspeth said, pottering around in search of the sharp, invasive tools of her trade as if behaving like a Nazi dentist would put me at my ease.

She talked me into it—I maintained. *I thought I'd get away with being forty-four forever!*

That was my go-to if I was ever restrained and tortured by the cosmetic police after they'd brought me to book for frightening

264 - GRANT MORRISON

consumers on Main Street with my new countenance born in the eighth circle of Dante's Inferno where frauds do your hair and makeup then present you as garish foregone conclusions for damnation in the lower *bolgia*.

Elspeth Beltane expressed amazement that I'd come this far without having any work done, which only set me to wondering—how far had I come and how bad did I look at the end of the expedition?

This crawling insinuation, this insidious suggestion that I'd spent my entire life fondly overestimating my attractiveness, brought with it an unwelcome and yet somehow irresistible new way of berating myself.

Where, prior to that day, I'd greeted the face in the mirror as a delightful and well-regarded caller, I was beginning to understand that what others saw in me might be a crudely thrown-together tribute to self-delusion.

I could tell this was a fresh scab I'd never tire of picking until the wound below refused to heal, its suppuration welcomed.

As I settled back in my "aesthetic practitioner"'s chair, I tussled with a brief blindingly reasonable compulsion to get up and run like fuck; the rebel patient in a hospital drama, tearing out the drip lines, hurling the oxygen mask in the trash, and lurching for the exit dressed in a flapping bare-arsed paper gown. This wasn't me! My lifelong commitment to decadent artificiality notwithstanding, there were levels of irreversible self-deception even I wasn't fully prepared to endure.

My girlfriend talked me into it—I said hoping to justify the whole misguided endeavour, as if to remind Elspeth I wasn't so ugly and malformed as to be disqualified from normal human relationships. *I say girlfriend, we're working together. Actors. I hate needles.*

There's nothing to worry about—she assured me. *All the young girls are doing it. Twenty-one-year-olds. Botox improves your muscle tone.*

As she gave me the sales pitch, Elspeth went to work on my skin, priming the canvas with cleansing wipes.

I thought I was getting away with it—I said. *That's all. I knew I wasn't.*

She didn't respond, instead asking—*Can you move some of the muscles in your face for me?*

Why?—I said as I smiled, snarled, raised my eyebrows. *I get paid for this sort of thing*—

A bit more if you don't mind—she said, prompting me to run through my Eva Fraser facial massage routine the way you'd practise a karate kata. *That's better*—she said, nodding. *It helps me find the best place to inject.*

Now you tell me—I said.

Seeing the look on my face, she did her best to console me—*You've not to worry, love. You won't need facial exercises after this.*

I hate needles, that's all—I began but she gave me no time to elaborate.

You won't feel a thing—Elspeth lied as she squirted air bubbles in a tiny fountain from a syringe, then moved in on me. *Think of this as liquid youth, my darling.*

I let out a thin whine, a rendering in pointed onomatopoeia of the needle's freezing tip as it glided under the skin of my forehead glabella in the middle of a sentence. I tried to take my mind off the moment by picturing a silver submarine slicing down through the surface tension of the waves, the flesh, delivering its deadly payload.

This goes in under here. We freeze the muscle there; you'll look fifteen years younger.

It feels like cheating—I said. *I don't deserve it.*

I knew that sounded ridiculous coming from me, mistress of the art of deception and Glamour. But I was feeling vulnerable there on the chair awaiting the next point.

She laughed. *What's wrong with cheating?*

I had no answer to that.

These at the outer corners of your eyes are your lateral orbicularis oculi muscles—she explained helpfully as she loaded another syrette with liquid toxic vanity. *Where we get crow's feet.*

That perked me up. Always alert to the potential of a pattern in random circumstance, I said—*Funny. I was thinking about crow's feet earlier. Not just the feet, the whole crow package. The complete crow.*

Swooping around among the circling crows again—I've thought about this for a while—and there's the mama bird teaching her offspring to execute a midnight holding pattern, spun flecks in the spiral playout groove of the thermals. With the focus on those ragged specks forming tea-leaf runes in my line of sight came an accompanying shift in the light, a brightening, a steep rise in definition and clarity that heralded the arrival of an unexpected altered state.

Ushered into Fairyland all unawares, I'd almost forgotten Elspeth was there until she responded to a question I hadn't asked yet.

She said—*I see things. I've got the Sight. The cards. The tea leaves. The clouds. The flight of birds. A third eye. I thought that's why you came to me*—she said emphatically, reading my mind as though it lay open like a webpage.

I nodded in the distinctive brilliance, the uncompromising authenticity of moments like these where commitments are made and honoured.

It was time to begin the next procedure; the moment I feared was all over me. Needles piercing my lips. It seemed like the kind of fetishistic ordeal a prospective Catholic martyr would opt to undergo as a fast track to the Pentecostal gift of tongues.

I thought of Jesus on the Cross, Baldur pinked by mistletoe, Odin on the ash, and the film *A Man Called Horse* where at the crescendo of his gruelling initiation into an indigenous tribe, they hung the man called Horse of the title, played by actor Richard Harris, on hooks and lines from the rafters of the lodge.

My extreme fear and discomfort in the new context of a ritual ordeal, came complete with the cries of scavenger birds and a face full of metal thorns.

Immersed to my eyelids in the purity of the present moment, way too deep to doggy-paddle back to shore, all I had left was capitulation, a surrender to the serpent's kiss of the syringe. The slim metal probe dug under my skin once more as Elspeth thumbed the plunger home.

There are more nerve endings in the lips than any other part of the body. I can verify that.

I counted as each individually caught fire. There were nine injections in all, before I gave up and went into a trance, nine points like the Nine of Swords in the Marseilles deck, a card otherwise known as "Cruelty."

I knew you did Tarot—I said and naturally, I was on the money, having already heard the answer to a question I'd only now gotten around to asking.

Thumbs up for pluck, three actors down, we persevered with the understudies, eager third-raters who don't even merit names or brief descriptions in this account of events. There are rules in this business. As every child knows, rule #1 is clear, unambiguous and to the point—*the show must go on!*

To keep the meat van of the production running as smoothly as possible in the absence of three of its vital wheels, we gleefully divided the leftover roles among the rest of the pack, like morsels of a primeval pig wrestled to its death and hauled back to the campfire in bits. Our most immediate concern was simple survival to opening night.

The Molly Stocking case trundled on, a media juggernaut where shiny new theories were minted then crushed by a twenty-four-hour rolling press, where seemingly-unassailable stories were shown to be as misaligned as ill-crafted bodywork, and where, devoid of a single screw of hard evidence to hold its component parts together, the clown mobile of the prosecution collapsed into wheel rims, door handles, and guffaws from the gallery. The traumatized songbird continued to tweet her innocence through prodigal tears. Her mental health was said to be "precarious" as if it had ever been regarded as robust by we the people.

Everyone agreed by this time—as more young women went public with new and increasingly perverse additions to his bucket list of "sex crimes to commit before you're forty"—that the boyfriend, Joss Weill, was a nasty piece of work and deserved much worse than execution by makeshift gallows. There was a groundswell of public support for Molly and online disappointment that the singer had stopped short of castrating her bastard consort while she had the opportunity. Offers poured in to chop the cock and balls off his corpse if anyone could identify its location.

The facts in the case revolved in a puzzling galliard around one principal piece of evidence, in the shape of a frustratingly-edited scene of impending congress.

A camera set up to record what should have been a potentially lucrative sex tape showed Molly Stocking in slick rubber and vinyl lingerie, her every gesture rendered into wind/rewind. The distinctive way she danced to the camera puffing on a jay was unmistakably her, while boorish Joss Weill, in background, worked his cock like a captive pithecanthropus to the robot beat of "Tigress." Dully enraptured by the liquid shimmy of Molly's departing arse, Weill snuffed coke off the flat of his thumb while coaxing his whimsical manhood to the approximate length and girth of a used eyebrow pencil.

There the video evidence came to an end as Molly draped a pair of lacy hot-pink knickers over the camera lens.

Audio briefly continued the story, delivering an *avant garde* radio drama where listeners were invited to guess what was happening and what variety of crime was being committed using quasi-surrealist sound cues. Was that the audible rasp of stripping duct tape on hairy skin, the barking of a dog, or the death-cry of a murdered young man? Did we just hear the gelatinous trickle of three-eyed goat's urine striking a steel pan? Was that a cabbage beaten to bits with a five-iron? It was anyone's guess. At one point a high-volume satanic snort seemed to rip open the fabric of being itself and the only explanation lay in the possibility of the TV remote going mad. Official sources tended to reject the option that the sound was a faithful record of the unlatching Gates of Hell.

Molly and Joss could be heard getting up and going in and out of the suite's acoustics, changing places to sounds of yelling and crying. Then there was the awful unmistakable crack of meat on meat, bone against bone. *Slut* and *whore* the vile Mr. Weill could be heard to snort, as he struck out, as she struck back. A window breaking only hinted at the beefy ogre's unstoppable priapic rage.

As the vultures of the media circled their injured prey, Molly and her lawyers were adamant: Their client couldn't have been present at this drama playing like the B-side of an old-school sound-effects record—she'd been fast asleep in her bed on a cocktail of drugs and cocktails, alone ahead of a breakfast TV interview where she'd have sniffled her way through a blow-by-blow account of her brave journey back to full mobility had an immediate warrant not gone out for the girl's arrest.

The case for the defence hung on an assortment of precarious discrepancies in several accounts of what happened after the audio—essentially, they claimed, it would have been impossible for Molly to do what she was alleged to have done.

This bulimic waif with an autographed cast on her leg clearly lacked the strength to roll the colossal ball of solid muscle and bone that was Joss Weill's head downhill, let alone drag his remaining 220 pounds of sedated muscular bulk to the balcony, where she was purported to have tipped the carcass over the railing with a bedsheet noose fastened tightly around his neck.

They had a point but through it all hotel staff stayed steadfast, swearing they'd checked Molly Stocking and "a clearly intoxicated" Mr. Weill into the Lady Ottoline suite that night. They had CCTV, signatures, even inconsolable witnesses, self-declared fans who'd worshipped at the altar of Pussyfever only for innocent selfie requests to be brusquely dismissed by the scowling ex-Pussy as she fled through the air-conditioned lobby less than five minutes after the hanged man's recorded time of death.

On the way back from the kitchen with chips and salsa—I stopped to close the door that lay ajar to Luda's room and something about my actions cast a line, a hook, shockingly landing a memory and hauling it out alive—there was Luda seated and beautiful at the little dressing table with her face dipped in close-up ambient screenshine, concentrating, recording every frame, every timestamped instant, of all those awful Pussyfever videos.

Somewhere during our first wet tech rehearsal, Dez Blue returned, all hip replacement and man sass, propped up on crutches and painkillers to stump and stagger his way down the aisle, bringing wounded Martian tripod realness to the runway.

Dez saw no reason why the Genie might not require some assistance with his mobility after being cooped up for centuries in the confines of a tiny brass lamp where, in any believable world, his leg muscles were bound to atrophy, right?

Why not a disabled Slave of the Lamp?—Dez demanded, advocating his latest trademark challenge to convention.

No one was awful enough to burst his bubble; instead, we cheered and applauded as Dez, fully resolved to represent a triumph of the human spirit over adversity, clambered onto the stage with the nerve-racking, gawky, sticks-and-skitters gait of an ill-conceived robot prototype struggling to negotiate an unforgiving assault course.

My previously fierce anti-Blue stance notwithstanding, I found myself warming to our Dez, gaining an insight into this born entertainer's determination and superhuman tolerance for pain as he gritted his teeth, sweated, spat curses, and lurched into our hearts like a man using ski poles to scale a hill of jelly.

I could practically smell the process of change occurring within myself as I developed a whole new appreciation for his abrasive style. His relentlessly uncompromising misanthropic act no longer served as blue touchpaper for my outrage but came instead as a welcome black-humoured shield against the demoralizing eldritch forces our production had attracted like so many flies swarming around the Ghost Light, blindly sensing decay.

Little did we know, as we gathered round Dez, our human Ghost Light, how readily his brave human candle would succumb to the merciless gale forces of impending doom.

Elspeth Beltane did Tarot cards and identified as a Wiccan "white witch," defying stereotype, I thought sourly. She knew I was "into the occult," as they invariably put it so as not to offend anyone.

"The occult!" There was a loaded phrase, trailing its own heady incense of dusty library shelves, forbidden volumes, clandestine convocations of gentlemen diabolists in panelled drawing rooms—implying in one word a scholarly upper-crust approach to matters of intoxicated and atavistic practice that made them seem almost respectable.

I hesitated before admitting to her that my own shamanic procedures involved a bit more fire and spunk and shadow than the average White Light Lodge prescription meds. I didn't really lend much credence to ideas about the supernatural and had my own ways of dealing with what they call demons and ghosts.

This went down like a lead *planchette* with Elspeth, who swore by the existence of angels and helpful spirit healers; she assured me from experience that reverberations of the beloved dead resounded on some diaphanous shuddering wavelength broadcast beyond the five senses.

She had no doubt that everyone we'd ever lost remained with us, woven through our circumstance, invisible on their own attenuated plane of existence, and I'm not ashamed to admit I might have indulged in some Olympic-level scoffing if what Elspeth said next hadn't effectively turned my spinal fluid to icy liquid nitrogen.

What she came out with seemed so unfeasible it called into question the nature of the afterlife itself.

There's a little girl—she said slowly, her beady eyes softening to focus on some plane I couldn't see.

H—she said, extending her corrugated necks to catch what might have been some passing scent so short-lived as to be barely there, some fleeting subtle flavour before it was gone. Then with increasing confidence—*A name with an H like a rare flower—or—a bloom—or—*

Heather—I said helpfully, grappling with a grimace I knew I couldn't control, semi-aware that the Botox would soon rob me of the ability to summon even the most basic scowl. *The name you're looking for is Heather . . .*

Heather. The first time we met, she would have been about ten. A little girl with light auburn hair. Serious and clever. Heather was my daughter, I understood, gathering armfuls of ling on the slopes of a grassy hill under the big round blue sky. Her wise sapphire-and-emerald eyes refracting the improbable colour of some rare, newly-discovered flower on a distant, heartbreakingly beautiful alien planet with rainbow rings arcing overhead.

I remember Heather's sunrise smile as she presented me with a posy of whispery white and purple and said—

I forgive you.

I woke up with tears dripping off my cheeks in the clear and scourging A.M. light of a mercy I knew I didn't deserve.

After that, Heather would show up when I was feeling especially low and she'd be there to laugh at my self-indulgences, a little more grown-up each time we crossed paths, as if her childhood had happened while I was too awake to notice the passing years.

As she got older and a little more independent, outgrowing her old clothes, I saw less and less of Heather, until one morning it came to me with a strange, sad start that I hadn't seen her for many years.

It occurred to me she'd have been twenty-one by then. Old enough to make her own way without me.

I'm so sorry—Elspeth said. I thought she might be apologizing for the pain I'd been assured I wouldn't feel but instead it was—*Did she die? I sense she's not with us but it's not clear*—

At this point, it could go one of several ways—and this is what I mean about life after death. Elspeth's impressive gifts suggested a fluffy outpost of freshly-laundered cumulus clouds, leaning Doric columns, and communal hymn-alongs; an airy upper storey where coffin suits were swapped for radiant immaculate nightgowns and everyone knew how to coax "How Great Thou Art" from the sparkling strings of an intangible golden lyre with all the natural grace and proficiency of Hendrix doing "Purple Haze"—perhaps, I could almost concede there might be a frequency, a waveband where the ringing reverberations of the dearly departed continued to resonate, ripple, and echo.

I was willing, I told her, to accept any convincing evidence for the existence of an astral plane but nowhere did there seem to be any provision in this spectral spa for lives that never were.

Did she die?—I said, so she could tell I wasn't willing to joke about this. *Did she die? Elspeth, Heather never lived.*

She didn't ask me to explain; placing instead an upraised, blood-dipped talon against her philtrum then swivelling those veined marble eyes to the ceiling before spinning them down abruptly, barrels on a one-armed bandit, to announce the jackpot.

So how is it possible she has a message for you?—she said.

I got into a taxi and rested my head against the upholstery, shaking, wrung out. She, Elspeth that is, had told me I might be a little unsteady after the jabs. As for the rest, I was still processing, still organizing.

Heather. What were the chances?

I still dream about her—I'd confessed to busty brilliant Elspeth. *She gets older in my dreams, like she would have done in real life*—I explained, adrift in my head on a captainless barque. *It's weird. I've always thought of her as Heather, I don't know why—*

That's her—Elspeth Beltane nodded, compressing her chins into three astounding flesh torques. *Heather.*

Are you saying she's real?—I hoped Elspeth could tell how close to being offended I was. *An abortion can have a ghost that grows up in real time?*—I said. She only raised a painted-on eyebrow as if the answer was self-evident.

All done—Elspeth said, briskly changing lanes. *The swelling will go down, and you'll start to see the difference in a couple of days.*

And that was that.

It takes two to three weeks to get the full effect and then you'll find it lasts for three months—she reassured me.

Elspeth Beltane cranked a lever or pressed a red stud to wind up the chair, elevating me to a seated position, in the manner of some old gilded pharaoh or other resurrected from the

tomb for a chat-show moment of honest self-appraisal. I folded
at the waist to face my new face in the patient mirror.

That wasn't so bad, now, was it?—she said, and all things
considered, I had to own up that it wasn't.

I touched fingertips to the tingling skin of my face, knowing
I should never have given in to pressure. I should have left well
enough alone.

I'd been warned to prepare for flu symptoms, bruising, a
frozen look as if I'd had a stroke. *Très chic!*

In the end there were no side effects, but I couldn't face
the possibility. I couldn't face my face. I'd betrayed the mirror. I'd admitted to Luci LaBang that she wasn't good enough
anymore. There was only one way to look attractive now and it
required surgical intervention.

The driver kept checking me out in his mirror. I'd made sure
I was sitting in the middle seat where I couldn't see my own
reflection. I wasn't ready yet.

Heather.

Crossing the sidewalk between the kerb and the door I
could feel heads swivelling to target me. Human gun turrets
rotated into firing configuration. What could they see that was
invisible to me?

Back home, I closed the door at my back and took a deep
breath. My heart was off to the races like a mechanical monkey,
banging mad cymbals together until its rusty key rotated to a
stop.

There's that bit in a film where the disfigured war hero,
hoping for the best, peels off the bandages only to reveal some
caved-in mask of horror with redistributed features that we, the
lucky audience, never get to see until maybe the last act after
the lady therapist has fallen in love with the man *inside*. It was
that moment. Time to peel the mummy wrap and face the hor-
rid music.

I prayed, head lowered, a repentant novice before a statue of Christ. The tears threading down my immobile cheeks made it look as though an android had been programmed to cry and some glycerine subterfuge was the result.

Contemplating the plasticized reflection in the mirror, my videogame countenance, I felt a prickle of arousal. At this range, with my bad eyesight in the flattering dim, I looked like an old photograph of the Troupe's androgynous sex kitten.

I looked like Luda too.

I looked young again, caught in an awkward moment imagining what it might be like to be forty. Motionless and unspoiled, a waxwork cast at high noon on my most resplendent day with the light just so.

That, or a monstrous and evil embodiment of my curdled vanity.

Heather.

I tidied. Set the mood lighting to "opaque" and then, on further consideration to "stygian" so that I could only exist as a perceptual smear on glass, lacking all identifying detail and outline. A mere prompt. A vague notion. Pepper's Ghost.

I was still there when the locks unlatched, and the door opened, breathing Luda's scent of Daisy Dream into the apartment.

So, it worked out that Luda was first to see what I'd done up close.

With sinking heart, I registered each swallowed gasp—her pupils expanding.

You look amazing—she breathed.

I talked about this up front, and I've known pro dames who'll swear they can do stage-ready makeup in fifteen minutes.

Maybe, and obviously I could if I had to, but I call that a stark lack of commitment.

It's not a dash to the final period of an appliquéd beauty spot, I tell myself and my listeners; it's not about how hurriedly you can slap on some tarantula lashes and lip gloss and secure a place in the *Guinness Book of World Records,* it's about responsibility to the role, about vanishing into Twankey, becoming the makeup. It's a rubbing-out and a filling-in.

What do I know?

It's not boasting to say I've been blessed with textbook cheekbones, but I like to accentuate them to achieve the Widow Twankey's trademark gaunt and hollow-cheeked pout, making her face an X-ray of her vanity. In certain lights she's a fashion skull in a frock. Maleficent of the laundry biz.

Me in a chair, on the throne, shitting it all out for the last time.

It's funny what you're prepared to spill to a stranger. There are no strangers, they say, just friends you haven't let down yet.

I told Elspeth how, in a distant epoch bracketed by my twenty-third and twenty-eighth birthdays, I'd made up my mind to give it a go as a traditionally-gendered young man on the alternative arts scene. I'd fallen head over heels for a design school girlfriend with the lips and bed-tousled hair of Brigitte Bardot, the eyes of a *lamia* from mythology, chain-smoking roll-ups with a fuzz-toned voice and a laugh like champagne bubbling in the gutter.

Over time I tried to convince us both it was her I wanted, but in truth, in retrospect I may only have coveted her wardrobe—the clingy Gaultier dresses, the sheer stockings, the spiky boots, the opera gloves—but I undertook to be the model man in our relationship, the breadwinner, the stoic, the rock, as based on some blueprint of masculinity I'd inherited from Dad and the dominant pa culture where I'd been grown like an experimental virus on a dish.

In truth, it might as well have been marriage and Rose encouraged me all the way, adding her social worker's wage to a weekly check from my job in the bookstore for six years while I honed my skills in bars doing comedy and music; I wanted to break new ground, to be beautiful and deadly like a pop cultured bacillus, an infection of unclassifiable positivity, non-duality, and sexual ambiguity. Rose hoped for a successful career, children, security. She wasn't boring, just practical in ways I still haven't mastered. She was fantastic. I wouldn't want that to be forgotten.

Rose spiked me with rocket fuel, and I left her behind on the launchpad. I put myself and my self-expression first and I'm not sure how I feel about that now.

We planned to get married, me and Rose. Rose and I. We became fiancé and fiancée in a Leap-Year exchange of intent beneath overhead garage girders I'd strung with candles and swags of tinsel and foil. There were always plans to tie a knot in it, to choke off all other possibility, but the closer they came to fruition, the more I became harder than frogspawn to hold in place.

Just Rosie and me and baby makes wee!

I couldn't face the oncoming tidal wave of nappies; I was twenty-seven years old. I couldn't cope with the freezing process I told myself was taking place. I was terrified I'd harden like cement, spending my imagined potential, setting into one permanent shape, one specialized role before I'd tried all the others and found the one that made sense of me. The prospect of being some ungrateful brat's dull dad for the rest of my life brought on ice-cold flop sweats, 3 A.M. to 4 bleak roundelays of recrimination.

I couldn't talk Rose out of it, not at first, so of course I had to bring it all down. I felt the need to make rubble of possibility. Reduce the girl I loved and her imagined future to a debris of impossible fragments. This was my last chance to prove to myself there was more to me than her and our rented flat with shared garden.

Enter Jet, Rose's younger brother by six years; Jet was the sort of man who could straighten out an engine, score a winning goal, command a room, but there was a part of him, a little ingress point I recognized as potentially queer.

I held off for a long time. I really did. But there came a brisk shining day in May with the blossom on the apple tree like Queen Anne's lace in that Larkin poem.

Jet had sourced some MDMA from a mate at work and turned up in our little back yard on a mission of home improvement. I'd promised Rose I'd put my back into it and help her brother till the soil and plant some shrubs and lay some tiles.

As for backs, it takes at least two to make a beast.

At the risk of slipping into Twankey as easily as Jet found himself slipping into me three hours later, it wasn't the tiles that got laid that day.

Jet convinced us both the powders would turn the work of setting paving from a chore to a pristine expression of our creative souls. He had a surreal sense of humour I liked although he skewed towards being a bit crude even for me. It wasn't a problem; I saw it as my duty to be the entertaining one and kept volleying setups in a quick-change revue of madcap scenarios, a jumble of accents—Geordie, Boston, Thai pimp—harvesting blue lines from him that I'd keep in storage and thaw out for Twankey to use all those years later.

In the intensely meaningful and heartfelt counselling-session intimacy that followed the peak of our trip, Jet articulated at great length all the ways in which he was straight. Whatever had happened between us at chemical Ground Zero could be filed under the not-unexpected effects of disinhibiting love drugs, whose complex molecules were, even now, in the process of stripping our workaday selves back to pure libido and steam-engine flesh. He was a highly-sexed individual, he assured me. That didn't make him gay. I agreed wholeheartedly—we were straight by convenience, straight as the line of least possible resistance—as we knotted our bodies quite naturally into a wet blue passionate kiss under the garage rafters where I'd pledged my future to Rose.

To her credit, Rose saw through the matey wink-wink banter when she discovered us some time later, like ruffians on a Caravaggio canvas, hoplites lolling spent and self-satisfied in the garden with its half-done path. By the time we followed her into the kitchen, clattering and bedazzled, practically hand in hand and twining posies into each other's hair, she was determined to make light of her obvious suspicions.

When she questioned him about the florid love bites blooming on his neck, Jet muttered something about his girlfriend's tooth-grindy passionate nature and fled. After a few inept attempts to lie by editing the truth, persisting over three days of strenuous cross-examination, I confessed. Looking back, I did it to be cruel. I did all of it to make sure there was no way home for any of us.

Naturally, this unrepenting confirmation that her fiancé had on that day sucked her little brother's cock with vim, vigour, gusto, and brio was one more betrayal than Rose could bring herself to forgive or overlook.

She wanted to make it clear that she had nothing against boy-on-boy action. She just didn't think it made a good foundation for a long-term monogamous heterosexual relationship. A point I was obliged to concede even as I assured her that Jet most definitely wasn't gay! He'd told me so.

And I'd be lying if I said I was gay either.

I'm fine with making up my face; making my mind up is beyond my capabilities. I hope that's clear by now.

I've always known I lack the commitment to be any one thing or the other. Selected as a spokesperson for any specific viewpoint, I'd be an affront to the faithful. The chances of ever doing my homework to the required standard were slimmer than the influencers on eating disorder websites. I preferred to have options. I was queer. I was a living mess of contradictions. I felt like an alien peeking through circular spaceship windows at the world and its folly. That was the best I could come up with.

Then came that final argument—where the compacted energy of our first meeting was all used up at last, dissipated to hoarse indifference—where everything we'd seen and done together was squashed down into the sad, awkward interlude between first kiss and last curse.

After my breakup, after the agonizingly unsuccessful next attempt to form a partnership with a ten-years-younger, more brilliant, tortured, and perverse iteration of Rose's basic type who came with the addition of a prominent shaved penis, the Imperial Years arrived, all massed platinum trumpets, pomp, and distracting dazzle.

At the height of the Troupe's TV success, I found myself in bed with underwear models, male and female, a film star, rock singers, two supremely evil, corrupt, and inked oligarchs, and a famous married footballer who was later captured for all to see splayed with mental black pupils staring into the true-life floodlights of some afterparty hotel suite, arms around a pair of underaged wild-boy hookers.

On the day Rose walked out, all that hedonistic abandon was still in the future, an adolescent dream of disregard, a rejection of convention only attainable after years of toil through a wall of plaited thorns, regrets, and emotional denial.

I'd gotten what I wanted. Self-expression at all costs.

It was only much, much later that it was pointed out to me during a course of Reichian body therapy how radically dissociated I was from my behaviour, how easily I'd justified the pain I was causing to people around me as collateral damage from my fierce commitment to individualism. What a terrible cunt I'd been!

It's been a long time and now I'm trying to be honest. I'm not proud. When it comes down to it, I had terrible rock-and-role models and no stop button.

She was better off without me.

But that's never a good enough excuse for selfishness, is it?

So then, what happened?

Elspeth's voice shocked me out of my disorientated, high-heeled stumble down the vomit-varnished cobbles of Memory Lane, after dark when it got rapey.

What happened was Rose sent "Luci" a final message, acquainting her soon-to-be-ex-fiancé of her decision not to have the frightful baby after all. My baby. Her baby. Rose wasn't having it.

Me? I didn't know there was a baby. By the time I found out, it was too late to prevent the termination.

That's what I told myself anyway.

Like me and Jet during those gilded, ill-fated hours of innocent pharmaceutical love in the Garden, you can see how it all starts to come together, how the cracks spread in all directions from the point of collision, setting off the unstoppable concentric avalanche of cause and consequence that is karma.

Karma is as good a cue as any for you and me to circle back on the map to Mercy Mansions. Maybe you remember the place from before, or maybe you're checking your notes and your little charts to be sure.

Think of an ivy-scrambled red sandstone enclosure in the Gasglow Gothic style, near Spiral Park on the city's South Side where I took you all for coffee at the Rendezvous. Picture iron railings containing a concrete courtyard, with shaved lawns and tended trees, willows mostly, hung heavy with that Pre-Raphaelite melancholy and grace they're serving up; they wore late Ariel communion dresses of powderpuff-coloured blossom that day, like the Lady of Shalot in her lonely canoe.

A neat sign affixed to the brickwork requested QUIET from passing motorists.

Heather, who might have become anything she wanted to be, was edited from the narrative here, all placenta and possibility, a bloody afterbirth gathered into its bucket taxi by the prayer-scarred hands of silent nuns in the sacred awful compassionate heart of Mercy Mansions.

I fully support every woman's right to choose, don't get me wrong.

What I'm saying is no matter what, something always survives.

I'd done my time, those years after the fall of the Troupe where I could be found most days buried up to my neck in bleak volumes of pessimist philosophy, anti-natalism, speculative realism and nihilism.

After the breakdown, I walked shellshocked and medicated out of Luci's frozen bombshell image, and left her behind, pinned there on the mood board of nostalgia.

I think of my voice cracking as I read the eulogy at Mum's funeral, carrying her film and fashion books and her perishing spider plant "Steadfast" back to the apartment on Prospero Road.

Waterproof black liner for the eyes now, sweeping down the runway to take off at the tips.

There was no hint of magic in my life between the disintegration of the Troupe into five disgruntled awkwardly-shaped pieces and Dom Float's call to arms, only stark reality, pure unalloyed being that felt like a daily sandpapering down to the exposed nerves. There was no Glamour, I told myself. The Glamour was the gutted space left after a narcissistic bereavement. Stripped of his illusions, me, him, Graeme Mott was a mousy little creep who'd tricked and ensnared others in his unsettling web of make-believe.

Mine was the sobbing pain behind the tattooed mask, the greasepaint grin daubed over melancholy, the Harlequin's chequerboard armour, the jester's makeup deliquescent with newsprint tears of ink. All of that, all the time.

Where I'd admired people having fun, always smoother, slicker, and more worldly than I could ever hope to be, I now saw in my friends drunks and addicts who fell to bits at the end of the night, cracked masks and bleeding hearts cursing taxis, sick into glass slippers.

Where I'd seen heroism, rebellion, I saw instead fragility. I'd failed to register the damage trailed in my wake like a surf-white bridal train yellowed at the fringes by debris and puke. I replayed every offhand remark I'd dropped to cut someone to the quick, every nasty comment, every expertly thrown six-pointed dart of wounding shade I'd been so proud of at the time.

Where pretence had reigned, cold reality swept through the broken backstreets of Luci LaBang.

Every sad small attempt my peers made to disguise their bulimia with a baggy hoodie and an upbeat fist bump, every stab at being brave about the unexpected cancer diagnosis, every refusal to knuckle down and accept their loneliness or their failure to succeed in spite of all that talent—all futility, all dwindling, all radiating potential lost, all visible to me as sickening Roentgen emissions.

The friends who fell behind, who stumbled, whose great paintings were never seen, whose heartbreaking poetry went unread, whose unforgettable songs were never played.

And there was nothing I could do about it, except cry my eyes out so I couldn't see properly any more through a gelatin blur, a smudge across the camera lens that helped soften the heartless edges.

In later years, I came to classify my positively Christ-like sense of hopeless compassion as more sentimental projection; my unquestioned certainty that to have a talent go unrecognized by the masses was just about the worst thing that could possibly happen to anyone was not necessarily shared by others with different priorities. Under the self-congratulating guise of empathy, I was reverting to my usual snobbery and writing people off for nothing more awful than failing to be famous like me.

That's how it was, in those T. S. Eliot "Waste Land" desert days when I was dying somewhere between the ages of thirty-eight and forty-four, before the Phantom wafted into my life, when I checked out of my right mind whatever that was. I chose to confront the void and face the absence of meaning head-on.

By the time David Bailey shot me for GQ when I staggered out of the *Superstar Survival* compound with my brittle broken crown askew on my brow, cruelly quoting those 'Altered Image' drag photos of Warhol, taken by Christopher Makos in 1981, my thousand-parsec stare identified me as a pop culture martyr, a media refugee, survivor of some irresistible glitterdammerung, some unimaginable apocalipstick, a ruination.

I had that T-shirt I wore throughout my mental health crisis—DEATH IS THE NEW BLACK.

If it can't condense to a slogan punchy enough to scrawl across your tits, is it a philosophy worth expressing? That's what I always say, but here I was screaming for help in Verdana Pro Black two-inch type.

Without Luci LaBang to hold my hand and guide my steps, I was out of control on the existential dance floor. My moves, once admirable, were the out-of-touch contortions of age, the cringey twists of the dad I'd never be. Past a certain birthday, even the most seductive disco shimmy turns sleazy, ill-advised, lacking in charm.

It was all of it pyrotechnics to distract us from that flaking perimeter of a black crater at the centre of everything, that waits for us to catch up to the hospital bed at the end where the days of our lives concertina behind us, when the claustrophobic collapse of possibilities into one terminal state, one inescapable impossible now, draws to its conclusion. Here. Now. Staring you in the face.

Steady on, Lu—I hear you say. Why don't we all just slit our wrists if that's all we have to look forward to?

And I know what you're saying, you're saying—*I thought this was funny drag queen stuff. All quips and innuendos, not this heavy-going.*

Well look at it this way, babes: The universe is laughing and that can only mean one thing—if you're not laughing along, it's laughing at you!

It wasn't worth explaining any of this to Elspeth Beltane that day in the chair, the Mercy Seat. The full story, even in *précis* form, would have chewed too deeply into her next client's valuable appointment time.

Are you sure you're okay?—she asked, with what I took, quite cynically, to be a naked, avaricious concern in her charcoal-black eyes. It was all too easy to picture her as a ravenous raven, pausing to ensure her roadkill prey wasn't 100 percent putrid before stabbing the beak back into the tender flesh.

I told her I had lost the conviction it would take to quantify or define "okay," but I could be certain of one thing.

"Okay" would never be good enough.

Twankey quivers with excitement as she hovers behind Aladdin, a carnival balloon inflated to emblazoned glory.

It's just an old lamp—she shrugs. The Widow can't bring herself to believe something broken and rusty might share in the powers of the gods. She's been let down by life too many times and it's only when she finds a way to compare the Lamp to herself that Twankey gives Aladdin leave to kick-start the plot.

Well, look at me—I said, using myself as an example of my thesis, while Luda sneered. *I may be past my best, but I still polish up a treat!*

If it polishes up like you, we're in big trouble—says Aladdin aka Luda, mastering her role, her technique, making the rest of us skip through hoops to keep up with her elastic improv. *The last time you stopped traffic you were passed out drunk in a zebra print dress in the middle of the road!*

Luda presented the dented, green-mottled, verdigris-encrusted, heat-blasted old Lamp so that it hung between us, our eyes meeting across the projecting wick of the outsized prop.

Let's SEE, shall we?

She knew I was hurt, wounded below the Plimsoll line and shipping brine.

She raised her cuff, like Batman sweeping his umbrella cape across his face, then she buffed the Lamp with three exaggerated Paganini arcs of her sleeve, followed by an accusing glare.

There was a single tremendous bang timed to a magnesium flash and the Lamp lit up from within, revealing its magic in a renovating blaze.

Dez Blue took his cue like the consummate professional he'd always been; despite severe hip and spine injuries, he spun like a barstool granted life to hit his mark so accurately I felt I was watching a pratfall run in reverse.

How may I serve you?!

Here's where Twankey does a double take, flapping away the rags of violet smoke that swirl around the Genie's return to the material world. She thinks about it then brings it back down to earth scanning a roll of paper with a weighted end that drops all the way to the floor.

As a matter of fact, I've had one or two ideas!—says the Widow Twankey.

After rehearsals, as I zipped up my belongings, Dom Float surfaced like Moby-Dick or an asteroid threatening mass extinction, blotting out the light.

I thought you should have it—he said, thrusting a fluoro-pink

Post-it note so aggressively into my line of sight I thought he planned to label me.

What's this?—I said.

We've had an enquiry—he said.

Scribbled on the note were a string of numbers and in all-caps the word *LUDA???*

Looks like someone from her past trying to get in touch—said Float, already moving on to the next phase of his life without a backward glance. *I thought you could pass it on . . .*

Five minutes later, I called the number and left a message.

The mantra I'd splashed out on all those years ago didn't help; I couldn't seem to settle. I knew there was something about what I'd done that could never be taken back. It was different for young queens, I told myself. Nothing you did when you were young had consequences. Those came later. Mascara runs at 3 A.M. made you sexy, not sad.

I'd betrayed my own skin. When the toxin dispersed under the surface, petrifying muscles I never knew I had until they were sealed in place, a horrible admission of fear would be tattooed on my skull for all to see. The wind-tunnel tightness suggested a supersonic ghost train ride, a thanatotic hurtle towards the exit doors.

What would it be like when I lost the ability to frown my displeasure, when that smooth, inarticulate forehead prevented me from ever again doubting? I had become a premonition of my own resting coffin face preserved in a snapped instant of time no mere emotion could shift, not even with a dynamite chaser.

I touched my cheek. It felt spongy, congealing to the consistency of loft insulation, as if I had to be careful not to leave my fingerprints in it. When I prodded my fat sexy lips, there was nothing there but anaesthetized negative space.

I'd revelled in flux and metamorphosis, until the Gorgon,

Medusa Madame Beltane with her viper's-nest hairdo, pinned me ossified and unawares in her glare. The needle fangs of Momma B's rattlesnake dreadlocks fastening deep in my face to pump me full of *botulinum,* freezing one uniquely dull moment of freakish unchanging stillness on my face.

From this day, I would wear the impassive artificial mask of the mannie-queen. Of all the shapes and faces I could be, I'd settled for this vacant passport portrait!

Glumly, I was forced to concede I had ventured into Von Aschenbach territory. The black toxic dribble of eyeliner through layered foundation would mark as a boundary the pad-locked Gates of Eden, where in yellow letters fifty years tall the universe confirmed in no uncertain terms—*You will never again fuck a golden youth* . . .

Trying to look younger is the essence of tragedy. With Luda around, the effort was laughably pointless.

And yet there it was again, that face, the face of Luci LaBang that I'd left behind in my hurry when I was unceremoniously shown the door out of my untamed thirties. There it was again, unchanging, serene as a trophy head in a wooden frame, behind glass.

And I had my wardrobe; I still liked to imagine her in all my old clothes, bringing them back to life. I took every opportunity to pass on some fabulous dress, pair of supernaturally-fitted thigh boots or stainless-steel boned corset ensemble. Luda would accept these hand-me-down gifts of my fashion history with a shrug, but she never wore them around me.

The only time I'd catch sight of her decked out in one or other of these secondhand extravagances was to glimpse Luda slipping out the door after midnight, going wherever it was she went.

And underneath it all, below the pack ice, in the substrate, among the roots of the underbrush, was the rustling creep of an ever-encroaching spookiness; shadows thickening to ugly psychic bruises on the self-esteem, their cobweb crookwork clotting as shady corners seeped across walls, ceiling, and floor to become the whole room with all the lights out. In that stifling, drunken obscurity, insidious possibilities spawned monsters.

If everything she told me was true about the Marvells, what was Luda, I asked myself, but a creature born and raised in an upside-down twenty-first-century fairy story?

I thought of the temperature drops, the stopped clocks, the mysterious upbringing.

Wasn't there, hadn't there been from the start, something about Luda that came with the joss-stick spice of the truly, authentically *supernatural*?

At this point in the narrative, it was hard to be certain of anything. Even the most outlandish explanations for the prevailing atmosphere of collapse and disorientation seemed worthy of serious consideration.

Was Luda a luscious *doppelgänger,* the Sister Hyde to my Jekyll, the Dorianna Gray to my rotting Picture?

Was she some manifestation of those small, personal crimes and misdemeanours we fuss over, those transgressions long thought buried, now disinterred to haunt anxious days and insomniac nights?

Was Luda the deadly avenging avatar of sky-blue possibilities I'd squandered in some mirror during some drug-trip breakdown half a lifetime ago?

Here's the elevator pitch: Narcissus absconds from the reflecting pool and makes it his primary objective to seek and destroy his ugly, compromised, disillusioned future self before it can happen!

Was Luda a Cautionary Tale made flesh?

Elspeth's last words to me had been—"Be careful . . ."

Careful of what? Drunk drivers? Loose bathroom tiles? Coughing strangers? Betrayal?

In all my elaborately-conjectured scenarios, you may notice

Luda relegated to the role of shadow projection, a troubling *tulpa* summoned into fleshly reality as some miscast spell powered by ugly personal neuroses. Looking back, I can see I was already trying to dehumanize her, already preparing my justifications for what I might have to do to survive her.

As I, Luci LaBang, narrator, basked in the soft, silent dark at the bottom of my tank, there was no limit to the contortions of speculation. The regrettable flipside of a colourful imagination is a flair for summoning night-horrors and floppy disfigured hell-things . . .

Ask the Romantics.

I say that but it's more likely these tales of mystery and imagination that preoccupied my mind were concocted to obscure a more troubling conclusion I could hardly bring myself to flirt with.

The idea's sole virtue, that of distressing plausibility, failed to make it any more palatable.

I trod the ugly writhing conjecture down into the mud at the back of my mind and decided to explore some brighter avenues of investigation.

But the unthinkable wouldn't stay unconsidered and bubbled up again as blossoming florets of filthy black silt . . . septic suspicions, infected qualms . . .

There was something about Rose and the baby that never was. Something incomplete. There was a rusty saw-toothed trap set to spring behind Heather's sweet smile.

During the breakdown I'd lived in denial of the Glamour and its implacable responsibilities, but I couldn't look away from the sequin dazzle forever, I couldn't turn my back on the promise I'd made the mannie-queen to at the very least be entertaining. Like a probing tongue, relentless self-examination revealed unfilled cavities, feeling out mysterious foundations, identifying Work that remained to be done.

Destiny had me down for something big I decided.

My comeback came first.

The Phantom, a play that consumed its cast. A story reflecting its own pathology, a dramatic brew so rich, a Glamour so heady it had begun to slop over the barrel into our real lives, recapitulating my catastrophic mental and physical breakdown, my emotional journey, into life-affirming drama and song.

I half expected a last-act reveal; the blurred lines that no longer served to separate fact from fiction in the case of *The Phantom of the Pantomime* would turn out to be a meta-marketing masterstroke as played by Dominick Float and the publicity department. There was still an open invitation for rationality to ride to the rescue.

The Glamour can be so seductive and so convincing it's easy to mistake it for the real thing—like those inexplicable discarded totems on shadowless beaches Yves Tanguy painted and J. G. Ballard wrote about—abstract driftwood and dream jetsam that stood in for more complex emotions, their obscure arrangement substituting for an urgent, untranslatable *cri de coeur* from the dark of the mind.

I mean, why not?

I pushed lightly with my fingertips and the door to what we'd both come to think of as Luda's room swung silently open on its oiled hinges.

She didn't have much, and what she had was concentrated like a white dwarf star into this space. I no longer believed there was a plague of cockroaches at her mythical place. There was no place.

When Luda wasn't here, she might as well be nowhere. Her whole life could be subtracted into a single bag of clothes and shoes, cosmetics and condoms. It was why she borrowed my heels, however reluctantly. She owned nothing.

Like I said, Luda was a quantum event, existing only when she was observed.

I know now and I knew then, I shouldn't have pried but pry I did. I felt compelled to ease our closet door open to rummage below the hems of splendid coats and dresses for her Goodbye Kitty! bag.

I paused to register the little key-ring ornament dangling from the bag handle—a plastic vulture from some cartoon or famous animation I could barely recall. *Lion King* most likely, or *The Jungle Book*.

The painted eye regarded me with scorn. A predetermined panic dug in—I knew what I'd planned to do could only lead to trouble, but I went ahead with it and fished blindly inside, unwilling to look at first—a premonition—a lucky-dip scramble through the contents—lipsticks smeared to stumps, brushes and mirrors, Q-tips, face wipes, an enigmatic tub of fish paste.

Intruders, my fingers searched by shape and contour alone, moving with a delicate prudence as if expecting to encounter a Black Widow's hairy feelers and dripping fangs in there. It wasn't long before I found what I instantly recognized as the things I didn't know I was looking for.

First there was a wig. No surprises there, you might think in this story of drag queens and drama. At first, I couldn't identify where I'd seen the familiar style. It wasn't one I'd seen Luda wearing.

When it came to me, it came the way it might to a passenger on a runaway train, careering downhill, with no way to halt the momentum of events.

I was reminded of the particular unnatural shade of Molly Stocking's hair extensions—a cut she'd made her own, bravely taking a bullet for a whole generation of women who might otherwise have gone out looking like that—it seemed impossible.

A further fumble and rummage only made things worse;

now I held in my trembling hand a *shoe*. In every way the shoe was ordinary but one awful detail made it special.

The shoe with its blunt and broken heel belonged to Molly Stocking. The left. Someone, I wondered who, had taken a hacksaw blade to the block heel, broken it carefully along the fault line where Molly had cracked hers on the day she bowed out of *The Phantom*.

It might seem like a moment of shocking revelation but looking back, I was mostly baffled. I held in my hands what seemed to be damning evidence of unfathomable crimes, but I knew Luda was a long way from stupid. I didn't have to make a trophy-winning standing long jump to the conclusion that she'd left these clues for me to find. This did little more than add to the mystery, as you can imagine—flywheels struggling in the cogwebs of the mindmills of your wind . . .

Where Luda was upon me. I froze like a pervert foraging through a neighbour's daughter's underwear drawer. A "knee-creeper" my mother used to call them.

I'd already put her bag away—in its place, I lifted a blame-less tin of rosin, posing with it like a housewife in an ad.

I've been looking for this—for you—put this on your shoes you'll fly across the stage.

She took the tin, suspiciously.

Roll us up a jay, then—I said, all innocent.

There had been something else in there that I recognized. This time I knew it by touch—the tactile memory of those fidgety buckles and straps came with an electric shock of recognition.

Next to the broken fetish, the talisman that was Molly Stocking's shoe, had been my Little Shoe Box peep-toe plat-forms, missing since the night of the party.

Crows glory in the most effortlessly cool, most defiantly metal of the animal kingdom's collective nouns so in order to compete, vultures have at least five available varieties depending on when you see them and what they're up to; when a gang gathers in a waiting huddle like swags of feathered fruit in the bare branches, they're called a "committee."

When they descend to feed, it's a "wake."

Where it got more complicated, more elaborate, baroque, and frankly Mephistophelean in its cat's-cradle intricacy was this . . .

Elspeth had been clear about one thing; activating her Spirit-Vision she'd peered beyond the veil—which I have to say feels like a bit of an invasion into postmortem privacy—where Heather was engaged in what appeared to be an ancient, star-shaped board game. Alice in the Underworld, only turning her head from the intricacies of the play when she sensed the presence of a Peeping Tom observing from the sordid solid world.

According to Elspeth, Heather shook her head solemnly and spoke three words—

She's behind you.

Oh no she isn't . . . I tried to convince myself.

Rehearsals took on colour and substance, a *ligne claire* drawing filling out with rim lights, shadow, texture. As we drew closer to opening night, we were pulling six full run-throughs a week, bone-weary from singing and dancing, drilled down to parade-ground war-machine efficiency.

When it comes to Aladdin's grand arrival at the palace, the Genie has it all worked out, arranging circumstances so that events flow naturally the way a stream joins a river, and, borne on a tsunami of hallucination, the boy-king arrives at the head of a parade of wonders.

With a start, the princess connects the young gender-neutral pinup with the vision she caught sight of in the Market scene. Confused and uncertain, she agrees to consider his coarse hand in marriage based on nothing more than good looks and a flair for performance.

Her wayward, scatterbrained, spendthrift mother, the Empress—a sleepwalking May Tang-Taylor, and I'm sorry but I've danced with livelier hat stands—is only too happy to forge an alliance with a fabulous and impressively polite, super-wealthy young prince from a land of gold no one's ever heard of. His arrival in a flying chariot pulled by a team of tame rocs suffices to quell all doubts, and the stacked treasure chests take care of any misgivings that may have survived the original quelling. Aladdin, let's remind ourselves, is a street urchin wielding the power of gods to reshape reality on a whim.

It's a big scene, exhausting when you've been playing it on

repeat a few dozen times, when you'd be forgiven for thinking, even hoping, it was the last scene. Sorry, we're barely midway through act 2.

I flapped offstage. Twankey, installed in the royal palace in the run-up to Aladdin and Jasmine's wedding, sports another outrageous fashion confection the *djinn* has conjured for her, this time a feathered overindulgence that fluttered around me like ghosts having a pillow fight.

Sat in the front-row stalls, pouffing feathers from my sticky red lips, I guzzled expensive springwater and surveyed how it might look from the house. The blocking was the work of a dangerous obsessive, but I had to admit, it was fabulous. It played from every angle.

I was part of something special. Something unique and un-repeatable. Like a thumbprint or a fart.

I'll say it again and not for the last time: Dominick Float is deserving of his genius reputation, there's no doubt about that. But it was his destiny to die obese and misunderstood like Orson Welles. Nobody cares how clever you are.

Following a short, disconcerting scene where the Phantom brings Abanazar kicking and screaming back into the story, we restart the action as the wizard fumes like an alchemist's retort.

Abazanar's sexual frustration is telegraphed to the adults in the audience when every soldier's pike he passes is gripped to sudden erection by tight gloved fists while the young couple finally sing their song of asexual oneness together on the palace balcony, the bright voices intertwining sinuously in fluid counterpoint.

We two can be two together!

On that note, Aladdin bows out in a flurry of stars, vowing to meet Jasmine again on their wedding day. He hasn't told her about the Lamp or the Genie or how he came to his illimitable power, his incalculable wealth. He's promised himself he'll let her in on his secret eventually, but Aladdin feels guilty. How can he kick off their relationship with a lie?

What if Jasmine turns him down when she discovers he's just a street kid, the dishonest son of a lowly, vulgar washerwoman?

Overhearing from the next room her beloved son's frank, dismissive appraisal, Twankey's heart breaks. Can he truly be so ashamed of her, after everything she's done for the boy? It's the first time we've seen the old Dame's soft side and the catch in her throat never fails to get a big *aaaah* reaction like wind through eucalyptus leaves.

What then?

As he departs, perking himself up with a reminder that tomorrow is another day, the lovestruck Aladdin makes the biggest mistake of his life: He leaves behind him the wonderful Lamp. No matter how hard the audience tries to alert him to his mistake, Aladdin's lost in self-censure and love, soused on a cocktail of contradictory emotions.

There's a last feeble warning flicker as Aladdin exits, then the Lamp goes dim.

They all think you look much better the way you do—she said.

And yes, we'd made up yet again and I had to agree with her. I couldn't say no to Luda.

I've been hard on you I can't deny it. And I know what you're thinking, but I didn't just say that to slip in a hard-on where you'd least expect it!

It can't be easy, tacked like helpless bluebottles to the adhesive strips of my delusions. How can you be sure I'm talking sense, let alone telling the truth?

I've admitted I live for deception, trickery, and illusion, which makes me the epitome of the unreliable Narrator.

What would they be like, the characters, the main players in this drama, if you met them at a party? Would you even recognize them from my sketchy, bitchy, shorthand descriptions, my cheap-and-easy scorched-earth, fuck-you stereotypes of lovers and colleagues?

How reliably could you identify in a "real life" lineup any of the cast of complex human beings I've reduced to comedy routines or handpicked to play enthralled planets in rapt orbit round my dazzling sun?

It can't be easy when someone you've never met, someone like me, asks you to reevaluate your definition of what's real and what's not. Especially in matters of the judiciary.

I know I've tested your patience with rambling accounts of dreams, memories, and drug hallucinations. I've discussed the deviant customs and beliefs of a quasi-pagan psychedelic sex, drugs, and drag cult as if dictating the minutes of the Annual General at the local Community Council headquarters. I've presented you with a gonzo cosmology for the nonbinary theatrical classes that puts all of us centre-stage where we belong, in the spotlight.

I've required you to keep up and keep an open mind and if you've managed to persevere so far, this next bit should separate the men from the goats, the women from the nannies, and the rest of you from everyone else!

At this point, when your minds are more than likely not just open but positively gaping and rosy, it's time to introduce a new concept, a new alibi, in the form of what they call a p-zombie.

I know what you're thinking, and I'm happy to give you all the time you need to compose yourselves while I get some cream contouring organized, filling in the painterly shadows on my cheeks and along my inked and adjusted jawline to mimic the favourable light of a California sun that isn't really there.

I'm with you; if you're anything like me, the words *pee zombie* are likely to set off predictable eruptions of mental video; scenes of golden showers, walking putrefaction, spattering rains of shiny urine sluicing through decaying flesh and rotten fabrics.

That's how I pictured it anyway. Your mileage may vary.

Then again, maybe you're way ahead of me on our headlong plunge into the unreasonable. Maybe you're thinking vampires drink blood, *ergo* it stands to reason these p-zombies have drawn the shortest of straws, cursed to survive on a diet of salty hot piss. With phlegmy cries not of "*Brains!*" but "*Bladders!*" they stalk their still-breathing game.

I like how your mind works, but in this case, we're dealing with a different flavour of horror altogether, and a more troubling monster. P-zombies are more insidious than the traditional shambling corpse brought up to date with a urine fetish.

I wish it were that easy.

The *p* in *p-zombie* stands for "philosophical," and I'll tell you how that works, and why it's relevant in a bit, but first we have to strap in and jet back to the progressively intense rehearsals for *The Phantom of the Pantomime* where a cracked, familiar voice can be heard above the empty lilt of the desert wind, crying—*New lamps for old! New lamps for old! New lamps for old!*

Dominick Float had made undeniably important, inventive adjustments all around by subjecting *The Phantom* to the same merciless, objective appraisal I'd brought to my flagging features.

In Dom's vision, the Phantom creeps around to the atonal lament of a desert sirocco, as generated by the prop boys and their antique wind machine.

Coming closer, ghostly, insistent on the still-warm October wind, we can make out a spicy jangle of cheap metals and the wavering cry of an elderly street vendor.

The Princess Jasmine swans in her nightie onto the balcony as gorgeous Dayanita Jayashankar, clutching protective talismans of all faiths in her impossibly pretty fist—I saw a Star of

David, a New Age crystal, a Christian cross, a yin-yang medallion, a Saint Christopher's, some Buddhist blessings taking the form of miniature hand-painted *thankas;* you name it, our Dee swore by its efficacy, as she stood in her unique moment, trusting this polyholy, anti-viral injection of full-spectrum devotion to inoculate her against all evil.

As Jasmine, trusting daughter of the Empress of Peking, turns Aladdin's battered and oxidized Lamp over in her hands, she concludes that the only reason her fabulously wealthy new boyfriend left it behind is its little obvious value. Perhaps he hopes someone in the palace will be able to repair it.

Or even better, replace it!

New lamps for old!—comes the fortuitous cry.

Eager to demonstrate her love with a meaningful gesture, Jasmine's song pushes the plot forward into the darkness of act 2's sombre conclusion—because what earthly use could a pockmarked oil-burner be to anyone, let alone the Girl Who Has Everything and the Boy Who on Top of Everything Also Has Her?

The audience by this time is cresting a crescendo of panic—*NOOOOO!*

What's that?—says Jasmine. *I can't hear over all this noise.* While she cups a hand to her ear, pretending to strain over the rising warlock wind now lifting the tassels on the awnings, bringing the clamour and clash of the approaching vendor's cart and the call—

New lamps for old!

That's it!—she cries. *New lamps! For old!*

NO!—they wail as one from pits to nosebleeds but it's too late. Jasmine has been raised expecting things to turn up when she wants them.

New lamps for old—the vendor screeches as his shadow elongates across the wall like spilled paint.

He's behind you!—

I could hear the crowd's multi-tracked warning in my head

as I scrutinized the performances and committed to muscle memory Float's clever stage proxemics.

It was impossible not to sneak an upward peek into the cranky *macramé* of the overhead bars, without expecting to see a glancing shadow bristling with murderous intentions.

My phone buzzed in its bag. Number unknown. I'd set something in motion. I'd sent out a signal. I didn't expect to be so surprised when it was returned.

As our play unfolds, with the prompt desk taking the place of Gofannon Rhys, you'll just have to imagine how Abanazar has sidled greasily into the scene, hunched and bedraggled in the guise of a superannuated peddler. In exchange for unwanted junk, he offers from a selection of fashionable golden lamps inlaid with faceted jewels, fantastic metals, and the colours of local football teams.

Aladdin will be so happy when he finds I've swapped his useless old lamp for a shiny new one—Jasmine tells herself, to groans and hisses from the auditorium. Dazzled deaf to their warnings, the princess freely trades the magical Lamp for a sparkly cut-price replica. Only a princess brought up in complete ignorance of the value of things, a young woman to whom diamonds were common as freckles, could make this mistake.

All hope lost, the devious magician throws off his disguise to stand tall in the ballooning canopy of his robe, sneering at the coterie of callow fools he's hoodwinked. Aladdin and Jasmine. Twankey. All our sympathetic cast members revealed as dupes, victims of the master manipulator and his crafty misdirection.

Boos and hisses attend his every exaggerated gesture as Abanazar hoists the Lamp aloft like a sports trophy, controller of the captive Genie within! Cackling possessor of a power supreme!

Rolling deep in his newfound supremacy, Abanazar's first miracle is to transport the entire palace, including Jasmine and her protesting mother, the Empress, back to his homeland in Egypt!

I know!

Can we try that over again?

I could have throttled Dom Float by then if it had been possible to get my fingers round his neck.

That day, another Wednesday, its scant difference from all the others measured only by an incremental reduction of daylight hours, we were twenty minutes into rerunning the show's second-act Street in Peking scenes and we'd still gotten the last five minutes on repeat, reliving every move, every reaction the way a goldfish gets through life, or the way mum got through her last year and a half.

Over and over and over again since opening night in this very theatre six years ago—I complained. *And it's always the same!*

Dom materialized beside me, a portly NPC respawning in a videogame, popping up from his Lamp, expertly sensing my suicidal impulses from fifty paces and curious to know if I was "okay."

I was exasperated—*You've got us drilled like clocks in Prague!*—I said. *Actors are human beings—I mean, let's not go that far but—*

It's going to be great!—he shot back. *When everyone feels the underlying framework like it's their own nervous system, that's when you can be truly spontaneous. Great's the very least of it!*

I said—*You'll just jinx us saying that*—already wondering which of our merrie band of sacrificial lambs was earmarked for the mint sauce. By the time the Phantom was done, there might be no one and nothing left but recipes for disaster. Dom suggested I take the rest of the day off as long as I kept away from blades, lengths of rope, and labelled bottles from the drugstore.

Isn't it a bit weird this is the exact plot of the Phantom?—Dee Jayashankar suggested somewhere near the end.

No one had a retort. We'd gone way beyond "a bit weird" some time previously.

She was trying to make light of it but there was a sullen overhang, a low ceiling of growing unease and suspicion.

What was the point if all this was already written?

Not quite home, I sat on the wooden bench in Observatory Gardens, bearing its scratched commemorative plaque to a Labrador service dog named Peter, with the rose window of our local church, a *faux* Sainte-Chapelle, framing my head in a stained-glass halo. The disquieting ozone charge of a whole new *déjà vu* sizzled bitterly on the tip of my tongue.

I faced an unfamiliar name in my inbox. CALLER UNKNOWN seeking another route to my attention. I opened the box, Pandora-style, to find a MISS SPALDING appearing like a shark breaking cover to toss the cat among the pigeons.

Can we talk about Luda?—Miss Spalding's brief message read, and I could almost taste the bait wriggling on the hook.

I called her. "Miss Spalding." Of course I did.

I'm calling about Luda—I said. *Your reply to my message. Do I know you?*

There was a pause before the phone went down, leaving a ringing burrrr.

In the time it took me to react as though I'd been stung by a hornet, the phone rang and rang twice.

I'd rather not talk on the telephone—she said, being she obviously. *You're familiar with the art museum*—

Accounting for the fact that Calvin's Gallery was one of the most famous buildings in Gasglow, visited as a rite of passage by generations of parents and their children, the question seemed redundant.

Friday?—she suggested. *Four o'clock?*

Friday afternoon was polishing, and I was expected onstage.

It wouldn't look good if I just walked out, I thought, but I couldn't see a choice.

So, I said—*Yes, Friday's good—I'll be the one wearing a pink negligée.*

She didn't laugh. Whatever the guttural werewolf growl she uttered was, it could never be mistaken for a laugh.

The palace in Peking has gone, as if it was never there at all.

Even the Empress is homeless. Following the supernatural evaporation of her opulent crib and its lavish contents, May Tang-Taylor who portrays her has been required to downscale. Airs and graces notwithstanding, the sovereign's struggling to adapt to a dung hill aesthetic where a broken China cup might as well be the Holy Grail or the Crown Jewels.

Aladdin, for his part, having endured a blinding glimpse of the promised land, is caught suspended between two magnificent harridans from opposite ends of the class spectrum. The Empress never tires of telling our Principal Boy he's a liar and a fake, the Widow never wearies of weighing in to defend her thirty-*denier* gloss-tights-wearing son.

Now the Empress huffs indoors, all Blanche DuBois with the back of her hand tacked to her expansive forehead, revolted by the smell, the noise, the everyday poverty of life in the backstreets of a Peking she'd only ever known as a gilded confection of soft cushions and attentive servants.

The spell has worn off. The Glamour has lost its sheen. Aladdin's back in the flashy rags he started with, turning out moth-eaten pockets, rich only in holes. Twankey, stripped of her Crown Jewels and ermine meteor trail, is reduced to thriftstore improv with shredded newspapers as a dress and a bin lid for a fascinator, contriving to look like she's turned up for an alternative fashion show dressed in a Vivienne Westwood fever dream.

We have to do something!—Twankey resolves, hoping she won't have to come up with what that might be.

You heard what she said—when Jasmine finds out I lied to her, it's over! Aladdin plunks himself down disconsolately, racked with shame and guilt at last, like the rest of us on a good day. Buttercup tries her best to console him but he's as desolate as the absence where the palace was.

You wouldn't be lying to her if you got that Lamp back from the wizard, would you?—Twankey observed slyly. *I'm just saying, Aladdin . . .*

But how?—Luda, as Aladdin, lamented. *All we've got left is this old carpet.* Luda was good at lamenting. Her performance kept improving; once fed the basic algorithms, Luda could self-propagate, self-progress exponentially.

Maybe we could sell it—

Twankey reappraises the carpet—*I could make that into a very chic evening dress! Hand me my scissors, Aladdin . . .*

As the Widow's son locates a giant pair of shears and opens them akimbo to cut, the carpet gives a nervous ripple and tries to escape.

Did you see that?

If I didn't, someone else saw it for me!—she exclaims.

Then they have an idea.

You said it yourself—Twankey reminds her downcast son. *Sometimes there's magic in ordinary things if you know how to unlock it!*

Twankey makes the reasonable point that seemingly useless old rubbish has turned out to have hidden worth before.

Maybe it's a magic carpet!

But how to make it work? Where do you put the key? Where's the start button or the hole on a magic carpet for a crank handle?

You polish a lamp—I said, after some thought, handing Luda one of two huge swatter props.

Here Twankey usually turns to the audience—*What do you do to a carpet?*

Beat it!—they'd chorus, and she'd place a hand on her impressive cosmetically enhanced bosom, mock offended. *You don't mean that do you? I thought we were friends . . . now you want us to leave?*

BEAT IT!

Oh, you mean the carpet?—I beamed, latching on with a big wink to the children and the slow-on-the-uptake in the audience. *Well, it might just work! What do you think, boys and girls and all the rest?*

Willing to try anything no matter how unlikely, Twankey and Aladdin take turns serving up mighty slapping strikes as if attempting to spank the pattern off the shag pile.

This is ridiculous—says Aladdin. *It's never going to work!*

Put your back into it!—Twankey urges, redoubling her own two-fisted efforts to whack the unresponsive Persian rug into life.

Until just as we're both on the brink of yielding to futile exhaustion, the old mat undergoes a magical transmutation. A scintillating cloud of glitter billows from the beaten drugget along with a spluttering voice.

Enough!—it yelps in its own peculiar carpet language, all fringed vowels and tightly woven consonants, as devised by Float himself, of meaning only to him.

Rippling with an ophidian vitality, the mat snaps tetchy fringes, shakes itself down in a rippling haze of stardust, then bobs and lilts and swoops between us, defying gravity with the help of near-invisible prop wires.

I mean, how lucky can anyone get? We've found a flying carpet! Almost immediately, Aladdin sets his jaw for adventure and vaults into position on the conveniently suspended plush aircraft.

Well—says Twankey. *Help me aboard. You can't do this without your mother!*

Aladdin's reluctant; and who wouldn't be? The last thing any brave boy wants on a quest to save his princess is a clinging, raucous reminder of his low-class origins. He tries to talk her out of it but the Twankey's not for turning, and resolutely hikes up her skirts to clamber aboard the now-stationary carpet, hovering at crotch height.

And off we went, courtesy of the props team, over the pagodas and inappropriate minarets of pre-Communist Peking to exit stage left; me hanging on for dear life, shrieking until my knickers flew off in the imagined breeze, gusting away on a whirlwind of laughs, while Luda guided our Persian glider by taking hold of its ponytail tassels to stabilize our frantic flight— vowing to rescue the princess, trusting our lives to Aladdin's pilot skills and his newly-revealed way with floor coverings.

Even the elevator seemed reluctant to rise, wishing it had been installed instead in a swanky five-star hotel.

I hate hospitals. I hate the smell of disinfectant and disease. I hate the way the light goes yellow and everywhere leads to another room you might never leave.

It's not just me, right?

Some things are universal.

When I arrived at the intensive-care ward with my unlikely bouquet of purloined tulips, and the latest issue of *Hey You!* Dee Jayashankar was on her way out, wearing a *chic* anti-viral mask.

I'm surprised to see you here—I told her. It seemed she felt the same about me. I'd missed rehearsal. I was *persona non grata.*

I know he's a bigot—a very lonely bigot by all accounts—she said wisely. *I came on behalf of us all.*

Gofannon Rhys lay semi-comatose, sucking ragged breaths through a corrugated tracheostomy hose.

So far, he doesn't have much to say.

I said I hadn't come for his conversation, which as we all know could be distasteful at the best of times. To be honest, I wasn't sure why I'd come at all.

Rhys uttered a splutter before heaving forth from his bony chest an alarming chain reaction of staccato ripping barks that threatened to pick apart his skeletal structure.

Unable to spew forth from his customary sewage fountain of arbitrary curses and xenophobic disapproval of the culture and culinary practices of Mundugumor society, the venerable actor's only option was a recourse to pre-verbal offence as he commenced to masturbate wantonly under the blanket.

They said it was fish oil—I shook my head gravely, politely drawing attention away from the rubbery slap of wattle. *It got into his Tom Yum. He ate there all the time . . .*

They'd rolled him into the ward with an allergic reaction, now he had pneumonia. I could feel myself catching it too and tried not to breathe, anxious to get away.

The nurse snapped her apron, Twankey-style, to clear us from the ward as though we were chickens in the yard, or three blind mice.

What do you think of Luda?—I asked Dee outside in the car park, under the pot lid of the overcast sky. *Be honest.*

She's very good—she said. *Getting better all the time.*

Dee's beautiful face was so clouded with misgivings the effect was well-nigh meteorological.

She took my hand. *Be careful*—she said.

All I could think was, It's a bit late for that!

I'll admit this was my attempt to stress a need for spontaneous Samaritan missions to the Goff's hospital bedside, using that establishment's proximity to the Gasglow art gallery and museum as cover for a longer assignation I had scheduled.

I assured Dom that Rhys was on the mend, having successfully regained the use of his penis.

Five days later, Gofannon Rhys died, barking vile slurs in a Micronesian language no one understood.

Call me an idiot, it was only then that I remembered the inexplicable jar of fish paste from Luda's bag . . .

I opened the door and after registering a big Deliverex box, I immediately sensed an occupancy, a tenancy as palpable as a magnetic field.

I found Luda poised at my dressing table, very still as if she was impersonating a photograph of herself. Her face hung in my mirror where my face belonged.

She'd made herself up to look like an android, a Franken-stein's porn puppet, a part-plastic androgyne with her own painted lighting.

There it was, the Golden Ratio squeezing down into the plane of her right cheekbone, fuck poverty, fuck it all, whatever confluence of genetics and math had sculpted her Pythagorean proportions, the mix was exquisite. Everywhere I looked, from heel to shoulder, eyebrow to index finger, I saw the living em-bodiment of the Golden Mean; in each gesture was a Vitruvian expression of the mathematics of being.

Luda was ratio and angle all the way down, a self-replicating vortex curling around its centre in her cellular, microscopic core. Bisected, trisected, divide her any way you liked, the numbers folded together serenely through $\frac{1+\sqrt{5}}{2} \approx 1.618$ reckoned to *phi* and factors of five. She was a found object, a ready-made Platonic pro-totype waiting to be unearthed from unhewn rock.

What?—she said, never taking her eyes away from their own blue copies. *What's wrong with you?*

You touched me that one time and now you never touch me—I said feeling stupid with each word that dropped like congeal-ing molten lead from my lips to clunk on the carpet. *It's hard, Luda—I won't deny. I can't help thinking about that first night.*

There was no way to take it back.

It was your idea—she said without changing her expression. *Platonic, you said. Otherwise it's a power imbalance. It's exploitation. You're my drag mother. It would be incest.*

Hearing her say that. What could I do? I broke down and told her about the fantasies, the feelings I'd had about her, and in doing so I handed over to her the very last shreds of what power I had.

She knew me for what I was: a fool seeking solace in the youth of another, projecting my fears and fancies, elevating Luda to a pedestal she could never hope to occupy.

She had me on my knees and she knew it.

You won't tell them—said Luda, not asking but instructing.

Last time I looked—I said, keeping an even tone intended to suggest not sobriety but fury. *Murder was regarded as a crime.*

When a crowd of them get together it's called a murder of crows.

Why should I protect you?—I said eventually.

Because you made yourself responsible for me—said Luda. *Because you love me*—and I was undone.

Ruminating on the curious shape of my life, I rummaged in the kitchen drawer for the Stanley knife I'd impulse-purchased on a trip to B&Q some days before Luda's arrival into my story.

I slid the safety stud into place and the razor blades slipped out like the lolling tongues of vicious robot dogs. I deftly sliced the brown tape on the Deliverex box and folded out its cardboard flaps.

Inside was the wig I'd ordered. The ultimate wig, the archetypal wig I planned to wear for Twankey's intro. The wig that would do more than half my work for me.

Custom-made, bespoke as fuck, it resembled a candyfloss tower, a piled-high Marie Antoinette shaving-foam cloud that was bleached Bondi blond and bubble-gum pink, bobbed and cut and teased to frame my face like a work of art.

Production had paid for it, my crown to my design, awaiting coronation day.

Nursing a watery screwdriver in the bar, I had no way of judging how long I'd been in this busy hotel talking through my problems to an old girlfriend/boyfriend with a cute bob haircut and breasts I caught myself coveting, but I'd planned to get to the airport early, so that I could avoid the stress of late arrival by killing time on-site before catching my flight home.

Something about the book I was trying to read gave me a feeling of unease; what I began to suspect was a wildly inaccurate and vindictive take on my biography had been written as a single line of Times New Roman text on a very long thin strip of material exactly like measuring tape winding out of its roller in my right hand.

Bells rang periodically. I understood they had something to do with the close monitoring of the phases of the moon, the essential function of the tides and the nearby ocean, which somehow corresponded with the date and relied on my precise posture to be fully effective. I became aware with a start of how late I was for my flight back home, still disturbed by the lack of content and complexity implied by the ticker-tape book format.

Was this the fate of the novel in a world with less time for the written word? To make matters worse, it dawned on me that I'd left my luggage back at the hotel, expecting to pick it up— when? What had I been thinking? I'd checked out hours ago and the hotel was already miles away, too far from the airport to make the journey there and back and still board my flight on time.

I needed very badly to get home, but how could I leave my belongings at the hotel and get on a plane without them? As panic expanded like gas in a vacuum, taking my last breath with it, I cast around me for my coat, knowing it too was back at the hotel.

My coat was gone, and along with it my plane ticket, my wallet, my cards.

I hurried to see if there was any sign of my bags at the Lost & Found.

As it turned out, the concierge was able to identify an item matching my luggage, although the soft sports bag they produced looked nothing like the sturdy Samsonite roller I'd described.

This was a holdall . . .—they insisted and when I tried to assert the difference between a cabin bag and a hard-shell, I was immediately placed under soft arrest.

Tall, uniformed officers frog-marched me, wearing my wig and heels, into a holding area where I tried to object but no one seemed willing to listen. As I tried to decipher the barking glottal snorts of the guards, it occurred to me I wasn't even in the country where I thought I'd woken up.

They had my clothes. Not the ones from the hotel but from the racks at home. My outfits collected over years.

Are these your clothes?—they asked. *There have been serious complaints.*

I thought, Have there?, and the worry grew that this had something to do with a new movement I'd been hearing about: a protest wave of clothes denouncing their owners, even allegations of lifelong garment abuse.

Why, I thought, especially in this sensitive climate, had I caused such a fuss and deliberately drawn the attention of the officers? I was my own worst enemy, and to prove it I'd behaved in a manner so suspicious I was now being held against my will!

Is this the one?

The Alexander McQueen dress I'd gone to great lengths to secure for that wasted, victorious TV awards appearance twenty-three years ago then never worn after a better offer came in from Christopher Kane, slowly, eerily straightened its hollow windsock arm. The policemen took note of my reactions as one by one the other garments followed suit, a regiment of haunted sleeves converging on me, an *haute-couture* firing squad united in voiceless judgment.

My clothes wanted me to understand they were divorcing me, as unfit to wear them. If I wasn't knocking them out of shape, I was leaving them to rot in dark closets when what they'd been born to do was party. The degree of neglect was an affront to the Lord. Things had to change.

I had nowhere to put them. No occasion to wear them—I protested.

The mute solemnity of my rebel garments' gestures could not be clearer. I was being sentenced to life in khaki overalls and wooden clogs.

I had no idea until now how much my clothes hated me.

You can see how it all relates—I said as if I knew what I was talking about.

Dominick Float, nodding abstracted, took a few moments too long to grasp that I'd stopped talking and now expected a response.

There I was, earnestly expounding on why this one dream among all the others had so imprinted itself and negatively impacted today, a Thursday's, mood that I was drifting, de-powered in its torpedo aftermath. My engine room was ablaze under what could only be described as a dour cloud blocking all light from my soul, but no one wants to hear about dreams, do they? Dreams are boring, we're told again and again like it's part of a lexicon hammered into our developing understanding of the world. Descriptions of drug trips are boring too. Any misguided attempt to describe what's going on in your mind is boring. That's what they always say.

It won't knock you off your rocking horse to learn I've always disagreed. I can't get enough of people's inner lives. You can't fake dreams, or visionary experiences.

P-zombies can't describe a healthy inner life, can they?

Can we try that again?

By this time, I shouldn't need any *he said, she said* cues—you know who's talking. *I don't mind you playing it a little broad, but can we have some nuance? Twankey knows it's all an act . . . she knows she's learned the steps. She's a chess piece! The Red Queen in* Alice! *But she's doing her best to outwit her controllers—*

Oh, fuck off, Dom! I bellowed, pruning his tedious mansplain at the root. *Is that nuanced enough for you!* And with that lip-rolled punk rock snarl I flounced off.

I could hear them shaking their heads it was so obvious.

Is it that time of the month?—I heard the ever-abrasive, unrepentant May Tang-Taylor comment under her breath in the way atom bomb tests happen "under" the desert.

You can't say that!—Aiysha Dyce blurted out, at all times attuned to the potential for offence. But it was too late. May had committed wholeheartedly to intolerance.

You haven't lost your timing—Float said. Sensing the abject failure of his previous attempts to reach me he'd finally opted for the approach he found most arduous; and here he was, shivering in the pitiless bright and Baltic chill of the moral high ground, on his ill-fated ascent up the north face of Mount Empathy.

He was keen for me to see something way up in the rigging above the stage, in the elaborate cross-hatching of the overhead bars that made it all possible.

Bit dramatic—I remarked.

I'd already worked out how I could evade him up there if our confab turned homicidal and I was left with no choice. Designed to support an incalculable tonnage of equipment, the rigging could easily tolerate my sylph-like proportions, but Float, I felt sure, would immediately fail to live up to his name if he dared set foot on the flimsy platform.

You know I like to get the god's-eye view—the overview—

From here, he explained, I could literally see how his mind worked. Peering down like Olympians through the hole of the sky onto the cubed entirety of our homemade universe below, he wanted me to know it wasn't all in vain.

The colour-coded marks onstage, as viewed from our dimensionally-elevated perspective, laid out a wireframe puzzle contrived by a mathematical savant—fluorescent tape tags set as jewels in an unfathomable cogs-out contrivance, so that their precise placement singly and in relation to one another encoded hidden forces, predetermined tracks of character arcs laid bare in the overview of this join-the-dots X-ray of *The Phantom of the Pantomime*. The entire show unfolded from a basic five-pointed star. A pentagram no less.

*Tell me you've not been using us to summon the Devil, Dom—*I said. *He wouldn't have my soul. He doesn't know where it's been.*

The proxemics of every costume change, every scene, every number were organized around the same witchy polygon vectors.

*I'm impressed—*I said. *You've really made this nervous breakdown work for you, babes. You must tell me the secret because I'm struggling to find the positives.*

*It's the Golden Ratio—*Dom said, keeping the conversation business-like. *Murdo McCloudie gave me the idea—*

*From beyond the grave?—*I said. *He's the gift that keeps on grieving.*

The Vallhambra was designed to embody the Fibonacci spiral. Like the Parthenon. It's obvious when you look at the plans.

That glint in his eye kindled to a firestorm.

*There's a reason why I've been making everyone go over and over it, Lu—*he insisted, mounting a spirited defence of his uncompromising artistic vision before riding it into the sunset. *Everything we're doing is non-naturalistic, every move is* *calculated, but I want it to feel improvised like it's second nature and there's no other way you know how to do it!*

I'm delighted you've managed to the lay the blame for months of torture on your Muse!—I said, and I don't know if it was the strong coffee I'd necked, but the ice on my tongue melted, and the river flowed—and flowed.

It's always the woman's fault—I ranted. *Which one is she? Terpsichore? Melpomene? No, it has to be Thalia, she's the only one who'd put up with you!*

Dom was beaming, a grin that reminded me of the widening split in a pair of gammon-hued rubber pants.

The last time I saw a face like that was a police photofit!—I said and put up my hands and pretended to back away from him. *I knew it. The real Phantom is the director!*—I told him. *We're hundreds of feet above the stage.*

Beat. Timing.

You only dragged me up here to toss me off, didn't you?—I said.

What happened to that sense of humour, Lu?—he came back with a pallid smile and the swift stroke of an axe felling a silly ugly tree. *How come this Lu is up here when I need her down there?*

I grew up a punk. An anarchist. Rebel without a job—I said. *That Lu doesn't take kindly to anyone telling her what to do over and over again as if she hasn't spent decades learning her trade.*

I did it to remind you who you are—he persisted. *You're playing a character who's filled with passion! Twankey is raw joie de vivre that defies entropy—but you seem spent, burnt out— where's the Widow?*

It came down to this. Why, oh, why couldn't I slip into character the way I always used to, the way you'd slip into a shimmering baby-doll nightie made to measure? That's what he wanted to know.

Too much of whatever's going on with you is showing through Twankey's front—he kept up. *Your worries, Lu, your distractions. I don't know what you're going through . . .*

You don't—I affirmed.

Late nights?—he said. *Drink. Drugs. Whatever it is with you and Luda . . . everyone's talking . . .*

We've already had this conversation and nothing's going on!—I snapped back, elastic. *Everyone can shut the fuck up!*

Luda's killing it! She's really come through—said Dom, his way of delivering a compliment on the point of a dagger.

All thanks to you know who?—I hissed. *Have you any idea what it takes to wrangle worms? To turn raw silk promise into luxury satin talent?*

Is that what it's about?—he honked derisively, a clown car in a traffic jam. *You've taught your replacement to be better than you, and you can't stand it? A Star Is Born? You're better than this*—

He wouldn't let go, just held me in his evil hypnotist gaze, those grey eyes in that face, like two nail heads in a pig's rump.

I'll throw myself over—I said. *Would that be spontaneous enough?*

The scrutiny went on and on, but the eyes visibly softened like chocolate buttons left in the sun until they were an accusing puddle. I believe he believed his puppy-dog expression telegraphed the sentiment—"I'm hurt by your behaviour, be reasonable"—but seething on the spot, all I was willing to see was a faded cushion sat on by so many arses over the years it had lost the will to maintain its former shape and firmness.

You can't always bring your A-game to rehearsals—I volleyed, and he came back with a bitter and world-weary death strike.

Well, maybe you could stretch to your X- or Y-game, Lu.

I bit my tongue, held my lip, kept my pride up, and swallowed my pecker. Here in this world bound in a nutshell, this Peking in a cabinet faked up by paint and carpentry, its superficial plausibility upheld by a hidden skeleton infrastructure, Dominick Float was Lord God Almighty. That was the important lesson to be learned and absorbed here. God had lifted me from the bell-jar confinement that was the whole of my existence, up into the rigging and the wiring, and asked of me only that I play my simple part as a good, functioning sprocket in the madman's contraption he had suffered to reveal unto me.

To Mega Therion—his Great Bestial Work. His monsterpiece. His overreaching pathology laid bare! Take your pick.

I will—I said rightfully chastened. I was nunlike. Humbled after a righteous tongue-lashing by the Mother Superior. *I will. I might even show you my R's.*

Let up—he urged. *Luda's hard as nails. She can hold her own*—

I let that one pass with only a raised eyebrow.

But if it comes down to you, or Luda—he assured me. *I need my Twankey. That's what I'm trying to tell you. I'll let Luda go if that's the only way to put an end to this . . . this* folie à deux . . .

The very thought was an ice pick to my aorta. What if she walked away? What if we never saw her again?

Our relationship is platonic, pedagogic. I'm her teacher—I faced him down, going as cold as I could manage without climbing into the freezer cabinet. *It's not what you or anybody else thinks. I'm sorry I can't be one more identical wedge in your clockwork chocolate orange!*

What's chewing at you, Lu? Honestly. All the occult stuff—he said, shifting the points on his train of thought so we split from the branch line and took a turn for the macabre. *I thought maybe you could put an end to this fucking Curse*—he said, really spitting out the word "Curse," as if it was a curse much worse than *fuck.*

I thought that's what you were doing—I said. *They use pentagrams to bind demons*—I reminded him, vague on who "they" might be. Rosicrucians? The Salvation Army? Zookeepers? Accordionists?

I reminded him how not so long before, he'd rashly extended a welcome to the denizens of the Underworld alongside the dregs of the Press, practically handing out free tickets that day to any stray *revenant* that wandered in off the eighteenth-century ghost of Gargoyle Street.

*Come one come all—PhanTom, Dick, and Harriet—*I said.

Perhaps an excess of spectres, I suggested, drawn to the Ghost Light by Dom's unrestrained hospitality, now struggled unseen in the theatre's latticework web of iron beams and girders, its cunningly-plaited wooden planks.

Impalpable, too weak on the mortal plane to free themselves from the sublime architecture of McCloudie's ghost trap, lovely mothlike "spirits" cried for help all around us, invisibly tugging against the sticky mortal restraints of crisscrossed cables and chains. Thirsty for the distilled passions of the dramatic arts, more of the spooks were sucked in daily, their increasing numbers bloating the guts of the theatre as trapped ectoplasmic wind . . .

*All the frustrated energies summoned here, with no way to escape these straight lines and angles. Maybe your Golden Section's a spirit cage—*I said all disingenuous, and if that wasn't improv, I don't know what is.

*What would I do without your voice of reason, Lu?—*he deadpanned. *Laugh if you like. We don't need any more bad luck—*

I couldn't agree more. On this subject of bad luck prevention, I proceeded to tell him of my Good Samaritan visit to the hospital bedside of Gofannon Rhys. Earnestly, I claimed to have revived the elderly thespian's personal spirits with a bracing dose of good cheer.

Midway through this unlikely admission of charity Dom cut me short with a curt flick of his hand and peered over the rail, listening for unfamiliar voices. The hairs on my arms and the back of my neck stiffened into quivering antennae tuned to bad-juju FM.

As we were lowered, unspeaking in the grinding scissor lift that now felt like a coffin inching its way into the grave on folding clotheshorse legs, two ominous figures came into view in a slow suspense shot, shadows at first, unrolled black rugs in the shapes of men. Then sprouting from the shadows' feet, two boys in blue stood tall like lovely twilight croci craning their heads on stalks to track our *deus ex machina* descent from the dusty, oily workshop of the heavens above.

The police are here to see you—said the prods manager although by that time he was simply stating the obvious.

I said—*What's all this about?* Well let's face it, nobody wants to find the police at the door. It's not as if they ever turn up to wish you a happy birthday or pose for a selfie, do they? They never deliver pizza. Instead, they deliver lines like this—

It's about the missing boy.

The missing boy, as it happened, was known to me by another name—Rentboy, we might as well call him, since that's who he was when we met. Remember Rentboy before he sloughed his skin and took control of the whole narrative?

According to the law, the missing boy's real name was Kenny Trace. Although even that wasn't his real name. Kenny Trace was the product label attached to an unbaptized foundling with no name of its own. A mewling newborn stranger to this world, a changeling, a fetch left quacking on the orphanage steps in the once-upon-a-time.

Kenneth Trace disappeared ten years ago. Wanted by police.

I do remember him—I said carefully. *We'd just started pre-rehearsals. June?* I turned to Dom for confirmation.

June it was June—he confirmed on cue. *Feels like forever.*

I felt emboldened to give him his money's worth as the

322 · GRANT MORRISON

policeman jotted down my freestyle in his little book, eager to keep the story exciting—

He was selling the Homeless Times *outside the Rendezvous—the café. I didn't want to give him money; he'd just spend it on drugs, right? So I offered to buy him a square meal instead—*

Do you do a lot of that?—he asked, still scribbling with his pen.

I thought about it and said—*Not really*—I said. *I do my best to bridge the gap between rich and poor but there was something about the boy's eyes*—I said, and the policemen reacted like deer catching wind of a rifle.

His eyes?

They were a very unusual colour—I recalled, having my wicked way with the filth. *Capri grotto blue. I don't know. I was moved is the best way I can put it.*

I held it there on a tender indrawn breath. I hoped I'd baited my line with enough tasty gobbets of truth to hook them wriggling there until I chose to lob them back in the lake none the wiser.

This kid had brown eyes. Cop two of the two, rising to the challenges of the sidekick role I'd assigned him, frowned, sensing a sure lead turn to ink running through his fingers. *You're certain they were blue?*

I said—*maybe I mixed him up with someone else*—having forgotten about Luda's brown contacts when we met in the Rendezvous.

I went on to tell them how yes, I'd talked to a boy or rather how I'd talked about myself while he ate and ate and ate. Me, I could gab for two, for a whole string quartet, a football team, a police department. The waif hadn't seen fit to pass on his name, or any other meaningful details.

I gave him a few notes and made him promise he'd spend the money on accommodation—I assured the policemen. *I told him to be careful and I wish I hadn't now*—I said. *You try to be a Good Samaritan these days but it's a minefield.*

They asked if we'd left together. I nodded, delighted to confirm that the homeless boy was gone on his way by the time I hailed a taxi. That much was true in the sense that I'd shared the cab with Luda not Rentboy, or Kenny, or whoever it was she'd been impersonating.

Could I remember what I was doing on the South Side that day? the cops wanted to know. Of course I could!

I'm working on a memoir—I divulged. *I know! You must be thinking, She's way too young to be writing memoirs!*

I knew that was the very last thing they were thinking. I twinkled—*All joking aside, I had a band, the Troupe, you might remember us from Channel 6, we first met up in the Rendezvous.*

I watched as they both misspelled *Troupe* on their way to the alphabetical pileup that was *Rendezvous,* before summoning my most solicitous, seductive voice—*I wanted to go back. See if I could capture the feel of the place. Trigger some memories.*

By now the even, toneless drone of my voice was causing the eyes of the detectives to blur with boredom.

It's a grim business, Officers, but it's heartwarming to know somebody cares—I said, as they left. *Social services. Police. He didn't think anyone wanted to know. He'd appreciate all this attention.* It was a near-faultless performance, if I say so myself, 9.9 out of 10 for gall.

My elation was short-lived; when I returned to the stage, it was to find Dominick with the separate pieces of a snapped pole in both hands standing like the last survivor of a bloody, pointless battle, clutching his broken lance in the smoking shambles of everything he'd thought worth fighting for. The shattered bulb of the broken Ghost Light lay deconstructed into pale shark-toothy shards.

That doesn't bode well—was all I could say.

Our lightning rod for grounding dangerous spirit energy was reduced to a fused and melted spar, good for fuck-all now, blown out by who knew what stupendous aethereal discharge.

When did this happen?—Dom said, and his desolate expression was that of a boy who thought they were both special but who's just found his adventurous little dog dead in the coal cellar. *Nobody saw anything.*

I wanted to say—*Nobody ever sees anything*—but I didn't. It broke my heart to note how Float's remarkable voice had lost its rich choral congestion. Stripped of the harmonic overtones he relied upon to convey his authority, our esteemed director had nothing to offer but his own first-rate impression of a Microsoft text reader.

You had nothing to do with this boy's disappearance?—he asked with big sad eyes, become now the innocent wife in a film, coming to terms with the bloody evidence of hubby's passion for serial murder, hidden beneath the marital bed.

I had nothing to say so I said—*Nothing.*

Is everything going wrong?—was all he had to offer in return.

Second Law of Thermodynamics says yes—I said, wishing I didn't have to be so clever and callous all the time.

We can't let this get out—he resolved, setting his lips in a ruled line.

There was more to come.

As if things weren't already much worse than bad enough, reports began to trickle in concerning an incident of extreme violence involving Dez Blue.

The story hadn't made the leap to headline status yet but, as far as Dom could glean, the whole seamy subplot began its slouch to Bethlehem when Blue limped into his spare bedroom to face down the primal scene that was his devoted wife Lol *in flagrante* with an up-and-coming club comic I won't even name. It wasn't the betrayal that set Blue's blood ablaze—God knows he had a reputation as a well-oiled extracurricular fuck machine himself—more the implied stripping of status, the indignity of this blow to his honour and especially his already compromised masculinity.

That Lol, his Lol would choose some penniless, ripped, and gifted young newcomer over her successful, out-of-shape, and currently disabled narcissist of a husband made all Blue's accomplishments seem worthless.

But what actually happened, Lu?—I hear you asking.

As I had it explained to me, the Fisher King Blue, lamed first, then horn-crowned and cucked, had chosen to refine his recent mastery of support sticks into a new experimental martial art.

Pressed into service as a pair of stabbing blunt spears, the most severe and prolonged application of Blue's weaponized walking aids had been directed exclusively between the wife's lover's legs in a crutch *vs.* crotch death bout the fork was doomed to lose.

Picture it if you dare!

Front-line bulletins hinted at irreversible injuries to the up-and-coming funnyman's penis, testicles, and rectum of a kind and in a manner that seemed unlikely to inspire many comedy routines or future affairs.

So far so good, except Dez Blue, ever the consummate pro, could hardly be expected to mount a suicidal defence of his dysfunctional relationship without throwing in a final comedic flourish when he'd overbalanced and clattered downstairs attached to two rigid metal poles. Working in tandem with gravity and torque, they broke everything that hadn't already been snapped in previous misadventures.

It all seemed too much to take in.

I hope it's not just me who's worried about Dee Jayashankar—I said, not entirely taking it seriously in that annoying way I have. *She's allergic to tree pollen and cat dander. Anything can happen . . .*

Dee. Aiysha. May's in a state of shock since she heard. Everyone thinks they're next. Dom swabbed his broad brow with a kitchen towel that turned immediately transparent with wet. *Thank God she's only in a few scenes and we can afford to lose her until the last week*—he said.

The Twins seem oblivious at least. They're probably immune to any curse—I pointed out breezily—*I saw them playing Ping-Pong earlier and I still have no idea which one's Ping and which is Pong.*

I'm worried about you, Lu. What if it's you next? All this scandal. Or me.

What scandal?—I shrieked, situating the pitch a little higher than I'd planned. My unfortunate yelp ricocheted off the rigging like the shrill cries for assistance of a seabird mixed up with a fisherman's net.

It does seem a bit weird—he said, troubled in an uncharacteristic way that troubled me.

I could only agree. What evil twine tied these random incidents together, what dread Prime Mover organized these serial calamities into prearranged conspiracy? What awful thread dyed crimson with Kensington Gore wound its way through all our human affairs?

The police, Lu—Float whimpered, going under despite his optimistic surname.

Assisting with enquiries—I explained without emotion. *You can use this, Dominick*—I said. *You can work with this.*

Looking back, I must admit that day may have been my one and only chance to come clean and stop Luda in her tracks, but we're all prophets and weathermen in hindsight, aren't we?

They had nothing on me.

Zero.

Zilch.

The police couldn't touch me. Nobody wanted to touch me, least of all the law.

The cab was a driverless, thank fuck! I couldn't face conversation. I'd lied to the police to protect Luda. For her, I'd made myself vulnerable again.

Did I expect gratitude?

I needed silence and calm to rehearse in my head what I planned to say next.

What have you done to get the police involved?—I said.

Luda's eyes flickered, and her lower lip vibrated fetchingly. It was all an act but like the death of Bambi's mother it would work on me every time.

They think I've got something to do with his disappearance—your disappearance—I explained for the fifth time. *I covered for you! What do they want with you?*

The Marvells sent them!—Luda was unequivocal. *Isn't it obvious?*

Backed into a *cul-de-sac,* I opted for adamant—*If this goes any further. If I'm implicated in anything, you have to come clean. You have to tell them Kenny Trace is you!*

But Luda held my gaze and flew me like a kite.

I'm not him—said Luda. *You don't know what I went through to not be him. If they find me. They'll take me back—you can't let that happen! You made a promise! You have to hide me! From them*—she shrieked. *The Marvells!*

What do the police want with Kenny Trace?—I said. *What did he do?*

Luda shook. *It wasn't me*—she insisted. *I wasn't born then*—and it was difficult to find the flaw in her argument.

Rules of the game of Golden Dames.
The game is played on a board that encodes the Golden Section in its angled geometry, with five sides making up a star pentagon otherwise known as a pentagram of the kind a working necromancer might slap up to confound a malignant spirit, as I'd pointed out to Dominick Float in the upper stories of the Vallhambra that day.

Play commences with nine pieces on the board placed at the vertices of the star, with one space left empty.

Two players alternate turns, capturing each other's pieces by jumping over them like chequers into the empty spot beyond. The winner is the player who captures the last piece and leaves one single token on the board.

There were other diversions like it; Pentalpha was the oldest, going back to 1700 B.C. Then there was Golden Star. In Mexico the five-pointed board was recruited to run a con known as *estrella mágica* and there was an even more narratively-perfect variant known as Vultures and Crows, oddly enough.

Once you know what's going on, once you figure out the rule book, you'd like to think you can turn it to your advantage.

The board, the spiked and star-spangled field of play that was our stage at the Vallhambra, pinned out like a starfish dissection, flayed bare, with each new vacant space the gap where a captured counter was stretchered offstage, still telling jokes, promising a return, a resurrection.

Like a sack of endless snakes that turns out to be just the

one wily ouroboros, all the seemingly random loops and coils of circumstance were braided into the same conclusion. The same step-by-step process led me prancing over the edge of reason into a waiting abyss.

Seen from one angle, the pentagram had two points down, one up towards the unity of pure spirit. From another it showed one point down, two points raised—the horns, the contending dual forces of the material universe.

The One snapped in Two.

The story picks up following the act 2 scene 4 climax where, as you'll remember, ladies and gentlemen, boys and girls, and all the rest, Abanazar has commanded the reluctant Genie to flit the palace across thousands of miles, through time and space to Egypt of all places, where the princess and all her palace infrastructure now appear against a red-and-gold backdrop of pyramids and the inscrutable Sphinx.

The painted flat depicted a romanticized Nile Delta, shuffled together with local Gasglow landmarks, Wonders of the World like the Millennium Wheel, Tatler's Tower, the university spire's cone of lithic lacework, and the double-D-cup dome of the Mandrake Library joined forces to assemble the half-remembered skyline of some liminal world.

Abanazar enters stage right to a crashing Niagara of hisses and jeers. No one wants the villain to win, after all, and the arrival of a new dawn, a fresh scene, brings hope that there's more to this story than just the unfair triumph of age, cynicism, and greed. No curse, no sibilant approbation can unseat this new, inflated Abanazar from his perch, strutting into the footlights in curly-toed slippers of pure gold thread, so puffed-up with pride he's popping like evil corn in an evil pan.

After all this time toiling in the pale shadows of the dreams of greater men than he, Abanazar has achieved everything he wants by resorting to subterfuge and deception; his power, as conferred by the Genie, is unlimited. His horizons are reliant only on the constraints of his imagination.

Thankfully, as one more demonstration of the pre-eminence of irony in the universe, Abanazar, learned, articulate, well-dressed, well-read, well-hung I'm sure, has the tiniest little imagination you'll ever set eyes on.

Stuck with this predictable dullard, the Genie follows his demanding new master dutifully, shackled and surly. You can tell by the spirit's hangdog expression how he chafes against Abanazar's orders, but he lacks free will. As a thing of pure power, he can only grumble and obey. While Abanazar shows nothing but contempt for the wondrous being that does his bidding, sending the Genie on boring errands, lavishing the omnipotent sprite's limitless potential on incessant palace redecorations.

The Genie does as he's told when Abanazar orders up another banquet featuring all the same exotic ingredients, the same golden cutlery and priceless diamond crockery—*Do as I say, you miserable creature! If you can't hack it, I can always call Deliverex!*

Then comes the entertainment! Dancers file in like sluggish rivers of mercury and molten bullion, dispirited jugglers tumble without conviction and describe mathematically complex but fundamentally unexciting arcs with balls and skittles. A dry physics lecture in clown's motley ensues, prompting Abanazar to burst into song, voicing the deep-throated confident bluster of the successful midlife man facing a predictable crisis.

Forget that wretched beggar boy—he sings with powerful conviction. *There's someone new in town!*

He struts, he soars—

Here Abanazar performs a textbook basketball throw, a move requiring stage effects to reproduce, in the form of a deflating balloon, a pretend backward toss underlined by the loop-de-whoop of a swanee whistle, and a real basketball plopped through the hoop.

He always scores!

There's a mirror where he preens, as Abanazar waxing his moustache with a coiling oiling twist of finger and thumb gives his gem-studded new headgear a rakish gambler's tilt.

He suits a golden crown!

This conceited inventory of the wizard's many attributes grows showier, more strident, while he strides with self-important assurance among the antic diversions he's conjuring from transparent air.

His retinue's spectacular, the master of vernacular, his reach well-nigh tentacular! It's TRUEEE!

Abanazar's ostentatious exhibitionism intended to spark the fires of desire in Jasmine's spent embers is having the opposite effect on the young royal kidnappee. Instead of reacting with the anticipated joy and gratitude, Jas averts her attention, too despondent to react to Abanazar's manic display with anything other than a stretched-out sigh. Then, as bitter smogs of pollen from the forest of rare flowers he's charmed to brighten her window box wring tears instead from her eyes, she sneezes and begins to sob.

Get rid of it!—Abanazar snarls in response, scorned and bewildered. *All of it!*

The Genie obliges, burdened by grim servitude, humourless and demoralized as he banishes the impossibly-coloured garden, so that all the imaginary performers scatter into the wings, leaving only silent dirt and sand where wonders lately cavorted.

No matter what the old man magics up to impress the captive princess, his threadbare powers of invention serve only to expose his innate lack of flair; his diamonds are never much bigger than the Ritz, for instance, while Jasmine's own private, personal chariot of stars is drawn through the firmament by only seven clockwork swans, each made of wearying quantities of the pure gold that every fixture, fitting, utensil, and convenience seems to be fashioned from these days in the relocated palace from Peking. With every new and more excessive nuptial offering, Jasmine only shakes her head morosely, deep-dipped in what doctors might diagnose as the marinade of clinical depression.

We all know there's only one thing she yearns for, and that's Aladdin. Aladdin. Aladdin!

But Aladdin will never find her, she frets! Not here so far from home!

Dee Jayashankar played a chef's kiss that day, her chops honed by high-pitched soap-opera performances every week-day for four years. Every articulate facial expression, every *hasta* gesture she'd studied and absorbed from the Bollywood dance routines she grew up replicating in her crowded family living room, each application of *abhinaya* now came into play to whet the edge of her performance.

Even in rehearsal, she was amazing to watch. I could hardly imagine what she'd be like when her dial was turned up for opening night and I wondered why I'd overlooked this young woman's cool, dedicated brilliance.

In fact, and this is me in a dark place emotionally, taking a moment to think about it, the whole crew was operating to the peak of its abilities at a very challenging time. So much so that I experienced an uncharacteristic surge of affection and appreciation for everyone's accomplishments. Our refusal to bow to adversity was remarkable and laudable. Naïve, you might say.

I gave Float a thumbs-up and regretted it. I don't do thumbs-ups and he immediately, correctly, suspected something was amiss in the inexplicable blue swamps of my interior world.

I'm master of the Lamp, I'm a winner, I'm the Champ!

It's plain to see, the clouds, the trees, all dance a jig at my decree!—sings Abanazar to his own perma-tanned face in the bright mirror, but as we watch, the pumped-up pride begins to leak from his posture.

Abanazar has everything he wants but none of it is how he wanted it to be so what's gone wrong?

The girl's his, but she despises him down to his biomolecular constituent parts. The Genie obeys his every command, but the miserable thing openly loathes him and ticks off his uninspired catalogue of wishes with a sulky disinterest that ruins all the fun. The only way he can get people to love him is to bully them and then punish them if they don't do as he says.

There must be more to supreme power than this!

Intelligent, I'm elegant, astride a golden elephant—he brags with growing uncertainty. *What can she see in him but not in me?*

What must I do—what's wrong—what's wrong with me?— he sings, and these last words break down into a forlorn spoken-word *récit,* an admission of frailty.

As his self-respect crumbles, as his big number wraps up in dejection and rejection, we may almost feel sorry for Abanazar, but that's the trick here. For the first time we see through the old fraud's desperate act; underneath the designer turban and the spangled shift, there's just one more silly goat losing his edges to the corrosive passage of days, imagining his power and privilege makes him young and attractive rather than something to put up with in return for six heart-shaped swimming pools and a holiday house on the moon.

Just as we're opening to the possibility that the embittered magus might hide a gentler, more sensitive side, he gathers his rage in a ball of haywire and spite and makes up his mind, pulling the corners tight.

What does it matter, he decides, if he has to twist people's arms up their ungrateful backs before they'll admit to loving him? He has the capability to do just that and he intends to use it, singing his song of agency with a renewed will to power.

If she wants a brutal tyrant, then I'll BE a brutal tyrant and my brutal boots I'll tie right up right now!

I'll stamp around triumphant, causing maximum discomfort—and in the end, I'll FUCK THE SACRED COW!

The actual line goes—*And in the end, I'll WIN her heart I vow!* but I include the multiply-offensive parody version for completists and in memory of the late, grating Gofannon Rhys.

It's decided there and then that Jasmine must agree to marry Abanazar, whether she wants to or not, the ceremony to take place, without further hesitation or delay, the very next day.

And in the end, I'll OWN her heart I vow! He concludes his song to the accompaniment of a scattering cloudburst of drab neon glitter.

I suppose it would ruin the story, along with the dreams of moon-drunk teenagers everywhere, but I always wondered why it never occurred to poor old Abanazar to have the Genie transform him into a fully authentic physical duplicate of Aladdin. Or even just make him young again in his own skin. Hooked nose and a tendency towards stooped cadaverous clutching aside, you can imagine Abanazar being quite freaky-sexy, in his dating days all those aeons ago, Byronic even.

I don't think the best of people in general, I admit, but you have to wonder how long Jasmine's resolve would hold out when she found herself in the experienced arms of a jaded, courtly libertine with the gym-sculpted body of a twenty-two-year-old man. Wouldn't Aladdin seem uncouth, ill-educated, and undernourished in comparison with the worldly, shredded Grand Vizier of gorgeousness?

Wouldn't an aristocratic girl like Jasmine choose the hard-to-get Bad Boy over the *gauche* and puppyish Good Kid if the playing field of years was levelled?

Digressions aside, Abanazar's destined to be a cartoon baddie with uncomplicated motivations, locked within his proscribed horizons. No matter how hard he tries, the story will never let him be evil enough to do what most of us would do, and as for Jasmine, she's written to be far too pure, too innocent, and too completely in love with her dream boy to dump Aladdin in favour of even the world's most powerful sorcerer.

It's a fantastic scene where Abanazar outdoes himself, while Jasmine in her gilded links tries her best to raise a smile at an autopsy.

As Abanazar blusters offstage in a litter swirl of metallic purples and flashing aluminium stars, Jasmine is left alone, sobbing into a watered silk cushion that looks from the gallery like a gigantic foil-wrapped toffee.

But there's movement. To anticipated audience whoops of delight, Aladdin shows his hand. Tentatively he raises his head from the laundry basket used to smuggle him into the throne room, wearing the wicker lid as a coolie hat.

For the first time since the windbag's dazzling display began, Jasmine breathes life, rising like a newly-watered springtime flower into the refreshing lemon slice of a sudden spotlight.

Extending long shapely pins in nude tights and kitten heels, a gender centaur with the strong wiry torso of a skinny hot twink, and the enviable legs of a hosiery model, Aladdin tiptoes across the stage to the sound of cheers from the audience. Ostentatiously quiet, his upraised finger makes a cross with his lips.

Shhhh!

Luda, eyes big and round as bike lamps trained on the gallery, instructed the purely notional audience to hold its collective tongue, lest the wizard twig to the escape plan. Then just to make certain we got it, she went on to deliver her message in a slapstick combination of International Sign Language and semaphore she'd learned for the purpose. Dee Jayashankar clapped a hand across her mouth and nodded like a dashboard dog into an imagined crowd.

The atmosphere in the palace has shifted, brightened. The

audience is surely cheering even though Aladdin's silently urging them to stop before they alert the sorcerer!

Too late!

What's that noise?—booms Abanazar's bad-tempered voice from offstage. The wizard's on his way!

Aladdin makes it back to the laundry basket's concealment with heart-stopping moments to spare as Abanazar blows back in like a recurring headache. He's grasped that something's not right; they're cheering. No one's ever rooted for Abanazar.

What's going on? What was all that noise?—he demands of the audience, who customarily respond like an overworked boiler room of hisses, a ghost stampede of boos. *Tell me, you ungrateful lot, or I'll order my Genie to turn you all into smelly camels!*

He sniffs, detecting molecules of scent, and turns on his heel in a fluster of spangled robes to berate the Genie.

You're supposed to tell me if you see anything!

I don't see Aladdin anywhere—the Genie replies with the current undeniable truth.

Aladdin's still hidden in the basket, but it can't be too long before he's discovered. A barely-stifled sneeze betrays his position.

That's because he's hiding, you idiot!—Abanazar barks.

My wish is your command, O wizard—and Abanazar says—*Flush him out!*

The Genie points his finger and one by one the baskets explode in a fusillade of sparks and pyro. Closer and closer to where we know Aladdin is precariously concealed. The audience screaming louder and louder.

The princess almost gives him away. If only a diversion could be arranged! Something so ridiculous and diverting it might work.

Something so tacky, tasteless, and unforgettable your eyes would deserve sensitive counselling to help them recover.

Delivery for Mr. Abanazar!—comes the shout as a pair of anachronistic Deliverex drivers played by the twins interrupt the Genie's target practice in the vital moments before Aladdin goes up in pink powderpuff smoke.

I didn't order anything—Abanazar objects. *I'm a powerful wizard! If I want something, I conjure it from thin air!*

It's got your name on it—the Deliverex dudes insist flatly, bringing the clipboard rules and regs of the real world. *You have to sign for it*—they say. *You have to own it.*

But—but what is it?—the wizard splutters, losing control of the situation.

It's the Magic Carpet, or at least a much bigger prop facsimile that the Deliverex boys can gruntingly lay down, unfurl like a huge scroll, and barrel the carpet's hidden contents into view.

Menopausal MILF realness ensues!

Twankey in the house!

The Widow Twankey, risen from the rolled-out carpet, in a lurid glam lampoon of Botticelli's *Venus.*

Float and I exchanged a blowtorch glare as I plumped up my tits and prepared to slay the tech run.

Abanazar's eyes attempt to divorce themselves from his skull on the grounds of cruelty. No one compelled to watch this *Danse Macabre* performed to a strutting *bom-sha-boom* of sleazebeat and limelight could be expected to hold on to sanity.

The wizard can barely process the horror as the veiled Widow advances with all the sex appeal of a beautiful, ungainly asteroid plunging towards Earth without warning. Fiery friction tracks struck by trailing chiffons in parrot red, yellow, and vivid blue stream behind her as Twankey immobilizes the cringing conjurer in the magnetic field of her smouldering stare.

The whole cast, what's left of us, steps back and hands the stage to *moi* as I swagger and bump in striptease rings around an Abanazar rendered impotent by Twankey's militant femininity.

So begins Twankey's climactic burlesque seduction of

Abanazar, so occurs his descent into the flowing primary colours and unstable forms, the deviant unchecked sexual menace of a savage bad trip, a fever vision of what can happen when ultimate power attracts into its orbit the supreme shameless gold-digger.

The Dance of the Seven Fails, I'd called it six years ago and the name stuck.

But really it was Twankey's Dance of Death.

Transcending time and mortality, Salvador Dalí's *Christ of St. John of the Cross* occupies its own mysterious alcove in the Gasglow Art Museum where the famous painting depicts a vision of the Christ as seen from an elevated perspective and witnessed by the tiny figure of Saint John by his rowboat on the shores of the Sea of Galilee. No prior artwork had taken a viewpoint that looked down on Christ seemingly skydiving on the Cross.

It was here I'd agreed to meet my mysterious contact during the hour Float had allotted to my hospital visit that day.

Sorry if it's all a bit cloak-and-dagger—Miss Bee Spalding apologized as Christ loomed over her shoulder, a solemn all-forgiving kite.

She seemed nervous and who could blame her? All in black like Mary Poppins by way of Hammer Horror, with her buglike Jackie O shades and anti-viral face mask, also black, she was an irresistible target for any nearby vampire hunters.

Miss S. took off her glasses briefly, blinking pinkly before putting them back on—*I hope you don't mind*—she said. *I have to wear them in strong light, I don't want to seem rude.*

At least I knew she had a face under there and not some inverted hollow, like the Invisible Man.

It did occur to me that the sacerdotal glow in Jesus's hushed and holy cubbyhole was no more an example of strong light than the sleepy sigh of a kitten is loud noise. The lighting of the painting evoked votive candles, the intimacy of the confessional, but I let it go. I wanted to cut to the chase and take my leave of the painfully-neurasthenic Bee—Beatrice?—Spalding ASAP.

I watched directions lock together under the varnished surface of the painting—an infrastructure of precisely-arranged triangles and pyramids that supported the composition.

I couldn't look at a work of art without discerning its horizon lines like this, its parallax and perspective. I couldn't prevent myself from seeing the underlying fretwork turned inside-out. And this was a painting I'd been coming here to admire all my life; I knew by heart the geometry of the bones under its skin of glaze and shadow.

When a reportedly "mentally ill" critic slashed the canvas with a chunk of sandstone, it was quickly repaired good as new by the museum's restoration team.

One urban legend speaks of Dalí himself, the great Surrealist, praising the passion of the vandal before jetting from his sunlit retreat in Port Lligat to Gasglow to personally repaint the damaged sections. It's a lovely story that seems almost convincing but it's no more nor less real than the suicide of Murdo McCloudie.

Young restorers with horsehair brushes in hand were able to reconstruct the original intent of the canvas even as its initiator imploded into crabbed moral decline in Franco's Spain.

Good as new, these radiant art-school alumni knew how to tart up the Redeemer with a fresh coat of slap and symbolism for future generations to argue over.

I like a bit of dagger with my cloak—I said, doubly alluding to the Dalí slasher incident, hoping to put the Woman in Black at her ease, seemingly accomplishing the opposite.

There was something alien about her. Reptilian. No, marsupial. Arachnid. I honestly don't know how to explain it. She had a way of drifting sideways into the corner of my eye, or was it that when she turned to face me it felt like someone turning away, deciding to leave?

There's a reason I chose this painting—she said. Hers was a clipped cultured East-Coast-educated accent salted with a weariness that seemed affected. *Do you know much about art?*

I met my band in art school—I said, mildly offended. *It's my subject. Practical and history.* I thought, I didn't spend four years listening to ten thousand hours of "Pansy" Millington's maddeningly comprehensive lectures to have perspective and proportion re-explained to me at my age. *The composition's based on two triangles . . .*

More than that—she said, clamouring to outdo me. *If you continue and extend the vectors, you can see a pentagram. Two points raised.*

Why would I want to see that?—I said, although I knew it was there. The Luciferic pentagram again, two horns raised in the triumph of materiality, duality, over the One. The serpent on the crossbeam suffering Time's industry. *Is there some sort of satanic subtext I've been missing this whole time?* And I don't try to be cruel, but now and again it comes out in one big *blahhh*. My Tourette's! *I always thought there were hidden satanic messages in the Bible. I heard if you read it backwards . . .*

No—not at all—she said, oblivious to the lowest form of wit. *It's the Golden Section.*

I don't know if I was shocked to hear her say that. I'd grown to expect coincidence spreading like knotweed around where the Glamour had taken root. We were in an art gallery. Hardly surprising the Golden Section was everywhere with that throwaway emphasis she gave to the word "Section."

I was her nanny—you could say I was her mother in a lot of ways.

I raised an eyebrow, hoping that would be enough, and it was.

I was Luda's mother.

There were tall shadows approaching, angled by the lights from the main hall into a procession of ominous backslashes.

She pulled me onto the stairs that led to the ground floor before the precise configuration of angles could assemble into a police pursuit.

Behind glass, suits of armour mustered in an intimidating polished mob as we drifted quietly between them, anxious not to wake the sleeping tin soldiers. Still belligerent, these vacant shells left standing after some old muddy battle or other, after the bodies they were made to protect had long ago withered into crumble, thronged the gallery. Judging by the size 5 iron sabatons, people must have been preposterously small in those days just a few hundred years ago, not so long a time you'd think as to adequately justify the differences between them and us. Or perhaps they'd avoided conflict by sending their children into war, tiny in their foil wrapping like candy kisses, perched on huge snorting warhorses. Maybe there were miniature ponies they'd ride into the fray with a neighbouring kingdom's army of killer jockeys.

Perhaps these suits never had anyone inside at all. Perhaps there could never be anyone small enough to fit inside what were to all intents and purposes shiny tiny mediaeval robots, remote-controlled iron-shelled crustaceans, piloted by alien brains to clash at Battlebridge and storm the walls of Cranston Castle.

These, my flights of fancy, sifted like the powdery snows of Villon, dusting hushed castle parapets, but I sensed in Miss Spalding a shuttered autistic withdrawal, an introversion that suggested no need for the companionship of human beings or their idle imaginings.

What happened?—I said.

We had come through an archway to the Egyptian rooms where glass cabinets showcased papyri and canopic jars robbed from the unguarded tombs of dusty blue and gold gods by the smash-and-grab merchants of a pith-helmeted colonial yesteryear. When it seemed as if we'd given the pursuing silhouettes the slip, Miss Spalding sat down in the shadowy interstitial between two tall and narrow windows where the sun shone through in brilliant ingots of absolute light.

I helped look after the boy. I was his wet nurse—she admitted with an undulating continental drift of her impressive bust that may have been offered as proof of her suitability for the task.

I asked her about the time frame, and she told me all this had happened nearly eight years previously, which hardly made sense. I said—*You were wet nurse to a teenage boy?*

It's complicated—she replied. By this time, I couldn't wait to hear the shocking story that lurked behind those two inoffensive words.

As she spoke, it occurred to me what made her familiar; I'd seen her in dreams, on TV. A bell rang: the cut of her coat, the little black kitten heels, and the bippety-boppity black hat.

When I came in at first—I said. *I could have sworn you looked like Mrs. Baylock. From* The Omen. *The film. She's the Antichrist's nanny.*

I haven't seen it—she said.

All you're missing is a big black dog—I assured her.

Unsmiling, she nodded past my shoulder, and I turned to face a statue of the jackal-headed god of death, Anubis.

I was a wet nurse, not a nanny. They raised Luda to be—exceptional . . .

As she drifted again among the cabinets, allowing pleather-gloved fingers to trail lightly across the cool glass, in and out of shadow so I couldn't see her face, she spoke in her neat clipped topiary accent of insanity and perversion.

First, Penelope Marvell, aged nine, disappeared. Suspected abduction. The couple never got over it. How could they? They were forced to endure ugly rumours they'd killed their

daughter accidentally and invented an abduction to throw police off the real trail. There were accounts of a neglected quarry
where Penelope's body was painstakingly disassembled by natural processes under a lurid green tarn. They were blamed, they
were condemned, even as a grief beyond measure sandblasted
the Marvells down to emotional stick figures, running basic
routines, surviving on the bare minimum of feeling.

They went mad. You can see how it might happen.

As Miss Spalding told it, Mr. and Mrs. Marvell found themselves in the slowly-tensing coils of a deranging obsession; it
began with a little red notebook where they set out imagining
in detail how Penelope might have developed and changed if
she'd been able to live the life they'd planned for her.

They redecorated their lost daughter's room every few years
to reflect how they imagined her body and her interests might
mature. Updating the décor as the trends changed, they selected posters of boy bands she might appreciate as a preteen,
before researching the latest fashionably retro young girl singers, rebels, iconoclasts, who spoke the authentic argot of bro-
kenhearted defiant adolescence.

They browsed for the books they would have encouraged
her to read, websites she might visit, handpicked by her parents,
hobbies she would gravitate towards; each carefully-planned
stitch assigned its preordained place in the tapestry.

There were charts and graphs, mapping the conceivable
peaks and troughs of a daughter's life that never was. There was
everything except the disappeared centre. Penelope's bedroom
wallpaper and Penelope's unread library shelves wrapped in
black-and-yellow virtual police tape sealing off the crime scene
of an assassinated future.

Brick by brick, memento by memento, the despairing parents built a house made for haunting by just one person—but
it wasn't enough.

Having assembled a context for her existence, the Marvells

set about reconstructing their daughter as she would have been, aged seventeen by that time, using as their raw material another human being.

Whatever they did to the boy they chose to replace their daughter, the result was to wipe him clean like a grubby window, erase his personal files. A character armour as impoverished as everything else in his life was no defence when the chemical bulldozers rolled in and the wrecking balls of shock therapy spun on their chain links to dismantle him. The whole rickety structure to which someone had tacked the name Kenny Trace came down like the first Little Pig's house of straw at the first meaty zephyr of Big Bad Wolf's breath.

But something odd happened; and the more they tried to redial the former Kenny Trace all the way back to primordial being, the deeper the well they'd drilled, the more insatiable the black hole where regression could be pursued infinitely into an all-engulfing logarithmic spiral.

With mounting unease, they'd take turns to drop exploratory stones into the all-consuming dark, waiting each time for a splash that failed to come.

Prolonged contemplation of Kenny's sink of no return came with consequences; first Charles, then his wife, lost their respective bags of marbles to be followed in the Bedlam parade by the very last of their accumulated shit. Figuratively speaking, obviously. Too much gazing into the Abyss and you come to the awful conclusion that there's nothing staring back at all. And that's why I'll take the Mirror over the Void any day.

That's where I came in—Spalding said, explaining to me how she was still working part-time at the orphanage when she received the call from the Marvells, that bereaved couple from the news.

It all made sense. They wanted to re-create their daughter. The boy Kenneth—and Miss Spalding tried to be careful and precise—*was undergoing a process of depatterning, to become a new Penelope.*

I shrugged, having some idea what she was talking about, hoping I could squeeze more out of her by playing dumb and pandering to her vanity.

A programme of drugs, conditioning, sensory deprivation and overload was needed—she said. *Intended to return the subject's mind to its original factory settings, I suppose. A blank slate.*

La Victoria Marvell's mental health, teetering precariously on the high wire to begin with, succumbed to a major Hollywood breakdown—a cosmic post-natal depression expressed as one emotionally-mutilated woman's insane coping strategy.

The gone little girl of the Marvells had spent the inaugural three months of her life as a living exhibit under the display canopy of an incubator, so whatever first-draft version of the boy Kenny Trace still endured in the aftermath of trauma induction was suffered to undergo the same ordeal in the adult-scale reproduction of a newborn intensive-care unit Charles had commissioned.

Shivering and choking while the temperature was slyly lowered to unbearable zero, the moment the new Penelope learned to sweat again was regarded as a breakthrough equivalent to baby's all-important mastery of its own body's thermostat. She might have died otherwise but she was strong with the life force. Penny pulled through.

I got the bit about mind control, but the rest had me dumbfounded.

Why a boy? To take the place of a girl? It made about as much sense as swapping your laces for spaghetti.

I told you—she said. *By this time, they were both mad. And they couldn't find a girl who fit the bill. It was harder to justify doing what they did to a young woman but if they had to, they could sell this as a means to pacify and rehabilitate violent offenders.*

As girls!—I snorted.

More to the point, I didn't like her use of the words "violent offender." I didn't like the way that you wait ages for a

346 · GRANT MORRISON

coincidence then five of them turn up at the same time, all going the same way.

You say you were breastfeeding him—I said matter-of-factly to take my mind off the step-by-step progression each new smidgen of information took towards an inevitable unthinkable conclusion. I still wanted to find an escape hatch, a flaw in the structure that made it all fall to bits. *You didn't think that was a bit unusual?*

I didn't have to do much to terrify him—she admitted. *I just came in wearing the mask and a sort of black iridescent kimono. They'd pump noise into the Nursery—babies crying, slaughterhouse screeches, loud death metal. The lights would be flashing on and off. Strobes.*

She painted quite a picture; like something Francis Bacon would have done but a picture, nonetheless.

Then I had to, well, dance around a bit, being creepy. I did my best.

It's not really something you can train for, is it?—I said with a withering acidity I hoped conveyed at least a hint of my disapproval.

They were doctors—she said, exonerating the crazed couple. In the hands of certified professionals torture, conditioning, and forced gender reassignment could be classified as medicine.

When the commotion in the Nursery reached its cacophonous climax, Miss Spalding explained, she'd swoop through billows of dry ice with the spectral oil-slick wings of her kimono flaring and snapping around her to scoop the screaming naked teenager into her lap.

Bee Spalding spoke lightly, using the same cropped diction she'd lately employed to debate matters of Renaissance perspective, of how she'd breastfeed the sobbing hairless Luda, stroking the smooth scalp of a naked young creature of seventeen so traumatized and dissociated it had lost conscious control of bladder and bowels.

As the atmosphere of abnormality she attracted curdled into free-roaming clots of palpable unease, Miss Spalding spoke fondly of the boy they'd shaved to a babyish softness and christened "New Penny," of how, in the throes of rebirth, New Penny would twitch under glass as her muscles attempted to release the stored tension of a violent past her waking mind would never recall. Cast ashore, shipwrecked and amnesiac among the potent symbols of pre-verbal consciousness, curled like a Nautilus shell on a beach, foetal in her outsized neo-natal incubator, newly-minted Penny nursed on a wizened, waterlogged thumb and filled her patient nappy with each new blissful uninhibited release of tension.

Laces tightening on a corset, the strands of the plot, the play, whatever had begun when I first met Luda, contracted sharply into shape, taking my breath, straightening my spine to look truth in the eye.

Was it really beyond the realm of the possible that an untamed hooligan could find himself the guinea pig in a social experiment conducted by wealthy, bereft parents?

Was it likely they scrubbed his identity with cleaning products courtesy of brainwashing pioneer Ewen Cameron and the CIA?

If there's anything I value it's the opportunity we're given to shine, to be authors of our own gripping biographies, directors of our own blockbusting movie franchises, celebrated actors slipping effortlessly into our starring roles.

Spalding's story was anathema, apostasy; so fundamentally opposed to my core values, so tailor-made by some consumer anti-algorithm to offend specifically me, I found it hard to swallow. It sounded like science fiction, but you know me, I did some looking into it later and it's all true about Cameron and KUBARK counterintelligence techniques.

Charles wondered if a soul could be constructed—she said. *Or reconstructed I suppose. Could Penelope Marvell's soul be rebuilt from scratch then housed in a body renovated for the purpose?*

I get it—I said, a bit troubled. *But transplanting souls, I mean—it can't be legal.*

Temporarily alive in this unlikely world, sensibly shod Miss Ess and I flitted brief as damselflies among the eternally dead. The stuffed, the mounted, the painted, the wrapped, and the embalmed. Among the sarcophagi, the dead bodies swathed in cloth cocoons, prepped for some unknown metamorphosis in the afterlife, in the Fertile Fields of Aru, the Sunset Lands . . .

She wouldn't be drawn on the judicial front, but I will say she was an absolute gusher of information when it came to the transmigration of souls.

Together we continued down broad sandstone-and-marble stairs to the expansive ground floor. Above us a blue whale skeleton hung suspended in its imagined X-ray ocean above the grand hall, participating in an inadvertent Surrealist dogfight with the World War I biplane strung a little higher, visible in sections through the rib cage of the whale.

We stopped again in the Ancient Animals gallery by the scale model of an allosaurus painted blue-green. Here since the 1900s, it reared up behind her, two tiny arms typing at an imaginary keyboard made, I like to imagine, from rib cage, monkey knuckles, and bamboo.

Charles, the spinster Spalding explained, clearly reminded of the man by the thunder-lizard's murder-clown grin, was obsessed with reincarnation. At first, he'd clung to the idea in the hope that Penelope would be reborn and that he might hasten her return to the world of the living by crafting a vehicle suitable for her return.

But set a pessimistic madman to ponder reincarnation and it's easy to see how the needs of an analytical mind might get scrambled together with articles of faith and led by the nose, by the heady aroma of reason sizzling to scratchings in the pan, in the direction of some far-ranging, some might say downright unreasonable, ideas concerning the brunt of overpopulation on the global supply of souls.

If it was true that human spirits were recycled into successive generations, in a closed system where population was doubling exponentially, Marvell calculated frantically, where were the fresh essences coming from to occupy all the new bodies?

In almost two thousand years, between the arrival of baby Jesus in his spaceship from the planet Krypton and the febrile death of Lord Byron at Missolonghi, the number of human beings living on planet Earth multiplied from an exclusive clique of 160 million to a jostling *hoi polloi* of 1 billion, kept in check by regular visits from one or other of the Four Horsemen of the Apocalypse.

I'm not just making this up. I've got it written down.

Since the last time the Black Death had its way with Europe, improvements in health and education, along with standards of food production and distribution, have resulted in what they call logistic growth of human biomass—in only two hundred-odd years from the Regency period to where I sit today doing my stage makeup, our human obsession with mass production in all areas has yielded a surly swarm of eight billion people, shuffling shoulder-to-shoulder around the increasingly shabby décor of the same old living room. Even the enthusiastic mass extermination of our animal companions has failed to free up enough space and it's not as if we can just knock up an extension.

In my own brief lifetime, the number of squabbling, competing, self-serving *Homo sapiens* has doubled. I'm no chicken spring roll but that does seem a bit excessive. I'd go so far as to say profligate but it's not a word I tend to use more than twice.

You're asking—*Where is all this leading, Luci?* Well, it's leading to Charles Marvell's theoretical breakthrough. A misguided *Eureka!* on a par with reaching the conclusion that the sun is a giant plug of flaming dung orbiting an Earth shaped like the lid on a tin of Pringles.

Could it be, the doctor speculated, that the accelerating human birth rate was outpacing the allocation of souls? I know! It's not my idea. It's what I heard that day, wandering through the display units, where stuffed wolves serenaded a painting of the January full moon in gouache, and kingfishers spread lysergic blue wings to take flight yet never left the sheet of rippled glass that stood in for their long-dried marsh, where nature was impersonated by taxidermy.

These same animals have been here since I was a kid—I said, pausing to admire my reflection superimposed over the blunt head of the black leopard in its shrunken diorama.

I'd come here with my art class when I was nineteen. I'd chosen to draw the panther because I felt sorry for it, adding a bleeding carcass spiked and limp between the All-Beast's open gate of jaws. The strawberry blobs of dripping bloody saliva I'd chosen to include brought the only splash of colour to my charcoal sketch.

The panther must have been shot dead a hundred years ago, longer—victim of an old-fashioned 3D photographic technique where, instead of emulsion, the subject was immobilized in a glass case, fixed by the taxidermist's art as a faithful snapshot of a day long ago when it muscled through the undergrowth in search of food, prowling through an afterlife among the artificial branches, the artful facsimile of savanna and distant tropical volcano. The panther pretending to live beyond its natural span as its own substantial ghost—its parents and its siblings, the cubs it was driven to care for gone to dust long ago, while it kept on into impossible futures padding on its habitat base, outpacing us all, eyes locked to an inner endless horizon as we grew old and passed and where other children, scowling students with pens in hand and screens instead of cartridge paper, sketched the immortal likeness of

Panthera pardus, the All-Beast, become one more ephemeral reflection among countless generations smeared across the convex curve of its inscrutable glass eyes.

The price of staying the same forever was to live in one eternal moment, shot dead then stuffed and mounted to look your best in a glass box.

In its shoulder-led gunslinger poise, in the glossy fur coat, the tanned and tempered hide held together by glue and string, was the ultimate performance—a cosmetic triumph of armature and cotton batting, wax and paint.

Death dragged up as Life Eternal.

I'd titled my drawing *The Kill* in a troubled attempt to shake the panther from her daze of permanence and restore her haemoglobin-speckled fangs to red currency.

My teachers regarded the addition of dripping cherry gore as needlessly sensational, and in flagrant violation of the strictly black-and-white brief, but I won a minor prize, nevertheless. At least one perspicacious critic saw in my title the ironic double meaning I'd intended.

Miss Spalding seemed disconcerted; the glass eyes troubled her, she explained, made her skin creep. There was something awful about the painted polystyrene dirt scrabble between the claws, the snarl forever young, forever defiant in the face of a death that couldn't be deferred because it had already happened long, long ago.

Charles Marvell was sure we'd run out of souls to recycle, she told me. *There weren't enough to go around, you see, new babies were being born without souls.*

I wasn't persuaded by the numbers. Marvell hadn't taken into account that some more populous breeding ground might supply the necessary discarnate ingredient—battery hens, for instance, slaughtered at the age of seventy weeks might be rewarded with an upgrade where they would blink to awareness in a different kind of incubator, as a human baby.

Who can tell? For all we know, especially virtuous and hard-working insects might level up to *Homo sapiens* after a lifetime of service to the hive. The soul of the whole honeycomb reborn as a banker's wife, or a corporate CEO.

None of that mattered. What did matter was middle-class Marvell's deeply held, deeply flawed conviction that some people, maybe entire generations, could be born without souls; some of us could be flat people with only one dimension, on the outside.

That perhaps this Invasion of the Charisma Snatchers was already under way, had already happened, and there was nothing any of us could do to prevent it, until the last of the truly human found themselves with cudgels in their hands defending a giant, black-walled city against the hordes of feral, amoral simulacra, was enough of a threat to justify in Charles Marvell his voyages beyond the pale.

This infestation of the unsouled, Marvell conjectured, accounted for the loss of meaning, the degradation of culture, the sociopathic narcissism characteristic of the Age of the Individual, the zombie apocalypse.

Where we saw simple alienation, Charles Marvell saw a literal plague of the p-zombies.

Sorry I'm late—I trilled, fluttering busily into an atmosphere so thickened with impatience and disappointment it seemed to set around me, stilling me into a cringe.

I was only three hours late. Abanazar's nervy understudy had given up and scuttled home to contend with a veterinary drama centred on an ageing red setter with a boisterous bladder. The first canine victim of the McCloudie Curse, I ventured, but Dom was immune to levity. His whole body seethed with the scrunched fume and scramble of those tightly-squiggled black balls cartoonists scribble to signify wordless anger.

There's only one thing for it, Dom—I said. I refused to give ground. *I'm willing to pay back the three hours and work all night but you'll have to be Abanazar.*

I didn't give him time to reply. I made a precise Knight's move into my start position on the massive cat's cradle of tags and with an imperious flick of my wrist directed him into place. Dumbstruck, he shuffled onto his mark and just as he found his voice again and was opening his mouth to speak like a blowhole gaping in a whale's head I cut him off with these words—*If it's a princess you're looking for, Abbey National*—I crowed. *You've come to the right place. If you're still straight after this performance, it's a miracle—*

With that, Twankey shimmers across the stage, a dreadnought in a frock on full steam ahead. As he faces down this vision of an oncoming force of nature, this pyroclastic mirage of glitter and polychromatic polyester fabrics, this unstoppable whelming slurry of lipstick and rouge, sarcasm and predatory sexuality, Abanazar's jaw flaps open like the back end of a cargo plane.

I didn't have to delve deep to summon Twankey to her pivotal scene. What I had to do was forget all about p-zombies and mind-wiped louts until we were done.

I swung my hips to a sinuous slut strut, taking care to stumble artfully on my heels, so that I didn't come across as too good or too overtly sexy. Twankey's function is to be funny and she's an underdog after all, an underbitch you might say, reaching for fruits she can never pluck. If I tell you I learned everything I know about throwing shapes from watching late-night documentaries about lap-dancers, or by imitating the blank-faced, serpentine flexing of caged go-go girls and belly dancers in '60s movie parties, you might be halfway to understanding the potential for taking it all too far in the direction of nausea-inducing erotica.

Swooping in on Abanazar, executing a *kamikaze* approach run, I trailed fluttering flags of silk as if they were coloured

354 · GRANT MORRISON

smoke pouring off the engine of a dying Mitsubishi G4M gliding towards the aircraft carrier on a wing and a *banzai!* The
wizard retreated, nipping behind his wall of bodyguards for
protection from the living single-minded flame that now swept
through his chamber, the named hurricane, Storm Twankey,
wiping out the contours of the weathergirl's map.

I was a nightmarish premonition of his young and wealthy
wife after twenty-five years of embittered cohabitation for
which even matching thrones could never compensate.

Everywhere Abanazar tried to flee, I was there already—
flapping my wings of trailing fabric, puckering puffed-up red
balloon lips, I was herding him, manipulating him into ev-
er-smaller safe spaces, leaving the wizard with fewer and fewer
options for survival.

I did a bit of research and I'm not saying I'm an expert, but
I think I got the gist; a p-zombie, or philosophical zombie, is a
living, reacting creature that looks and behaves exactly like a
typical human being would, except for one all-important difference: The p-zombie has no inner life, no sense of self or self-reflection. The p-zombie is a living robot, driven to respond to
stimuli in certain ways, but incapable of free will.

Tickle a p-zombie and it will beg for mercy like anyone else
but only because it has learned or been taught that's the correct
response given the circumstantial parameters.

In fact, the p-zombie can feel no pain, no surprise, no sensation, nothing at all. Even when it insists it's in pain you know
it's not. It's entirely mechanical.

Think behaviourism. Skinner's pigeons. Pavlov's pooches
trained to slobber at the sound of a bell.

The maddening thing is how would you know if you met one?
The only way to be sure that any living thing other than yourself
has an inner reality of hopes, dreams, is to have that internal life
described to you in some way that can be acknowledged and

recognized as human. We like to think Marcel Proust had a world inside his skull because he went to great pains and filled thousands of pages with words to explain how it felt to be him, dining on cake-shaped memories in bed.

I can't help thinking about the crumbs from Proust's madeleines. Doesn't matter how comfy your silk pajamas are, it must have been like sleeping in a cat's litter tray!

Could a p-zombie describe that sensation? I ask the question in all seriousness.

Charles Marvell came to believe that "Kenny Trace" had been born without the appropriate USB port for a plug-in. All attempts to endow the Trace with a prosthetic soul invited the same inevitable reckoning, the same reenactment of Baron Frankenstein's cautionary journey—from a boast to a scream.

If any of this was true, Luda had been conditioned to respond appropriately to sensory input; she'd been schooled by experts on how to reproduce the physical signs of caring and affect, but she didn't care, she wasn't affected in any meaningful way by events in her life. I'd met narcissists and sociopaths before. I'd fucked more than one and had stories to tell about how they operated according to strict guidelines and dependable routines.

Like so many girls and pretty boys, I'd been the centre of attention, flattered, wooed, and then insulted, ignored, betrayed, and accused. I knew the standard type: rock-star boys who couldn't abide to be out-glammed, who indulged their bleak banal appetites by immersing unsuspecting pretty faces in the suppurating cesspit of self-loathing they kept nailed down behind the eyeliner and Jack Daniel's. Or there were coked-out Patrick Bateman city boys scrubbing search histories that would put anyone else on the Register.

Luda was something else, something I couldn't put my finger on. Something I had no vocabulary to describe until this new appreciation of the whole p-zombie hypothesis made it clear to me that something was seriously wrong.

There were hollow people. They lived among us and we knew them when we met them but refused to believe the evidence of our senses. Of course we did. They came from beyond our common understanding.

In the unsuspecting yellow soil, the sprawling untended garden that is my imagination, a Pepperland of thistle-whistles, glitterhorse trees, coffee apples, and wonderwear, Bee Spalding had sown the leprous seed of a *fleur du mal* grown so purple and so virulent its dripping tips oozed the wine of all intolerance, all othering, all "ethnic cleansing."

To suggest that some people might not be real people at all was to sound the bugle, blow the conch, press the button, and board the express train to one inevitable terminus, and the camp gates of sanctioned genocide.

Welcome to the world according to Charlie Marvell!

Speaking of hollow, Spalding seemed drained when I left her, as if the effort of absorbing all available light in the room had taken its toll on her liver. I, on the other hand, was bursting with energy, a mosquito topped up to capacity at a human filling station.

I promised I'd keep in touch, my current most regularly-deployed fib.

As she walked away, shoulders bowed by the weight of her own insignificance, a living silhouette lost in the high-contrast shadows between the tall leaded windows that let in flying buttresses of light, I remembered what I'd meant to ask.

Were there others?—I called after her. *Copies of her? Luda said she'd seen others.*

She turned to face me from the bleached darkness beyond a forty-five-degree-angled rafter of sunshine and dust and spat out her words the way you'd flick a coffin fly off your tongue—*Don't believe a word Luda says.*

Alone in the shadow of the allosaurus, I felt the ineluctable hand of circumstance fashioning, from bits and pieces that didn't fit a Victorian *portmanteau* grotesque, a platypus with wheels, tits, and a unicorn horn.

I flagged a cab.

I had a lot to think about, don't you think?

While Abanazar stands riveted in place, justifiably stupefied, I enact the mock-seductive extinction event that is Twankey's obscene Dance of Death; designed by me and Elena Novac during golden afternoons we'd spent absorbing YouTube footage of the cannibalistic courtship rituals of preying manti and trapdoor spiders. Aladdin goes to work, ducking in between his mother's flapping curtains to reach the Lamp on its pedestal by Abanazar's throne.

But there's trouble afoot when the Genie clocks Aladdin dodging and rolling commando-style just out of Abanazar's sight line. The *afrit*'s torn between sounding the alarm to warn his new master or keeping his mouth shut long enough to give Aladdin his chance.

Shall I instruct my Master Abanazar that Aladdin still lives?— he asks the audience.

NOOOO! The crowd yells one great command.

Shall I help Aladdin?—our supernatural fly in the wizard's ointment now inquires of the fully-agitated spectators, and this time of course they all bellow *YESSS!* at the tops of their various voices—fully aware of how, in this enchanted bounded micro-world, so unlike the real one, the clear difference between what's right and what's wrong must be insisted upon.

Abanazar has other things on his mind, such as dealing with the equivalent of battlefield trauma as Twankey all but wrestles the cornered conjurer to the floor, subjecting the man to what in any other context could only be described as aggressive non-consensual sexual assault disguised as a collapsing circus tent.

As Abanazar drowns beneath billowing bales of stoplight- and acid-drop-coloured chiffon, struggling as frantically as a man failing to attract the attention of the lifeguard, Aladdin and Jasmine seize the Lamp with a bit of teamwork—she throws it to him, he catches it, gives it some elbow grease, and hey presto! The natural order of things is restored with six words!

Your wish is my command, Master!—announces the Genie smiling proudly, winking at Aladdin. We knew we'd get audience cheers for that moment loud enough to be heard above the rush-hour rumble on Gargoyle Street. *As long as you don't ask me to suck your*—time the beat carefully—*toes!*

And there on the laugh, we hit pause on the action one last time. The lights shift ominously, the music warps into minor chords, ambient electronica, clicks, burrs, and impending thrums that leave the audience paralysed, dumbstruck with tension.

The end is close now. The curtains tremble in anticipation.

Friday night. Me, home, decanted into the cushion scoops of the sofa in a blue fluffy robe. I drank too much coffee and filled a notepad with shorthand doodles, spidery drawings of stars and triangles, pentagons, polygons. Me trying to work it all out, mapping Dominick Float's intricate proxemics, the stage directions and fluorescent marks that explained the seeming chaos onstage and elsewhere in our lives.

Pythagorean underpinnings. The whirling Fibonacci helices of atoms and galaxies and Renaissance paintings, the Golden Sections spinning into a conclusion that can never come because there's always more down there to divide and explore. The deeper you go the deeper it gets.

Foremost in my ruminations that evening was Charles Marvell's obsession with the Golden Mean, Vitruvian Man, the Ratio. The crucified Christ. Dragons and fives.

Phi breaking down into the 1 as penis, the 0 as vagina,

womb, receptacle for the force and intention of the thrusting phallic "1," the matrix where the impulse is brought to term then turned out *à la mode* onto the merry butcher's block of the world of everyday things you can touch and divide, buy and sell.

Binary notation being all that's required to conjugate a universe of dynamic opposites. All it takes is an on and an off. A dark and light, a yes and no. An up, a down. A push and a pull, reaction, dialectic thesis, antithesis, synthesis, new thesis, antithesis, peristalsis triggering karmic landslides of consequence. The In. The Out. The Give. The Take. Cock and cunt creating copies of another *ad infinitum*.

I left school when I was eighteen, but it didn't take a philosophy degree to figure out where Mr. Marvell had gone awry.

I drew the Golden Rectangle, separating it with boundary lines into flawless fractions, into Mondrian divisions of space I knew by heart, into fractals, where each tangram tile repetition of the pattern dragged me around and deeper into a ceaseless pressurized intensity, a quintessence of meaning and symmetry where all of this made sense as the simple Möbius twist of one simple thing, seen at last from a distance, recognized as the final period at the end of a long, long sentence a bit like this one.

The unsatisfying answer to a pointless question.

I read and took notes, as somewhere out there, east of the apartment and Charity Row, Luda made her way through the gathering dusk of another year's November, weightless traveller through the moonstruck streets of Gasglow, coming closer.

I was sunk into the sofa's soft fathoms two-thirds of the way through *Some Like It Hot* for the millionth time when I heard the door locks clench and unclench, and Luda pitched into the living room.

I waited for her to go about her routine: opening the fridge, drinking the probiotics, munching on dark chocolate, crunching

a raw carrot until slowly she became aware of the mounting tension in the room, sensing my eyes on her, my taut silence.

What?—she said, and I said—*What do you mean by "what?"
There's something up. I can tell.*

She paused in the doorway, leaning nonchalant, poised on
the threshold, subliminally dividing the space in the frame, and
made a dainty rabbit wrinkle of her nose as she sniffed for what
you'd have to guess were single molecules.

Were you doing one of your rituals or something?—she said,
making it sound like the accusation it was meant to be. *Did I
miss something at work?*

There was a half beat before I'd had enough. I was a little
fizzy, a little spangled and self-righteous and it was time to pull
rank.

You didn't—I said, meaning "you did." *You fucked Molly's
boyfriend and—and then—and then what? You can't blame
Kenny—this is you!*

In reply, Luda dropped all the pretence to show me what
she'd been learning. With a reptilian sine-wave shimmy, she
stretched, undid herself, then clinched into a near-faultless
reproduction of Molly's posture, and when I say "near" that's
what I mean; we were back at Uncanny Valley city limits, with
this oozing, sexed-up Stepford simulation of Molly Stocking's
distinctive voice and mannerisms.

Who's been talking?—she said.

Luda's over-the-top posturing was delivered with a side of
satirical cruelty that laid bare in each entitled attitude and sulk
Molly Stocking's self-conscious pretensions. Sweet, silly Molly's
every unguarded flaw was amplified by a single gesture, a slur
of syllables, a graceless sashay extended to parodic, hyper-camp
extremes, so much realler than the real thing it made you gag
like an overdose of candyfloss.

This is what you did with what I taught you?—I said, vindicated, horrified.

It was and I'd never seen anything like it. The attention to detail that made this spiteful venomous caricature so effective was maddening in its scrupulous, microscopic fidelity.

He thought I was her!—she said with distilled and bottled contempt. *Even when I showed him my cock, he wouldn't believe it was real! He thought I'd had it strapped on to get back at him for the anal rape*—Luda wide-eyed waved her arm, seeking praise, seeing validation in my eyes. *I told him I'd always had one and he just hadn't noticed before.*

Did you? I wanted to laugh and go mad to get out of the trap. I was in the presence, tightly-wrapped in the spiky fractured glory, of the Fallen Angel, celestial, young, and forever. Luda.

Last time I looked—I said, keeping an even tone intended to suggest not sobriety but madness. *Murder was regarded as a crime.*

So is rape!—she said.

What else have you done?

Luda said nothing. She didn't have to.

I held up the shoe, Exhibit B in the case for the prosecution. Not Molly's tap shoe but the other one I'd found in Luda's satchel. My Little Shoe Box peep-toe platform.

You need to get your shit together and get out of here—I said, best boss bitch.

As she gathered her meagre belongings and left, Luda winked and flashed a red-outlined klieg-light smile that made it all seem like a move in a game, with skin so smooth and elastic her expression was streamlined to an emoji.

Like the back cover of a book with the saddest of endings, the door closed on Luda. Her shape atomized to coloured spray in the pebble glass, the hot simmer of pixels that receded until she wasn't there any more. The light of her dwindling off-screen, with the sound, much slower, of her typewriter heels on the stair chasing after her into silence.

With that, I burst like a balloon. I could have filled a basin and washed a week's worth of dishes in the tears I cried that night.

When I'd given up gulping and snuffling, when my body was wrung dry of its saline and mucus quotient, leaving me sluiced out, serene, and faceup on the living-room carpet, I charted the backslash graphics across the ceiling and walls without granting them the succour of significance. They were *shunyata*—physical optical processes occurring as a result of prior conditions and subsequent outcomes.

I knew it was likely to get worse.

Fortunately, I also knew what had to be done.

What's on your mind, Lu?—thus *sprach* Dominick Float and by this time, I was fully receptive to anyone willing to take more than a statistician's interest in my shambolic so-called life.

Family stuff—I offered, keeping it nebulous, adjusting my lipline.

You told me you had no family—he reminded me, and I could see I'd let him down again.

Luda had failed to appear for weekend rehearsals. I could tell Dom held me responsible for her behaviour.

It's not what you think—I said. *It's nothing like what you think*—and he said—*You think?*

I held my ground until he opened the *News of the Sun.* I almost started crying when I saw what had happened. There in declamatory sixty-point type I read the words nailed, like the Romans tacked INRI to the vertical crossbar above Jesus's skewer-crowned head, to the page beside my picture.

DAMES IN DISGRACE!

Grimly, Dom unfolded to a double-page spread. Archive shots of me in the Troupe days, then hunched, furtive, and overweight on *Superstar Survival* dodging out of view, trying to escape off the frame—

IS TV HAS-BEEN TELLING THE TRUTH ABOUT MISSING BOY?

I was staggering now, on the ropes, too stunned to defend myself against the feeble punchline.

OH YES, HE IS!

YOU DECIDE—it went on, offering an alternative as a joke.

OH NO, HE ISN'T!

What about HE'S BEHIND YOU!—I countered dismissively, scuffing tears off my cheeks as if they were bothersome insects. *They haven't used that one yet.*

PANTO CURSE CONTINUES AS BANNED COMIC'S DATE WITH MISSING YOUNGSTER SPARKS MANHUNT . . .

Gravely he said I could take the day off. I was touched but he had a reason.

We can't do any of this without her—Dom gibbered pale as a sweating cheese. *You have to get Luda to rehearsal.*

She walked out, Dom. After the police. I'll find her—I said, a film hero vowing to save the day at the end of act 1. *Whatever it takes.*

You don't understand—he started, then shook his head. *This is life and death*—

Dom seemed snapped, his spine rotted and shattered all the way through, bones of biscuit crushed in a heartless fist.

Don't let this fall apart, Lu—he pleaded with me, flattened beneath the rubble.

I told myself not to dwell on "TV has-been" with its ugly double meaning. The implication that I may have been involved in the disappearance stroke buggery, prior to murder, of a scrawny homeless waif surely outweighed the stinging throb on my self-esteem and yet . . .

TV has-been!

What kind of has-been can handle the starring role in a prestige theatrical production? Show me the has-been who can dance out the meaning of each of the Seven Veils five nights a week!

Mirror, mirror on the wall, I thought glumly.

The oak frames of the dressing-table mirrors were shifted slightly off true from a configuration so long established they'd left thin, clean spaces in the dust of years. The frames had been newly angled, so I looked splintery, schizoid, with my unity split into queerly-canted fragments of face; the broken plates of cheekbones, the mouth and teeth relocated below my ear as an artistic experiment.

Sealed inside the three golden rectangles of the mirror's varnished oak frames, powerless to resist my creator's lack of talent and time, I was a badly-drawn comic-book character with hexagonal mouth agape, eyes wide and marbled in some moment of awful revelation, undone by the corkscrew twist at the story's end.

I was a microscope specimen divested of the dimension of depth, glued and mounted beneath the glass slide.

The frames around the semi-silvered surface were sawn from recycled train sleepers. A friend who sometimes worked with the prop department back in the Troupe days had measured, cut, and handcrafted the mirror's folding triptych panels to complement the immense and intimidating four-poster bondage bed I'd commissioned from him as a night-boat constructed with voyages beyond decency in mind. With that in mind, the headboard had a built-in working stocks. I can't say I was ever especially drawn to S/M or B/D or any of that alphabet sex, but it looked good and separated out the timewasters and faint of heart.

The bed's just here as texture for the story about the mirror. I felt cordoned off within its lines and limits, entrapped in carved and jointed bones of tree, for all eternity, facing my face as it hastened towards a promised end in leather and dust.

I reset the panels, restoring balance and harmony. The central portrait staring me out, the flanking semi-profiles disengaged, eyes on an elsewhere, a vanishing-point unavailable from my vantage.

I knew myself to be in a kind of free fall, a chaos of doubt between the jump and the chute opening. Suddenly I found it impossible to mangle any meaning from the scratchings on the newspaper page. The only thing that made sense was the photo-spread shot of the waitress from the Rendezvous in her under-wear and then only because I recognized the Marlies Dekkers set as identical to one I'd ordered online and last worn twenty years ago.

Hers was secondhand.

The waitress from the Rendezvous—"Nataliya Nowakowski, 21" my arse—was willing, nay duty-bound, to testify that she was certain beyond any and all possible shadows of available doubts that she'd waited on Luci LaBang off the TV, aka Graeme Mott, and with him a sexy-cheekboned homeless boy matching the description of the et cetera et cetera.

You can see how it happens: Some juicy stray gossip crystal-lizes around a single seed of truth, half-truth, or no truth at all if the rumour is intriguing enough to put down roots. A loop of narrative coils around real people and events until there's no untying the knots it makes. Fiction lashed to reality as the Ship of Theseus goes down between Scylla and Charybdis.

The noose tightened.

Luda had contrived her glittering Glamour, her diamond snare, with care and elegance.

If they find me, it's sure to be obvious I did it. Whatever it is. The Crime. Somebody must have done it, so why not me? I've got so many motives I don't know what to do with them!

Think about the plot of *The Phantom,* the framing story where the embittered older actor, obsessed with her looks, resolves to wipe out her imagined rivals one by one until she reaches her star pupil. Dame *vs.* Principal Boy.

What was to become of my big comeback? The crown-ing achievement that should have been *The Phantom of the Pantomime.*

What if there are police pounding a beat beyond the purview of workaday pigs and plods? What if Flat Police patrol a bigger more splendid yet far more dangerous version of Gasglow that exists where dreams and reality meet and shift on the shore between solid and liquid? What if there are Hollow People?

What if I'm one of them?

Would it make any difference?

It was bad, but it's been worse. One valuable side effect of being dragged kicking and screaming through a few decades is the accumulation of emotional scab with its accompanying merciful loss of sensation.

I'd survived the gruesome deaths of treasured parents. I'd lost lovers and animal companions. I'd lost myself. I'd made mistakes. I'd hurt everyone including me. I was a disgusting mess and I was uniquely beautiful.

I was fucked if the Devil was going to bring me to book. Pot. Kettle!

It all made sense. All it took was the calm, the stillness of that first-page face before the words accumulated as overwritten lines, plot wrinkles. Webs and snares are among the most seductive and deadly of the Glamour's tools and weapons.

Thinking back to some of my outfits and especially the Hervé Léger bandage dress I used to own, I was confident I could wriggle into and out of pretty much anything.

How can you possibly go up against someone who plays five moves ahead?

It's a reasonable question.

Closing the front door behind me, I shuffled bills, rejecting emergency red demands from the electricity company on the grounds that I had a direct debit and they'd made a mistake, and waited for the tub to fill.

Then, as if slipping into a mink coat, I inserted myself into the hot bath I'd drawn and settled into steaming orchid-house buoyancy. I pressed my right foot into service as a prehensile hand to twist the hot tap until the incoming wave of boiling water churning up my shins and knees to my thighs, to my balls, was deliciously unbearable.

Sinking below the surface, just a nose and lips, yacht and dinghy, I hung in suspension, rocked in a cradle of bubble bath as I listened to the blood sawing through my bones.

Hauptprobe is the German name we give to final rehearsal.

After *hauptprobe* there's no safety net.

1101
Devil Woman

A longside the boxes of fashion magazines and newspaper clippings in the untidy, unlit broom cupboard, side by side with examples of the "art" I've inflicted on unsuspecting audiences, I keep a locked Louis Vuitton suitcase. Inside this item, purchased for the first Troupe tour, are what might be described as totems, fetishes, items of power and significance I've accrued over the years like barnacles stick to a hulk; give value to any object and it will acquire a thicker skin of meaning and importance as the years go by. You won't want to let it go, even if it's only a frayed bus ticket from that first date. Preserve the chosen object for long enough, it might become an obscure object of desire, a Stone of Destiny shaping nations, a Holy Grail inciting spiritual quests.

I opened the suitcase with the key that normally spends its time in the top right-hand corner of the top right-hand drawer on the desk in my small study, where I used to write sketches and songs for the Troupe, where I've been writing that memoir I told the police I was working on.

My senses blunted to a blind man's cane tips, I was only numb. My entire body was one big sexy phantom limb as I split the case like a clam and retrieved the folded pearl. I held in my hands the glittering dress that cracked my family into fragments.

I seemed to watch myself from a distance, as a granular Rorschach blot on an antique TV screen, observing the ancient rites of the Glamour.

I stretched out and carefully rolled the flexible tube of the spangled LBD down over my head, over my stuffed bra, clearing the lowland downs of my stomach. Elastic and celestial, the dress graciously adapted its contours to my changed shape.

The hemline, I have to say, was nothing less than scandalous. Cut to compliment the baby-horse legs and elevated posterior of an eleven-year-old boy, there was something obscene about its unwillingness to disguise my flabby thighs and sagging cheeks; something awful and occult that suited my midnight purpose.

Facing first the East and the element of Air, the intellectual faculty, I brought together the elements. A quarter-turn left I was facing North, which is Fire and passion, then West and Watery emotion, until a final rotation situated me in the Eastern corner informed by Earth and practicality. As I spun in stately slow motion, I called on the Presence at the Crossroads, the one astride the in-between. The notion nailed alive to materiality. The Manageress!

Come among us my Mercurius
Lightning-tempered, fast and furious!

I spread my arms wide, vogueing onto an imagined runway in a Daliesque glam crucifixion. My dress road-tested and discarded new constellations, temporary star charts as I swaggered, its redirected disco-ball shimmer thrown in eight directions, a shower of phantom coins at an anti-gravity wedding. The cornicing bled from the ceiling, crowning me with old paint and new meaning. The sense of living contact was stronger than I'd predicted but I should have known.

Resorted to in existential crises only, this dress meant life-and-death business.

Quite unexpectedly, the words in English I was improvising lost their shape, tearing off constraining vowels and consonants along with any need to make sense. They ran naked as pure sound, pure sensation, pure expression. I started to sway and croon in tongues, inviting possession, giving voice to

Pentecostal torch songs of passion and regret, composing bar-room laments in alien dialects that were all wordless keening expressions of yearning, loss, and a sozzled sincerity.

A sacrifice will be required—the arch-mannie-queen Mercurius solemnly informed me, turning colours inside out.

The price of not just victory but survival would be something of great value.

Under normal circumstances I'd be expecting to hear from the call boy any minute now.

The wig completes the transformation, seals it with a dynamite kiss. My act 1 showstopper is a towering candyfloss castle of sparkle and weird coral colours only bees and poets can see. Twankey goes through six complete costume and wig changes over an hour and fifty minutes but her first appearance demands an unforgettable creation, a flaming Eiffel Tower, a bargain-basement Sun King confection in every imaginable shade between purple and pink, with modernist lightning zigzags in black and white inspired by Elsa Lanchester's Amy Winehouse look in the *Bride of Frankenstein.*

Twirling bangs bracket my contoured face. The geometric fringe obscures my frozen brow as I prepare my ascent to Elizabethan Gloriana majesty. Drag Tutankhamun, *ersatz* Nefertiti.

No longer Luci LaBang, I become the Washerwoman, archetypal, Mother of the Sun.

I tried to wrinkle my brow. The glaze refused to crack. My days of registering disapproval with a frown were behind me. Instead I lightly painted one in place.

Next, humming along with "Pretty Vacant" on repeat, dialling the strobe light to twenty-five hertz, twenty-five flashes per second, until it seemed as if the flawless mask was melting, peeling in ribbons to expose something real hidden underneath the rank pretence. The florid countenance of an immortally-beautiful chortling fiend made of flame showed in flickers at first through spreading burn holes in a blazing black veil. In the rouged cheeks, the hyper-contouring, the tragi-comic battle against age and irrelevance could be seen as the painted bloody mask of Kali on the rag, at the end of all things in red fire and yellow flame when galaxies combust in the hot breath of Siva the Destroyer, her consort, dancing down the constellations.

The Crone, the Beldam, the Widow Twankey.

From the back stalls she could pass for half her age!

House is open!

The end of that Monday, when I danced into the lion's den, as it unreeled in the cab windows, was all travelling textures of brick warehouse and train-yard corrugated shed, a scrib-ble of fencing, and packs of shuffled guard-dog warning signs that gave way to cropped hedges and suburban approach roads pebbled with five-stones, pressure-hosed clear of brittle rust-coloured leaves, as I thought again of the countless things I knew I shouldn't do but did anyway. It was my *modus operandi,* the wayward by-product of Luci LaBang's personal Glamour. Nobody was going to tell me what to do, especially not me.

Truth to tell, I'd figured most of it out when the Twins let slip they'd received their sex party invitations from Luda, and not the other way around. Some light sleuth work did the rest, and, as I deduced, the Marvells were at the heart of it.

I'd taken a chance and called ahead. The hesitant voice on the other end of the line reminded me of someone but I couldn't place the ripe intonations, even when she suggested I call on her in a manner suggesting the heated incitements of a brothel madame.

The taxi scrunched into a gravel driveway. I felt a clench in my bones to confirm I'd been here before. The apologetic hungover atmosphere the house and gardens wore like a damp dressing gown made a stark comparison with the last time I'd seen this place done up in its glittering glad rags.

There had been fireworks then.

I jilled the bell and waited, wondering what I'd talked myself into. I'd find Luda and cheerlead her into a third-act comeback that would break the curse and rescue *The Phantom,* that was the strategy.

A voice crinkled over the intercom saying—*House is open*—as an electronic echo and the door buzzed to let me in. Before me was a soberly-furnished hallway, pensive in the low sun's claret light. Shorn of best bib and tucker, it seemed bigger, emptier, expanded lazily to fill the cooling silence where a party had been.

I recalled the inflatable guillotine and the framed *Guitar Lesson* while closer inspection of the assembled art treasures, some mercifully draped beneath canvas, provided further hints of an ever-present morbidity lurking beneath the floorboards; an ominous aesthetic bass line, counter pulse of impending dread, underscoring the bourgeois respectability of polished marble, of tasteful wood panelling and original parquet, of icing-sugar cornicing scrolls.

I followed the music, wafting like dope smoke from a room with double doors. I may be a bit of a philistine in some ways, but I'm half proud half ashamed I recognized the tectonic triumphalism of *Glagolitic Mass* by Leoš Janáček; it's not that I'm especially cultured, but the music had inspired a sketch in *The Troupe* series 2, where I played the Statue of Liberty as a strippergram. I sang "Happy Birthday, Mr. President" at groaning subsonic levels while teasing off my robes in extreme, disturbing slow motion to the clanging mallets of *Glagolitic Mass.* Jeremy and the other three played the parts of the four presidents carved into the granite rock at Mount Rushmore, or Six Grandfathers as it's known to the local Lakota Sioux people; George Washington, Lincoln, Roosevelt, and Jefferson with foghorn voices hooting and cheering a lap dance that took ten thousand years to undertake, as registered on a "century counter" in the corner of the screen, before I crumbled into bits. It seemed hysterically funny at the time like so many things that now seem deadly serious, possibly borderline-offensive.

Come in—the woman's weary, enervated voice had an upper-middle-class register; a ringing enunciation tempered by sandpapery exhaustion. *I knew you'd be back in the end.*

I could have said—*What makes you so sure it's the end?* Like James Bond would do but I wasn't quick enough and only came up with the reply much later when it was too late to make a difference.

She sat waiting for me in the cavernous gloom of a living room with hefty curtains drawn so the only light was an artful blade of winter red sun striking beams off enormous nova-burst mirrors to refract as stars through pendant chandelier crystals. Candles, baroque with melted wax, were stationed around the room as grace notes of illumination, their flames burning dead straight, unmoved by the slightest breath of air.

I found myself face-to-beak with a proud figure perched on an ostentatious throne, dominating the stagey set-up while dressed in black and wearing a startling crow mask I'd seen before, on what I'd judged then to be a more padded, more middle-aged body than this frail phenomenon.

Sometimes I like to surround myself with life—she said, anticipating my questions. *What better way than to advertise a sex party?*

It was quite a night—I nodded. *I brought this*—and I fetched the creepy music box from my bag. *It must be worth quite a lot of money*—I said with a sneery implied ellipsis . . .

The demonic music box had been assembled twenty years ago by a local artist who never amounted to anything, she told me; it wasn't worth shit. So ascertaining its worth, she lobbed the contraption over her shoulder where it broke on impact with the floor, still doing its mechanical best to crank out "Devil Woman" as it died there, winding down to an aggrieved hush.

I might have kept it if I'd known you'd do that—I said.

She said it was nothing, the kind of nothing Luda fixated on when she was developing, the way newly-hatched geese and ducks fixate on pencils and straws if Mom's not around.

"Developing."

I love what you've done with the place—I said. *The way you've combined the smell of decaying flesh with just the right hint of bleach is an unexpected highlight.* I knew I was talking too fast and she could see right through my nervy attempts at nonchalance.

The woman in the mask shifted so her leather corset creaked beneath the black dress. The fabulous, feathered throne framed her with exuberant giant quills dipped in beetle-black India ink and tipped with thick gold paint.

Like personal treasures stacked in her own desert tomb, her morbid enclosure, the artworks and the lacquered chess tables, the glimmering lamps, gave the woman an extended presence that went far beyond her frail body. She'd arranged it so that she seemed to be wearing the room itself as a complicated dress. Hollywood style. Surrealist *noir.* Cecil Beaton, Angus McBean.

Was it a family? Sniff! *I'm sure I can smell more than one body*—I said.

She settled, adjusting her posture until she resembled a Tarot Major Arcana. The Black Queen. The Wire Mother. Classically composed, precisely centred. Drawn with compass, set square, protractor.

The beaked head tipped abruptly to one side then the other, unnerving.

I was surprised when she picked up on my obscure Troupe

ref, my Easter Egg, quoting dialogue from our almost classic Murder House Realtor sketch.

More than one generation actually—she finished brightly.

I came to bring her back—I said as pieces fell into place, a punched, fragmented jigsaw filmed in reverse until the blast shards reorganized into a placid pastoral, a waterwheel, an eighteenth-century English country village where everything might make sense at last. *She's Principal Boy. We can't do without her.*

And then the woman in the raven mask identified herself as Victoria Marvell. At least, I think she did.

Deep breath! In my head, I was beginning to solve the Rubik's Cube I'd hammered into incoherent clashing rows of colours.

I'm just a fifty-year-old woman trained in behavioural science, but I thought you'd appreciate a bit of theatre. The truth is I'm bald underneath this mask. Chemo.

I told her I was sorry to hear it but if it was any consolation, she looked like a Surrealist superhero, and I was in awe of her mastery of the Glamour.

We looked forward to a normal life—she said quite suddenly as if a tap had been turned on. *We were a normal family, imagining all the normal things that would happen. Then Penelope was gone . . .*

This is where Luda comes when she goes—I wanted to say but I was too slow off the mark. La Marvell was entering full spate with her cracked chime voice going up and down the *do re mi*—beaky dominatrix of the aviary.

With no mercy, an unendurable grief was all over the Marvells like a snarl of hyenas, a murder of crows among spring lambs, tearing them apart again and again. They couldn't even protect each other, each taking turns to hunt with the pack, husband savaging wife, woman tearing man down to size.

With the evil miracle of each new morning patched together from a moth-eaten tapestry of circumstantial evidence, booze, sleeping pills, and man-sized tissues limp with wrung-out tears, came another bleak recuperation where there was nothing they could do but shudder in each other's arms and await the next round of psychic mutilation. No resources existed to help them deal with their loss.

Part of me wanted to give Victoria Marvell a big teddy bear hug but there's the whole consent thing to be taken into consideration these days and I couldn't be bothered filling in a form and sitting an exam before I was allowed to comfort someone, so I didn't even make the effort.

Somewhere partway down the harrowing track of tears, the insufferable load caused the couple to crumble into constituent ingredients. Too many nights writhing insomniac in the thorned paws of demons as the sheets soaked through, as they sobbed through repeated ineffectual mantras they'd been given in more innocent times at the TM centre.

No longer parents, no longer normal, no longer inhabitants of the sunlit world, whither the Marvells? A little family fallen prey to sadists and sex fiends, their home was a place haunted by murder, contaminated with imagined snuff-porn cruelties starring their little girl. They needed something to glue them back together, something that wasn't just a shared plunge down the same well.

Another baby was out of the question; Charles had opted for a vasectomy after the first.

How were they supposed to create new life in the face of its livid absence?

A gifted surgeon like Charles.

A behavioural psychiatrist like Victoria.

There had to be something these two could come up with!

As a novel way of passing the time, while he figured out what that something might be, Charles took to cruising around town, Mr. Hyde on a fact-finding mission—east to Dunedin and the capital's infamous Pubic Triangle, bristling with its chiming penny arcades, lucky-dip glory holes, and dance bars, then west to Gasglow's bus termini and train-station toilets where junkies were easily persuaded to trade inexpert hand jobs for pocket money.

On one of these compulsive scouting trips, as we know, Charles chanced upon the ideal subject for his increasingly elaborate, ever-more-mental schemes—I nearly said *came upon* but that didn't happen until later—in the form of what he, Charles, chose to capitalize "the Eidolon."

The Eidolon; picture a teenage boy hugging his bony knees against the penetrating cold. A desperately-malnourished seventeen-year-old with seeping needle tracks crusting in the bruised hollows of both arms and behind his knees, between his toes.

When the boy didn't move a single whittled muscle or exhibit any of the traditional signs of life, Charles sprinkled a shower of small change into the polystyrene hamburger box beside the vagrant youth that already held a few pennies and had the words PLEASE HELP felt-tipped on the side.

Determined to provoke a reaction, Charles let some more coins fall from his fingers in a sequence of clatters and chinks that seemed intended to express a sneering condescension as they slowed to an intermittent drip-drip of metal.

Finally, rung to attention by the tinkling patter of change, the boy looked up. Charles later described the moment—*as if the Mona Lisa suddenly turned to look me in the eye—I felt the drag of a singularity—I saw eternity—*

I'm paraphrasing what I was told but you get the general idea. He seemed fixated on the clenched curve beneath Luda's eye, the spinning fall into beauty's true proportions. I don't blame him; staring at the pristine aquamarine section can be enthralling.

Mrs. Marvell, Vicki, if we can call her that without having

met her in any meaningful sense, rose in painful stages from the bum-dented royal purple of her cushion, black-kid-gloved fingers gripping the curved handle of her cane, a silver crow's skull, I noted.

You don't need to—I started, shooting a meaningful glance in the direction of her cane, but she seemed offended.

I can get around my own home—she snapped, before her voice relaxed a little, processing pain she didn't show. *The exercise is good for me.*

With these words, the tripod Widow Marvell led me from her bad dream gallery to a hallway lined with more disturbing or thought-provoking paintings, and a procession of stressed or spidery sculptures squatting in arched alcoves.

This is where she grew up—Marvell said, and I have to say it explained a lot.

Is she here now?—I asked, trying to keep this on track.

She ignored me. *Luda was made here*—was all she seemed willing to say.

I couldn't help noticing her strange way of walking. Hers was a *geisha* hobble, a constriction that hinted at laced-together ankle boots while the elegant cane added its own touch of decadent theatre. A surgical boot bolted to her lower leg would only have oversold her supervillain status so at least she'd had enough dignity to know when to stop.

Something about the way Victoria Marvell moved seemed manufactured. I'm not saying I had it all worked out at this point, but the clues were beginning to form a huddle.

The house has many mansions—she said portentously. *I haven't lived here since Charles ran away with his boyfriend.*

We had come to a door that opened onto what appeared to be narrow stairs to a basement or cellar; a portal that had loomed in my memory as the entrance to the Inferno or Orpheus's shortcut to Hades. *Abandon Hope All Ye . . .*

Like most remembered epiphanies, the reality was smaller

and more commonplace, the shadow of a Chihuahua mistaken for Cerberus, Hound of Hell. Inebriated recollection's cavernous stairway lit by flashing traffic light reds and greens was sobriety's flight of ten or twelve shallow steps illuminated by strings of party lights.

Our brief descent brought us to a modest wine cellar with its bouquet of damp and powdered stonework. She apologized for the Dracula's Castle mood lighting on the grounds that it was surprisingly hard to get the electricians to replace bulbs down here.

You may have noticed the cellar's a bit lacking.

I had noticed. I'd remarked on that the first time around when I'd pointed out to Luda how few bottles were stacked on the racks. Or maybe I pointed it out to myself, or to you.

I'd offer you a drink otherwise—she added.

And I'd probably take it, I thought, but I'd promised myself I would do this straight.

She's scared of you—I said. *Scared you'll send your policemen to bring her back*—

She has issues—Mrs. Marvell said carefully.

Hoping she'd trust me enough to elaborate, I gently supported Victoria Marvell's knobbly elbow as she negotiated the way down another short flight of stairs that brought us to a curtailed passageway where arched recesses were crammed with bundles of outdated newspapers bound with string. Set in the wall ahead was a green door with frosted-glass panels. Touch-sensitive, she shook me off abruptly.

I know this place. I know that room. We came down here—I said.

We called it the Nursery—she told me. *This is where Kenny Trace died. This is where Luda came to life and outgrew our ability to contain her.*

I remembered the circular Bakelite switch too and there it was again, the white moment of Genesis when Luda flicked the toggle and we were there.

Stripped of its numinous intensity, all the meaning had seeped out of the basement to expose a dull sump.

There was no room beyond, no depth; the door in the far wall opened on a shallow pantry with wooden shelves. No hallway there linking to a secret underground complex, no corridor from which the bureau's finest could emerge in their polished brogues. No faceless agents with sharpened pencils and T-squares joining forces to repair the wounded world after whatever *contretemps,* atomic, bacteriological, ideological, terminal, had rendered it irreparable.

I'm disappointed—I said. *It's a lot smaller than I thought.*

Isn't everything?—said Mrs. Marvell and who could disagree with that?

I was right about the mirrors—I congratulated myself, examining a folding screen of five reflecting panels, tall and thin as church windows or test tubes.

Something else was real, I'm pleased to say and almost as impressive as I'd remembered it, if less animated. There propped against the wall was the map of MYSTERY CITY.

It was, in fact, a deliriously detailed painting of a map, the crude portrait of an imaginary Gasglow as seen from Dareport and Carnock downriver and to the east, out Witherwell and Landry way.

It's always nice to discover you're not completely mental—I said, looking up close to read the eye-straining names of streets that didn't exist in the real world—Buchanan, Argyle, Cathedral, Cathcart.

It was an astounding piece of work.

The man responsible for the painstaking eighteen months of creation that went into rendering the bas-relief effects and labelling every thread-wide alleyway, every postage-stamp park, was the late Andrew Moncrieff, artist, activist, and author of post-modern Gasglow novel *The Dare,* along with several others I'd never gotten around to reading.

The mural was commissioned by the old Cobblestone Bar before they shut down—Mrs. Marvell explained, adding chatty and knowledgeable tour guide to her menu of personae. *Charles gave Andrew the money to complete it and add all the little surreal touches from his dreams*—

Charles, it seems, had been compiling notes in little books since he'd been eight years old. Drawings and jottings, records of nightly adventures in a folded-out version of the city where he'd grown. The Mystery City of his boyhood fantasies was an expression of his faith in a grander Gasglow hidden in the folds.

Those luminous grey remembered playing fields, housing estates, shipyards, expanded parkland, industrial estate, and quarry he knew by heart from a lifetime of nighttime voyages beyond the beaches of consciousness.

A violent slash from top right to bottom left made a non-representational portrait image of the Golden Ratio in Luda's face, ever smaller, ever tighter spinning deliriously into a zero that threatened but never arrived.

Did Luda do this?—I said running my fingers down the rough spine of the gash. *Is Luda here?*

This was his house—she said, as if I'd never mentioned Luda's name, and it took me a little while to understand who she was talking about. *Murdo McCloudie had this place built. He lived here between 1900 and 1910, the years of his greatest success.*

Well, he's been haunting us long enough—I smoothly retorted. *It's my turn to float around his corridors frightening the staff.*

Pointedly popping the bubbles of my attempts at levity, she explained how the Nursery had played many roles during Luda's dismantling and her re-education; dressed and redressed as a schoolroom, a lecture hall, an existentialist Purgatory concretizing Basic Perinatal Matrix 2 *leitmotifs* of stifling subterranean authority, chained confinement, learning, reward, and punishment.

In much the same way as gone Gofannon Rhys had cornered the market in decent, still-viable retired coppers, the Nursery's speciality lay in its blankly efficient ability to become any kind of horror film set you might conceivably require, from creepy playpen to nightmare hospital or existential gaol for the human spirit, four walls with many faces.

It seemed we were getting down to the nitty-gritty, the origin story, the how Luda came to be . . .

We called her Penny. Both of us thought we could build a living monument to our daughter—Mrs. Marvell explained. *Instead, Charles began to use Penny as a sex doll. He justified it by saying she was a zombie with no inner life. He said Penny was a collection of programmed behaviours, that she felt nothing. He kept saying she'd been a brutal thug, lacking in scruple, deficient in liability, ignorant of kindness. She deserved it. She'd been born and lived as a mockery of civilized virtues. She had no soul and no rights. How could anyone prove otherwise?*

I think I might have put it better than she did, but that's direct from the raven's beak.

I'd come here apprehensive, fearful of what I might find, but the Heart of Darkness, the inescapable iron womb of Satan, was just a sad, mad experiment in a soundproofed cellar. Having scouted out the terrain upriver, I felt secure in my belief that fear was the wrong response to whatever was happening or had happened in this soul-crushing hypogeum.

But it was Penny who seduced Charles—she insisted. *She corrupted my husband. Not the other way around. They were carrying on an affair right under my nose, in this place. Goading each other on. More perverse as it went on. She brought out the worst in him. In me.*

I'm trying to do her justice but it's hard to capture the artificiality of her voice, the gelatinous quality of her overshare.

You may want to sit down—she said, and her advisory was hung with icicles. Her entitled air of total command came as an affront to my rebel spirit. I wouldn't sit down. I wanted to sit down after a long day—but I thought no. I'd rather stand, I explained.

It's for your own good—she said, but that's what they always say, isn't it? People who like to order the rest of us around.

I can take it standing up. I smiled without a muscle moving. *It's one of my proudest personal achievements.*

She'd failed so far to come up with anything capable of plonking me back on my ass—not yet—but I held on to my high hopes.

Victoria Marvell, twitching her beak, went on in great, I might say tiresome, detail about "unpatterning" and breaking up pathological behaviour routines.

She told me how they'd set about scrubbing Kenny's whiteboard, erasing his recollections, his biography, until the desired blank slate was achieved.

It began in total isolation with goggles and headphones disrupting his sense of time and space.

Electric shock therapy came next, an accelerated course of six consecutive jolts from the Page-Russell device, intended to shatter his links to any coordinated Self. Techniques like these can convert the strongest adults to dependent children in a matter of weeks they say.

Drugs were used to disinhibit "Kenny:" uppers, downers, psychedelics, stimulants, to further breach his defences and disorganize his sense of himself as "Kenny Trace"—as he became incontinent, they put him in adult diapers, reducing their victim to helplessness.

United in madness, the Marvells took turns to fashion the ideal daughter of their shared dreams; a superbeing, a new artisanal human fabricated for a harsher world of metastasizing billions, where life-and-death choices would have to be made without emotion or reflection.

By week 6, the last dregs of Kenny were fully squeezed from his imprint-vulnerable brain, his exhausted spent body.

Another Ship of Theseus I'm thinking, another boat of segments leaving dry dock. How much do you take away, an arm a leg, a mind, before the original no longer exists?

In the cave-painting simplicity of pure inexplicable sensation that was its moment-to-moment understanding, the Marvells' Eidolon was surprised to discover it could no longer walk without support or feed itself.

It cried a lot, perhaps it was the hormone infusions or maybe the newly-forming Penny was remembering the last fading flavour of a prior life, the haunting shape where something precious and important had been that would never return.

Vicki Marvell described to me in zoom-lensed pornographic close-up how supremely adorable the former teenage violent offender became, bumbling around in a bulging nappy, with a mind wet-wiped as clean as its bum, a neocortex buffed to the same slick smooth featureless polish as the now hairless, androgynous body.

As I'm swithering between *is this mind-control erotica or a horror story,* she guns the narrative engine and skid-drifts into high-geared black mirror-walled bio-sci-fi mode.

As test results piled up, as information visibly purged from the captive boy in a digital sweat of ones and zeros precipitating onto hard disk and thumb drive, the Marvells constructed a cast-iron defence of their philosophy; one they'd be unafraid to defend with vigour should, God forbid, anyone ever find out what they'd been up to in this seedy basement with its stink of mothballs, ozone, cum, and ugliness.

They knew the whole misguided enterprise was, if not morally suspect, certainly professionally indefensible. They did what we all do in situations where convention breaks down, convincing themselves they were doing the right thing. Not only the right thing, but the very best thing they could do, in an act of creation that would benefit all of humankind.

They were offering the world a unique gift by road-testing a radical new solution to the problem of violent young men raised on a diet of hardcore coercive pornography. A way to safeguard women.

No judge in the land would convict them. Instead, they assured each other, the criminal justice system would immediately franchise their programme, declaring them visionaries. They foresaw prison populations cut by factors, the streets scoured of vicious Dickensian ne'er-do-wells and crowded instead with well-brought-up young ladies promenading for pink and pretty things to pass the time.

If there truly were essential selves inhabiting bodies not always fit for their needs, did it not follow we could evict unwanted tenants and replace them with more compliant residents?

A nation of soulless wicked lads would be exchanged for obedient girloid consumers with prosthetic souls tailored for algorithmic mass appeal to complement the fillers and implants, the pre-programmed hapless giggles, and the enticing need for approval.

A lofty, noble objective of such supreme calibre justified the cruelty, the revolting class exploitation, the breathtaking entitlement to someone else's body as if it were windfall in an apple orchard, shaken from the tree by Darwinian economics.

Beset with personal infernal legions for as long as they could remember, the Marvells weighed it up, and all things considered, what were a few new demons?

They plunged ever onward, galvanized by a Shelleyan creative lightning storm. Forbidden possibilities arced and sparked from their Van de Graaff globes, lewdly crawling up and down the Tesla coils of their shared fever. The new brightness in their eyes was the crack and snap of naked wires, the exposed, blue-white voltage of a mad Promethean *hubris* the rules of Greek drama would fail to favour with a Hollywood ending!

I took over—she said.

It was Victoria's turn—as she told it, she greeted each day on a smorgasbord of mind-bending chemicals and gin, wielding her expertise the way a madman wields a hammer as she set about guiding her blank, autistic daughter-thing through the four stages of Piaget's scale.

I could bore you with the whole process. I did read up on it, but I'll stick to the major milestones in the family album—Penny's first steps, for instance. Penny's first words.

Cognitive development invariably follows Piaget's sequence like one square follows another on a Monopoly board.

Stages cannot be skipped or omitted. Those are the rules of the five-sided Game of Life. Each level brings a wider more inclusive understanding of the world, all of which leads to new intellectual abilities making it a bit like standing on your own head to reach higher ground.

"Penny" was violently accelerated to recapitulate sixteen years in twelve months of intensive renovation.

It started with what they call the sensorimotor stage, the early foundational stage that lasts until you're about a year and a half to two years old.

Here there's a fixation on sensation, with the subject investigating its environment by touching and biting until, between seven and nine months, which in Penny's case equated to a fortnight, object-permanence comes online, and the development of memory begins.

That was where Beatrice Spalding from the orphanage had come into it to play her part as a totem bird from the Left-Hand world, dispensing terror and mother's milk in equal measure.

It was Charles's bright idea to bring the mask into it. To incarnate the Wire Mother from Harry Harlow's experiments with infant chimpanzees. Mrs. M. was preoccupied with her personal mental-health issues, leaving her husband, who had already surrendered to the dark side, responsible for their new-born teenage child.

Crawling at first—mobility encourages cognitive development as it turns out—"Penny Marvell" struggled towards Selfhood in a series of off-kilter baby steps that grew in confidence with each month that inched by in days stretched to lifetimes. Together Charles and Victoria watched their creation awaken with sparkling eyes, recognizing her new parents as a more miraculous extension of herself, remote-controlled by her squeals and giggles, sobs and jobbies, to bring her everything she might need.

Somewhere during this phase of the proceedings Charles Marvell crossed the line that separates medical research from mad science when he strapped her down and syringed saturated dye into Penny's pale blue corneas, activating an electric unreal glow that was cyan teal cobalt cerulean inexplicable . . .

Day 12 was when Penny uttered her first word. Marvell told me in a breaking raptor voice of her pride as Penny picked her skinny body up on wobbly Bambi legs and, faltering, took her first steps at the age of seventeen across the living room in a ragged stumble that became a toppling rag-doll collapse into her new daddy's awaiting arms, coincidentally uttering her first word.

This should have been an occasion for champagne celebration and may well have been if Penny's first momentous utterance had not been "cock."

All right I may be exaggerating, but you get the gist.

The pre-operational stage takes us from age two or thereabouts all the way through early childhood to age seven.

Here we find Penny, seventeen going on six, dressed in gymslip, ankle socks, and Mary Janes, deeply implicated in the soap-opera comings and goings of a miniature world she's been curating inside the scaled-down drawing rooms of her beloved doll's house—the prop was still here somewhere apparently, according to Ma Marvell—applying rich dimensions of playset reality that turned the model three-levelled Georgian mansion into an unfolding series of vastly significant spaces, brought to life by imagination and emotions.

Now came ABCs. Number games. Multiplication. Long division. Fellatio.

Penny began to construct elaborate stories, crayon-coloured high-fidelity simulations, to explain her world, inventing her own language and instinctively crafting a domestic mythology tinged with creepiness and incest, horror, and rape.

I can't say I'm entirely surprised that someone who'd been electroshocked, terrorized, drugged, re-gendered, and abused by her step-parents might exhibit one or two symptoms of PTSD, no matter how stringently you thought you'd deleted her files and flushed her stash down the toilet.

When I tell you it was around about then she started constructing ornate fantasies concerning a long-lost family from space you won't be surprised, I hope. She postulated a super-human mother and father who'd abandoned her among the throwbacks, the *Homo sapiens* proto-men still learning how to live together without fights breaking out every five minutes.

During the concrete operational stage, encapsulating the years between seven and eleven, there came to the Marvells the uncomfortable insight that Luda was figuring them out even as they scrutinized her.

Charles began to fret: What if Penny's transplant didn't take? What if sweet deleted Penelope Marvell's rebuilt soul was rejected by the Eidolon? His paranoia intensified, fronding with reckless effulgence to absorb conspiracy theory, fringe theology, apocalyptic prophecy, and wonky biology.

As the Marvells raised their homemade daughter in an atmosphere of increasing deviance, they were forced to admit they might be losing control of the experiment altogether.

They rewarded Penny's efforts to mimic their lost Penelope, punishing any resistance with a coronation by lightning crown in another scream-lit expressionist ECT session.

When she rampaged through a rebellious tomboy phase in dungarees and chopped hair, the Marvells were keen to encourage this gender insurrection, knowing it would trigger a powerful reflex action in the opposite direction soon enough.

So that when Penny began to favour longer wigs and more feminine looks, her self-appointed mummy and daddy were already waiting with a whole wardrobe and a list of new rules.

If they hadn't gone out that night—if they hadn't left Penelope to come home alone from school—if she'd never met a monster who took her by the hand—if Penelope Marvell had lived and everything had stuck to the pre-ordained script, it could never have turned out like this steaming psychosexual playground where Luda was raised and nurtured on soul-sick depravity.

Luda was Penelope as she might have been, but only if she'd been reared in the backstreets of Hell.

Penny asked awkward questions about everything, continually. She distrusted the consensus. She took notes. Analysing how her scary parents spoke and moved, she taught herself to mirror their distinctive robot gestures and default modes of speech using NLP and pre-suasion techniques she appeared to have developed naturally. Soon she had the Marvells wrapped around her finger like an engagement ring.

Meantime, if she was old enough to manipulate symbols related to abstract concepts, if she could think in systematic ways, if she could generate theories and consider possibilities, ponder theoretical relationships and concepts such as justice and free will, then she was capable of juggling her stepfather's cock and balls into her face—that was the prevailing wisdom according to Charles Marvell.

Here Penny cultivated her singular worldview over years.

Using felt-tipped coloured pens she cultivated revenge plots of Spirographic intricacy. She sublimated her rage into obsessively-crafted strategic webs of yellow, purple, and blue ballpoint.

She memorized her parents' routines; New Penny knew by heart their timetables, their repeated, habitual behaviour patterns.

She paid close attention to the microscopic nuances that told her where we'd be at any given moment of the day—Vicki Marvell told me. *My own mother was dying at the time so it's possible I was too distracted to notice*—Mrs. Marvell mused, only making it worse, feeding into the connective tissue of associations, correspondences, analogies that supported a life.

Oblivious to his daughter's subterfuge, Charles Marvell, like some unbalanced Gnostic god inclined to blame his twisted Creation for his personal failings, had returned to cruising the mean streets in a hire car, on the prowl for Penny's sisters, dreaming a sorority, a harem of programmable dolly boys seated obediently at their desks in the Headmaster's classroom. But he returned home disappointed each night, finding no other who could match Penny's geometrical allure. Compared with Penny's insufferable loveliness, every ordinary human face seemed bent out of true, crooked, and deformed. Commonplace people seemed cackling feudal idiots in a Bruegel daub.

What else could Charles do but take out his rage and frustration on his lovely malleable young daughter?

What else could she do but play along while plotting then executing her bid for freedom?

Penny had the Marvells worked out down to the fine stitching so that when she escaped, she did it between blinks, in the space of breaths. Having accurately determined every move they'd make, she countered with another of her own that edited her from their line of sight, a teenage drag ninja slipping out the back door in the company of shadows while her parents argued and looked the other way.

The next time they saw her it was five years later, as backstage colour in outrageous local news stories about an unlikely Curse dogging the Gasglow revival of *The Phantom of the Pantomime.* And there was Penny all grown up, all unmistakable as Luda as Aladdin in a story about the ghost and the Phantom.

It was too much. Too much of everything. What felt like falling tons of implication crashed down around me.

Where had "Kenny Trace" come from? Before Charles Marvell found him on the run from the law? Before he was judged to be no more than a convenient vessel to be scraped out, excavated, and prepped for occupation. Before he was gentrified as Penny.

She told me: Charles Marvell discovered his exemplary guinea pig, the so-called Kenny Trace, living rough, eighteen months after the urchin's conviction for the attempted rape of a thirteen-year-old girl.

That took my breath away, I have to say.

I'd been having my suspicions obviously but to have it served up like that with no sugarcoating went below the belt. All I could say was—*At least it was only attempted*—regretting every word as it came out.

There was something about him, or so went the story, something about Kenny Trace that wasn't right from the start. It wasn't just the drugs and the neglect. Cold turkey, antibiotics, and a nutritionally balanced diet took care of those stumbling blocks. As Kenny grew in strength, he waxed intimidating, a raucous underclass cuckoo outgrowing its upper-middle-class nest.

Kenny Trace was at the very least sociopathic, the Marvells agreed. Kenny's pale cancelled eyes, frosty demeanour, the expressionless pearlescent beauty of his flawless skin concealed dimensions of rage and revenge.

That's why a primal scream rebirth was called for. A re-creation from square one. Kenny to Penny with Luda the unexpected result.

It's quite a story—was the best I could come out with. It was all I could do not to start laughing. *I might have that seat now*—I said. *Go on.*

And go on she did.

There's that moral conundrum—*if you had a time machine would you go back and kill baby Hitler?*—she said and that's when I knew I was in for a long drawn-out night in the company of a troubled cosplayer unless I made my excuses and scuttled. I wondered why I'd come here at all—what did I seriously expect to learn from this clearly unhinged woman in her feathered headdress?

I was able to answer without hesitation that it wasn't any kind of conundrum and as far as I was concerned if I had access to a working time machine, the last thing I'd be doing is dicking around with baby Hitler when I could be riding my Silver Machine all the way to the thirty-first century to bring back marvels from tomorrow, like Barbarella's Paco Rabanne breastplate! That's if they even bothered with a tomorrow, which all this apocalyptic song and dance seemed to suggest might be wishful thinking on my part.

You say that but what would you do?—she pressed, as if this crackpot scenario were ever likely to happen anywhere outside of stoned speculation. *If I showed you a sweet plump baby in its cradle then revealed to you that this little bundle of joy was destined to grow up to be a soulless destroyer of hopes and lives, would you be able to stand by as I throttled the monster in its cradle?*

I raised my hands in surrender. Honestly, who's got an answer to that?

Except I did have an answer and I said—*I wouldn't trust anyone who said they were a time-traveller. Especially not if they handed me a gun and told me to shoot a baby in the face. I'd be suspicious.*

You must remember what he did—she kept reminding me as if to justify the family secrets watered and cultivated down here in the stuffy dark where inhumanity was given sanction.

When you said attempted rape—I began, unsure where I was going.

I'm talking about before she was Luda, or Penny—Mrs. Marvell cut in. *Luda can't be held accountable. If I were to tell you the Antichrist had come among us, in the form of a soulless child*—Mrs. Marvell probed ever deeper.

I'd have to say grief can do strange things to the mind—I argued.

As far as Luda knows, her birth parents left her as carrion, a sacrifice—she cackled in return.

I stood my ground as best you can manage in six-inch heels. I mean, I'm joking about the heels as I was wearing ridge-soled Oakleys, but there comes a time when all you want is a break from the unrelenting morbidity. I know I do.

Penny—she intoned, allowing the thrill of a salacious shudder to travel in a Mexican wave from crotch to crown—*Penny was the Devil.*

What did you expect? We're down in the dungeon with the Black Queen. It could hardly get any more Goth if it wore a fishnet vest and played bass for the Brides of Dracula.

We can do it again—she wanted me to know. *It's a process we can repeat. What we did to him we can do to anyone.*

My spider-senses alerted me to where she was going with this and it felt to me then as if evil had crept naked into the room.

We can delete Luda—she said. *If that's what you want. We can take her back to basics. She won't be able to tell the police anything because she'll be someone else entirely*—

If I so desired, she wanted me to know, she could take an eraser, a kind of blackboard duster to Luda's private personal diary. She could swipe away the crime scene outlines of Luda's half-arsed jerry-built personality setting free the vacant space they enclosed. All I had to do was nod my head and Mrs. Marvell would arrange for things to happen that would leave Luda wide-eyed, openmouthed, abridged to a cipher, gender-neutral and box-fresh for fucking.

Consider it an exorcism—she finished with relish.

I hoped that, stiff and doll-like as it was, she could see my reservations on my face.

You're not using your imagination—Ma Marvell said, certain I could be tempted as easily as Eve who only knew one sex, victim with a womb of a dull and judgmental Dad God. Eve, whose only crime was to find the serpent persuasive.

My god/dess was different; where Mercurius was concerned, three heads were better than one.

You can use her blank slate to redraw your own youth for new circumstances. She can be you, now. You can live it all again, better, through her.

I was way ahead of her. The needle spun on my moral compass searching for ethical north, a spinning dervish motion lost at sea and lured onto the rocks by false lights, deceptive magnets. I wrestled with inevitable consequences. I ran scenarios, risk-assessments, outlooks, outcomes.

I'm offering you a choice. I want to know the kind of person you really are.

I thought, good luck with that! Even I don't know what kind of person I am most days of the week! And this wasn't most days of the week . . .

Then slowly, wringing out maximum drama and conviction, I shook my head from side to side, grinding pepper with my neck.

It wouldn't be right—I said. *She's Luda now—she's worked hard to make something of what you did to her.*

I felt proud of myself, holding the line, gazing down from

that chilly plateau, the moral high ground. The crow, silent, considered.

I'm sure you won't mind if I take a moment to bask in what must be your admiration here; can you believe my selfless devotion to someone other than *moi*? My staunch refusal to concede even an inch of territory deserves some applause surely.

Oh well—she said dismissively. *It doesn't matter anyway.*

I didn't come to be put on trial. I came to tell Luda she's needed at work—I said firmly. *I came to bring her back.*

She'll destroy you—was the reply. *That's what Luda does. That's what she was built to do.*

But why?—I asked, not unreasonably.

Because you're guilty—she said with a juicy pursing of blackberry lips. *And because Luda is the Devil.*

That plummy diction was a hallmark of storytellers on the old 0898 telephone sex lines we'd sampled for a couple of the Troupe's musical numbers. Her lascivious scenery-munching reminded me of those tall tales of aunties feminizing stud jock nephews with hormone injections and DIY tit jobs. Michael to Michaela. Paul to Paula. Joe to Josephine. They'd narrate the stories in a fabulous lip-smacking pro-domme cadence I spent ages learning to imitate, all rolled *r*'s, sibilant hisses, and spiteful condescension.

Victoria Marvell had one of those phone voices, camp, OTT. Her story was a Golden Oldie, a standard chaser fable: violent teen hooligan to pampered pretty sex toy, a Nuclear Family deformed and glowing arsenic-bottle green in the dark. Mum getting off on Son sucking Dad.

The distinctive seasoning of the Glamour was all over every staged element. When it was sprinkled too liberally, as with an excess of chilli powder or garlic cloves, the taste was overpowering.

I hoped it wasn't too obvious I didn't buy a word of any of it. I hoped she was blind to the webs I was weaving right in front of her stabbing beak. The ghostly cat's cradle of the Glamour interlacing spun strands of wool over her beady scrying glass eyes. I hoped experience counted for something.

Now here's where you can all get together and shout—*OH NO, IT DOESN'T!*

And I shoot back with *OH YES, IT DOES!*

There are only so many times someone can be told they're the Devil—she'd said offering one last gnomic crossword clue—*before they give up and shrug*—

If the hoof fits . . .

I let out a long-held breath in the back of the taxi home, filing my bitten nails.

I can be down on myself a lot of the time but there are and have been times that I treasure, and that ride home in the heat of a winter sun after the chilly basement of the House of Marvell was up there with the best.

Now and again, I'm given permission to remind myself I can be quite good at this!

Victoria the Crow Queen had clicked her head to the right and back with that staccato motion I drew attention to earlier, contrived to suggest birdy glitches in the replay, missing frames. Her beak had tipped and tilted, sniffing for a perfume called Deception.

Would I lie to you?—I said, and Botox provided the lack of expression that allowed me to get away with it.

When she couldn't for the life of her detect a trace of guile anywhere in my personal aura, my audience with the Morrigan had ended abruptly. I was dismissed.

The Glamour has tricks, secrets I never got around to teaching Luda. Certain sleights and arcane arts of the wizard's sleeve went without elucidation that night we had our fight, that Saturday in the sulks of September.

There are some things you just can't hide—and some things you can—but Luda's diva tantrum had caused her to miss out on these essentials of a Glamour education.

It may have seemed inconsequential in the grand scheme but sometimes it's the things that don't happen that turn out to be the things that matter.

No matter how you choose to look at it, my second visit to the Marvell Mansion, my appointment at the table of the Crow Queen had provided some vital scraps of intelligence.

I must admit to a manic hormonal rush; I felt like a soldier preparing to go completely over the top: the glitter bombs, the gummi Dum-Dums, the pink bubble guns of the camp fusiliers locked and loaded with Fairy Liquid.

I won't fib; I can't say for sure what would have been my real answer to Victoria Marvell's question. If I could have a tailor-made living toy to twist and remake in my own image, a human blank page on which to exercise my creativity, what would I do?

What would you do?

If I was offered a breathing dress-up doll to improve upon, make better, guide, or control, would I be the kind encouraging mentor I want to be, striving to make her better, stronger, more self-confident?

Would I be the cruel domme taking advantage of my puppet's breached walls, her smashed defences? Would I choose to twist her into ever-more-grotesque shapes in my well-meaning attempts to teach her how to be me?

Me in love with me.

Wouldn't that be something?

I ask myself what I would have said if I hadn't seen what Madame Vicki Marvell didn't want me to see. If I hadn't figured it all out, right there and then. I'd called it all along; the carefully-curated set and setting, the destabilizing narrative delivering random electroshock therapy so you can hardly think.

I could tell by the way she'd been sitting. It's a subtle thing but if my ultra-critical eye couldn't always detect the smallest flaw in perfection where would I be? They may have been shaved and taped, but you can't hide the tricks of the drag trade from an old pro.

Victoria Marvell was not who she claimed to be, nor what she claimed to be.

Victoria Marvell, the Crow Queen, the Morrigan, had a cock and balls sandwiched between her smooth thighs.

I knew I'd find Luda in that house of Marvells. I wondered how long it would be before she showed up for the big climax.

By the time I got home, I'd sandpapered my fingernails down to the bleeding raw pulp. These things happen. Thank fuck for press-on talons.

Let's not beat about the bush. In fact, let's leave the bush out of this altogether. Consider the shape of the game plan, the pentagram, the horns raised in a divided universe, emblematic of a severed alienated Creation much like the one I've had so much fun with.

Let's lay our Tarot spread on the table.

Double is Dual, is Deuce, Trump 13, *Le Diable, Diablo,* the Devil.

The Horned Gambler. Two-fingered gesture. Lord of the Divided World. The Player of Games. *Magister Ludi.*

Luda.

Get thee behind me, Satan!

Isn't that what they used to say?

If you ask me it's practically a proposal!

BLACK WIDOW TWANKEY

I t wasn't necessary, Elspeth informed me, but against her best advice I chose to have my fillers topped up. I regarded the injections as equivalent to polishing a protective battle visor.

There was bright work to be done. I was determined to scintillate.

When she was done with my procedures, I gave Elspeth five free tickets to an opening night I knew would never come and told her to expect some surprises.

She said Heather had another message for me, but I didn't want to hear it. I knew what it was.

She's behind you!

We were drawing to the close of what should have been the last full rehearsal before curtains up at the end of November and the whole thing was in pieces.

Props and wardrobe threatened industrial action, the catering staff remained as elusive as Borrowers, while the publicity and administrative departments continued to firefight the sun with water pistols.

May Tang-Taylor, citing a bird flu diagnosis, opted to relay her contribution remotely, which meant the Empress now appeared onstage in the form of an open laptop, a radical rendering of her character as a rogue AI in some flattened-out post-human sci-fi variation of our production.

For her part, Aiysha Dice, the influencer influenced, had

400 · GRANT MORRISON

resorted to a series of excuses so complex and self-referential, we were left with the bewildering impression that she had somehow installed her ailing grandmother in a cattery and was now struggling to secure a comfortable bed in a senior-care facility for Burmese Blue kittens Tabby and Toby.

With Luda a no-show, Dee Jayashankar, weighed down with protective charms that were effective against jinxes and maledictions but powerless when it came to health and safety regulations, doubled briefly as Aladdin while we went through the motions with the apprehensive air of convicts rehearsing their own executions.

Abanazar, thoroughly defeated, remains unrepentant until Aladdin offers him a simple choice. On one hand, he can face exile, banished into the desert to live among the wild creatures.

Abanazar, mollycoddled in silk sheets, mosquito nets, and warm baths for most of his life, is horrified by the possibility that he might have to share a bed with nature.

He protests, demands another option.

Or—says Aladdin, adjudicating—*you can stay here in Peking.*

Abanazar shrugs—*obviously duhh*—but there's one condition.

One condition? The wizard's Adam's apple bobs like a yoyo, sensing his future closing in like the rungs of a bamboo cage.

Here's where Twankey makes the closing scene, wearing a wedding dress of such scale and construction it could pass as a marquee tent capable of hosting the royal reception. In full sail, a sugar galleon, I enter like Queen Bod in Derek Jarman's *Jubilee.* Punk Gloriana. The shotgun Wedding of the Faerie Queen.

Fluttering massive spangly Venus flytrap eyelashes at my cornered groom releases a clap of wind that blows the toupee off his head. The wizard, bidding farewell to any vestige of backbone, twists and turns to wriggle invertebrate out of his obligations. *Err, I think I'd rather go into exile*—he admits and as I stalk him across the stage, a plus-sized hunter-killer shuttle-cock, he scrambles aboard the Magic Carpet screeching—*Get me out of here!*

But the living carpet hates Abanazar too and gives up its animating ghost, collapsing the villain to the floor as Twankey tears the bridal wrap from her body like a Band-Aid off a star-tling wound . . .

The Widow steps on sky-high heels from the deflated cream blimp of her dress, the feathered *frou-frou,* fishnet, and frill that froths around her knees. Abanazar screams. A single immense gasp from the audience would suck all the air from the front rows, causing the short of breath to briefly black out with the shocking reveal soldered into those last instants of conscious awareness . . .

Underneath the avalanche of that dress, emerging from a bang and a landmine glitterburst of mauve smoke and tin-sel, comes Widow Twankey buttoned into the Phantom's trademark tuxedo with its withered lapel rose, its mildew of twinkles.

One by one the cast is blanked into shadow until only Jasmine, Aladdin, and Abanazar remain. The wizard hides his face. Thunder rolls among the rigging, as the Phantom lays his hand on Jasmine's brow, as she turns pale and breathes her last, as Aladdin cries out, only to be silenced in his turn.

The Phantom's hand attempts to close to a fist around Aladdin's slender throat. The deafening crack of the crash box comes as an elemental shock wave resonating into the lightless soundless void out past the footlights. The scooped-out sound of a night wind is all we hear, until the first nervous coughs come from a shaken audience set adrift in darkness . . .

A distraught, solitary Twankey begs the onlookers to for-give her ugliness as she fastens a crablike hand to her face and casts around for a mask to obscure the frightful sight of the terminal mutilations of age. Some thaw in the Phantom's glacial psychopathic veneer is embodied in the spotlight that now begins to flash on and off, following the plotted course of Dom Float's stage proxemics to starkly isolate one motionless standing figure after another—the Genie, the Wizard, the Slave, the Princess, Aladdin—arranged as upright bowling pins on an invisible five-pointed star, lifeless in a pallid freezer-cabinet half-light.

In that failing heartbeat pulse of the overheads, in the random sequence of beam and blackness, the Phantom undergoes a startling process of metamorphosis.

Crushingly aware of how alone he is on the darkened stage, the Phantom tries his best to repopulate the immaterial palace of his mind.

He twitches, jerks, and jolts, a puppet strung all wrong, and becomes in rapid turn each actor, fluent for moments and snatches of dialogue in the body language of every character he's dispatched till another takes its place; Jasmine's sweetness unhinges its courtly delicacy, extends quivering girl-power daring to become Aladdin's reckless acrobatic bravery, before developing from his youthful optimism the restricting carapace of Abanazar's age and skulking guile. A chameleon rippling on a Transactional Analysis Personality Grid, the Phantom twisting, turning, boasts and laments, sobs, guffaws, until worn down by emotional erosion, polished smooth by the rough edges of all those big personalities, he crashes to his knees, an upside-down letter Y with all his focus, all his grand intent, draining to a fork, a split, a dual runoff where the energy seeps from his body, neutralized by the Magic Carpet spread beneath him, bleeding into the pattern.

Proceeding with slow ceremonial steps and gestures, the policemen Ping and Pong are first to rise from their joint grave to join the Phantom onstage. More summer sundown shadow than form, they take position and together use unnaturally long spatula fingers to press the Phantom's mask into place on

Twankey's skull. The faceless lawmen don't seem all that funny any more. The desert atmosphere evokes the Egyptian Book of the Dead. The Coming-Forth-By-Day.

But then—There comes a time—I croak, and the Flat Policemen begin to nod along with the lamenting rhythm—*in every life to draw a line—repent your crimes and count your dimes and this is mine—*

Escorted by Ping as witness or most likely evidence, Aladdin is summoned from the shadows to stare accusingly, lips sealed in mute disillusion.

This court demands the full name of the accused . . .

You can feel the sidewinder flex of disquiet passing through the audience. It can't end like this! Our stories can't have such bleak conclusions, can they?

I give them just long enough to lose hope then I lift my head with a mischievous grin—*My name?*—I say. *Start with the hard ones first, is that your game?*—and I mobilize the power of audience participation to save the day.

I'm not sure—I start by saying—*I don't know who I am right now, but I do know I asked you lot to remember for me*—cranking the pressure until they're close to eruption. *Now, it's not something like Tom, is it? Fanny? Fanny Tom, is that it?*

OH NO IT ISN'T!—I'm assured by a wall of sound you'd feel deep in your womb if you had one.

I can never remember—I go on. *I'll tell you what! Can you help me boys and girls and all the rest?*—the energy is accumulating, compressing to power a two-word explosive discharge.

If I asked, you'd be able to tell me who I am, wouldn't you? Can you help me ladies and gentlemen boys and girls and others? Can you tell me who I am?

WIDOW TWANKEY!—comes the two-thousand-voice salute from a crammed auditorium.

What's that? I cup my hand at one ear. *I can't hear a thing. WIDOW TWANKEY!*

What's that?

WIDOW TWANKEY!

As I said at the beginning, three's the starter's gun; my posture cracks loose from the Phantom's wretched self-defeating hunch, decrinkling to full height, chest out, tummy in, pre-ZENT ass! And with a music-hall flash and flourish I strip off the Phantom's penguin suit intact as one piece, as it might be a poster from the old regime, torn from pockmarked walls on the first day after revolution.

Did I hear someone say Widow Twankey?—I enquire at full "Hello Wembley . . ." volume, accompanied by a sassy shoogle of my simulated tits.

WIDOW TWANKEY!

Underneath I've been hiding a mini-smock, all fizzy orange and chemical blue-striped tights and a washerwoman's apron so brief you wouldn't get your money's worth blowing your nose on it.

It's as if I've never been away!

Then I take a bold step forward on my platforms to hit Dom's mark, a play-token skipped into place by an expert gamer.

It's quite routine—Twankey winks as the tempo shifts up to suggestive bump-and-grind. *To take a good long look*—kick! *At all the books you've cooked*—kick!

At all the things you've seen and all the dreams you've dreamed!

And don't forget the chances that you took!

Kick! Bump!

And here on the brink overlooking the orchestra pit I come to a hipshot standstill. Twankey counts the pauses under her breath. We lean into the hall, deploying our right palm as an amplifying parabola behind our ear, and we listen deep into a stopped hush such as might follow time's last orders.

Before the lazy drift of silence can settle, Ping first, in a tentative whisper, joined momentarily by an emboldened and,

I'm scandalized to report, visibly aroused Pong, begins to hum along.

But as you reevaluate—
Remember that it's not too late
To choose a different character to play

Now Aladdin comes to stand by his mother's side adding his clear-running young voice raised in forgiveness, seasoned with fresh wisdom and experience, to this conclusion, this musical summing-up of our shenanigans.

The play's the thing but here's the thing
As actors we just put away
The doubts and deeds of yesterday
Forgetting all the drama's phantom pains!

The orchestra launches itself like a supersonic ICBM into the closing number, where everyone we thought had died is alive once more on the Day of Judgment, or an amateur musical-theatre version thereof, performing the Resurrection reprise in formation under Twankey's outstretched wings—

As strident harmonies braid into a complex single human voice uttering wry defiance into the unimpressed toom, our whole ensemble returns from the ghost world to reassemble onstage like a tour party around their guide through the dodgy East End of Erebus.

Reborn with each repeated scene
A slate wiped clean, a haunted screen
No trace of anywhere we've been remains be-cause . . .

Cheers vent with a sound that's a sudden monsoon downpour. Abanazar snarls, curses, shakes his knuckled fist, and is gone forever in a blast of violet smoke and tinsel pyro while those of us who remain onstage blast into the recurring earworm chorus.

We're phantoms at the pantomime!
Come paint your face, rehearse a rhyme!
Everybody! Clap in time!

That's not to forget how what's played as an upbeat plot reverse, an act of good magic triumphing over bad, can just as easily signify the apocalyptic schism where the Phantom loses his, her, their minds, rupturing into multiple contending components in a last-ditch effort to cope with the punishing jackhammer-wallops of self-awareness and guilt followed by guilt and more guilt and guilt.

The only way out is a volunteer disassembly where Self throws in the flannel and surrenders to jabbering Legion, to become asylum choir, belling out *Spem in Alium* in forty different clashing keys and tempos.

We're phantoms at the pantomime!

We're ghosts in grease, all fog and lime, we're peak performers in our prime!

Twankey's retreat into the comfy validations of psychosis leads us by the hands into the grand finale.

Where 5 is 5 and 9 is 9!

Everybody! Sing in time!

We're phantoms at the pantomime!

It's a soaring heartwarming outro, except the chorus repeats too many times for comfort, repeating as police lights repeat, as the house lights go up, repeating like a copier turning out duplicates in an empty office as if it intends to continue repeating indefinitely, still harping on long after the audience has dispersed into the jagged wet slap of Storm Ingmar, still humming the nagging repetitive refrain, repeating, repeating.

Phantoms at the pantomime

Phantoms at the pantomime

Phantoms at the pantomime . . .

There was sarcastic applause from the front stalls. A steady handclap.

The pigs were back. After all I've been through, I don't see why I should put it any more delicately than that.

Speaking of sniffing around, that's me wrapping up my nose now. Brushing contour down both sides from the bridge to a point above the tip, sculpting a narrow doll-like shape. A dab of white down the centre seals the deal.

I'm eking out the second bottle of Mumm, trying to make it last the way you do when you're a kid with a can of fizz, timing to the moment before the last bubble pops and all that's left is an oily flat treacle.

Now, where was I?

That's right! Under investigation!

This time I got straight to the point of the air-drawn dagger and asked the policemen why this boy's case was so important. Did they understand the damage to my reputation these unfounded allegations were causing? Had they seen the newspapers?

The more charismatic of the pair, which only required him to demonstrate all the personality of a coat on a hook, asked me if I'd had any dealings with the Marvell family. I tried not to jump but it felt like every cell and molecule farted at the same time.

Are they the ones with the daughter?—I ventured. *She disappeared*—I said.

They wanted to know if I'd met Charles or Victoria at any time during pre-production, but I could honestly say I had not and in addition had no idea why I might have reason to.

Dom cut in at that point—red-faced—*Lu*—he said—*the Marvells were major sponsors. I don't think you ever met them, but they were patrons*—

All at once, all the ghosts swept in on a chilly inwardly-drawn breath of rags and dry ice. The policemen stayed alert to my every tremor, waiting to pounce if I moved to get away.

I never met them—I said. This much was true.

There were irregularities. Rumours of corruption. Backstage

jiggery-pokery. Offshore transactions. By that time, I'd stopped listening.

I had no idea what was real and what wasn't. It was like Ping and Pong. I couldn't expend the energy it took to distinguish one from the other.

In the end, what could they do, those boys in blue? There was no crime, no evidence. Not even a body. There was only a hole in the world where a homeless boy had been with no explanation of why he was so important. The puncture might fill with theories, speculations, conjectures but it remained a boy-shaped hole.

If there's anything you think we should know—the marginally more interesting of the two policemen said tentatively. I nodded gravely trying to put boy-shaped holes out of my mind. There were a million things I thought he should probably know, encyclopedias of data he might find useful in some other line of work.

I've got your number—I said, clarifying our relationship.

The missing lad was crossed-out software, while the hardware remained at large.

The rest of it: The Marvells? Whereabouts unknown. Molly Stocking? Ruined. Dez Blue? Finished. Gofannon Rhys? RIP. Luda AWOL. *The Phantom* shipwrecked. That much was real.

They were shutting us down.

I breathed a premature sigh of relief for Dee Jayashankar that we'd hit the buffers before her brave ghost-repellent wore off and left her exposed to an influx of spectres bent on affirmative inaction.

How was I to know about Dee's history of clinical despair, her unfaltering abuse of meds? How could I have guessed at Dee's plucky refusal to let depression ruin her life even if it killed her?

How could I have predicted how the imminent loss of her only gig might silently whistle up a hunting pack of black dogs bent on mauling Dee Jayashankar all the way back to the pill dispenser and oblivion?

Ticket sales went through the roof at the precise moment the floor opened to swallow us up and we sank. Audiences, it seemed, were more than happy to shell out for the opportunity to witness the outcome of vindictive lethal poltergeist activity, but it was too late. That particular skeleton horse had made a bolt for it from the bone barn.

I'm so sorry, Dom. I didn't know what else to say. *What a fucking mess.*

You look good—Dom said wanly. *Wow! Night out?*

This was the first dress I ever wore—I told him, tugging the hem down over my thighs as the minidress scintillated in today's different light. *I kept it for special occasions. It's my Ghost Dress.*

I think I've had enough of ghosts—Float said wearily, then he looked me in the eye. *I'm dying, Lu*—

We're all dying, Dom. Me, I'm dying for a drink—I fired back but faltered before the raw revelation in his expression. Levity was the wrong response.

Pancreatic cancer—he said with a new manly gravel in his resplendent intonation. *This was my masterpiece.*

And I said, with pinprick fireworks going off in my field of vision, I said—*Dom, I'll make sure they all know. Just promise me one thing—you won't end up haunting this dump.*

If I do, you'll have to be my Ghost Light after all, Lu—he said.

Then I threw my arms around him, which was a bit like trying to comfort Mount Kilimanjaro but it's the thought that counts, and we stayed like that for a while with the years we'd shared running as tears down our silly sagging cheeks.

Outside, on the flared steps of the Vallhambra, I took a preparatory yogic lung full of Gargoyle Street's deep-fried urban

410 · GRANT MORRISON

BO, that savoury salt and sauce, fast-food essence infused with an aerosol of carbon monoxide that carried the battery-terminal taste of the Hell that is other people, that everyday bacterial tang of adrenalin, pizza, halitosis.

I drank all of it in, feeling myself on the brink or the cusp or the edge of that little world where I'd lived in two squashed dimensions without ever turning my attention to the accumulating power of the Real at my back.

Evening, arriving a little earlier each rerun day, bestowed its wintry burnish. The afternoon light's run-down copper glow electroplated all the windows down Gargoyle Street with a brief sheet-metal flare that had to signify something. The mirrored silhouettes of nude girls adorning the black-painted walls of the Sugar Shack across the street caught fire like a photoset with Joan the Maid pirouetting in her birthday suit, the sign spelling ADULTS ONLY in capital letters of fierce light.

It was all I could do to hold my breath, as if a mistimed exhalation could shatter the brittle moment into powdered glass of the sort long-suffering wives might use to season a brutish husband's stew.

I checked the text message on my phone again, hesitating one more time before taking the plunge and sidestepping the homeward-bound traffic to reach the far side of Gargoyle's busy intersection with Charity Street and the South Side entrance to Circle Station.

Standing at the bus stop under the rail bridge, basking in a pure and welcoming nostalgic reek, as sincere as the boozy unwanted hug of a drunken uncle, with its punter's fug of bookies, game arcades, football scores, and expectation unwinding into disappointment. I couldn't remember the last time I'd travelled by public transport, let alone the legendary number 36 bus route, now extended in an endless circle round the city limits, describing one half of a Venn diagram containing the set that was Gasglow. In the clingy, sparkly LBD, in my classy

Prada heels, my auburn bob, my stage makeup, my Yves Klein International Blue and orange *faux*-fur coat I seemed to be drawing quite a bit of attention. I'd only worn the coat so I wouldn't have to keep adjusting my hem every thirty seconds. I'd barely made it across the road and already the LBD had rolled like a peeling uncut foreskin up my thighs and butt; the length of the coat ensured that no one would ever know but me.

Are you? . . .—a girl with picket-fence teeth enquired.

Now and again. I grinned and posed for a selfie. Then another.

My bus—I apologized as the 36 heaved its boxy bulk around the corner at Gargoyle and Charity.

I extended an opera-gloved hand to halt the bus in its head-long progress through spacetime. A catalyst, there was a commotion around me, a stirring of the silt that reminded me I was still infamous.

Pretty art student girls fetched breathless fey and blank-faced boys who couldn't wait to tell me I was their heroine, their trailblazer.

You're a pioneer!

And where did I get my dress?

As I boarded the bus to wolf whistles and paid my fare in coin, as I waved mock-regally to my awestruck young audience, I felt like Cleopatra stepping onto a barge of hammered gold, with sails of illustrated silk, with winds of affirmation blowing at my rear as I prepared to face the consequences of my actions at last.

Upstairs on the 36, I reread the message that had pinged its way into my box during that conversation with our esteemed director, Herr Float. I didn't recognize the number and the name was unfamiliar, at least at first.

Ariadne Welcome. Ariadne Welcome.

When it clicked who she was, I felt icy mice scamper up and down the rungs of my backbone.

Out of nowhere, I'd been extended an invitation to meet

from a woman I'd only ever known briefly: Mrs. Ariadne Welcome, Rose's sister, and it ended with the words.

I'm surprised you didn't know.

Rosie's dead—said Ariadne.

Three syllables, three vivid hammer-strikes, three terminal nails, and I don't mean the kind you manicure and varnish, driven through Rose's casket lid, as we crossed the Knox Bridge heading south from the city centre past shabby car dealerships and the railway yards where blackened brick or concrete sheds hunkered behind fishnet chain-link, tough guys trying on stockings in furtive hours when the wife was out. After decades in taxis and limos, the top deck of the number 36 bus felt like the lead carriage on the world's biggest and most famous roller coaster. Front seats on the right. Where I'd kissed Rose for the first time, and we'd hugged all the way home to keep warm, those decades ago.

I really am so sorry to hear that—I said, and I really was. Rose was the first person I'd fallen in love with after myself. Or was it the other way around? There was love certainly. For some reason, it was a day trip to the coast that came to mind. Home on a train, both of us wiped out walking country roads, with a flimsy bag of groceries between our legs locked at the ankles as the peripheral towns raced by like dim rockets on the return journey to Gasglow.

It's lucky I saw—she started. *I kept her phone. I don't know why I still check her messages.*

I thought about it for a long time—I said. *It preyed on my mind. I wanted to talk to her.*

According to Ariadne, they'd tried to get in touch with me just after it happened, but as she spoke all I could think about was the shopping piled in a fat recycled paper bag at her feet.

I remembered deleting her message without reading, anxious to avoid the scouring inquisition I fully anticipated.

Shopping for two, a middle-class couple in their forties with children at uni. I wished I was her. The necessities of life abbreviated to a bag of health foods and yogurt, bran, seeds, a till receipt from an upmarket chain.

Ariadne told me she headed up the Accounts Department of the Dareside Bank headquarters in the centre of downtown—she usually took the train home, but she'd remembered me from the old days, thirty years ago, talking about how much I loved the number 36 route. It seemed appropriate to meet here.

I was touched, if overdressed for it.

We'd played an exploratory game of Truth or Dare one dismal family Christmas in a fruitless effort to get to know each other not long after Rose and I first got together—but I never had much to do with Ariadne and her husband, a home-brew-loving junior vet.

Aside from the sure and certain knowledge we had nothing in common, what came out during this agonizing attempt to break the ice—every bit as successful as the ill-fated effort of the SS *Titanic* to do the same—what stuck in my mind, was Ariadne's owning up to her unusual hobby.

In her spare time, Ariadne was the author of unpublished dystopian fiction; she'd written dozens of interconnected short stories narrated from the points of view of various cloistered homosexual priests in what may or may not have been a near-future or possibly far-future throwback to the Dark Ages. Now, anybody else might have stopped there and been content with inventing queer Harry Potter, but for Ariadne that was only the springboard as she embarked on a world-building binge to imagine a whole planet in a post-nuclear endless midwinter ruled by decadent vampire aristocrats. You'll be more than halfway there if you can imagine the Marquis de Sade writing *Dracula meets Justine* . . . undead lords and ladies and what have you, relying on the repressed celibate clergy to record their horrific, perverse stories in extravagantly-illuminated comic-book manuscripts. Revolted or aroused by the depraved tales they were forced to chronicle, the monks lived short, grim lives anticipating their own gruesome twist endings.

Ariadne specialized in stomach-churningly forensic and inventive descriptions of an eclectic range of ghastly carnal torments and cruelties regularly visited upon these battery-farmed ecclesiastics by the jaded bloodsupping elite, and the result was a kind of priestly lyric pornography with page after page of demented sadomasochistic sex and extended torture scenes occurring in a feverish Gay Gormenghast that offered little in the way of serious characterization, or forward plot momentum.

I suppose she could have squeezed the Lowest Common Denominator cordial of a TV season or YA fiction series out of the idea if she'd cared about entertaining anyone other than herself, but she didn't. Hers was an absolute self-expression.

I thought that's why you'd gotten in touch—she said. *After all this time. I expected it would be something to do with the baby. Not about Rosie.*

My turn to be gobsmacked. The baby?

The bus rattled on its predetermined course past the replica Flatiron Building at Boothcross where posters for touring bands were plastered over skinned, wounded brickwork.

Nobody had ever hurt her the way you did—*she went to pieces*—

I took my lumps with, if not a grin, a stoical acquiescence. I knew what she said was true.

I had no idea she was pregnant—I lied. *Never mind the abortion. I only heard after it happened.*

Ariadne sighed, composing herself as if she'd carried this for a long time.

There was no abortion—she said. *She had a C-section.*

With those words, my world was folded down into a claustrophobic cube, where the colourful moving pictures drawn on its walls did nothing to prevent the suffocating sensation of premature burial.

Was it a girl?—I said, thinking of Heather, thinking of the ghost of someone living. Praying she'd say yes and get it over with.

I don't know—she said. *I wasn't there. First time I heard about any of this was when she was dying, Graeme*—and then she said—*I'm sorry. I'm sorry. Luci*—

It doesn't matter—I said.

And she said—*I know I shouldn't call you that.* A pause, a concession. *We all knew you were gay. After what happened with Jet . . .*

I thought better of asking after her brother. I preferred to convince myself he'd found equanimity.

Well, I wasn't—I wanted to reply like I always did without thinking, all wintry and self-assured. *Look at me. I don't have the commitment to wear a label or be part of any community. I liked sex and dressing up and roleplay, that's all it is.*

Instead, I bottled it like moonshine. The last thing anyone needed here on the top deck of the 36 was me trying to articulate my questionable views on gender and identity. I couldn't make room in my head for the idea of Rose dying. Being dead was one thing. Death was an absolute condition but dying was a process I was reluctant to imagine her going through. Not Rose, with her sailor's laugh and her funny cigarettes, her special way of being unique in this old world that thinks it's seen it all before until someone like her happens.

Something happened—she went on. *There was something wrong with the baby*—

It wasn't like that—Ariadne assured me emphasizing italics when she read my expression. The baby was premature but physically healthy, "normal" in every way. I hadn't passed on some family taint, some rot in the bloodline out of Poe and Usher.

Or had I?

There was something missing, she said. Ariadne tried her best to talk her sister out of a conviction she was gradually coming to parrot like a creed.

I think it had more to do with post-natal depression—she said. *She wrote it all down, all her feelings, the doses of medication. It's no wonder. I couldn't read it.*

What had?—

Ariadne looked uncomfortable. She turned to me and lowered her voice—held my gaze with a "can you keep a secret?" passion that gave her the appearance of a child reading from a special storybook and said—*It was two or three months after the birth when Rosie started to say the baby wasn't a real person.*

A changeling, I thought but I didn't say. Instead. I asked her what had started it.

They'd kept the baby in an incubator for six weeks. She didn't get to bond. She went through all that pain and then—nothing . . .

Do you know what happened to her? To the baby?

I thought of Heather again as Ariadne bent double to root in her bag, producing an A4 padded envelope.

I don't think it's much but it's in her own words—she said. *It's a copy anyway.*

How did she die?—I asked, unwilling to be told but nosy all the same.

Swearing at nurses—said Ariadne.

You'd want to keep the original—I said. *You might read it one day.*

It felt as if gravity had shifted underfoot; in one jarring cut scene, I'd gone from starring in pantomime to skulking through a bleak kitchen-sink spy drama. Swapping classified documents on a tram in Belgrade's Cold War monochrome. Exchanging passwords, trading double-meaning *non sequiturs* about the pigeons in Red Square or the weather in Prague.

I'm so sorry about Rose—I said, with a hitch in my voice

that was hooked into a real emotion too big and suffocating to admit. *I still turn the cover inside out to wrap the duvet, the way she showed me.*

She got that from Mum—she said, and you could tell she'd grown up sick of hearing how wonderful her sister had been at absolutely everything. You could tell she'd cornered the market in private undead sado-porn because it was her fate to be the involuted dark twin to Rose's bright extroversion, the voice reliably ignored at the family table.

I'd walked away from all of it. My own mum, God rest Her Optimistic Soul, even bought a ghastly hat for the wedding, so sure we'd tie the knot around our necks.

Ariadne was admonishing me with that little smile I had begun to remember and detest. The smile that told me I was being measured in feet and inches, divvied up as pints of blood and pounds of flesh, the incline of her head that confirmed she was sizing me up for the racks and rods, the thumbscrews, razors and stainless steel drinking straws of her vampire Inquisition.

There it was, the old sardonic "I can see right through you" look that left her so transparent I could draw her inner workings; the wireframe dunes of her desert marriage scintillant with arid vampire mirages, moonlit apparitions she drifted through of Gothic blood-soaked orchards by lakes of human milk and honey, haunt of undead Valentino *sheikhs* on carnivorous camels, the umbrella wings of leather that overshadowed her passionless sleepless nights.

Don't try to turn this into a Romantic tragedy of your making either—said Ariadne, correctly identifying the tenor of my thoughts. *She got over you, Graeme, Luci—she fell in love—he was nice. They only separated because of his drink problem.*

Sounds like quite a catch—I nodded sagely.

I assured myself Ariadne had lived long enough to know the world ran on unleaded irony and absurdity. The best response

to everything was a shrug of defeat or denial. It wasn't like being judged made it worse. I'd disappointed her a long time ago.

I don't generally resort to that name except in emergencies—I
said without conviction but peevish, nevertheless.

Her kids are incredible, like she was—she said, intending
each word as a spinning kick, a deadly dragon-strike in a *kung
fu* double feature.

Ariadne gathered her shopping bags into a dangling testicular
mass and got to her feet, adjusting her centre of gravity to compensate grimly for the drunken sway of the bus. She paused at the
top of the stairs, stationary and precarious till we slowed to a stop.

What happened to the vampire monks?—I said to paper over
the yawning conversational stasis.

She seemed genuinely surprised. *You remembered that?
They're quite popular online. You can find me under "Anonymous."*

We should keep in touch—I vogued. *You can tell me what
happened in the end.*

She smiled more warmly this time then remembered her
emotional armour with a wry, tight shake of her head, an elaborate eye roll, effectively telegraphing—*Nothing ever ends, does
it, babes?*

Without the *babes* probably. She'd never say *babes*.

We agreed we'd catch up, both of us aware we'd never find
common cause to speak again in this lifetime. The three or four
Christmas dinners we'd spent in each other's company over
decades of our lives were all we'd ever share. Our endless in-
conclusive *Truth or Dare?* where we never fucked behind her
sister's back or explored the implications communicated in our
torrid eye-to-eye contact all those years ago.

Nothing ever changes. Until everything does.

It was there, then, with Ariadne's head sinking below the
chrome horizon of the handrail, that fate saw fit to allow me
an uninterrupted view to the rear of the upper deck, where the
Flat Policemen sat.

I do declare.

It was as if the sun had set, in the form of Ariadne, making her way to the exit doors, and in the first moment of twilight the awful machineries of Night were laid bare so that the hideous guts, the pulleys and levers, were no longer hidden.

There were two of them, tall and thin enough to prop up a sizable tent, plainclothes in overcoats and hoodies. Both were scribbling in unison in black notebooks, scratching out the same observations. Then one of the men rose abruptly to his feet, snapped a rubber band around the cover, and folded his book into an inside pocket. Or perhaps it was only his phone. Perhaps there was nothing strange about him at all. Perhaps it was me.

I turned away. I wanted to let out a yell, to warn Ariadne, but the bus had stopped already. There was the bottom-deck door huffing open on its hydraulics to let passengers disembark. Facing front, I froze to my seat finding a new rictus appreciation of Hampton Row as it extended into leafy middle-class perspective lines, all converging politely at the same vanishing point lying directly, inescapably ahead.

I could feel the midwinter chill of the tall Policeman's unquestioned authority as he hurried down steps at my back. His partner stayed still and seated neatly in the rear, his presence a nagging wound in the space between my shoulder blades.

I checked him out in the overhead convex mirror that allowed the driver a periscope view of the top deck. The seated Policeman angled his head, presumably tracking Ariadne's progress onto the Row. There was something almost indecent in the intensity and eagerness of his searching eye. What next, I thought—a rasping cry of *show us your tits, love,* from the top deck?

I craned my neck to see Ariadne safely cross the street. No one followed. I waited for the tall Policeman to lurch his way back upstairs, braced myself for a cold, leather-gloved hand to refrigerate into place on my shoulder—but nothing happened, as if he'd never been there at all.

The second shadowy man jerked up his head suddenly as if to catch me measuring him up. I stared directly ahead. The railway embankment. The park gates. Left turn.

The Policeman was still there twenty minutes later, an itch on the periphery of my senses that I couldn't stop scratching. My body tightened into a boxer's glove of muscle and sinew each time he caught me looking and made another sharp scribble in his jotter.

As we circled back to the Dare's south bank five miles downriver from the crossing at Knox, I was able to piece together the approach of Darewater through the rain-spittered window on the left across the aisle.

The Flats were Gasglow's answer to the glory and the Romance of Greece and Rome, a numinous wasteland of abandoned building projects, corrugated iron, cinder, and blaes. Derelict husks of old-model cars and burst chain-link brought the World War IV afterparty mood.

Occupying, I should say more like squatting, the former site of a wartime "aerodrome" was a half-finished expressway junction whose colossal concrete pylons with their spray-painted graffiti tags supported unfinished roads to nowhere, truncated Rainbow Bridges to Valhallas that never got past the draughtsman's board, projected superhighways of a future stopped dead where budgets and imaginations expired in the dirt of fifty years ago at the End of the Age of Dreams.

Generations of Gasglow bands had shot promos here since the '70s, beguiled by the area's seeming debt to the novels of J. G. Ballard and their charged panoramas of urban decline. Brutalist, sublime, the fragmentary ramps and cryptic sections of deserted roadway always made me think of fossilized mega-dinosaurs with rusting iron sinews, plated with cracked tarmac and radiating indefinable significance. Then again, I'll take any opportunity I'm given to think about fossilized mega-dinosaurs, meaningful spaces, and anything that isn't the here and now of my mangled life.

Pigeon wings fluffed up the busy shadows under the flyover spans. Slashed mattress and split vinyl lay stacked and heaped against the concrete piers. Shopping carts stuffed to bursting with cardboard and plastic were parked unattended, shipwrecked on garbage reefs of splintered tent and torn awning. Even the homeless never stayed long, tormented in methylated slumber by monstrous spectres of unfinished futures here in the Cardboard City of Tomorrow.

The second Policeman—one too few for Flann O'Brien, I noted—finally got to his feet and hopped off the bus, trailing the same draft of icy ventilation as his partner before him.

There he lingered, at home in the convening shadows of the valley of the concrete cryptosaurs.

Praying for the bus to move again, I saw the detective flipping open his black ring-bound notebook. He licked night-blue ink off the ballpoint tip of his government-issue biro, jotting some curt, incriminating observation into his notebook as he glanced up to spot me staring down . . .

The engine bunched its shoulders noisily, the door wheezed shut. Wheels bit the road and turned.

No one would deny the atmosphere aboard the bus improved immediately now he'd gone. I'd hardly moved a micron since spotting the Flat Policemen and at last I could feel my entire body releasing tension, siphoning off the cortisol as cooling sour sweat.

On my right were the comforting square chimneys at Craigend Crematorium where Mum and Dad had both gone to cinders, overlooked by the art deco high-rise blocks at Bellamy Court, resembling a Space Fleet Headquarters manned by refugees, while ahead were raised the ugly modern aesthetics of

Southside General Hospital where Dad was sent to diminish at the last.

Sliding into the strip-lit throat of the Dare Tunnel, I felt secure on home ground again. Safe enough to slit open the A4 padded envelope and scan for key words.

In those last few miles and minutes, I can almost remember just how good it felt to be out of the house, far from the maelstrom's comet-spangled rim, riding the edge of the vortex with Luda. But I knew this stilled, contained moment of time on the top deck of the 36 bus couldn't hope to last much longer than the approximately fifteen minutes that remained before I was returned almost to where I'd started out earlier, decanted on Stables High Street in what would soon seem like another world, another century.

The number 36 route traced a wobbly circular path around Gasglow's city boundaries. In its inevitable orbital timetable, there was the assurance of seasonal, eternal return, but that was another harsh illusion.

In truth, even the 36 bus on its majestic trans-urban trajectory was constrained by irrefutable entropic laws of physics and urban transport scheduling. Even this noble trajectory was a childish ring-a-roses around a confrontation with devouring singularity it was impossible to avoid.

Curiosity got the better of me there on the return curve, the ecliptic. I slipped from the envelope a sheaf of stapled copies, scanned pages from a handwritten notebook. Birth records. A paper chase from the delivery room to the orphanage.

With a pang I recognized Rose's joined-up wavy art school scrawl from Post-it notes, to-do lists, birthday cards, and love letters. The last thing I noted before the world turned topsy-turvy was the massive red-brick grain store conversion at Porlock. All my attention was funnelled directly into the folded documents I held in my hands.

By the time the bus pulled in to pick up wan passengers

decanting from the office blocks at Porlock Cross, before its rumbling right-angled left turn onto the lower numbers of Stables High Street, passing the Indian restaurants, rare vinyl stores, charity outlets, and long-running award-winning cafés, I was shaking, and the whole panorama of reality through the cinemascope dimensions of the upper-deck window had sharpened to a malicious transparency where there was only one predictable outcome of every action.

I'd opened the envelope. I'd scanned the document and isolated the pure hot signal beneath the emotional noise of Rose's post-natal drugs hell. It could no longer be undone.

I tried my best to evaluate the contents calmly, but calm seemed an inappropriate response to the developing situation. The existential onslaught I was experiencing called for nothing less than bug-eyed hysteria. With the playa face and butcher's efficiency of an assassin Ariadne had delivered the death of a thousand paper cuts. Biding her time with the patience of the Immortal Undead, she'd waited until I was old and weak before slipping her blade, Rosie's, Jet's, between my fourth and fifth ribs into the thumping muscle of my wayward heart, completing a death strike begun twenty-five years before.

Still, I kept arcing back to Ariadne's shopping, bulging through the overstuffed skin of recycled paper, the hernia protrusions of fruit and veg, kale fan and celery truncheon that told of restricted diets and the 5-12 gone authoritarian.

Rose and I had just one bag of all the groceries and cat food sachets we could afford on the day we came back from the coast, its empty spaces revealing more about our lives than any physical contents. Not that there was anyone to notice. There was no Flat Policeman then to leave a long blue-black stripe on his tongue as he licked his pencil and wrote three words—*Justice is done . . .*

E verything about my meeting with Ariadne Welcome is very clear in my recall, but I couldn't tell you a single thing about the walk home from the bus stop on Stables. As it appeared to me, I was the only moving object passing through a single suspended solid moment. I was a neutrino signal zipping between atoms of rock like a wish. Like a thought experiment. If pushed I might be able to remember a tall thin man matching my pace some fifteen yards behind me on the hill but honestly? He was more likely my shadow, elongated by the year's fading light.

It's hard to explain, but under the deceptive glow of that low, artificial Hollywood sunset it seemed as if the whole world and everything in it had been replaced by its own luminous, lifeless duplicate. It looked real but it was a body double, a floodlit facsimile dressed for the camera setup.

I walked home from St. Pat's, along Stables High, dissolved to snow-globe Brownian motion among the student crowd and the weekenders thronging the boutique cinemas, Chinese takeaways, renowned art deco ice-cream parlours, independent bookshops, and thrift stores dedicated to feline welfare or starving children.

By the library, another left turn brought me in a Pac-Man chess-knight move onto Observatory Hill, where stood the scale-model copy in Rayonnant-period Gothic style of Sainte-Chapelle on the Île de la Cité in Paris I mentioned briefly before. It was here Jeremy and I made a point every year of turning up for the Watchnight Service on Christmas Eve, belting out carols in eyeliner and fishnet stockings, dyed hair, leather man stag and bimbo blonde drag.

And after the first couple of times, when our sincere love of singing Yuletide hymns was no longer in question, everyone accepted us.

I remember the interference ripples forming in the trees around the Fuzzy Felt square of the bowling green. Through what I came to understand were the pinprick prisms of my tears, I hoped the rainbow-fringed and dappled super-people passing by couldn't see me crying like this but of course everyone could, all the way back to where I'd climbed from the bus stop at the subway station on Stables.

Not that anyone cared.

The bells in the spire of the replica church of Sainte-Chapelle chimed the passage of replica hours as they dropped away into the deep well of the past, leaving concentric splash patterns, diminishing farewells, echoes, and ripples.

One.

The momentous late afternoon seemed fixed, an emotional capstone upon a pyramid of hourglass sand.

Two.

The sky was a John Martin extravagance, a volcanic red-black apocalypse no one else could see for what it was because, to them, it looked like any other November twilight. Only I had been shocked awake to perceive a biblical catastrophe happening so slowly it could be savoured and dreaded at leisure. An intimate *Dies Irae*.

Three.

There. Was. No. Abortion.

Four.

Rose went ahead with the baby, but she couldn't cope. An orphanage was recommended.

The church bells rang a death knell for Heather.

Our child would be twenty-five now. I imagined a double exposure, Rose's features superimposed on mine to make a stereoscopic third image, a composite face that was all too familiar.

I knew then there was no Heather. There was no lost little girl. Heather's imaginary life was the sacrifice I made, the burnt offering, in exchange for wisdom and power, the wavy-bladed Aztec knife buried to the hilt in her flat breast.

Five, and the bells chimed out their count then rang the vast silence that followed.

The baby Rose gave up had been a boy.

Dressed in the dress my mother never wore, I climbed the stairs, one gloved hand gliding like a chairlift on the polished wooden banister rail, the soles of my shoes counting the stone flags, flight and landing, welcome mat and brass nameplate.

The door was unlocked; of course, Luda had copied the keys along with everything else she'd reproduced.

I stepped over another electricity bill with its bloody capital letters reading URGENT, treating it with the contempt it deserved.

There was almost nothing left but decaying sonic-trace vibrations, but I knew all too well the resounding concave hush that followed a performance of *Spem in Alium.*

I wasn't sure what I expected to find, I don't count precognition among my many accomplishments, but it made so much sense it became inevitable and like the controlled demolition of a cooling tower it all fell into place, in bits.

I knew she had to be there by the chill; the air in the apartment was at least ten degrees colder than outside and I recalled the first day she'd strode into the rehearsal room heels clicking like bullets loaded into the magazine. Outside, the wind drew itself up, and the first sharp rains of Storm Ingmar swept down as tin-coloured diagonal scratches on the windowpanes.

Luda was seated at my mirror and there was something about her deportment, the way she carried her whole body, that gave me instant chills and an unexpected erection. She was primping her hair.

I came back—she said, doing my lopsided smile. *I've waited ages.*

When I looked at her, there was a disorientating stereo-scopic feedback.

Into the transcendent silence came the opening eight-bar riff of "Pretty Vacant," with its unstoppable cavalry charge of drums and shattering glass.

She hefted her fake tits in both hands. Luda preferred a manufactured rubber breastplate to my DIY lentil-based cargo cult fakes. I couldn't blame her. When it came to breast substi-tutes, I'd failed to keep up with the times.

You suit them—I practically spat. *Almost knocks the last of the boy out of you.*

She was me, her makeup reproducing each wrinkle I'd tried to conceal, every broken line of my face. Luci LaBang split in two, like Superman sundered from Clark Kent, facing each other across a sensational Action Comics cover. She wore my wig, the one I'd personally designed and had made. The one I'd sliced from its box only weeks ago. My crown on the young queen's head where it looked so much better.

Only the eyes were hers. She hadn't copied mine yet.

I thought of poor Molly Stocking and I wondered what Luda had been up to, looking like that, dressed and made up like me. Where had she been before coming here? What footage of me now existed, committing fuck only knows what obscure crime?

The Crone—she said with a smirk. *I did it myself, but it might as well have been you.*

Don't flatter yourself, babes—I came back, unsettled by the sound of my own voice, how much it sounded like her parody. *Some things you should leave to the experts.*

I made a move, in this case a shrug, and she gave me the action replay, then reading my every facial tic and tremor, my giveaway body language stutters, she got ahead of me by anticipating where my exact posture and attitude would go next, getting there first.

In defence, I chose not to move at all, ossified in the petrifying eyeline of the Gorgon Girl. Anything to call a halt to the stomach-churning caricature.

I know who you are—I said. *I know what you're trying to do*—I said even though I was only grasping at straws.

I know who you are—repeated Luda. When she spoke, there came that mild astringent shock of hearing your own recorded speech for the first time.

Luda smiled and repeated in my voice, using my gestures, *I know what you're trying to do*—as another spot-on impression, certain she had me moused into her trap.

I didn't know about you—I said. *I still don't*—

They've got this story about the missing homeless kid in the paper—she said calmly, sipping the cold black coffee that was my favourite.

He'd been seen by witnesses at his pitch, selling Homeless Times—*then he was gone and I'm to blame!*

Yet more than just unsettling, her imitation of me was *marvellous* to behold. Luda had me down to a crossed *t*. Not just the *t*, Luda went from *a* to *z*. The mimicry was so meticulous it became more real than the real thing, an immaculate satire, or master *pastiche,* that was at the very least the equal of the original in a dim light.

I saw in her what she saw in me, how people imagined me to be, and I won't lie, I was impressed. I was enlightened.

In spite of all the self-aggrandizing shallow affectation for which I was rightly notorious, her take on me exhibited an angry determination, a fighting spirit, a defiant refusal to be entirely serious that I felt showed me in a very positive light. In so many ways she was kinder to me than I'd ever been to myself.

She made me look fabulous.

I was flattered, disarmed. How could I not be? Serious study and effort had gone into this disturbing creation, and part of that rigour was meant to impress as well as terrify me.

In stories like this one, the Pupil always feels the frankly tiresome need to amaze the Master with some final dispassionately-executed killing blow capable of condensing all the lessons they have learned into a death strike against which the guru is powerless.

Instead, as reflected in Luda's blue-sky eyes I was old and powerful, funny, complicated—even likable in my cranky way.

Luda was my double, I reasoned, counting backwards and forwards from 1 to 0 again and again.

Her plan had always been to duplicate me, replicate me, reproduce my every thought and gesture to advance her plan.

Have I mastered the Glamour?

It was clear: Only one of us was leaving this space, this room, this house.

Every day is initiation, babes—I said. *You're not done yet. You're never done.*

All my life's representation in all my tender jetsam, all the bird-of-paradise feathers, wigs, and secondhand books, the cantankerous TV, the beloved pot plants and special pictures, *La Petite Voleuse* in its frame . . . it was time to breathe out and let go of things. Time to say goodbye and shed no tears and stop worrying about how it would all get on without me.

It's all a bit much, don't you think?—I said. *It's like a terrible slasher movie, or one of those old ones with Vincent Price in a mask, killing theatre critics*—I said—and she parroted every syllable, closing the gap between my words and her duplications until we were lip-syncing.

—theatre critics—

Luda and I faced the symmetry of one another, matter *vs.* antimatter. Drag bookends. Mirror-universe counterparts. If Einstein had any idea what he was talking about, it seemed inevitable one of us would cancel out the other in a blinding gamma-ray wash.

I know who you are—I said.

And she said—*No, you don't. You never will.*

You're the Devil, I wanted to say but couldn't. It seemed so ridiculous. It was too much to explain and if she really was the Devil, she wouldn't need me to remind her. I couldn't bring myself to admit she may have been my son, then my daughter. Born without a soul or otherwise.

It all makes sense—she said. *You couldn't handle growing old. You had to kill your young rival. It's in the script.*

I've never seen you as a rival—I told her then and there and I meant it.

Thinking it through, she thumbed the box-cutter blades into position and ruled red rails across the pale flesh of her forearm with the cold, detached composure of a veteran self-harmer. As if she'd struck oil and rubies, the gashes welled up with generous garnet overspill.

Her blood is all over—she said. *Or it's the missing boy's blood. Either way it was Luci LaBang who did it.*

With a few jazz flicks of her wrist Luda cast slaps and spots of her blood in three directions.

Luci LaBang did both. She bared her teeth in a pumpkin-lantern grin, ignoring the pain, the frenzy, the strewn slashes of drippy haemoglobin. *Hid the bodies.*

Luda spoke as if revelling, luxuriating in the intake of new data. Luda was a calculating machine updating her previous reality with new input, a new programme.

In my heightened state of hyper-vigilance and microscopic awareness, I tracked a heavy ruby globule sliding in slow motion down the mirror's chilled glass, a resplendent VIP slug laying its own red carpet.

Luci's found dead—I said, working it out. *Killed herself to evade the law. Video evidence proves it's her, like it proved Molly*

Stocking lynched her boyfriend. Case closed. Luda vanishes into the night, never again to be seen.

The way your mind works—she said. It was a threat rather than a compliment.

I'm just like you—I said. *Older and more fucked-up but just exactly like you.*

I knew this would get under her skin deeper than any needle; as she postured there in my clothes with my every accumulated line reenacted by paint and contour shading, Luda could hardly say—*I'm nothing like you!*

I can swipe the years away with some wet wipes and baby oil—she struck. *I can wash your ugly old face down the plughole and be young again. You're stuck with it.*

I'm out of here soon enough. If you've come this far, and I do sincerely hope you've been obliged to go over this mind-numbing testimony not just once but dozens of times, or more, you might be able to forgive me for stringing it out a little until the conclusion.

I don't want to stop, I don't want it to end this way and just like the show, just like *The Phantom,* I could run and run and run—but there's always curtains.

You become me in the end—I said. *I hope you're ready. It happens so fast. Twenty-five years is nothing. It's what the Phantom learns at the end. Beauty doesn't last forever, not even a single lifetime.* I was on a roll by this time, edit if you can. *You can't copy who I am, where I've been, what I've been through*—

There was a skipped heartbeat that didn't come and then—

What if I could?—she said, activating a smile.

In languid slow motion, she set down the bloody cutter so big fat drips spotted coffee rings stamped like particle-collision diagrams across the cover of the *Phantom* script on the G Plan Astro Coffee Table by the Martinelli Serpente lamp. I asked the only reasonable question.

Why?—I said. *Why go to all this trouble?*

And Luda said—*It wouldn't be much of a Hell if the Devil didn't make the effort. It's all about Pride, after all.*

The table was exactly five paces from where I stood, three from where the Devil preened, or it might have been Luda drawing herself up to full height, thrusting out latex bosoms, gathering the Glamour around her in crackling folds and fissures with such intensity I saw a blood-black *borealis* that might have been her charred angel wings red-shifting back to the eternal Fall.

Rentboy. Kenny Trace. Bee Spalding. Victoria Marvell. Luci LaBang. The Double. El Diablo. Luda, the Player of Games. My son and my daughter. My custom-built destroyer. Mephistopheles in a lace-trimmed push-up bra.

You asked about my drag name—she said. *You wanted to know why Luda*—

And so she told me one last mesmerizing story; how after she'd fled from the velvet gaol the Marvells prepared for her, she'd gone back to the sheltering streets, home to her wastrel kind's ancestral hunting grounds, roaming free among the refuse sacks and temporary cardboard townships.

With her instinctual grasp of their behavioural inclinations, she'd calculated correctly that the estranged Charles and Victoria would eventually meet on Wednesday lunchtimes to get drunk together and negotiate the conditions of their inevitable separation in McCloudie's bar adjacent to the Vallhambra Theatre where they were sponsors. Neither of them ever paid attention to the grubby strip joint opposite on Gargoyle Street's north side let alone stopped to register the waifish afterimage shuddering under black awnings across the busy street. Diluted once more to an anonymous transparency in the ever-reliable Gasglow rain, Penny came each week to spy on her parents as their marriage fell to bits behind glass.

The gluey bonds that held the Marvells together were undone as she observed. And even as they quarrelled, her undernourished reflection stood between them unseen, a ghost attending an empty chair.

It was on one of those waterlogged Wednesday afternoons, she told me, when Luda went into a kind of meditative trance and from the still centre of her altered perspective became aware for the first time of a line of fiery letters suspended above their three heads, spelling out the words *adults only* in McCloudie's big window but in a blistering neon reverse clipped by the edge of the glass after the letter *n*.

It could be read as the title on the cover of a book or show poster, she thought as she mouthed four syllables O ST LUDA, and that was it. The universe had bestowed on her a custom drag name, her very own. She was in that moment christened by unlikely circumstance in a backward-masking baptism.

When I get around to being a pop star, I'm going to call myself Saint Luda—she assured me. *Like Madonna.*

What could I say? Naturally hers was a better story than mine, but I couldn't resist poking holes.

If you'd seen a bit more—I said—*it would have read no st luda . . .*

She stuck out her tongue. You!

For a moment it seemed we'd reached a stalemate. I was still standing. We could both still smile at each other, creating feedback.

But she wasn't done yet. Luda had something else to tell me, something I needed to know and to understand before she was finished with her implacable formally-constructed vengeance.

She'd been messaging an old friend of mine, she explained, a bitter ex-lover. Or was it that she'd contacted him with a business no-brainer back when she'd set this whole ornate scheme in motion? She couldn't quite remember where the loop had started to loop.

Prompted by a young "fan" of the Troupe's sketches online, Luda went on disingenuously, a moribund Jeremy Painter had found the motivation, the willpower, to lift his shorn skull from the bar where it lay among the rest of the empties. Mounting a last-ditch effort to remind an uncaring world of his undying worth, he'd pitched and sold a tell-all biography, parlayed by his agent and ghostwriter into a six-part drama series bible based on Jeremy's life and experiences with the Troupe, his tussles with genius, scandal, and addiction, his forerunner status as a gender rebel, his betrayal at the beringed, red-nailed hands of Luci LaBang, his side of the many-splendoured story.

How many of you were in on this?—I said, addressing Luda's multitude of faces as well as any other possible accomplices. I didn't need an answer; all I had to do was count the bodies, the broke and bitter, the left-behind I'd trampled thoughtlessly beneath spike heels on my red-carpet strut to this reckoning.

All it takes is setup—said Luda. *Set dressing. Glamour. You see what I want you to see*—

They can't do the Troupe without Luci LaBang—I quavered, my substance evaporating in a shock wave. *It's my story too. You wouldn't—he's not capable*—I heard myself try to explain, as if she'd gotten the script pages muddled up again—but she hadn't.

It's got nothing to do with what you think. They don't need you—said Luda, who could rinse my years from her face and step into the spotlight as the me I would never be again. *It would be easier if you just went away altogether and left this to me.*

When she exposed white teeth, her face, my own exaggerated to perfection, became an oncoming locomotive snowplough.

You're too old to be Luci LaBang—said Luda, making festive roadkill of me.

They say how could you do it? How could you take on the Devil?

How can you go up against someone who plays the game of Golden Dames five moves ahead?

Plan six moves ahead.

Stop at nothing.

There's a common mistake Old Nick makes in more than one of His Satanic Majesty's celebrated attempts to outwit chess players, backwoods fiddle *maestros,* or saintly blacksmiths, and it's to view the world at all times through the bifocals of Duality, as if it's all blurred or all sharp. All buy, all sell. All power, all weakness. All rise and all fall, like empires and economies, with nothing in between.

Mercurius, on the other hand, has three faces, the Good, the Bad, and the Absurd, the Up, the Down, the In. The Left, the Right, the Sideways. Maiden, Mother, and Crone. The Bought, the Sold, the Free.

They offered you a chance to reset me back to zero—Luda said as if I needed to be reminded of Victoria Marvell's clammy basement transaction—*What did you say?*

Would it make a difference?—I said and it was hard to know what else I could add without spoiling the charade she'd worked so hard to make convincing.

I decided not to tell her how she'd given herself away in the Ancient Animals gallery, and again at the Marvell house. Only I would ever know how badly she'd failed her final exam.

Cast your minds back, if they haven't been lulled into an irreversible vegetative retreat by now, and you might just find there some trace memory of that leaden Saturday night when Luda and I argued for the first time. Our pointless row interrupted the lesson I had planned, quite fortuitously foiling my attempts to serve up a mighty Secret of the Glamour I considered she'd finally earned. It had been time to instruct Luda in the *Grand Mystère* that is how best to obscure the telltale swell of a smooth cock and its attendant shiny balls by easing the whole kit, cue and all, into the conveniently placed snooker pocket of one's own unsuspecting inguinal cavity.

That was before it all went to hell in a handbag.

The demanding role of Victoria Marvell was in all respects but one a *tour de force;* for want of a hole into which to hammer a nail Luda's Oscar-baiting triumph fell afoul of the judging panel at the last hurdle when it became clear that straps of gaffer tape in Union flag crisscrosses were insufficient to censor the bereaved mother's ballooning nads.

That was when I was sure they were all her; each scrupulously-crafted Glamour she'd woven like I'd taught her gave her away like a school crest, or the chrome badge on a car grille. Some say style is defined by all the things you do wrong, the quirks of the teacher passed down that prevent you from achieving a faultless performance, the tics that make you human and distinctive and relatable, and in every imitated move Luda made I could see my own ham-fisted techniques learned and repeated. Molly Stocking. Miss Spalding. Victoria Marvell. Maiden. Mother. Crone. Reduced to cartoons.

The whole improbable three-act Hollywood hero fable told *à la ronde* from several different points of view remained uncorroborated by anyone but Luda; the damned boy-become-girl hero, the twisted and powerful fairy-tale parents, the escape.

The Crow Mother, the Nursery, the Homeless Boy; every improbable kink and bend in the story of Luda and the Marvells spun by a single unreliable narrator.

It's up to you to decide if that narrator was Luda, or if it was me.

Given my insider knowledge, it was inevitable I would occupy the ethical uplands and reject Mrs. Marvell's generous offer of my very own obedient sex genie. It was a Brothers Grimm bargain, a moral hypothetical with no real-world penalties. I had done the right thing and Luda had been there to witness.

But Luda licked her lips. *You should have taken your chance to bind me*—she said, deftly volleying my show of mercy back at me as an act of mortal stupidity. *I could have been everything you wanted for as long as you wanted.*

I noticed she'd closed the curtains, to deter any nosy neighbors with a *Rear Window* fixation.

You were—I said.

I'd made up my mind, or had it made up for me by circumstance. Only one of us would flounce out of that room. My room. You'll know that already, which makes this even more frustrating, I expect. Me talking, you listening, judging.

It was me who closed the door at my back in that final gladiatorial arena. I surrendered to the inexplicable Random that lay between Good and Evil. I opened myself to opportunity, offered up a prayer to pretty Mercurius.

Are you mad?—I heard her say. And I held my breath the way you'd hold a conviction, just long enough to make it seem convincing.

She said—*Being you would drive anyone mad.*

There's one last thing I should mention about the Glamour; you may think after all this it's the sort of "magic" that relies on dope smoke, mirrors, and gullibility, and I'd be the last person to tell you that old grab bag of gimmicks isn't a big part of what we do, but sometimes the Glamour is all about accomplishing the impossible and being in exactly the right place and moment when coincidence strikes.

If I was mad could I do this?—I smirked, and snapped my fingers, throwing caution like a well-fed Christian to the starving pride, abandoning myself to the quicksilver rapids of contingency in the sure and certain conviction the Glamour was pumped, primed, and willing to deliver on my rash confidence!

The reward for this leap of faith came almost instantly, doing its best impersonation of chance, when all the lights in the apartment decided to go on strike at the same time. The quite magical result of all those unpaid rouge-red demands was to provide me with a once-in-a-lifetime opportunity to seize an advantage.

One other thing to note about the Glamour: It's hard to

maintain in total darkness but not impossible, not if you know the terrain like a cat knows its way around a fragrant litter tray.

Mentally dividing the room into golden sections, I listened for the syrupy decelerated plop of blood hitting paper and moved like spilled ink through a darkness that was total and familiar when it came.

Use every trick you've learned, bitch—I heard that awful gloating voice in my head like a cheap Gasglow gangster as I went for the scent of Daisy Dream—*here's some lines you won't forget*—

Fingers curling on the rubber grip of the box cutter, I was blindfold justice swinging my hand in an upward arc to unzip the Golden Section.

Into the tightly-woven gloom, where Luda and I were both as blind as bats, love, faith, and mice arose a shattered glassy shriek.

Whether it came from me or from her is a mystery you may have to solve for yourselves.

There wasn't much anyone could do, that was the real tragedy; with its principal players, its star talent scooped off the board like captured tokens in the Golden Dames play-off to end them all, *The Phantom of the Pantomime* was cancelled two weeks before opening night amid a Storm Ingmar squall of recriminations and ill will. Tickets were refunded at great cost as lawsuits sprang snarling from the margins like unmuzzled mutts. Scandal mounted scandal and in unsavoury congress begat more scandal. Dom, not simply overweight but overbudget, stood crumbling by degrees, a barrier between his cast and crew and the unleashed ire of investors who could never recoup. In the final analysis, as my dad used to say, spin it any way you liked, the holidays were ruined, especially for children and the underprivileged.

I still think of the coachloads of shuffling shock-eyed seniors who might never sit through another "super saver" discount matinee they'd have any hope of remembering. My heart bleeds tears for the down-in-the-mouth men and women with learning difficulties who waited all year to clap along with the songs, gathered up in something bigger than themselves for just one night where the dreams came away all sticky and lovely in their hands and all the stars on top of all the Christmas trees were five-pointed unsolved puzzles.

With the dreary inevitability of prison dead bolts clanking into place, the story condensed and quickly gelled. To Murdo McCloudie was attributed an effective revenge he'd never set out to enact in the first place. There was only room in this theatre for one Phantom, as waggish hacks had it, oblivious to their own spectral participation in our production's downfall.

Poor Murdo; resentful spirits oozing from every crack in the walls and he, who died by all accounts wishing nothing but goodwill towards man and beast alike, was made the scapeghost for a *Haunted Mansion*'s worth of unseen bad intentions.

Me, I wasn't sure I'd survive the tabloid attention, suspecting it would propel me to the realms of the pop immortals for all the worst reasons. I could expect to be cancelled, amputated from the cultural discourse, with the yawning wound I left cauterized and sutured neatly behind me to leave no scar of my misshapen ugliness to blight future generations.

Even now when I close my eyes, I can picture Dom Float's headstone, with those six immortal words chiselled into marble . . .

When production ground to a halt yards from the finish line, Dominick Float's revival of *The Phantom* was doomed to inhabit an unproduced afterlife. I've tried my best to build for you a dressing room, a theatre, a cast and a world made of nothing but language where Dom's *tour de force* in all its tearful symmetry can play to record-breaking crowds in the only auditorium big enough to hold our beefy *auteur*'s vision intact without breaking everyone involved, in the Hollywood Bowl, the cavernous Budokan auditorium inside all our skulls where he traced his pentagram, invoked his Devil and left the rest of us to pay the pie-eyed piper.

Luda wanted to learn how to disappear. She should have hung around a little longer.

All that talk; the transmigration of souls, sarcophagi, cloisonné scarab shells, who's to say I didn't empty out Luda's personal contents just as the Marvells had done before me, shimmering from my worn and baggy corporeal bodysuit before easing my active consciousness into the factory-fresh driving seat of a new blood-and-bone machine, stretching Luda's boundaries as I poured inside to set like concrete?

Or why resort to the supernatural? There's no requirement for body-swap shenanigans or an easy retreat into the Twilight Zone after all.

What if Luda went too deep, the ultimate sleeper agent in a superspy saga—a Comrade X who's forgotten how to break character? What if her systematic imitation of me couldn't be so easily shaken off and instead clung to her like a possession, a monkey on her back, until one day twenty-five years from now she would look for herself in the mirror and find me waiting patiently with open arms, bingo wings, and missing teeth?

Could there be an ending where, in her single-minded dedication, her Method compulsion to understand me completely, to become me, she succeeded, and to all intents and purposes it was not Luda who walked away from Ground Zero of our predestined collision but me?

In truth, isn't this how a tawdry episode of human obsession and madness looks from the inside, with all its self-justifications, its attempts to maintain control of the narrative, its personal pocket-size mythology rendered in scar-tissue purple prose?

Let's go with it, let's say Luci LaBang bladed, bummed, and buried her rival, the beautiful up-and-coming young entertainer known only as Luda. The triple threat to Luci's throne. Mirror mirror on the wall!

Rather than face patriarchal justice, rather than endure the gavel and tip the blindfold lady's scales, panto queen Luci LaBang, TV has-been, chooses instead the high-drama opt-out, snuffing herself in a bomb-burst of fire and confetti.

Drunk on lethal champagne and ninety-proof guilt, here's Luci LaBang a collapsing star at her dressing-room mirror in a blazing Golden Rectangle of immodest bulbs, forever ten years younger in the ring light, composing a typically flamboyant Cleopatra swansong with cryptic overtones of ritual transgression, cranky diva drag witchcraft, and flames old, naked, and unashamed.

Can you honestly see me, climbing into a frock the size of a cathedral bell without the assistance of a dresser, a knight without a squire, huffing and puffing into awkward slabs of armour, contorting to do up the zips and lock the hooks, all painted, stiffened, set to strut the empty stage, rehearsed and psyched to play not only mine but everyone's parts, sing all the songs—and in this way conduct Dom Float's divine vision to its supreme articulation before I bring down the house with a squib?

You must have a very vivid imagination.

But there's proof in the case for the prosecution, you'll say: Luci LaBang's straight-legged, hip-led gait is unmistakable; CCTV shows the aforesaid La LaBang in her shaggy neon mane of a coat entering the vacant playhouse toting a Goodbye Kitty! shoulder bag plump with yellow canisters of lighter fuel and later, when the inferno shrugs off its red velvet smoking jacket of crackling timber, its black topcoat of crumbling brick, and the Vall is deconstructed back to McCloudie's ground plan by powerful thermodynamic forces, the TV has-been finally consummates her wicked revenge in rubble and char.

Now you've started down a path towards bewilderment, you may as well picture me in the sonic afterburn of the last chorus, gliding in state to the front of the stage, floodlit by lines of turquoise flame that, even as you watch powerless to prevent it, race across the boards to link Float's markers, sketching his grand five-pointed design in livid rows of igniting petrol.

Think of me if you must, silhouetted by luxurious furnace colours, arms outstretched, dreaming of Boudicca's sweat and her blood drying in the city-sized bonfire heat of a Londinium she'd delivered to embers.

Imagine all this as I put the cursed, corrupted Vall to the purifying torch. If you're confident your imagination's big enough to contain her, feast those prurient third eyes on the Widow Twankey orchestrating it all to ash. Visualize the Vallhambra, ghost-riddled, worm-haunted old whore, lit like a witch fallen foul of Matthew Hopkins, fluorescent chemistry and combustion consuming her stale-cake mouldings in coral shades of flame, her terraced rows of scuffed-velvet folding chairs—devouring in white-hot glory her stalls, grand circle, gallery, her backward-facing shame, in five-storey towers of exuberant fire that made of the immense ceiling rose a blistering Buddhist mandala, a supernova of flickering paint flakes and plaster!

Maybe that's exactly how it went down. You'll know better than me if Luda's plan played out as arranged.

Was it Luda who walked out of the apartment on Prospero under the hand-painted impassive tolerance of MRS. RAIN and MRS. SHINE, that pair of stalled wedding-cake brides neatly coffined in the carved rectangles of two little doorways on the transgender barometer I bought in Schöneberg on that dreamy post-coital Sunday with Jeremy Painter?

Or was it Luci, banking until the *dénouement* her signature special move, her Hecate-level mother of all spells, her last reverse, her inevitable post-credits plot corkscrew?

Was it Luci who took it upon herself to spare Luda the horrors of growing old? Preserving her in the Polaroid flash of light on a Stanley blade?

If you can't be sure, I wouldn't worry about it, that's just the Glamour doing what the Glamour does best.

Except, there's the troubling audio evidence to take into account . . .

I can't be sure why this came into my head at so late an hour, but I suppose it's obvious.

When I found it smeared and slimy on the wooden deck at the back of the old house, all those years ago now, I thought it was a rat at first, mauled and left for dead by some halfhearted predator, but it was a newly-born kitten, lying in its own watery afterbirth and too much clotted black blood while the flies crawled over its tiny severed back leg—bitten off by a terrified mother who was only a baby herself.

A living embodiment of the barbarism of the everyday delivered in a sticky slurry of biological snot from blissful and drifting uterine completion into our lovelorn world of savage deconstruction and pain.

The torn and bleeding scrap had to be dead but as I overcame my horror and looked closer, I saw two wee clawed pads batting weakly at the air, while hacked bone sawed in and out of fur where a meticulously-constructed scale-model leg stopped suddenly, and with a shock of pity and revulsion came the incendiary desire to help, to rescue, to do whatever I could to fan that spark of life to a flame that might endure for two decades, or 140 cat years.

Rose and I fed her with a syringe, and she learned fast how to create suction and drain the tube. We would have sworn she rallied on the third day, like Jesus flexing his muscles in the cave, warming up for the Resurrection, so much so that we became complacent, certain she was destined to pull through. We imagined her grown and confident, darting on three legs with nothing but boundless confidence and the model-girl elegance of a fur-trimmed modernist barstool.

We saw in the gasping will to survive, the kindling of pure potential, a future in the making. We strove to give her the tools to realize that destiny as a three-legged prodigy.

Our kitten died on the fourth day, emitting pin-sharp whines of pain I can never seem to put out of my mind.

The more we thought about it, and tried to make sense of it, the more we agreed that we'd delivered that kitten from a harsh unforgiving hell into a world of soft pink blankets and heat pads, a world of regular food and love where she passed into nothing via whatever eyeless dark of warmth, comfort, and attention four-day-old baby cats inhabit.

If there is mercy, we told ourselves, it's because we good people choose to bestow it. We alone have the capacity to imagine better worlds, kinder worlds than this awful self-munching cannibal engine dreamed up by our elusive Creator after one too many sleepless nights before Time.

Too bad we lack the technology to correct the Almighty's amateurish mistakes, we sniffed, lamenting as we buried our two-inch corpse with her sleek black fur in a chocolate box whose transparent window made her look like Snow White, waiting forever for a kiss. We assuaged our grief and a nagging guilt by taking pride in our kindness, stoking the fires of sentimentality like a boiler.

Some people see vulnerability and feel the need to protect it. Some see potential and wish to nurture it to its full expression.

Others live to take advantage of the weak. They see the same potential and feel the need to crush it.

Then there are people like me.

As it turned out, I'd been underfeeding the kitten. My failure to grasp lines and measures, my disconnect from the arithmetic of volume and content, resulted in the swift amputation of a potential future.

A four-day-old severely injured kitten died of malnutrition thanks to my stupidity. She had struggled with every scaled-down resource she could muster to survive a violent birth, a mauling, a general anaesthetic, and the loss of a leg, all in the first few hours of her life. She fought hard to live and relied on me not to fail her, which I did, so she gasped and died as her tiny rudimentary organs packed in.

There hasn't been a day gone by where I haven't berated myself for letting that kitten down.

This confidence we're qualified to play God leads the best of us astray.

And so, ladies and gentlemen, boys and girls and others, before I depart with my good friends the fairies and will o' the wisps, I'm duty-bound to demonstrate the full and final power of the Glamour.

Before we get to that, I couldn't have scaled my way to this glassy summit without you, sweet enduring audience and your all-important participation.

As a hero of mine once said—*I've suffered for my art, now it's your turn* . . .

I do my best work when someone's cheering me on or when they're hissing round my entrances and exits, and I'd like to think we've built up a rapport that's gone beyond comfortable and into unsettling by now.

There. The music stops and in its place a silence drops, a haunting expectant hitch that catches like your breath, that changes everything . . .

Can we have a show of hands ladies and gentlemen, boys and girls and others?

How many of you are beginning to believe mad Charlie Marvell might have been right? Half right? Onto something? What if there were too few recycled spirits for too many greedy, selfish bodies? What if the insensate ones, the unfeeling ones are everywhere, anaesthetized against affect, fast-breeding like contagion in the petri dish of the mirror? Hordes of naked p-zombies gorging on the wealth of nations and lives, consuming finite resources without conscience.

It almost makes sense.

How could you look at your loved ones in the same way? That's if you don't already regard them with justified suspicion. Do they really have souls or are they just faking?

Do they feel real pain, or do they just squeal like that when you break their hearts because it's what we've learned to do to pass as human?

I ask with the full thimbleful of seriousness I'm able to muster, do you feel equipped or authorized to determine whether this whole ridiculous story has been brought to you by a human being with an inner world of self-reflection or a soulless automaton only pretending to recognize its gurning DIY face in the vanity glass?

How discerning would you need to be to tell the difference between me and an identical copy?

Could there be a lampoon more uniquely and exquisitely tailored to my vital statistics than one deliberately crafted to waste 135,000 words faking my voice to drivel on about nothing while spunking malevolent antisocial philosophies into your cavernous minds?

How sweet Luda's vengeance, if she succeeded, if she was able to convince you I was only ever a thing pretending to be a real person. Or worse, if I couldn't persuade you otherwise— no matter how much of the dictionary I burned through in my attempt to kindle a beacon fire that could be seen and felt from miles away by others adrift like me.

What can I do but have faith in you not to be hoodwinked? You'd be able to tell if I was some two-legged scout drone for the p-zombie vanguard, wouldn't you? After all this time we've had, hand in hand skipping through my Perfumed Midden, you'd be sure.

Tell me you would!

But then I think, what if you decide instead there's something artificial about my story, a lack of genuine emotional inflection, a flippancy perhaps, a fondness for camp performance where nothing's taken as seriously as it ought to be. My lifelong love of the shallows, my disinclination towards the deep could easily play against me.

How much *gravitas* are we prepared to concede to words the author stitched together for no purpose higher than frivolous display? Can we trust words pimped and paraded into fanciful arrangements too delicate to support real meaning?

In this etiolated account of mine, human passions that deserve to soar on the wings of eagles find themselves reduced with self-conscious regularity to the coy flutter of revue-bar feathered fans quivering and darting over teased nipples, implicit ass crack. If there was any beauty to such a narrative it could only be skin-deep, recklessly glib, fundamentally lacking in the essential solemnity that gives a life its epic, unavoidably Glagolitic mass.

Wouldn't you say?

If you still can't be certain after all we've endured together whether the person talking to you is even human or not, who are you to judge anything, let alone me, let alone a mind like Luda's?

Nevertheless, as the jury, good and true, *vox populi,* it's up to you to make a critical decision shortly, partially based on everything you've just heard.

If it's any help at all, as a rule of thumb, I've found you'll never erase a blank. No matter how hard you rub, it only gets blanker.

The trouble with me is I've always aspired to be what's left when the Invisible Man relaxes, takes off his fedora and his Ray-Bans before unwinding the bandaged shape into a discarded bog-roll bundle on the lino.

That unfettered absence, that unlimited potential!

That's why, when you scrape away the slap and ditch the wig, when you unzip the dresses, unbuckle the heels, and roll off the stockings, you'll find there was never anything else.

There was only ever drag.

Which brings me to the concluding stroke before I face the critics, the ladies and gentlemen and others of the jury—a single application of Crystal Clear Shinelighter.

This last immaculate dab, the painter's signature, leaves a bright white highlight on the tip of my nose. It manifests as spark from nowhere, a vacuum fluctuation in some imagined initial source, the ignition glow of the primordial atom.

The makeup's ace: For now, this version of my preserved face in its glass cabinet is the one to beat.

The spiral galaxy, the starry involutions tensing in my cheekbone when I raise one corner of my mouth then the other, make me feel immortal. It's too bad about the backslash crack across the mirror's façade.

This is how we disappear . . .

There's another reveal I saved till now: The kitten who died had a four-legged litter mate, a twin we rescued at the same time. Her name was Babes, and she lived and was loved for almost 140 cat years.

It wouldn't be panto if she hadn't!

Together then, let's conjure the setting together one last time in outline: a backstage dressing room where the scintillating world of showbiz meets Death! Feather boas trailed seductively through cold bony knuckles. Clothes hangers twisted into butchers' hooks. A star of Satan on the door. Stage directions marked out with half-eaten body parts. Is that lipstick or is it spilled blood, or lines of fire? Is the fizz laced with cyanide or something much worse from the Dark Web, something to deaden the senses, to kill the nerves so the flames feel far, far away and a long time ago, breathtakingly chill against bubbling, blistering skin?

Disgraced TV has-been Luci LaBang abstracted to smoke and tallow in her Sunday best! Case closed and padlocked.

Luda, by this time missing, presumed shallow-graving it up on the peat bogs, would evaporate into the dead of morning, never again to be seen. She would make her way back to Purgatory, or Mystery City, for debriefing by Flat Police, awaiting her next mission, her latest seduction. As her power grew, so would her ugliness.

Luda would resort to a porcelain mask, a Bond villain plotting reprisals from an underground lair where slashed tailor's dummies stood guard like those terra-cotta warriors that march us in ranks back to China, to those streets in a Peking that never were and the Widow's laundry.

Whatever the precise sequence of events, the chances of Luda securing the juicy prime role of Luci LaBang in any six-part dramatization of Jeremy Painter's forthcoming auto-hagiography had fallen to zero. I'd made sure of that.

Framed three times for her crimes, I'd be vilified in folk memory as an unenterprising serial butcher, shunned as an out-of-date offensive stereotype: hysterical cross-dressing psycho, commemorated forever in a series of trumped-up charges that validated the status quo and made all of us hysterical cross-dressing psychos look bad.

The Vall would rise from its ashes as cheap student accommodation, or it would carry on gracelessly decomposing back to rotten foundations. In either outcome, stories would accumulate that spoke of monologues whispered in an empty room, of a garishly made-up apparition manifesting on certain nights of certain seasons in certain mirrors, as if perched intangible at a dusty dressing table backstage of the Land of the Living on some flat and disconcerting plane between the glass and its aluminium backing, choosing to attract the attention of the breathing classes by painstakingly slathering over its skull holes a half-remembered Halloween cake face, presenting the drag tutorial from Hell.

This is how the Glamour proceeds. Like false eyelashes and a faultless bee sting of glossy fire-engine red on a pouting porker, the strange allure of the Glamour can be achieved quite easily by simply and artfully obscuring certain qualities while emphatically underlining others for heightened effect.

The Glamour is that which is known to be false but felt to be true!

Time to discard Salome's Eighth Veil, to stand at last bare-arsed before the court and admit with a puckish crimson grin that while my wardrobe does indeed and without doubt include the items in question, at this moment in time and in defiance of everything I've been leading you to believe, I'm not wearing a giant cumulus cloud of a wig or a knock 'em dead senior supermodel ensemble. My Twankey drag, my Glamour was tailor-made with words, anecdotal gold thread sewn into fanciful textures and pigments of my own devising, triggering your assumptions and dressing me in imagined regalia, the shiny apple of your mind's eye!

It's not like I didn't make any of this as plain as your face in the mirror; I'm a *fata morgana*, a *trompe l'oeil* where all it takes is a change of position for the illusion of tangible mass to reveal itself as an embarrassing misapprehension, a grab bag of perceptual cues mistaken for a room, a house, a person, a reflection.

I told you Widow Twankey and the Phantom were one and the same!

Round about now is when even the slowest members of the audience see through the trick, when the penny drops as four Golden Rectangles fall suddenly flat, and the spangled cabinet is gone with a bang, taking the magician with it.

When the long arm of the law yanks open the dressing-room door, expecting to catch mad Ma Twankey in the act, all done up for a one-woman suicide performance on an otherwise deserted stage, all they'll find, those policemen and detectives, flat or otherwise, will be the basic ingredients for a ghost story: an unoccupied chair, a three-faced mirror scoured clean and disinfected of my radiation print, a drained triptych with the brightness and heat fading from its surface in smears of ectoplasmic talc. They'll find a mystery recording on a phone left talking to itself from beyond the grave, beyond the pale, and on into the wild mauve where mystery citizens retire to lose themselves.

Perhaps the sensitive ones, God forbid they'd have any in the force, might register the last faint traces of the features of Luci LaBang as a scorched afterimage, a retinal flare more gone than there, leaving only condensation, and an evaporating mask of makeup to show where a face had been. The Widow who wasn't.

Let them dust for the Devil's fingerprints and dab for the spoor of the Horned One's cloven stilettos in the powder and the sparkle dust. All they'll find is this voice, and these words, the bittersweet aftertaste, the cooling lip-print where I checked out.

Maybe then, boxed in uneasily by the multiplying corners of the scornful looking glass, the inescapable perpendicular tracks of the story, they'll consider the frame.

I promised you an irrefutable demonstration of the Glamour and I always keep my promises. Don't I?

Here, and then here, and now, where the words run clear, where the spell's tied up in ribbons and bows, all that's left is for me to dedicate my performance to you, long-suffering, treasured, unseen audience in your higher world of law and proportion, crime and consequence. I'm happy to take my reward in applause. Thunderous ideally, from the flats to the vaults. A vatic standing ovation like fine hairs thrilling to attention on a forearm in a lightning storm.

And curtain calls. I won't get greedy; three should cover it!

"Graeme." Luci. Twankey makes three.

The Phantom is where that trio of faces blurs and dematerializes to a bodiless voice inside your head where your own voice normally provides narration, arriving back where we started, and not for the first time either. We've been here before, you and me, mirror and voice, a squirrelly feedback of alluring reflections and siren echoes propagating back to zero, back to the Bang.

Thought for the day: If you must stop somewhere, stop at nothing!

I leave this impossible pre-recorded confession, this voice *de Profundis* with a wink and a leer to the gallery, a flash of synthetic cleavage. In my dearest wishes these words will come to haunt them, all the policemen and detectives squandering valuable years, centuries of their lives to the rewind, pause, and play buttons trying to figure out exactly who did what, when, why, and to whom?

In the event I've failed to say enough, or if instead it's all too much, I've left a three-word kiss-off for the impatient ones who prefer to cut to the end; the abridged version, the T-shirt slogan I promised writ large on glass in swishy Mon Rouge cursive across those flat reflected faces.

Where is it coming from, this voice in your heads?

All together now, ladies and gentlemen, boys and girls and others . . .

SHE'S BEHIND YOU!

ACKNOWLEDGMENTS

I'd like to thank my agent Peter McGuigan at Ultra Literary for cajoling me into finally writing a novel without pictures after twenty years of false starts, my editor at Del Rey Tricia Narwani, for her brilliance, insight, enthusiasm, and support for the vulgar and extravagant outcome, and Christopher Potter with Michael Kerrigan for their deft work on the Europa Editions version.

Thanks also to Gillian Paterson for invaluable proofreading and comments.

Love times love to my wife Kristan for holding up the sky, apologies to family—OSPD Leigh!—and friends who hardly got a word out of me this year, and respect to the latest generation of cat companions who did everything in their power to prevent me from working too hard . . .

And to the denizens of the *demi-monde,* my sisters, my brothers, and others, to the Fabulous everywhere, I raise a glass of fizzing gratitude and solidarity . . .

Sparkle on!

About the Author

Grant Morrison is the author of the *New York Times* bestseller *Supergods*. They are also well-known for their innovative work on comics, from the graphic novel *Batman: Arkham Asylum* to acclaimed runs of Superman, Batman, Wonder Woman, and the X-Men, as well as their subversive creator-owned titles such as *The Invisibles*, *Seaguy*, *The Filth*, and *WE3*. In television, they have developed adaptations of their comic series *Happy!* for Syfy and Netflix and Aldous Huxley's *Brave New World* for Peacock.

Grant Morrison is an award-winning playwright, a musician, an occult practitioner, and a stray-cat magnet. They were awarded an MBE for services to film and literature. *Luda* is their first novel.